BALLAD OF THE HIRED BLADES

THE SECRETS OF THE ROK-SENN

J.D. RAJOTTE

authorHOUSE®

AuthorHouse™
1663 Liberty Drive
Bloomington, IN 47403
www.authorhouse.com
Phone: 833-262-8899

Published by AuthorHouse   11/23/2024

ISBN: 979-8-8230-3877-5 (sc)
ISBN: 979-8-8230-3876-8 (e)

Library of Congress Control Number: 2024925215

Print information available on the last page.

Any people depicted in stock imagery provided by Getty Images are models,
and such images are being used for illustrative purposes only.
Certain stock imagery © *Getty Images.*

This book is printed on acid-free paper.

This book could not have been made possible without the support of my incredible wife, my amazing son, and my eternally encouraging family. Last but not least, all honor and respect goes to the Commander in Chief; The God of Abraham, Isaac, and Jacob, who's given me all of the tools to rightly serve.

CONTENTS

PROLOGUE

Sticks and Stones

It was quiet. A silence so stark; one would think sound itself was afraid to turn the dark corners of the Mirage Pyramid. In the pitch black, four would-be Hired Blades carefully stalk the halls of the ancient ruin. Guided only by the golden, auric light of a mysterious glowing stick; the quartet carefully tip-toe round the corner of a long, narrow, and desolate hallway. Unable to see ahead, the holder of the stick draws the glowing beacon to his face.

His sagging skin, a dark shade of mocha; covered in dark, unrecognizable tattoos. The stark bags hanging below his eyes tell the tale of a life of hardship and tragedy. Brown, matted dreadlocks flow past his elbows, swaying to and fro beside the glowing, wooden stick in his hand. A wooden *drumstick*, with mysterious patterns carved along it; the glow itself taking the shape of a golden knife blade, maybe seven inches in length. The man squints down the hall, barely able to make out anything ahead.

"Brotha, *the hell* are we at now?"

Stopping in place to scan his surroundings, he halts the momentum of his crew. The first behind him; a peach-skinned young man with an indigo-tipped mohawk, is forced to halt in place. This of course causes the other two to bump him from behind.

"Hey, tweedle-dee and tweedle-dick, watch it!" Hissed the mohawked man. He turns to the man in front. "And what's the deal, Danba? You forget how to walk all the sudden? You put one foot in front of the other, and fall forward. Duh?"

"Shut yer face!" Muttered the third member. Jet black, wavy hair of medium length, with a goatee to match. He carries an electric guitar across his back. "Quit makin' a ruckus, Lukah! We don't know what's around the corner, ya know? Anything could jump out at any time and try ta kill us... ya know?!"

"No *you* shut it Clint!" Howled Lukah, now increasingly forgetting to mind his volume. "I'm not the one who stopped anyway, it was Danba!"

Danba swiftly whips around, holding the glowing knife aloft to illuminate the group.

"Would yall two *both* pipe it down?!" He hissed. "We gotta be walkin' these halls all quiet-like. You never know when a big bad *boogieman* could come walkin' on through, with a big ole' *whoopin'* stick for each of our asses."

They both look at Danba with a befuddled glare. Lukah retorts.

"I just wish I could record the shit you say, so you could hear it. *Just once...*"

The last of the group's line up, tall and lanky; with long, warm ginger hair that covers his face. A bass guitar along his back, swaying back and forth as he melodically shifts his hips to the music in his earbuds. He waits patiently for his friends to quit bickering, standing peacefully in place while silently jamming to himself. That is, until he looks down and sees it...

A foot. A stone foot. Barely peeking out of the darkness before him. Attached to a body of course, but the likes of which is not reached by the light. As the ginger bassist shakes the hair from his face in shock, the foot quickly retracts, fleeing into the darkness once more.

The bassist quickly pops out his earbuds, staring wide-eyed into the pitch-black before him. His skin begins to clam, as the hairs behind his neck stand on end. He turns to Clint, incessantly tapping on the guitarist's shoulder in fear.

"Not now Svenn." Said Clint, brushing his hand off while barking at the others in frustration. "Now look here, I ain't scared of no "Boogieman", ya know? And *you,*" He points to Lukah. "I'm just sayin' that if you don't watch yer volume, the baddies are gonna come crackin' down on us, dontcha know?!"

Lukah mirrors Clint's movements, crossing his eyes and repeating everything he says mockingly.

"The baddies are gonna come crackin' down on us, dontcha know?!" Man shut up! If somethin' were gonna jump out at us don't you think it would've done it by now? We're good bro, can't *nothin'* handle the Funk Munkeys.

Clint and Danba both grin and nod.

"For once, I'm agreein' with what you sayin'." Said Danba.

With the stone foot now multiplying into ten, and the dark silhouettes of the five bodies attached, Svenn's shoulder tapping evolves into a full-blown swatting of Clint's back. The mute bassist struggles to get his allies' attention.

"Svenn, my friend, what the hell is it man!" Said Clint. With this, he, Danba, and Lukah all turn to see what he sees. "Oh..."

"..."

There is a brief pause of silence. The Funk Munkeys stare blankly at the row of five stone men, peeking more coming up behind them.

"..."

"Let's haul ass!!" Hollers Lukah.

Clint grabs Svenn by the back of his collar, pulling him back just in time to evade the wild swing of the stone man. The stone fist smashes a hole into the wall, effortlessly cracking the place where it stood.

"Holy crap!" Said Clint, as the four begin their sprint in the opposite direction.

The Funk Munkeys draw their weapons. Svenn and Clint rip the Stinger, plasma pistols from their hip, firing blindly into the crowd behind them. Danba pulls another drumstick from his back pocket, thumbing at the stick to activate a second blade of light. Lukah pulls a golden microphone to his face, beginning to methodically beatbox into it. His beatboxing causes the mic to glow with increasing fervor, before Lukah jumps out between his two comrades and the encroaching stone men.

~"Stick-and-stones might, break-my-bones but, this-sick-beat will *crush ya!"*~

A powerful shockwave of aura bursts forth from the mic, crashing into the waves of enemy forces. They topple back, giving the Munkeys precious moments to gain distance.

They run forward, diving into the darkness before them with reckless abandon. More stone men get close, nearly grasping Lukah and Clint, before Danba slices clean through them with his auric drum-blades.

"Damn!" Said Lukah. "That's a close shave!"

The Munkeys continue barreling through the darkness, coming swiftly to the large, open clearing of a dead end. Torches begin to light themselves along the wall, a mystic shade of teal, showcasing the large empty space upon a slightly elevated platform. An ancient fighting pit, to which the Munkeys have been expertly trapped in.

"Shit!" Exclaimed Clint. "What're we gonna do now?"

Svenn swiftly rips the bass guitar from around his back, strumming wildly at the chords while pointing the headstock at the incoming stone men. With a rush of fury in his hair-covered eyes, Svenn releases an auric flamethrower from a hole in the headstock with a mighty squeal of the guitar. The mystic flame blasts the oncoming foes, slowing and partially melting them into magma. Lukah points to Svenn and grins, brushing his mohawk to ensure every hair is erectly in place.

"*He's* got the right idea."

Danba and Clint both smile devilishly, as the quartet put their backs to the wall facing the enemy.

Danba reaches into his pocket, pulling from within it a small green seed. He whispers into the seed, chucking it to the ground with swift force. In an instant, the seed grows, sprouting from within the concrete from several places. Suddenly, a wooden stage is made below their feet, with a wooden pair of bongo drums growing from within as well. Danba takes a seat at a stump before the bongo drums, rhythmically beating them with an ominous undertone.

Svenn and Clint take to the stage, firing shockwaves of aura from their guitars at the enemy crowd. Lukah clears his throat, looking back at Danba just once before engaging.

"I wonder how the other teams are dealing with this bullshit."

Danba begins strumming faster and faster, as a mystical, golden glow takes to his bongo drums.

"I bet King Killer's squad ain't no worse for wear. That brotha's got no brains, but his nuts of steel make up for it. Ain't you more worried about *us*? Bonehead?"

Lukah chuckles before facing the approaching stone-army with a defiant smirk.

"I thought I already told'ya." He lifts his golden microphone to his lips, a devilish glow overtaking it. "Can't *nothin'* handle the Funk Munkeys..."

CHAPTER
ONE

Race to the top! The Mirage Pyramid

The dim lighting of wall lit torches adds an eerie energy to the lobby of the Mirage Pyramid. The walls are covered in the ancient language of the pyramid's creators, as well as grandiose images of battle scenes and sacrifices, carved into the limestone walls themselves. Three doors lay at the end of the lobby at ground level, while two parallel, curving staircases lead to a balcony above them, yielding yet another set of three doors. Various pottery and fine dinnerware are displayed on miscellaneous stands throughout the lobby, somehow undisturbed from the initial, violent rising of the pyramid from beneath the desert floor. Two, long tables running parralel each other line the lobby, with old, rickety chairs pushed into their sides.

After waiting for their team's turn, Pilet Whydah and the members of the Hidden Blades gain clearance to enter the ancient fortress. The last of his crew to step inside, Pilet quickly catches up to the others at the center of the lobby. Sporting a pair of baggy blue jeans, a dusty, white tank-top, and desert-stained white running shoes; The youth from Chamboree village sets his mauve eyes to his comrades in the dim light. He brushes the rogue desert sand from his buzz-cut styled hair, watching as it falls to the limestone floor. Some sand grains bounce off a pair of sharp, infrared long-knives at Pilet's side; the "Dragonfly" model.

The first to speak; Faith Sierro.

A gifted auracaster from the forests of Miantha, with an impressive storehouse of knowledge for all things archeological. She sports a blue, spaghetti string top, fitted-white denims and tan sandals. And across her shoulder lay a brown satchel, with a green leather-bound book peeking out; covered in Rok-Senn lettering.

"These murals..." Said Faith. "They're so fascinating. Look at this one." Faith points to a mural to the right of the group.

The mural depicts the image of a group of warriors pointing their daggers out towards a massive beast. The beast's maw juts open, showcasing its many, saw-like teeth and the outspread wings of a bat. It's eyes glow a devilish violet, almost radiating the vicious intensity of its glare off of the wall at the prospects.

"This is strange." Said Faith. "I've never seen this monster before. *Really* ugly too."

Faith's younger sister; Yuuna Sierro, is next to reply.

Short and petite, with long, platinum blonde hair. Covered in dazzling crystal jewelry; she wears flowy, baggy clothing, with a myriad of fun patterns of stars and cosmic entities embroidered into the thin fabric.

"And look over here!" Said Yuuna, directing the group further down the wall. "This one is crazy! See, there's the monster again. But this time it's like, dropping a whole lot of sand on a bunch of houses! At least, I think it's sand?"

The final member of the Hidden Blades adds his thoughts. Max Quinn, mighty young swordsman of the Sanda Tribe, of the island of Hachidori.

His skin, a warm chestnut, with rows of meticulously cornrowed dark hair atop his head. One particular row to the right, *his* right of course, is a colorful yellow braid unlike the rest. Short and muscularly dense, Max is fully suited in gunmetal black, half-plated lamellar armor; the likes of which holds a yellow gem in the center of the chest plate. Two, deadly, single-edged longswords cling magnetically to his left hip.

"It's almost as if it's drowning them in a massive hourglass." Said Max, scratching his stubbled chin inquisitively. "The sand seems to cover such an expansive region, and where did it come from?"

Pilet feels the mural with his fingertips. He looks into the eyes of the beast, almost lost in a trance at something he sees in them.

Faith snaps her fingers in front of Pilet's face.

"Hey hey, Giganus to Pilet, you still there buddy?"

Pilet shakes his head and blinks rapidly.

"Whah? Oh, yeah sorry. Wow, what a wild picture..."

"Well at any rate, we should continue forward." Said Max. "This lobby seems safe, considering nothing has leapt out at us yet. But the clock is ticking, let's not forget why we came here."

"Right!" Replied Yuuna. "Lets goooo!!"

"Right, but go where?" Said Pilet. "There's like, six doors. I mean if you'd ask me, I would go with the ones up the staircase. We're trying to reach the top right? Those *have to* lead upwards."

"Not necessarily." Said Faith. "The Rok-Senn were notorious for creating very confusing floor plans in their vaults. Those stairs might very well lead to a dead end, a staircase downwards, or even worse... a horrible trap."

"Oh ok, well then let's trick them!" Replied Pilet. "Let's take the bottom ones. If the top ones might lead down then the bottom ones might lead up, right?"

"Well, I guess it couldn't hurt. Yeah sure, let's take the third one from the bottom." Said Faith, pointing to the ground level door to the far right.

But as Faith was pointing, Pilet was distracted again by the mural of warriors fighting the ancient beast. The eyes of the beast pierce his mind, peering into his very soul. A wave of primal nostalgia overtakes him, as Pilet gets tunnel vision glaring into the violet pupils.

"Who, who are you? What is this feeling?" He murmured.

After a moment's pause, Pilet shakes himself out of his trance. He turns to see that his team has left him behind during his intrinsic episode.

"Oh shit. Where'd they go? Uhh, she said the third from the bottom... Like third from the right? That would be on the left... Right? Because, well, yeah! Third *away from* the right would be the one on the left. Right? Yeah that's it!"

Pilet runs to the left door, opens it and rushes inside.

"Yo! Where are you guys!!" He shouts.

His voice echoes throughout three long corridors directly inside the door. Upon entry, auric symbols begin to glow on the many wall mounted torches lining the halls. The torches light themselves, their arcane glow burns a bright cerulean hue.

"...Shit. Which way did they go? How could these peabrains leave me behind! Alright, eeny meeny miny... Oh tah hell with it, let's go this way!"

Pilet rushes off down the narrow corridor in the center in search of his lost comrades.

First Blood

Meanwhile, after taking the lobby door to the right, the rest of The Hidden Blades converse.

"Man, it's so dingey in here." Said Yuuna. "This hallway is so plain and gross, just a bunch of aura-lit torches and cobwebs!" She inadvertently walks into one. "Blergh! *Gahh! It's in my mouff!!* *Pthew* *Spew* *Spit* Oh my *God*!!! I hate this place!!"

"Shhh, be easy Yuuna." Said Max. "You never know what's around the corner in a place like this, and we do not want to alert the enemy should they be nearby."

"It *is* nasty though." Said Faith, taking her sandal off and pulling cobwebs out from between her toes. "Ugh damn, I'm gonna need a pedicure after all this. Can't let myself get *jungle feet* like Yuuna's."

"Heyy! It's more natural this way!" Yuuna replied. "Who knows what chemicals they put in nail polish, and you're gonna put that on your body?? Nope, not me!"

"That's fine but at least clean the dirt from underneath your nails, and would it kill you to trim those toe knuckles? People are gonna start mistaking you for the missing link!"

"This is a very awkward conversation to be stuck in between, and to be frank I think I will go on ahead." Said Max. "Wouldn't you agree, Pilet?"
"..."

"Pilet?" He continued. Max turns around, confused at the silence following his question. He notices that Pilet is nowhere in sight. *Gasp* "Oh... Guys? Where's Pilet?"

The girls turn and come to the same realization as Max. Yuuna holds her head in her hands in a panic.

"Holy cow, no way! We lost Pilet?!"

"Are you kidding me?!?." Exclaimed Faith. "Ugh that idiot! He probably went down the wrong corridor at some point, not paying attention as usual. And *now* we're down a teammate if we get attacked! Dammit!"

Max folds his arms, shaking his head in disdain.

"I *thought* it was too quiet back there, a very welcome change that was..."

"Well, let me at least try to call him." Said Faith.

She fiddles with her Chatch, a wrist mounted device which has largely replaced the modern cell phone in recent years. Finding Pilet's contact information, she sends him a phone call. The Chatch rings lowly for but a moment, before abruptly hanging up.

"What? Oh, damn it! There's no service inside this dusty old pyramid!"

"Well it can't be helped then." Said Max. "Pilet is on his own for now. Just the same, if there's anyone who can handle themselves alone, it's him."

"Fine." Replied Faith. "I'll leave him a text. Hopefully he'll get it whenever one of us gets service."

Just then, a subtle creaking sound is heard nearby.

"Huh?" Said Max "What was that?"

"I, I heard it too." Said Yuuna. "But I didn't see anything! Is it... Is it a ghost?!?"

"Oh stop, stop that right now." Replied Faith, reaching for her tome. "Oh God I hate ghosts, I absolutely hate ghosts. There's no ghosts here Yuuna, don't even talk about it. Don't even *think* about it!"

As the three argue about the mysterious sound, the blood curdling scream of a familiar voice is heard in the distance.

"Aaaaaaaagh!!!!" Cries the voice.

Max's right hand clutches his drawing sword.

"Let's move!" He said.

"Right." Replied Faith.

Yuuna trembles, but nods her head in agreement.

"We've gotta help them, no matter how scary. I can do this!"

They rush off down the long corridor. Bumping into the wall at the end and continuing down twists and turns, they follow the sounds of clanging metal and stone. Auric torches continue to light their way as they approach, until they see a broad path that was already lit by the presence of another group.

"There!" Said Yuuna, pointing at the pre-lit corridor in the distance.

They rush to the corner of the corridor, hearing pistol fire and war cries but unable to see the action taking place. Just as they are about to round the corner, they hear the sound of ripping flesh and a gurgling cough. They reach the corridor; but as they do, a fleshy mass the size of a bowling ball flies by Max's head. His reflexes kick in, as he smoothly dips out of the way of the projectile. But a spray of blood follows the mass and splatters all over him and the Sierro sisters as it passes. The mass bounces off of the wall behind them, and continues to roll until it stops at Faith's feet. The severed head of Martin Monroe, of the Cobalt Killers team lies before them; with a look of sheer agony frozen onto his lifeless face.

Faith stands before Martin's remains, stiffened to the bones at the gruesome sight. She feels her stomach bottom out, and her gag reflex nearly upchucks a hearty breakfast of Flarepheasant eggs.

"Oh God... Oh no..." She said.

They turn to see a long legged, spider like creature with sharp stone claws holding up the body of Martin in front of it. A green, glowing auric rune shines beneath its underbelly. The hide appears to be of some form of stone, with articulate joints fashioned between its many legs. Behind it lies the bodies of Samantha Wendigo and Medhi Balma, and further down Kenny Brown can be seen dual wielding two papercut longswords by himself against a second spider-like foe. The creature before them smashes the headless body into the ground beneath it, as pools of blood rush from forth like a geyser from the decapitation site.

"What, is... that?..." Said Max in shock.

"Get ready." Said Faith, reaching slowly for her tome. "That's the one thing I was hoping *not* to see..."

The Silver Stone

In another corridor much further away, Pilet struggles to find his way through the maze-like halls.

"Man, what the hell!" He said. "How could they leave me behind! This place is so confusing. There's no way points or markers, or even a damn arrow saying, "Bathroom this way."! And I have to piss something fierce!"

Pilet notices the Dragonfly seeker camera following him around.

"And you! Why didn't you follow the others or something? You had to pick me?! At least give me a second of privacy so I can loosen the load!"

The Dragonfly seeker does not respond, it simply continues to follow Pilet, buzzing by in a random pattern.

"You know what..."

He swiftly snatches the Dragonfly seeker out of the air and points it in a direction opposite him. Unzipping his pants, the King Killer begins to urinate profusely all over the wall. But as he does so, he begins to forget to point the camera away, exposing himself to the viewers.

In the boardroom of The Hired Blades Association, the spectating executives all cringe and cover their eyes at the sight.

"Yuck kid! No one wants to see that!" Said one executive.

"What are you doing you idiot!" Said another, banging his hands on the table and covering his face.

Chairman Yang lets loose a deep, bellowing laugh.

"*Baahahaha!* I knew I liked this kid! He's got *spunk*! The boy beats to his own drum!"

Pilet finishes and releases the Dragonfly seeker, as it frenziedly flutters around for a moment to find its equilibrium.

"Sorry little buddy. Next time look away when I tell you to, got it?"

Suddenly, a subtle, mechanical squeak is heard around the corner.

"Huh? The hell?..."

Pilet grows suspicious and casts "Callous" in response. He draws his Dragonfly knives and engages the infrared edges. The sharp edges glow a vibrant orange in the dim light of the corridor, letting off mirage-like heat waves. As Pilet turns the corner, he notices the hall is far broader than the previous ones. Ancient writings in the Rok-Senn language are displayed along the wall. Statues of various Rok-Senn Deities sit on thrones along the hall, in between the many inscriptions. One such inscription draws Pilet's attention. While the writing is illegible to him, the golden lettering catches his eye, as well as an etching of one of the sword wielding warriors from the lobby. The warrior's swords are sheathed this time, as his hands and eyes glow a silver hue. Around his neck is a glowing crystal necklace with a chrome-like finish. At the center of the chrome crystal is a small symbol in Rok-Senn language.

"Woah... Cool bling dude..." Said Pilet, touching the stone with his fingertips.

But while Pilet's attention is elsewhere, a dense stone pillar begins to shift and shake. A bright auric rune activates on the pillar's center, as it starts to shapeshift mechanically into a one-armed, human-like figure. Somehow so distracted by the image, Pilet does not notice any of the sound that it makes until the figure is right behind him; standing menacingly with it's one, massive arm winding up to swing. The figure's joints creak softly while drawing back it's arm, pulling Pilet out of his trance.

"Whah?..."

He turns around to the sight of the stone creature, its arm cocked and ready to strike, but frozen in place as if playing possum. The two stare at each other silently for a moment. Pilet, confused at the stone figure's appearance, taps it on the forehead.

"Who put this statue here-"

Crrrack

He's interrupted by a thunderous straight punch from the statue, cracking him square in the jaw. The blow knocks him directly through the mysterious mural behind him with ease, crumbling the wall like soft dried clay.

"Aggh!!"

Tumbling and rolling, Pilet crashes into a hidden room, nestled covertly behind the hollow wall of the warrior's mural.

"Ow, what the hell?!..." Pilet wiggles his jaw.

The Callous cast took the brunt of the blow, but the impact leaves him dazed and confused. The rocked King Killer begins to scan his surroundings.

Several wall hung torches activate at his presence, illuminating the hidden room and revealing its many treasures. Golden sets of armor, swords, daggers and axes line the walls. Entire buckets full of Rubies and Sapphires sit at each corner.

A sarcophagus lined with silver and tiger's eye lay behind the grounded Pilet, with a wall mounted stone bust of a falcon's head hovering over it. Around the falcon's neck rests a chrome crystal on a black chord of a necklace, identical to the one on the now crumpled mural.

The dragonfly seeker camera buzzes by the stone figure and into the hidden chamber. It flutters around the room, scanning its contents fervently.

Members of the HBA Board of executives all stare at the room's monitor, lost in awe of the new discovery.

"Chairman Yang..." Said a member of the board. "Are you seeing what I'm seeing here?"

Chairman Yang folds his arms and rubs his beard, glaring intently at the chrome crystal. After a brief pause, he reaches into his coat pocket and pulls out a similar crystal necklace of iridescent crimson. The crystal bears a different Rok-Senn word, but shares the same arcane glow. Yang holds the crystal up to his face, comparing it to the one seen on screen.

"Well would you look at that... The boy's found one..."

Inside the hidden chamber, Pilet stands up and wipes the dust from his clothes. He notices the crystal necklace dangling from the falcon's head and becomes entranced in its glow.

"No way. It's... Real?"

Unable to resist, Pilet gently removes the necklace from the bust and places it around his own neck, feeling the crystal curiously with his fingertips. Just then, the crushing sound of the stone foe stepping on crumbled debris can be heard nearby.

"Oh, that's right, I have a guest... Alright, want to play hardball? You asked for it!" Excaimed Pilet, turning around and pointing arrogantly at the statue. But as he points, he realizes that his Dragonfly knives were knocked out of his hands in the tumble, lying at the feet of the stone foe. "You've *got* to be kidding me. Ok then, plan B it is."

Pilet lifts his arm and begins to ready a "Hollowpoint", an explosive aura technique he's known for. But as he does so, the crystal necklace begins to glow an alchemic silver. As Pilet cultivates aura into his palm, the typical hollow ball of violet aura begins to fill with a glowing, silver light. Pilet's hands take to this same phenomena, as he releases a volley of three silver Hollowpoints at his foe.

Ripping across the distance with dizzying speed, the silver-lined Hollowpoints explode fervently on impact. But this time, they leave a mysterious, boiling hot metal splattered across the hide of the morphing foe. The metal swiftly hardens where it lies, seeping into the joints of the figure and immobilizing it in place.

"Woah?! What is *that*?" Said Pilet, befuddled at the heated substance.

He then notices both his *hands* and the *crystal* glowing that same silver hue from the mural. Startled, Pilet looks down at his face in the reflection of his Chatch. He clearly sees that his *eyes* have also taken to the metallic shine.

"I... I'm like a God-damn superhero or something!!"

As he fauns over his new appearance; the stone figure struggles to free itself from the hidden rooms entrance, as its welded joints creak in protest.

"Ah shit, now you're in the way... Well, if this thing can fire super hot metal-" Pilet readies another silver Hollowpoint. "- I wonder..."

This time he takes aim, focuses his mind and charges a larger blast. He watches as the liquid inside becomes more and more solid. As the Hollowpoint grows larger, it also increases in weight in his hand, beginning to solidify in its violet auric shell. Finally, the King Killer makes his move.

"Eat this!!"

He fires the solid metal Hollowpoint at his foe, sending a heavy ball of mysterious metal crashing into his foe like a medieval cannonball. With a deafening boom, the cannonball smashes its target to bits on impact. Whatever is not instantly blown to smithereens, spills over into the broad hall, as the auric rune across the figure's chest halts its arcane glow.

"*Sweet!!*" Exclaims Pilet, elated at the carnage of his newfound ability. "I got me some magic *Rok-Senn* bullet hands now! Nothing can stand in my way!"

Pilet steps back out into the hall, gathering and re-sheathing his Dragonfly knives whilst hobbling past the remains of his assailant. But as he does so, he's greeted by the sight of over a dozen small, insect-like stone figures. Each one sports a similar auric rune glowing along its underbelly. They cling to the ceiling, walls and statues around him, intently staring at the fiery prospect.

Pilet smirks and holds his fist up to his face. His clenched hand begins to shine an arcane silver.

"Alright bitches. Who's up for some pinball?"

Morphing Menace

Somewhere across the pyramid, Max, Faith and Yuuna steel themselves for combat.

The long-legged spider creatures' stone claws clack across the floor, as it rushes towards the three prospects. It lunges viciously at the group, as its forelegs reach out first for Max.

"Bring it, you atrocity!" Exclaims Max, drawing his dueling Lacerate and parrying the claws to the side.

Faith and Yuuna rush past the spider as it collides into the wall behind them.

"Help... me."

They hear a voice faintly cry for help, as they see blood pouring from the mouth of Samantha Wendigo. A hole is torn through her chest, as blood spills out from the wound. As they run to her aid, Yuuna trips over the corpse of Medhi Balma; flipping him over and revealing his lifeless face to be completely ripped off.

"Hoh, oh my God!! What ddid, what did that thing do!!" She exclaimed, holding her hands to her mouth in horror.

"Please... help." Cries the faint voice.

The sisters turn to see Samantha holding a hand out towards them in desperation. Yuuna springs to her feet and runs over to her.

"Hang on, just hang on ok?" She said, rubbing her hands and cultivating a platinum aura. "Overmend!" She casts.

Her hands radiate with platinum aura, as such energy pours forth into Samantha's chest. This begins to swiftly seal up the wound created by the ghastly stone spider.

"Aagh!!!" Cries Kenny Brown, further down the hall.

His spider-like foe holds both of his severed arms in its claws, as the armless Kenny Brown falls to his knees in defeat. His hands still tightly clutch the Papercut infrared longswords as they glow in the darkness. The spider raises its long foreleg in the air and swiftly smashes-in the skull of the fallen ex-con with its stone claw.

A tear begins to fall from Samantha's eye, at the grisly sight of her last comrades demise. The stone spider turns to Faith and Yuuna, picking up one of Kenny's arms and throwing it directly at Yuuna.

"Skarrya!!" Casts Faith, as a crimson blade of fiery aura juts forth from her fingertips.

The flying, Papercut-wielding, severed arm is parried out of the air by Faith's blade just before it reaches her sister.

"Keep patching her up." She said. "I'll deal with the Morph."

"The what?!?" Said Max, dodging and parrying blows from his foe at the corridor's entrance.

"It's a Rok-Senn *Morph*." Faith replied. "The Rok-Senn used runes written in blood to store aura into inanimate objects. They'd create transforming pillars, vases, and other objects and bring them to life with aura. The unlucky passersby trying to steal from their treasures would trigger the rune and be met with a swift and deceptive end. It's one of their most used traps-"

Faith is cut short by the claw of the second Morph reaching for her head. She draws her Skarrya blade to her face to block just in time, before turning a page in her tome and casting, "Ruug Yah!" with her free hand.

Vibrant, rainbow colored scales cover the Rok-Senn auracaster from head to toe. Yuuna can't help but glue her gaze to her sister's form-change, a glint of envious admiration in her eyes.

"I do love that cast, sis." Said Yuuna. "It's so pretty..."

Faith ducks and rolls under a horizontal swipe from the Morph, drawing it away from Yuuna and Samantha.

Max continues a bout of swordplay against the first Morph, managing to slice one of its hind legs off at the joint.

"One of their "most used" traps you say?" Said Max. "This would have been useful information maybe ten minutes ago, or am I mistaken for thinking that?!"

Faith fends off her foe, chipping away at the stone claws as they continue to reach out for her.

"Well like I said I was hoping *NOT* to see it, and plus I didn't want to worry Yuuna. And what's with the sass Max?! Just focus on your fight and let's get out of here alive!"

As Yuuna continues to heal Samantha, the wounded ex-con gives her a warm smile in gratitude. Yuuna smiles back.

"It's ok, you're gonna be ok. Ok?" She said. Her lips quiver ever so slightly as she delivers this line.

Samantha smiles and nods, but begins to cough uncontrollably and spits up blood onto Yuuna's chest. Shocked at the sight of the blood, her hands start to shake and tremble. But she takes a deep breath and closes her eyes, finding mental clarity and continuing her "Overmend" cast once more.

"I'm s, I'm s... I'm sorr-" Samantha attempts to speak.

"Shhhhshshshh don't speak, save your energy." Said Yuuna.

Faith continues to slice and scrape at the Morph with her Skarrya, as bits and pieces of stone continue to fly off of it. The Morph leaps into the air, attempting to body-slam Faith on the way down. But as it Descends, Faith rolls nimbly out of harm's way; snipping off one of the Morph's formidable forelegs on the way out. As the severed limb flies narrowly overhead, Faith lunges for the Morph's underbelly and slices directly along the glowing rune.

A piercing, teeth-gnashing sound is made as her Skarrya blade runs across the stone surface of the glowing rune. The cut in the rune begins to make the stone beasts latent aura visibly seep out, as its legs begin to wobble and shake. Faith takes a step back and observes the phenomenon at play.

"Hmm." She ponders. "Hey Max! Cut away at the rune underneath! You'll make it bleed aura!!"

Turning his attention to Faith, Max fails to see a hindleg of his Morph foe jutting out to kick him in the stomach.

"Ooof!" Grunts Max, as he's kicked square into the wall with a powerful thud.

Winded from the blow, he falls to his knees for a moment in pain. On his knees he sees the glow of the Morph's runic underbelly and understands Faith's request. He springs to his feet and raises his Lacerate, readying to strike.

The Morph flings its claw at him, but Max swiftly slices the stone weapon down, relieving the Morph of its arm in the process. It swings its other clawed foreleg at the young swordsman like a baseball bat. But Max promptly cuts right through the stone, taking both of its primary weapons from it.

"The steel of The Sanda does not yield to such petty stone."

Finally, without either of its forelegs, the Morph stands on its four hindlegs in an attempt to slam itself into Max. But as it does so, it exposes its runic underbelly. Max sheaths the sword in his hands, opting instead for the wickedly sharp blade of his homeland; the *Drawing Lacerate.*

Visibly identical to the *Dueling Lacerate*; the Drawing Lacerate bears a sharpness to its honed edge that to this day is unmatched throughout the history of the world. This blade is to be drawn only when a fight can be settled in a single slash, in order to preserve its merciless edge.

In the blink of an eye, Max draws and releases a wicked slash from this *Drawing* Lacerate, resheathing the blade just as quickly. The cut is so fierce that the solid-stone Morph actually separates in two, falling to the floor in halves. The stored aura of the Rok-Senn Morph releases from within and dissipates into thin air, as the writhing legs of the ancient monstrosity drop lifelessy to the ground.

"...Well I cut the rune as you said..." Said Max, peering into the split Morph. "That and more..."

Faith stands before her quivering foe, as the Morph struggles to swing its heavy limbs at her.

"Good that's good, this one's almost fried too!" She said, clipping and trimming the appendages of the Morph in its slowed state.

As she slashes the final leg off of her foe with her Skarrya blade, the Morph falls to its belly, squirming on what's left of its limbs. Faith closes her fist, retracting the Skarrya blade into thin air. She turns the page of her tome and points her fingertips in a cone towards the Morph.

"Frisio!!" She casts.

A powerful frost cone bursts forth from her palm and freezes the Morph in place. A moment later, the final stores of aura bleed out into the air, as the sounds of the Morph trying to escape come to a halt. Max approaches from the rear.

"Why didn't you do that in the first place?" He said with a grin.

"Well I've never faced one of these before, who knows if the damn thing would have just shook Frisio off and ended up with a huge ice-club on the end of its arm. And what about you? I didn't know you could just cut through stone like that!"

Max laughs.

"Ha! Neither did I. This blade for more accustomed to ripping flesh from bone..."

Yuuna cries out to her partners.

"Guys help!"

The two rush over to their teammate and cast "Mend" to assist her. They hold their hands out toward Samantha as their healing aura seeps into her chest. But despite their best efforts, the battered candidate continues to choke and cough up blood. She warmly grasps Yuuna's wrist, gives the trio her warmest smile and with the last of her strength, she forms her last words.

"Than. Ttthank. You."

Samantha's gaze peers off, her eyes fixed in place like a child's doll. As the last of The Cobalt Killers passes on, the red Dragonfly seeker camera assigned to their team zips away down the hall. Stunned, the Hidden Blades release their auracast and share a moment of silence. Max finds a Stinger pistol with a spent magazine on the ground beside her. He takes the weapon, puts it in her hand, and sits her hand in her lap.

"You were a true warrior." He said in a somber tone. "It was an honor to share the battlefield with you." He turns to the sisters Sierro. "What terrors await our fellow candidates..."

"I'm sorry guys..." Said Yuuna. The subtle frown before one cries a genuine cry of sadness creeps along the sides of her lips. Her eyes begin to gloss and water, as she tries not to choke up. She clears her throat. "I did the best I could... It's just, the wound was too deep. Not even Overmend could save her..."

Faith puts a hand on Yuuna's shoulder.

"You did great sis. You did great."

The group gets up and continues their journey through the halls of the ancient pyramid, ever aware of the new dangers they may face.

The Veteran's Lament

Outside the pyramid, Faxion of the Deadeye sits beside his Hired Blade colleagues, by the edge of the Cool Oasis. Sporting a black, long-sleeved compression shirt, and light gray cargo pants tucked into his black combat boots, the Veteran Blade's signature olive fedora shades his eyes from the harsh desert sun. The lean, fair-skinned, middle-aged mercenary digs into the pocket of his olive trench coat on the ground, drawing a piece of candy from within and popping it into his mouth.

He sits in a ring of beach chairs with the attending Hired Blade proctors, sipping from a mug of warm tea. The Veteran Blade convenes with his peers about the progress of the exam thus far. He sits between the two marksmanship proctors, both of whom wearing navy and grey camouflage uniforms. One with deep-blue eyes and tanned skin, with a shaved head and brunette goatee. The other, dark-skinned with green eyes, sporting a dark brown chinstrap and faux hawk combo.

"So Dex, how about those Mystic Marauders?" Said the goateed proctor. "Remember that big one who got stuck in between the dividers? I hear he took down two desert lions infected by the Wurm with his bear hands!"

The green eyed proctor responds.

"No kidding?" Said Dex. "Oh yeah... Cornelius right? Damn Dustin, it's a good thing we didn't piss *him* off. Those Kettlenian Elites are really no joke. I heard Lazlow's boy gave a royal *ass* whooping to the King Killer, pun intended."

"Are you surprised?" Replied Dustin. "You saw his shooting skills, there was more sizzling plasma in the wall behind the range than there was in his targets! King Killer's gonna need more than those hot knives he fileted the Wurm King with to deal with that kid."

"Ahem..." Faxion coughs deliberately.

Dex and Dustin pause for a moment, remembering Faxion to be The Hidden Blades' sponsor.

"Oh... Sorry Fax." Said Dex. "Hey, at least he pulled through in the end, right? I mean..." Cringing, Dex looks to Dustin nervously.

"I meannn, yeah!" Continued Dustin. "Hey, didn't he merc *another* Wurm King? He and his squad took out Kuweha, right? Good shit that is! About time that acid-spitting bastard got what he deserved!"

"But I heard the solo candidate did all the work in that fight." Replied Dex. "In fact, I think Kuweha was kicking their ass too, until the flamecaster showed up-"

Dustin begins motioning a hand across his throat and silently mouthing the words "Shut up" to his colleague.

Faxion silently sips his tea. He stares off into the distance for a moment before flashing a subtle grin.

"*I* killed Kuweha, credit where credit is due boys." He said.

Dex and Dustin's jaws drop.

"Wha- How the hell did *you* kill it?" Said Dustin. "Wait, did you use your sponsor save?!"

Faxion nods and grins.

"Oh you're a damn kill-stealer you are! See Dex, people don't change! Remember when he used to do that shit to me?"

Dex begins laughing hysterically.

"You mean back at the Dacklio outpost invasion, when Fax was landing head-shots on every insurgent that you only dinged or grazed? Yeah, I remember!! And he got paid for every one of 'em!"

Faxion grins from ear to ear trying not to laugh at Dustin's expense.

"Gotta hit the mark the *first* time gentlemen! You *might not* get a second chance."

"Yeah, second chance my ass... I took home half a paycheck for that one, Deadeye! I was gonna buy my kid one of those fancy hoverboards..." Replied Dustin.

Toste, both the prince of the land of Menanois and the Hired Bades swordsmanship proctor draws near. Thin and lean, with a dark handlebar mustache and his hair combed flat and to the right. In navy slacks and a white button-up, his red bowtie is loosened in the heat of the desert sun. A gently-curved sabre sits at his left hip, instead of the previous ball-tipped rapier. And to his right hip, his notorious parrying dagger lies sheathed.

"Hope I'm not interrupting." Said Toste, taking a seat beside Dex.

"What? No not at all!" Dex replied. "Hey sit here Toste, I was about to grab a cold one anyway."

"Why thank you sir." Toste replied, taking Dex's seat by Faxion.

"Ooh that sounds good, count me in!" Said Dustin.

Dex and Dustin head for the coolers to quench the thirst of the desert heat. Toste unbuckles his sword belt to sit down, and rests it on his lap. Faxion raises his teacup to the Menanois swordsman.

"Hello, brother." He said.

"How can you be drinking that in this weather?" Toste responds. "Do your insides not boil over?"

"It's chamomile!" Faxion replied. "A natural remedy for a racing mind."

"You, Faxion the Deadeye, suffer from a racing mind? Now I've seen everything. What's wrong, stressed about the boy from Minago?"

Faxion recounts the harsh words of Lazlow the Enforcer; when Pilet, his young prodigy was presumed dead in a bout with Lazlow Jr..

"The only shame is that you took a kid out of high school and told him he could make it as a Blade."

"Just a tad, yes." Said Faxion. "He's young. *Gifted*, but young. And he lacks almost any experience. Who *knows* what dangers lie inside that pyramid? You know I was quite confident in my decision to train him for the exam because he showed such promise. But now, I'm not so sure..."

Toste leans forward in his seat, a serious look upon his face.

"Well you're a master marksman, you know what happens when you hesitate to pull the trigger. You had your sight set on a candidate; you aimed, and you fired. And I believe you hit the mark beautifully. Now I'll have no talk of this nonsense of uncertainty." Toste raises his saber, the sun glints off of the sterling blade. "He beat me, fair and square. To me, there's nothing *uncertain* about that. He'd better succeed, if not there'll be hell to pay from this blade."

Faxion laughs.

"You're right, old friend. What was I thinking? Well, I hope he's doing ok in there. I hope they're all doing ok..."

Clash: The Mystic Marauders V.S. The Tree of Granite (feat. Pilet)

Back to the hall of the hidden chamber, Pilet walks triumphantly past a myriad of desecrated mini-Morph spiders. Their bodies, an assortment of welded to the wall, shattered to bits and sliced into pieces. Both; spheres of hardened, and splattered metal riddle the hall in a painted mess. The buzz of Pilet's Dragonfly long knives comes to a halt as he deactivates the infrared edges, waiting a moment for them to cool before sliding them into the holster on his hip. He exits the hall and begins walking up a steep ramp, leaving the carnage of an arcane metal tirade in his wake.

"Hmmph, too easy." He scoffs, cracking his knuckles and stretching his triceps. "Still, persistent little twerps. Made the big ugly bastard from the desert look like a puppy dog. Both *Blondie* and the Wurm."

As he treks up the ramp to what appears to be the next level of the pyramid, he sees a bright light from a large room at the top.

"Hmm, wonder what's going on up there…"

As he reaches the top, he enters the room and sees rows upon rows of lit torches, lighting the cylindrical walls all the way up to the incredibly high ceiling with azure flame. The walls are covered in Rok-Senn hieroglyphics, the characters lined with silver and bronze. The floor of the room itself is relatively bare, save for what appears to be a gigantic stone tree standing tall in the center. The tree has two thick branches, parallel to one another towards the middle of the trunk. Both branches are devoid of leaves, as well as the canopy, which comes together in one barren point. As Pilet walks into the room, he hears a familiar voice a ways off into his peripherals.

"Get ready guys, it's probably going to Morph soon." Said the voice.

Pilet turns to see Puerto and his exam team, "The Mystic Marauders", standing in battle-ready positions.

"Man O' War" Puerto, a tall and lanky young man from Port Lyso, with a deep-blue bandana atop his slicked back, dark hair. A dark tattoo of a jellyfish surrounded by runes covers the back of his left hand.

Wendy the sniper; a young woman in fitted, crimson athletic apparel, with a blood-red, 9mm "Arcane Pierce" rifle strapped around her shoulder.

Dunya; a young, Zardenian woman with long, wavy hair. Covered in gold bangles, she wears a long, magenta and pearl colored dress with a slit down the side; showcasing a Stinger pistol and a retracted papercut longsword holstered around her right thigh.

Finally, Cornelius; the fearsome pride of The Kettlenian Elite. A mountain of a man, dwarfing most in attendance. He bears the powerful, trademarked suit of the Kettlenian Elite forces, "The Alabaster Armor". The armor a mix of white and gunmetal gray, with a pair of high-tech cannons mounted onto his forearms.

As Pilet spots his fellow candidates, the many doors leading into the large room all slam shut at once, locking the five candidates in. Immediately following this; a large, forest green auric rune begins to glow in the middle of the stone tree, as the branches begin to shift. Wendy suddenly spots Pilet out of the corner of her eye.

"Hey, is that... King Killer?" She squints and covers her brow with her hand. "Look, over there!"

"You're kidding, right?" Puerto replied, drawing a Pilum beam rifle from around his back.

"No no, that's totally him! Hey, King Killer! Where's your crew?" Said Wendy.

"Yo!" Replied Pilet, drawing his Dragonfly knives. "I got lost. No biggie though, they can handle themselves."

Wendy turns and looks at Puerto with a jovial smile on her face.

"What an idiot." She said, trying not to laugh loud enough for Pilet to hear.

Puerto simply shakes his head and takes aim at the morphing tree.

"King Killer, if you want to help, feel free. Otherwise, stay out of the way. Got it?"

· Puerto turns to see Pilet missing from where he stood but a moment ago, only to hear the sound of hot metal searing through stone. His attention is then drawn to see the fiery prospect digging his Dragonfly knives into the stone tree Morph, using them to climb up the trunk.

"Damn this shit is hard!" Exclaimed Pilet, pressing his super-heated blades into the hide of the tree. "Harder than those little shits in the hallway, that's for sure!"

"*Sigh*. Why do I even bother? Alright guys let's make this quick. Remember, aim for the rune in the center."

The plasma weapons of The Mystic Marauders unload viciously on their target, knocking the tree slightly back as it finishes morphing into the shape of a man. The massive Morph forms two immensely thick legs, beginning to march towards The Mystic Marauders. The two branches mold themselves into long, gangly arms with articulate hands and ghoulish, pointed fingers. The canopy folds itself over, forming a sharp horn over a pair of devilish glowing green eyes. The titanic Morph slowly but surely stomps its way toward the team, shaking the earth with every bounding step. A lesser group of warriors would quake in their boots at the terrifying sight, but the Mystic Marauders remain calm and collected, readying a volley of plasma. Puerto and Wendy aim their rifles at the glowing rune at its chest, Dunya draws two Stinger pistols and Cornelius begins to charge a blast from his mounted forearm cannons.

"*Readyyy......* Fire!!" Shouts Puerto.

Crakoww

The firing squad unleashes a wicked barrage of shots, each of which with deadly precision. They land flush onto the glowing rune, sending the massive Morph stumbling back.

"Bull's eye!!" Shouts Cornelius in triumph. "Did you see that?! Right on the money I say!!"

"Calm down honey." Replied Dunya. "With a barrel that big you could probably shoot a squirrel out of a tree a mile off."

"With his luck, he'd blast the whole tree." Said Puerto.

The tree Morph finds its footing and continues its forward march, much to the chagrin of the Marauders.

"What?!" Said Wendy. "We hit the damn rune! Why is it still standing?!"

As the smoke clears, the team notices a forcefield of pure aura surrounding the rune, liken to a translucent dome of auric Callous armor.

"Wow, the Rok-Senn really knew how to make 'em huh?" Said Puerto. "Alright, time for a new plan. Battle stations!"

"Right!" Clamours his team.

Cornelius draws three thick metal batons from a strap around his waist.

Clink

The batons join together at sophisticated joints to form a long, staff-like object. He then pulls a large, round shield from his back, folds the shield in two at a special joint in the center, and sets it atop the staff like the head of a hammer.

Dunya begins to belly dance in the traditional style of the Zardenian people, cultivating aura in her palms and the soles of her feet. Her bangles create entrancing sound waves, as she begins to sway back and forth, creating mesmerizing afterimages of herself. With every step she takes, the glowing red soles of her feet leave behind a footprint of crimson flame.

Wendy tosses a dense metal disc aloft that transforms into a floating platform. She hops aboard and begins flying about the room, looking for a good angle to fire with her crimson Arcane Pierce.

Puerto hoists his Pilum beam rifle over his shoulder, in favor of a standard-issue Papercut, infrared longsword. He pulls the small metal bar from a holster around his right thigh and presses the release, triggering the folded blade to shoot out in segments from inside. The blade quickly begins to heat a bright orange, much like the Dragonflies of Pilet. Puerto then lifts his left hand, as his auric tattoo of a deep blue jellyfish begins to glow.

"Azure colony!" He casts, as a slew of translucent, azure, auric jellyfish begin to manifest and float through the air.

The jellyfish begin to fill the room, surrounding the tree Morph in a sea of shining blue. The Morph spots one of the many afterimages of Dunya beneath its feet, lifting its leg high into the air for a vicious stomp. As the stone titan brings down its foot, the afterimage of Dunya vanishes, leaving only her flaming footprint beneath it. The footprint explodes like an arcane landmine, chipping away at the bottom of the Morph's foot and knocking it off balance.

"*Woooaaah!*" Exclaims Pilet, still very much attached to the stone behemoth. "Careful down there! I've got him right where I want him!!"

The tumbling Morph continues to tilt backward, falling back into a herd of floating auric jellyfish. As the stone bark makes contact, the many jellyfish explode in a similar manner, blowing chunks of stone off of the rough hide of the Morph.

"Gah!" Cried Pilet, flailing about while holding onto the handle of his Dragonflies.

"Told you not to get in the way!" Yelled Puerto.

"Here honey, I cleared a nice path for you." Said Dunya to Cornelius, creating a line free of fiery footsteps behind the Morph.

Cornelius darts down the path, holding the oversized handle of his warhammer behind him. As he closes in on the leg of the Morph, the hulking Kettlenian Elite leaps into the air, swinging his mighty weapon with a powerful horizontal smash to the inside of the Morph's knee joint. The Morph's leg gives out under the power of the extraordinary blow, taking a knee to the ground and subsequently landing on a plethora of flaming footsteps.

With a mighty barrage of auric explosions, the heavy stone leg of the Morph is blown clean off, sent flying into the corner of the room. Dunya returns to Puerto and releases the aura from the soles of her feet, falling on her buttocks and pouring water on her soles from a canteen.

"Ouch! Thank God the hard part is done. That's enough of the hotfoot honey, my *dogs* are killing me!"

"Good job Dunya. One step closer to victory." Puerto replied.

Continuing his momentum, Cornelius runs up the back of the kneeling titan, passing Pilet along the way.

"Care to tag along King Killer?!" Said Cornelius.

Pilet grins.

"Hah! Sure thing. Last one up owes the other a pint!"

"I like the sound of that!" Replied Cornelius, as the two begin to rush up the back of the downed Morph.

"Fleetfoot!" They cast in unison.

On the way up, the Morph begins to claw at its own back with its wickedly sharp fingers, hoping to grab hold of one of its foes. Its hand gets dangerously close to Pilet, before each of its fingers are shot off by a series of powerful plasma shots. Pilet looks up to see Wendy in the distance, aiming her Arcane Pierce and giving him a thumbs up.

"Get 'um King Killer." She said, pulling the pin on a plasma grenade and tossing it at the right elbow joint of the titanic tree.

The grenade blows chunks out of the Morph's elbow, hindering its ability to bend the arm.

Pilet continues his dash, passing a peculiarly colored golden spot on the back of the behemoth.

"Huh?" He said, looking back at the strange spot.

He reaches the top before Cornelius, leaping high into the air above the Morph's head.

"Take this!!" He cried, dropping both of his knives into the base of the Morphs canopy and digging mercilessly, deep into the stone. But to no effect, as the Morph simply raises its good hand and flicks Pilet away in an instant.

"Gah! Oh shit!" Exclaims Pilet, headed directly towards the wall of the room at top speed. "Callous!!" He casts, covering his body in a translucent golden aura to brace for impact.

But just inches away from the hard stone wall connecting with his spine, Pilet's whole body envelopes itself in the bronze exoskeleton inherited by Kuweha the Melter. A sturdy, copper-colored breastplate covers his chest, as a similar armored plating overtakes his back. His forearms and shins are blanketed by the copper armor. A sleek, hard bronze helmet covers his head, leaving only a slit for his devilishly glowing violet eyes.

Crrrasssh

Pilet slams into the wall, but briskly bounces off without more than a headache from the initial impact. Puerto and Dunya look on in confusion.

"What the hell?..." Said the two simultaneously.

Seeing Pilet's plight, Wendy flies by and catches him by the wrist to save him from the fall.

"How many times am I going to save you, dude? And what's with the shiny new duds??" She said.

"Uugggh, wha-" Pilet groans, shaking his head clear from the blow.

Cornelius now reaches the canopy of the Morph, leaping into the air for an aerial strike liken to Pilet's.

"That looked fun! Let me try!!" He said, lifting his hammer high into the air.

At the height of his jump, he twists a segment of the handle, releasing infrared axe blades from within the folded shield. The blades immediately take to a bright red hue, loosing intense heat from its edges. On his descent, Cornelius readies for a mighty overhead swing down onto the head of his opponent. But the Morph tilts ever so slightly to the left, having merely the sharp horn of the canopy severed by the hulking Marauder's slash.

As the horn falls to the earth, the sharp point plants itself directly into the ground. The severed end of the horn creates a platform for Cornelius, as he breaks his fall landing directly before the massive tree.

"Let's try something else." Said Puerto. "Fleetfoot!" He casts, as he rushes towards Cornelius, nimbly avoiding the flaming footsteps of the Zardenian belly dancer.

"Cornelius! Give me a lift!" Said Puerto, leaping for his teammate.

Cornelius holds out his massive palm, as Puerto perches upon it like a trained hawk.

"Show no mercy!" Cried Cornelius, tossing his teammate effortlessly into the air at high speed.

Puerto flies directly parallel to the trunk of the mighty stone tree, drawing his Papercut as he nears the Callous protected rune. On the way up, he closely inspects the texture of the Morphs hide.

"Hmm, granite huh? Duly noted." He thought.

Puerto flies by the translucent, auric armor over the rune, scraping it with his Papercut along the way. The infrared blade reacts to the aura; causing sparks to fly, but leaving it completely unscathed.

"No notable effect from the infrared, maybe aura will do the trick..."

At the height of Puerto's ascent, he holds his left fist aloft, the jellyfish tattoo glows an arcane cerulean. Puerto points his glowing open palm towards the Morph's rune core.

"Tendril!" He casts; releasing a set of four long, frilled tentacles of pure cerulean aura, and launching them toward his foe. The tendrils wrap around the base of the tree, encompassing the Callous shield of the Morphs rune. Puerto follows up with an arcane combination.

"Nematoshock!!"

A surge of cobalt electricity fires along the auric tendrils, sending a shockwave throughout the trunk of the Morph. The electricity crackles over the Callous shield, but again leaves it relatively untouched. Puerto releases the tendrils, dissipating them into thin air.

"Damn!" Exclaimed Puerto. "Still nothing? How strong *were* the Rok-Senn?"

As Puerto begins to descend, Wendy flies by with Pilet still in hand. She catches Puerto by the wrist with her free hand, clearly putting a strain on her hovering disc.

"Ok sheesh, one of you has got to go!" She said.

"I'm stumped here, no pun intended." Said Puerto. "That shield is strong, *very* strong. Both physical and auracast attacks can't break that shield. What can we do?" He looks over to Pilet, still covered in bronze armor. "And what the hell happened to you?"

Pilet remembers the gold patch he noticed on the back of their foe. While the three fly bye, the tree Morph raises its left hand and swipes its sharp claws at the flying trio.

"Woah woah!" Exclaims Wendy, narrowly dodging the gangly fingers.

As the titan's hand passes by the group, Pilet hops off of the disc and lands on the back of it.

"I've got an idea, watch the rune shield!" He said, nimbly dashing down the arm and around the Morphs' back.

Pilet uses his Dragonflies to scale the trunk, holding on tightly as the Morph begins to violently flail in protest. Looking about 30 feet across the way, Pilet sees the golden patch. But, distracted by the sight of his target, Pilet fails to notice the shot-up, fingerless right hand of the Morph approaching from behind.

A hefty thunk is heard, as the clubbed hand knocks Pilet right off of his piercing Dragonfly knives. The fiery prospect swears in frustration l, as he begins to fall much further down the back of the trunk.

"You piece of shit!!" He exclaims, tumbling down the granite titan.

In an act of desperation, Pilet calls upon his large forearm stingers first seen with the death of Kuweha. The stingers jut out of the top of his wrists, scraping along the hide of the Morph.

"Here goes nothing!"

He raises his arm and drives his stinger into the granite bark. Surprisingly, the sharp stinger manages to penetrate up to two inches into the granite before the hardness of the rock halts its progression.

"Oh, that actually worked!" He thought. *"Wow! These things are serious. They're no Dragonflies, but they'll do for now."*

He looks up at his Dragonfly knives, sticking out of the upper back of the flailing Morph. Pilet begins rapidly scaling up the back of the granite behemoth, working his way back to the prized weapons.

On ground level, Dunya draws twin Stinger pistols and starts firing at the Morph, chipping away at its granite bark. The Morph swings an arm towards Dunya in an attempt to thwart the barrage. But as the massive arm branch nears the belly dancer, Cornelius relieves the Morph of its hand with a vicious skyward slash of his infrared battleaxe.

A mighty klack and a seismic thud resound throughout the massive chamber, and the earth shakes beneath them as the granite hand falls to the ground.

"What do you plan to accomplish with those little *water* pistols Dunya?" Said Cornelius.

"At this point honey, anything." She replied. "What are we to do? The damn thing doesn't seem to have an off switch!"

Wendy drops Puerto off with the two and continues her ascent around the room.

"I'll keep scanning for something, *anything* that might stand out. You guys just distract it!" Said Wendy, reloading her Arcane Pierce. "I'll try not to let the King Killer die too, *whatever* that psycho is attempting."

"He said to watch the rune shield." Said Puerto. "I'm not positive what that was supposed to mean, but at this point I'll try anything. I just want this thing to die!" He draws the Pilum beam rifle from around his shoulder. "*If* for any reason that shield comes down, *rain hell* on that rune!"

Cornelius clangs together his forearms. His alabaster vambraces begin to shift and change, as if preparing to transform. He turns to Puerto.

"Do you think it's time?" He said.

"No, not yet." Puerto replied. "That's a last, *last* resort. It's hard to control, and the last thing we need is this whole damn pyramid collapsing on our heads."

Cornelius nods, as he clangs his forearms again, returning the vambraces back to normal.

"A sibling thing, it is..."

Many corridors away, down countless halls and dozens of chambers, Yuuna, Max, and Faith proceed through the Mirage Pyramid with caution. Faith looks at the blood on her hands, the image of Martin Monroe's head rolling across the cracked tile floor flashes through her mind. She takes a deep sip of air, exhaling her heavy thoughts into the wind.

"Man, there *really are* levels to this, aren't there." She said.

"Levels to what?" Replied Max, cautiously checking around a dark corner before motioning the sisters to proceed. "The pyramid? Yes, I believe there are probably *several* levels. Too bad we have yet to find a staircase."

"No, not the pyramid." Said Faith. "I meant there are levels to *us*, the exam candidates. I mean, and I don't want to be morbid mind you, but we just watched the Cobalt Killers get completely eradicated right before our eyes... And as sad as that is, I can't help but marvel at our ability to take on those Rok-Senn Morphs by oursleves. Even though Yuuna was preoccupied, I could guarantee you she could hold her own against one too. But the Cobalt Killers were all, well, literal killers! If not skilled, they had to have at least some form of mental toughness and experience. But there were *more* of them, and they still never stood a chance..."

"It's sad really, it is." Said Yuuna. "I had no sympathy for them at first, being that they *were* murderers and all. But after seeing what happened to them... I mean, I don't think anyone deserves to go like that."

"You know Yuuna, as Licensed Hired Blades, I can promise you that there will be missions that require us to take life as well." Said Max. "The fact that the Cobalt Killers had done so already should, *if anything*, be indicative of an advantage on their part."

"Oh here we go again, picking on me because I don't want to hurt anyone!" Exclaimed Yuuna. "Look, I know we're probably going to have to... *kill* people... but at least it's for the greater good!" She looks to her sister for approval. "Right?!"

"Shh Yuuna, lower your voice." Faith replied. "And nobody's picking on you, especially not Max! I mean come on." She motions to him. "This guy wouldn't pull the tag off of his *own* mattress! And he probably doesn't kill bugs either!"

"I, well..." Said Max. "I mean it's dishonorable and cowardice to take the life of such a small creature, that fight is simply not fair. And I do apologize for offending you Yuuna, I had not intended to do so."

"See!" said Faith. "He's a marshmallow, a teddy bear, and he's right! And I've been saying it all along. One of these days you're going to have to learn to show no mercy, that hesitation is going to get you... well it's going to get *you* killed!"

As Faith continues to berate her sister, the three approach a set of limestone double doors at the end of the hall. Their arrival triggers an auric rune to glow, as the doors swing open on their own.

"You two will need to halt your debate for now." Interrupts Max. "I think we've found our way to the next level."

Tearing up, Yunna folds her arms at her sister and pouts, abruptly turning her face away from her.

"*Sigh* Fine, be like that." Said Faith, turning and briskly walking into the newly revealed chamber.

Torches light upon her arrival, lighting the cylindrical room to reveal a pitfall filled with spears beneath them. The ceiling is quite high, with limestone pedestals protruding from the wall in an ascending spiral pattern, all the way to the top. At the height of the rising step stones, a narrow platform awaits with a sealed doorway. Looking up at the myriad of rising stones, Faith fails to see the spears lining the floor past the entry platform.

"Wait!" Exclaimed Max, lunging forth and grabbing Faith by the arm.

The young auracaster takes a step past the platform and begins to fall, but finds her balance in the grasp of her Sanda colleague.

"Woah!" She said. "What is this? Oh my God, the floor!"

Wide-eyed for but a moment, Yuuna looks over to check on her sister. Seeing Faith unharmed, she sighs in relief, then pouts again, averting her gaze with arms folded.

"You are the expert here." Said Max, pulling Faith away from the edge of the platform. "Have you any knowledge of this form of trap?"

"It looks like a basic pitfall." She replied. "Sorry Max, I should've known better than to just waltz in like that. Thanks, you really saved my skin. Now the goal here is to reach the top platform without getting decimated by whatever traps are set within the walls. It could be everything from poisoned darts, arrows, stored auric bolts of fire or lightning... *honestly,* your guess is as good as mine."

"I see..." Said Max. "Well, this should be fun."

"Kite stream!" Cast Yuuna.

She flies past Faith and Max, surrounding herself with a powerful layer of Guardian Mist, her defensive armor of wind. The glow of platinum aura enshrouds the Wind and Star caster, as every pour of her skin releases a concentrated wind; like a mystical air-hockey table.

"Yuuna stop!" Exclaimed Faith. "What are you doing?! It's dangerous!"

Yuuna gives her sister the cold shoulder, slowly flying up the center of the spiraling chamber. Glowing auric runes activate as she passes by, firing bolts of fire, frost, and lightning at her with vicious fervor. But the Guardian mist of the young prospect holds true, easily shielding Yuuna from the onslaught of elemental fury.

"Amazing." Said Max, stunned at the performance of his teammate. "She's, triggering all of the traps for our safe passage."

"Yeah. Yeah, she is..." Said Faith. She turns to Max, letting out a heavy sigh. "Max, do you think I'm too hard on her?"

"It's hard to say." Replied Max. "My father was very hard on me, and it turned me into the fierce warrior I am today. But... his harsh lessons were always taught with an underlying love, and not once have I harbored disdain towards him for it. I will say though; he is my father, and you are her sister. If my older brother tried to scold or reprimand me, we would fight until one or both of us bled. Mind you he would likely win, and even, then I'd *never* yield. A sibling thing, it is..."

"Wait, you have a brother?" Said Faith. "Huh, I never knew that."

"I have several. But one of them, the oldest, has a penchant for torturing me." Max gazes off toward the ceiling, a glint of rage mixed with frustration in his eyes. "It's part of the reason I'm set on this journey, to get away from him..."

The sounds of the elements furiously firing from the walls come to a halt, as Yuuna reaches the top. She lounges across the platform like a resting cat, posting her head on her shoulder.

"The hard work's all done, hurry up down there." She said.

"That's our cue." Said Max. "Just give it some thought. Your sister is her own person, as you are yours."

Faith takes pause, the wheels in her head turning with the advice of her peer. She flashes Max a quick smile, before readying herself for the trek up the spiraling staircase.

"Thanks, you're right." Said Faith. "And, I know. I've always known..."

Faith and Max step out to the furthest point of the platform and cast "Fleetfoot", nimbly navigating the scattered stepping stones with ease. They hop from stone to stone, weightlessly traversing the spiraling chamber. As they reach the top, Max slips, beginning to fall before Faith catches his arm in a split second. She drags him up, hoisting the Sanda warrior to the top platform.

"Phew!" Exclaimed Max. "Many thanks."

"Hah! Consider us even." Replied Faith. Struck with a somber expression, she turns to her younger sister. "Sis... I'm sorry. I... I've been really hard on you. You don't have to listen to me. You have your own life, and I don't have a right to tell you how to do things..."

Surprised at this act of humility, Yuuna unfolds her arms and twiddles her thumbs bashfully.

"Well, I mean... *Good!* At least you know now..." She grows silent for a moment.

Faith looks back at Max, who gives her a nod and a subtle grin.

"Now let's get out of here, there's spears down there!" Said Yuuna,

Looking down at the heights they've scaled. "And who knows what they put on them. What if they smear their shit on them, there are people who do that, you know? I read about it one time. Who needs to fall on a shit smear, I mean a shit spear! You know?!"

Max and Faith laugh.

"What are you afraid of? You can fly!" Replied Faith.

"I mean I don't know, what if I trip like clumsy Max and run out of aura at the same time or something? Then I'm getting shit speared!"

"What?! I'm not clumsy! The Sanda have the reflexes of a fearsome Wisp tiger!" He replied.

"Not today they don't!" Retorts Yuuna.

"I... How dare you!" Said Max. "I assure you I could have saved myself from that fall! Faith, you never should have helped."

"Oh yeah?!" She replied.

Faith winks at Yuuna before pushing Max off of the platform.

"Aaaaaahhh!! You swine!!" He shouts at the sisters.

Yuuna effortlessly flies down and grabs Max, who's still light as a feather from casting Fleetfoot. She drops him on the platform, landing herself beside the door to the next level. Max furrows his brow at Faith, who simply shrugs her shoulders.

"That's what you get for being ungrateful. Bitch-ass." Said Faith.

Max shakes his head.

"The two of you will be the end of me, I swear it. If Pilet does not get me killed first, it's one of you for sure."

The girls laugh, as Yuuna pushes open the door to the second floor. They walk through, triggering more arcane torches to light their path. As they proceed, a familiar voice begins to ring throughout Yuuna's mind.

"I sense it, an unpleasant surprise... You're in for a treeeat."

"What?" She thought, feeling an eerie presence from within her bag.

She rummages through it, pulling out the Black Onyx harboring the inprisoned soul of Besmith; an ancient, criminal Necrocaster from Rok-Senn time. The stone emanates a ghoulish, black aura, liken to a midnight fog.

"Oh, it's just you. Quiet down." She grips the stone and suppresses the latent aura, quieting the voice of Besmith.

"But wait, you ignorant girl! I'm trying to tell you somethi-"

"Click, I'm not buying what you're selling buddy." Said Yuuna.

"What are you talking about?" Said Max. "Or rather, *who* are you talking to?"

"Oh no one, just a telemarketer." She replied.

Max looks to Faith, who returns his puzzled expression with her own. The three continue their way down the narrow path, wondering what dangers are in store for them next.

Roar of the Arcane Eraser

Back on level one, Pilet and the Mystic Marauders continue their battle with the titanic granite Morph.

Pilet, still adorned in his bronze exoskeleton, scales the back of the massive Morph with his razor-sharp wrist stingers.

"God, this is tiring!" Exclaims Pilet, retracting the exoskeleton helmet and wiping the sweat from his brow. "After all this, I need a vacation. I hope that tatted-up old Chairman gives paid time off."

"Let's give King Killer a diversion." Said Puerto. "Whatever he's doing up there, the Morph doesn't seem to like it."

"Sounds good to me!" Replied Cornelius, readying his mounted forearm cannons. "Give it some plasma!!"

Dunya, Puerto, and Cornelius all begin to unload their firearms onto the granite bark of the Morph, drawing its attention to the firing squad and away from its unwanted hitchiker. A barrage of red, hot light pummels into the hide of the creature; as the ancient stone tree flails its arms to keep from toppling over.

"Took ya long enough!" Shouts Pilet. "I thought I was the only one workin' here!"

Wendy fires a powerful beam from her Arcane Pierce, knocking a hunk of granite from the massive tree.

"Just shut up and fight would you?!" She retorts.

Finally, uninterrupted by the flailing foe, Pilet reaches his Dragonfly knives and pulls them from the back of the titan. He swiftly works his way to the golden patch on its back and lifts his knives overhead.

"I sure hope this works..." He thought, anxiously digging his hands into the weapon's rubber grips. "You're dead!!"

With a swift stab, Pilet plunges his knives into the golden hull, finding it to be a surprisingly easy task. Underneath the gold appears to be hollow, allowing wiggle room for his piercing blades.

"What?" He said, a befuddled look upon his face. "What's... this?"

He notices the golden patch begin to shake and move with his blades, revealing it to be a thin plate of gold covering a hollow chamber beneath. He slashes and slices at it, looking for a way to open the golden covering. Eventually, he manages to cut a large hole into the golden plate, revealing a glowing auric rune underneath.

"I knew it!" He exclaimed. "Guys! Get ready!!"

"What?!" Replied Puerto. "Ready for what?!"

"Just watch!"

The King Killer drives his heated blades into the glowing rune with a vicious thrust. Suddenly, the rune begins to dim, as if the life force sealed within many centuries ago is fading away. Instantly, the Callous force field around the frontal auric rune shatters and falls to the earth, finally leaving the ancient rune vulnerable to attack.

"Oh shit!" Yelled Puerto. "King Killer, you're a genius! Crazy, but a genius!! Marauders, take aim!"

Wendy swiftly flies over to her team, as the four ready their firearms for another synchronized barrage. As the Callous shield goes down, the vulnerable tree covers its rune with its arms and takes a knee, blocking the rune from the line of fire.

"Fire!!" Exclaimed Puerto.

"Grrraaaaahhhh!!!" The Marauders let loose a fervent battle cry.

Like a finale of fireworks, the sound of bright, hot plasma escaping the barrels of each gun fills the room.

With a mighty crash, the arms and knee of the titanic tree are chewed up by the onslaught of plasma. But they hold true, protecting the rune from further harm. Suddenly, the rune begins to glow beneath the guarding limbs. Glowing veins begin to appear within the layers of granite bark, releasing a high-pitched whistle. The tree falls face down to the earth, completely covering its auric rune to the ground.

"Shit!" Said Wendy. "How are we supposed to hit it now? The rune's completely covered."

"We've got bigger problems to worry about." Replied Puerto. "I was afraid it was going to do this."

"Do what honey?" Said Dunya. "Keel over and do the worm?"

"No, it's going to explode. The Rok-Senn programmed some Morphs to do this. If they *really* wanted someone dead, they'd make a rune capable of self-destructing as a last resort."

"They *what?!*" Replied Wendy. "What the *hell* are we supposed to do about that?!"

"Calm down!" Said Puerto. He nods to his Kettlenian Elite ally, peering at his mighty forearm cannons. "Cornelius, it's time. Do you think you can stop your *big* guns, before they fry a hole through the walls?"

"The Morph is pretty thick." Said Cornelius. "With luck, and I mean lots of luck, I can stop them just in time."

"Alright, good enough for me." Replied Puerto. "Then let's do this! Everyone stand back! That means you too, King Killer!"

"What's he saying over there?" Thought Pilet, pulling his Dragonflies from the golden hull.

Cornelius takes a knee for stability, clangs his vambraces together, and holds his arms out in front of him. The vambraces begin to shift and mechanically change. They combine to make a cannon, 3 feet in diameter around his fists, clenched around a mechanical throttle in each hand. The palms of Cornelius' hands begin to emanate azure aura, feeding such aura into the clenched throttles. These throttles send the aura into the cannon, causing the massive barrel to begin to rotate. All the while, the tree continues to glow, growing brighter and hotter with each passing second. Pilet finally notices this.

"Woah buddy, what's the big deal?" Said Pilet, shielding his eyes from the light. "What's up with the lamp act? What am I, a moth?"

"Move you fool!!" Bellows Cornelius from across the way. "Do you wish to be ground to powder as well?!"

The rotating cannons begin to cultivate azure aura in a small sphere at the center of the cannon barrel. This sphere grows larger and larger as the cannon's rotation picks up speed, releasing a wicked hum.

"Oh, shit!!" Exclaims Pilet, dashing away from the line of fire. He reappears swiftly behind the hulking Kettlenian Elite. "What's with the shiny new toy, big guy?"

"It's not a toy King Killer, it's a weapon of mass destruction!" Replied Wendy. "And so is that tree! It's gonna blow!"

"Hwhat!" Exclaimed Pilet in horror. "Let's get out of here! What are you guys doing standing around trying to blast it?! It's a bomb!! You're gonna shoot a bomb with a cannon?!" Pilet begins incessantly tapping his temples. "Does that *sound* like a solid plan to you?!"

"Just watch." Replied Puerto sarcastically.

Pilet furrows his brow at Puerto.

Suddenly, streams of air rapidly begin pouring out from the back of the rotating cannon, as built-in fans begin to cool the heating weapon. The streams are so powerful they force the candidates to cover their eyes and mouths. Cornelius braces himself, tucking his chin into his shoulder. As the giant morph begins to shine like a dying star, the Kettlenian Elite releases a mighty howl.

"For Kettlena!!"

The cannon fires with a deafening boom, creating an 8-foot-wide beam of pure cobalt aura aimed directly at the glowing granite titan.

The ear-shatterig sound of stone being melted down and turned to dust encapsulates the chamber. Progressively, the beam begins to chew down the mighty stone log until it nears the guarded rune. As it does so, what's left of the Morph begins to release an epic shine of light, ready to trigger the final explosion.

As the light blinds the candidates, Puerto fights the wind from the blast and cups the eyes of his massive comrade, shielding his vision.

"Get ready! You're almost there!!" Yelled Puerto over the sound of the powerful beam.

Wary of the impending blast, Cornelius cries out, giving every last ounce of aura he has into one final push.

"Grrraaaahhhhh!!"

The beam suddenly widens by three feet, vaporizing the shining rune in a blast of auric fury. Just as the beam passes the last few inches of the glowing rune, Cornelius begins to power down his cannon.

The impressive, gyrating weapon begins to slow, as the cobalt beam shrinks down three feet, then five, then eight. Finally, right before burning through the last of the granite Morph, the beam dwindles and the cannon simmers to a halt.

"Uuughh." Grunts Cornelius, falling face down and plummeting toward the ground. With his last ounce of strength, he points the cannon away from his team. The fans in the back deactivate and switch to the front, letting out a massive blast of steam before their eyes. As the weapon cools, it disassembles itself, once again forming alabaster vambraces.

"Are you ok honey?!" Exclaims Dunya, running to Cornelius. "That was amazing! You really came to the rescue!!"

Puerto brushes his face in his palms vigorously, takes a deep breath, and falls to his knees.

"Cornelius, if we make it out of here alive... remind our sponsor to give you a raise."

The exhausted Cornelius flashes a labored thumbs up.

"*Pant* All in a day's work. *Pant*"

Wendy sits cross-legged, staring blankly into space. A traumatized shade over her eyes.

"I can't believe I signed up for this shit..."

Pilet deactivates his Dragonflies, giving them a moment to cool before holstering them at his hip. He takes a seat by Cornelius.

"Dude, that was some serious firepower." He said. "What kind of gun is that?"

"It's not a gun." Replied Puerto. "It's an Arcane Eraser. It's not powered by plasma, electricity, or even old-fashioned lead bullets. Just straight-up aura. Something that Cornelius has in spades."

"Are you serious?" Said Pilet. He turns to Cornelius. "You used *that* much aura? How are you still breathing?!"

"..."

Cornelius fails to respond.

Visibly worried, the group works together to roll his heavy body over.

"Nngguuhh"

The bulky Marauder begins snoring incessantly.

"Oh thank God." Said Wendy. "The big oaf had me scared, thought he stopped breathing for a second."

Ping

Pilet's Chatch notifies him of a message.

"*Hey dipshit, good job getting lost so early. Meet us at the center of level two. And try not to die, ok?*" -Faith-

"... *Smug bitch*" He thought. "Welp, guess I found my team. Sounds like they're waiting for me upstairs."

Krkrkrkrkrkrkrkrkr

The low grumble of seismic activity begins to occur, as a vertical line of auric runes begins to glow along the wall.

"Oh crap, what now?!" Yelped Pilet.

Each rune takes up a 4-foot space of stone tile, which separates itself from the wall and begins to form a floating stairwell to the upper level. The stairwell ends at a set of double doors, as the doors shift and open on their own.

"That looks like the way to level two." Said Dunya. "Sweetie, you should go on ahead and find your team. I'm sure they're worried sick about you."

"Yeah, please." Said Puerto. "I mean, we'll stay here a bit... Cornelius needs a break after that, *crazy* shit."

"Alright then." Said Pilet, releasing his bronze exoskeleton. The insectoid armor slips off of his body, clanging along the ground in an erratic fashion. Puerto, Dunya, and Wendy exchange puzzled glances at the outlandish sight. "Pleasure doing business with you folks, glad to do all the work." He looks at Cornelius, sprawled out on the ground. "Well, most of the work."

"Shut up and get going!" Said Wendy, as she tosses a grenade at his head.

"Ouch! Oh, what the hell! Fleetfoot!"

Pilet vanishes up the floating, stone steps in an instant. Wendy walks over and picks up the grenade, its pin still firmly placed inside. The Mystic Marauders let out a unanimous laugh at Pilet's expense, waking Cornelius from his slumber.

"GAH!" Exclaims Cornelius.

The startled giant flails about for a moment, smacking Puerto in the back of the head with his massive forearm.

"Oof!" Grunts Puerto, swiftly falling on his face unconscious.

Wendy and Dunya look at each other with raised eyebrows and take a few steps back. A few seconds later Cornelius falls back to sleep, snoring with an intensity that rivals Pilet's.

TWO

The Vessel to the Unknown

On level two, Pilet paces up and down the halls of The Mirage Pyramid.

"The center of level two. The *center* of *level two*... How do they know where the center is? How am *I* supposed to know where it is? But I'm the dipshit for getting lost?! This place is like a God damned maze! All the walls look the same, even the torches are all still blue!"

The sound of Pilet talking to himself attracts a multitude of small, Rok-Senn Morphs. The Morphs begin to transform from colorful, limestone pottery lining the walls; taking the shape of vivid, bulky scarabs. The scarab Morphs start to take flight, heading straight for Pilet with their mandibles snapping open and shut viciously. The fiery prospect takes notice, drawing his Dragonfly knives and holding the blades out towards his flying foes.

"Tch, bring it!" He scoffs.

He launches himself at the stone insects, slicing and dicing at dizzying speed. Wings and mandibles fly through the air, bouncing and clacking off of the tiled walls. His infrared blades whirl gracefully in rapid succession, like flaming pinwheels in the dimly lit corridor.

Shink *Clack* *Kshh*

The Dragonflies' infrared edges effortlessly flay chunks from the limestone Morphs, sending clouds of grainy particles wisping through the air. Pilet cuts down each morph one by one with ease, littering the floor with severed beetle limbs. But the persistent Scarabs keep coming, seemingly endless in number. One Morph creeps past Pilet's blades, nipping him in the ear as it flies past.

"Aaagh, damn!" He exclaims. "How many are there?! What kind of *ass-backwards* beehive did I just step in?!"

In a mad rush to reach the next chamber, Pilet darts and dodges in between the scarabs.

"Callous!" He casts.

A golden, auric overcoat protects him from the razor-sharp mandibles of the flying insects, as the jaws and claws scrape and scratch over the surface layer. But as Pilet turns a corner, he sees another hall lined to the brim with pottery.

"You've got to be kidding me..."

In an instant, the pottery morphs into large hustling soldier ants, snapping their mandibles savagely at the fiery prospect. They rush Pilet, flooding the hall like an endless rogue wave. Pilet turns around, pivoting on the back foot to sprint to safety. But the thorax of a flying scarab smashes him in the face, as the stone insect wraps its legs around his head.

"Hmmmmmmmppphhh!!" Pilet releases a muffled cry.

Unable to see anything or free himself from the grip of the scarab, Pilet rolls around on the floor in protest. The ants and scarabs cover his body, biting and clawing away at the protective Callous layer.

"God damn it! Thought Pilet. *"No! I can't go out like this!! God, I hope the others are having this hard of a time... because this is bullshit!!"*

As Pilet continues to struggle with the impending swarm of insectoids; Max, Faith, and Yuuna make their way to the center of the second level, completely undisturbed.

"It's quiet... *Too* quiet..." Said Max. "Faith, we've been walking for the past half hour, and not a single trap has sprung. Am I crazy to believe there is something wrong here?"

"Be grateful Max!" Said Yuuna. "I don't want any more scary spider things coming after us. You saw what they did to the others..."

"To be honest it's rare, but not unheard of for a route to be completely clear of danger." Replied Faith. "In those examples, it typically tends to be more of a psychological test than a physical one. The constant fear of impending doom plays tricks on the mind."

"Is it working on you?" Said Max.

"Please, I have nerves of steel." She replied.

Fsst fsst fsst fsst fsst

A subtle grinding sound causes Faith to abruptly stop and hike her shoulders to her ears.

"Shit, i-is, is that a ghost?!" Said Faith.

Max and Faith turn back and see Yuuna trimming her fingernails with a nail file. She looks up at them puzzledly.

"What?... Oh, sorry." Said Yuuna, packing the file into her satchel.

Max grins and puts a hand on Faith's shoulder.

"Those steel nerves must be starting to rust, huh?" He laughs.

"Tch, I... Who files their nails at a time like this?!"

The trio takes a sharp left, followed by a quick right. They immediately find themselves standing at a sealed door covered in Rok-Senn writing. Faith approaches the door, feeling the etched lettering with her fingertips.

"What does it say, sis?" Said Yuuna.

"It's a riddle." She replied. *"It serves no master, it keeps no servants. It works with time, it works against time. Embraced by some, scorned by others. The Vessel to the unknown."* How interesting..."

"Sooo..... Hmmm." Said Yuuna. "It has no master, *or servants?* Sounds like a jobless bum."

"Embraced by some... scorned by others..." Said Max, brushing his stubble inquisitively. "Defeat. Is it defeat?"

"Well, is *defeat* the vessel of the unknown?" Said Faith. "Defeat is the vessel to... well, loss. Right? And what if you make a bet and lose? If you lose, you *know* what you're losing; that which you wagered. That's not *unknown* right?"

"I see, this is true. How very strange." Replied Max.

The group takes a moment to think, standing in silence while assessing the potential answers.

While these three inquire within to solve this ancient riddle, Pilet's plight becomes more dire by the second. Back at his end of the pyramid, he tumbles and rolls about, desperately trying to shake free from the swarming morphs.

Crunch *Crack*

"Aaagh! Damn you to hell!" Pilet cries out in agony.

The powerful mandibles of the limestone insects begin to pierce the arcane armor surrounding Pilet. They reach the soft flesh of the prospect, biting and gnawing him open. Almost instinctively, Pilet's bronze scorpion armor emerges from beneath what's left of his Callous, shattering the auric layer like sugar glass. The bronze exoskeleton proves strong enough to withstand the jaws of the maniacal morphs, thwarting their attempts to penetrate.

Pilet then manages to pull the rogue scarab off of his face, giving him a clear line of sight down the hall. He staggers to his feet and casts "Fleetfoot!", dashing down the hall with nimble haste. But the joints of the armor prove difficult to maneuver in, cutting off his ability to make a sharp turn.

With a heavy crash, he smacks face-first into the end wall, tumbling backward uncontrollably.

"Agh! If it's not that slow-ass monkey suit, it's these awkward duds! Why can't I get some kind of *useful* special powers?!"

As Pilet relents on his labored mobility, the humming of his countless, flying foes echoes through the hall. Before he can stand to his feet, The scarabs and soldier ants quickly overtake him. They crawl across his bronze hide, gnawing and snapping their jaws at his exoskeleton. As the faux insects soon realize the strength of the armor, they begin to attack the joints. They bite and chew between the crooks of Pilet's elbows and behind his knees, his ankles, his wrists. As Pilet cries out in agony, the ravaging morph swarm begins to find weak points beneath the exoskeleton, peeling the bronze hide from Pilet's flesh.

"Gggaaaaaagghhhh!!" He cries, frantically flailing about.

In a desperate, lastish effort; Pilet takes a deep breath, releases his bronze armor, and activates his risky ace in the hole, the "Fever Point". His eyes take to their devilish violet hue, as the Fever Point's trademark indigo aura begins to seep out of every pore of his skin. He exhales indigo steam, as his skin swelters and takes to a heated shade of maroon. Violet, auric patterns shine vividly across his body, lighting the darkness of the chamber with an otherworldly glow. The glow startles the limestone beasts for a moment, causing them to backpedal in shock.

"Just remember." Said Pilet, glaring at the endless army of stone insects before him. The look in his glowing eyes could pierce steel. "*You* wanted this."

After a moment's pause, the insects collect themselves and go on the attack. They rush back down the hall, frantically buzzing and snapping at Pilet. But as they reach the fiery prospect, all their stone mandibles taste is fresh air. Pilet's speed yields a convincing afterimage where the young warrior once stood. As the scarabs and soldier ants realize this, they begin to fall apart; singed and sliced mercilessly by the heated edges of Pilet's blades.

The fiery prospect darts and blitzes down the halls of the Mirage Pyramid, hacking and slashing at the vast army of his insectoid foes feverishly. His speed renders him nigh invisible, baffling the morphs and leaving them flying aimlessly in search of their prey. But as the slices of limestone begin to pile up in the chambers of the Pyramid, it becomes increasingly difficult for even Pilet to maneuver. Suddenly, he trips; tumbling and rolling into a pile of crushed limestone.

"Shit!"

The insects immediately take note, swarming him yet again in response. Some soldier ants and a scarab manage to latch on to him in the scuffle, each taking a generous bite of his flesh.

The King Killer cries out in agony, slicing and scraping the insects from his peeled-back, fleshy wounds.

Pilet lets loose a wild flurry of spinning slashes, decimating the morphs attached to him in an instant. But he's soon met with countless more creeping foes, following up the assault of their fallen brethren. In a panic, he continues to dart down the halls, searching for a way out of this limestone hell...

Meanwhile, Faith, Yuuna, and Max continue their attempt at solving the ancient riddle. Faith and Max sit cross-legged in front of the sealed door, peering up at the gold lettering of the inscription. Yuuna casually floats by in the air above her teammates, arms folded behind her head as if looking up to the night sky.

"It works with time, and it works... *against* time?" Said Faith. "Pick a side! What a confusing riddle!"

"Maybe it's like a double agent, sis." Replied Yuuna, pulling a wooden flute from her satchel. "Or what if it's like apple juice? At first, it's sweet and tangy, but *over time* it turns into tart apple cider! But if you let it sit too long, it becomes applejack! Nothing but straight alcohol, no good for your tummy... or your liver." She begins to play a mellow tune on her wooden flute.

"I... What?" Replied Faith. "Yuuna, it's not apple juice. Remember, *"It serves no master, and has no servants."* An apple serves a tree, or at least it comes from a tree, and it's full of little seed servants that turn into more apple trees!"

"That's just your opinion." Said Yuuna. "The tree is the apple's Mommy. *And,* the seeds aren't the apple's servants, they're its babies!"

"There's a difference?" Said Faith.

Max flashes Faith a concerned glare.

"I fear for your future children..."

Yuuna continues to play her flute. The dry, unkempt wood fails to capture sound very well, as the flute begins to screech and creek. Faith and Max cringe painfully, covering their ears in disdain.

"Ugh!" Grunts Faith in frustration. "Yuuna! You never oil that thing!" She turns to Max. "She does this *all* the time. Playing that damn, dead-wood children's toy until the late hours of the night with her friends in the backyard. It annoys me to death!"

"*Gasp* Children's toy?!" Said Yuuna. "This is the traditional instrument of the Wind and Star tribe! And it's not *my* fault you hide in your room and cover your head when they come over. If a little music and fellowship ends up *killing* you, I'd hardly imagine being a mercenary to be a good fit for you."

While the sisters continue gawking back and forth, Max remains deep in thought.

"Death.... Killing.... I wonder." Thought Max. He interrupts Faith and Yuuna's heated debate. "It's, death."

The sisters pause their exchange.

"What?" They replied puzzledly.

"The riddle." He said. "I believe it represents death."

Faith rests her chin on her palm inquisitively.

"I feel like I know where you're going with this. But please, go on."

"Well death is inevitable, it's unstoppable; therefore serving no master." Said Max. "It keeps no servants because any who meet with death, well... *Die.* Now, time works with death by causing age, which brings decay. But time will also *prolong* life, slowing the course of death."

"Wow Max, you've really got this fleshed out." Said Yuuna. "But what about the whole "embraced and scorned" thing, or the part where it says, "The vessel to the unknown"?

"Thanks. So, death is scorned by most of those who *value* their life. But unfortunately for some, those under great suffering have shown to embrace it with open arms... Finally, no one in the world of the living knows the secrets of the other side, making death truly "The vessel to the unknown".

"That's astounding!" Exclaimed Faith. "What an observation Max! Here, let's give it a shot." Faith stands to her feet, walking up to the door and feeling the inscription with her fingertips. "Krohh." She uttered cryptically. "It's Rok-Senn for "Death"."

Suddenly, the inscriptions on the wall take to a radiant golden glow. The dust begins to shift within the crevices of the side hinges, as the stone door starts to rise up into the ceiling.

"You did it Max!" Exclaimed Yuuna. "I knew we kept you around for a reason!"

"Thank you... I think?" He replied.

As the door fully lifts, the three are greeted with the sight of a wide-open, hexagon-shaped room with a tall ceiling. Several other doors liken to their entrance line each wall of the hexagon. Inside, the floor is riddled with mounds of piled sand. The center of the room boasts a large, golden sarcophagus, encrusted with rubies and sapphires. The head of the sarcophagus is lizard-like in appearance, boasting turquoise scales and sharp, ivory teeth. Six ivory horns protrude horizontally from the crown of its head, as a row of clear, sharp quartz spines line the center of its belly. Max, Faith, and Yuuna proceed with caution, weary of their cryptic surroundings.

Yuuna peers over a mound of sand, taking note of a small bronze plate peeking out from within.

"Hmm, looks like there's something inside."

As she reaches for the bronze plate, Faith grabs her hand in protest.

"Yuuna wait, we don't know what will happen if you do that. The Rok-Senn were crafty. *Who knows* what dangers can be triggered from touching *anything* here."

Max approaches the sarcophagus, examining the lush details of the precious gems encrusted upon it.

"What immaculate work these people have done. To think that whatever creature lay inside was given such an honorable resting place, I wonder of its significance."

Just then, a violent wail can be heard from a distance. The sound echoes from behind the door directly across from the three's entrance.

"Aaaagghhh!!" Cried the voice in agony.

They instantly turn their attention to the farside door.

"What was that?" Said Faith.

Yuuna jumps at the sound, her hiked and frozen shoulders tickling her earlobes.

"Holy shit, that scared me! It, it almost sounded like-"

"Uwwaaagh!!"

The voice cries out again, this time closer in proximity.

"That's Pilet!" Exclaimed Faith. "What the hell is he doing?! He's going to spring every trap in the pyramid yelling like that!"

"He must be in danger!" Said Max. "I've only ever heard him scream like that the moment he was stabbed by Toste. He does not yield to pain or panic that easily, something isn't right!"

They run to the door, banging and shouting for their teammate in hopes for him to hear.

"Pilet! We're here!" Yelled Yuuna.

"What's happening?! Pilet!" Shouted Faith.

"Follow our voice Pilet! Stay strong!!" Bellowed Max.

The sound of Pilet's screaming grows in intensity, as a wicked humming begins to follow.

"Do you hear that?!" Said Max. "Faith, what is that?!"

"It sounds like a damn swarm of bees!" She replied. "I think he ran into some kind of morph nest! Guys, get ready!"

"BEES?!" Exclaimed Yuuna. "I hate bees! Why do you do these things Pilet!?"

They continue banging and hollering, hoping to draw Pilet's attention before it's too late.

Just then, a loud thunk hits the other side of the door like a sack of potatoes. The trio back away in perplexity.

"... Pilet?" Said Yuuna.

Suddenly, the sound of merciless scraping can be heard coming from the other side. A moment later; the vibrant, orange, infrared edge of Pilet's dragonfly knives begins peeking out of the door like a nail through someone's boot. In an instant, the other Dragonfly peeks through, as the two blades slice the door apart like a pizza cutter. This door instantly falls to pieces, crumbling to slivers under the bladesmanship of the fiery prospect. Pilet bolts through the debris before it can even hit the ground, tumbling and rolling before finally coming to a halt.

"Wait, you can just... *cut down* the door?" Said Max. "Why did I not think of that?..."

The Kekehio Shriidah

Pilet lies there, facing away from his team in a fetal position, as a pool of blood begins to form around him. Yuuna slowly approaches, putting her hand on his shoulder. She rolls him over gently.

"Pilet? Are... are you ok? *Gasp!*"

Yuuna leaps back in shock, as Pilet's intestines line the floor between them. His skin, covered in cuts and fleshy gashes. Pilet's body, still glowing from the Fever Point, tries to rapidly regenerate. But the usual healing properties seem to be labored and slowed, taking much longer to seal wounds and restitch flesh. Yuuna drops to her knees and immediately clasps her hands together.

"Overmend!" She casts, forming a platinum capsule of healing aura around her wounded ally. "Guys, he's hurt *bad*... And he's not healing!"

"He's not healing?!" Replied Faith. "What do you mean? Yesterday he took a *missile* to the face and brushed it off like it was nothing! How is he not healing?!"

"He's been using his powers a lot lately, maybe his body is just burnt out." Replied Max; drawing his custom plasma bow, the Hachidorinese "Sunshower". He fixes the bow around his wrist like a wrist rocket, as the bow unfurls itself, forming a full weapon. "Never mind that, Yuuna can take care of him." The Sanda warrior glares warily down into the dark hall from which the King Killer arrived. "Something is coming..."

Max pulls back the drawstring on his sunshower, charging hot, golden plasma in all three barrels. After a moment's pause, the silhouette of the swarming morphs begins to take shape at the end of the hall. The flood of insects takes Max by surprise, as he unleashes a barrage of plasma arrows down the crowded corridor. Firing at will, the plasma arrows knock the limestone scarabs out of the air with blinding speed.

"Come at me! Ancient demons!"

Max fires volley after volley of scorching plasma down the hall, reducing each unfortunate target to dust and rubble. After felling several dozen maniacal morphs, the plasma barrels on Max's Sunshower begin to billow clouds of steam.

"Great Serpent Dragon, how many of them are there?!" Said Max, twisting the handle of his Sunshower. The twist activates a mechanism in the bow that releases the hot steam in thick pillars directly from the plasma barrels. "My bow is overheating, at this rate we'll be overtaken! If you've any ideas as to how to stop them, now is the time to share."

"It's just as I thought, a swarm." Said Faith. "There must have been a nest nearby that Pilet ran into." She begins sifting the pages of her tome, stopping on a green bookmark. "There's no point in trying to destroy them all, we need to stop them in their tracks. Luckily, I have just the thing for that." She kneels, placing her free hand flat to the floor. "Oaaknilifo!!"

The ground in front of the sliced door begins to crack and fissure, as verdant aura shines from beneath. Suddenly, rows upon rows of thick, oaken tree trunks burst forth from the limestone floors. The trees completely line the morph-infested corridor, congesting the path so greatly that even their incessant buzzing ceases to be heard.

The group waits with bated breath, listening intently for some subtle sign of enemy resistance. After several silent moments, they each sigh in relief, resting assured that the advance of the Morph swarm has been halted. Faith shuts her tome and flashes Max a grin.

"Phew, I'm beat from doing all the work!" She said, strutting past Max to check on Pilet and Yuuna.

Max retracts his Sunshower, pouting and shaking his head in disdain.

"Hmmph, life must be easy with a magic bible..."

Faith and Max return to the others, to the sight of an unconscious Pilet splayed across the floor. With his wounds now mostly sealed, the Fever Point naturally deactivates. His steaming hot, brick red skin returns to its peach tone. The glowing runic tattoos and violet aura surrounding him begin to fade, leaving behind a wispy pillar of violet steam wafting away in the air above. Yuuna turns to the others.

"Ok, he seems stable. I just... don't know what happened to him. I mean, his guts were *literally* strewn across the floor!"

"Holy shit..." Said Faith, her face contorting in twisted shock. "How the hell did you fix that?"

"I didn't! I cast Overmend to help him heal, and his body just kinda, *sucked* his intestines back in! It was like some... some *alien* shit! Ugh, poor Pilet..."

Max scans the room, looking for a sign of what to do next.

"Faith, where do we go from here?" He said. "Clearly Pilet's entrance is blocked. *I could* just cut down the other doors, but we had to solve a riddle just to enter here. One would think this room must have a certain, significance."

"It most certainly does." Replied Faith, walking over to the sarcophagus in the center of the room. She begins to pat the top of it with her hand. "This bad boy is what we're looking for."

"A coffin?" Said Yuuna. "What, are we grave robbers now?"

Faith shoots her sister a contemptful side-eye, shaking her head in frustration.

"*No* sis, this is the resting place of some form of animal. Maybe the pet of an important Rok-Senn figure. We've gotta open it to see what chain reaction it'll cause. Hopefully, a door somewhere will open, leading us to level three. Of course, chances are a morph or two will show up to crash the party."

The voice of Besmith begins to echo throughout Yuuna's mind, as her black onyx pendant emits a dark fog.

"Stupid girl, soon I will be free of this prison!"

Yuuna clasps the onyx in her bag, silencing the voice yet again with a pulse wave of aura from her palm.

She ignores the warning of the trapped necrocaster, encouraging her sister to uncover the sarcophagus.

"Let's do it sis." Said Yuuna, activating a quartz crystal from her satchel and placing it around her neck. "I'm ready for anything!"

"That's the spirit, Yuuna!" Faith replied. "Let's get to the top of this madhouse and become Hired Blades! Now quick, help me get this thing open."

Max and Yuuna walk over to the massive sarcophagus, prepping to push the lid off of the base.

"Disturbing one's final resting place, how shameful of me." Said Max. "Let us make sure to replace this when all is said and done."

"Oh hush Max." Said Faith, spitting in her hands and rubbing them together. "Do you want to be a Blade or not? Let's get this show on the road!"

The three push with all their might, slowly but surely sliding the lid inches off of the base. As they tirelessly continue to uncover the ancient coffin, the group starts to clear the face of the deceased. As soon as the face is discovered, Faith steps back, gasping in shock.

"Oh my god." She said, covering her mouth in revelation. "There's... There's no way. That can't be what it looks like."

"Woah woah woah." Said Yuuna, backing away from the sarcophagus with her hands up. "What are you freaking out about? Did you see spiders in there?! I am *not* getting spiders in my hair right now."

Faith collects herself, coming back to the sarcophagus and examining the corpse. The mummified remains of a 16-foot-long reptile lay face up, arms crossed in front of its chest. A row of sharp spines line the creature's underbelly like the teeth of a saw. The crown of its head bears six, pointed horns in a horizontal row across the top. The right side of the beast's mouth has decayed, exposing sharp, jagged teeth lining its jaw. Its left eyeball is missing, leaving an empty pit where it once lay. A tumbled stone of red jasper lies encrusted into its forehead. Faith stares intently at the remains of the ancient beast.

"Kekehio Shriidah..." She said.

"I'm sorry?" Said Max. "I didn't quite catch what you said."

"It's, it's The Kekehio Shriidah." Replied Faith. "It's Rok-Senn for "The Shredding Reptile". A fearsome, mythical apex predator of the ancient world. But, what is it doing *here?* And this stone..." Faith points to the red jasper burrowed into its forehead. "Why is *this* here?"

Suddenly, an auric rune appears across the brow of the Kekehio Shriidah, glowing eerily in the dim of the sarcophagus. The mounds of sand surrounding the room begin to shift and tumble, revealing small sarcophagi identical to the large one. Just then, the other eye of the Kekehio Shriidah opens, revealing a glowing, blood-red iris. Faith leaps back at the ghoulish sight.

"Get back!" She exclaims, motioning the others to do the same.

Max springs back from the sarcophagus in the blink of an eye, clutching the handle of his Drawing M7 Lacerate. The lids of the small sarcophagi begin to shift and slide, as an arcane glow begins to emit from inside. Little "Shredding Reptiles" rear their decayed heads from within, the crimson glow in their eyes glaring devilishly at the unassuming prospects.

"Great Serpent Dragon!" Exclaimed Max, anxiously clutching his Drawing sword. "What is this?! They've returned from the grave!"

"They look like babies!" Said Yuuna. "Faith, you don't think this is..."

"I, I'm afraid it is. It's... the art of unholy revival... Necrocast."

A hot wind starts to blow from behind Faith's head, gently whisking her ginger hair past her ears and over her shoulder. The fine hairs on the back of her neck stand up like a threatened cat, as she freezes in place. Max and Yuuna both look at her like they've seen a genuine ghost.

"...Sis..." Muttered Yuuna. "Don't freak out, but..."

Max points over Faith's shoulder, his jaw almost unhinged at the frightful sight.

"What have we done, we've entered the home of a Devil."

With her eyes wide as a deer in headlights, Faith begins to slowly turn her head. She feels the hot wind continue to rhythmically blow onto the back of her neck, sending chills down her spine. As she finally turns around, she's met with the ghoulish sight of the Necrocasted Kekehio

Shriidah, glaring intently with its one eye into her very soul. The beast's foul breath wafts into her face. It begins heaving steadily while the skin above its nose starts to curl and wrinkle. The demon-like arcane glow of its iris sends an unwanted memory flashing through Faith's mind...

In a graveyard behind their Miantha village home, she sees the faces of her parents, decayed and long dead before her. Their skin rotted and torn apart by maggots, the same blood-red glow of the Necrocasted reptile in their eyes.

"Faith lookout!!" Shouts Yuuna.

Faith shakes her head, snapping out of her unpleasant trance. The long neck of the undead reptile retracts, coiling itself like a cobra ready to strike. Frozen in fear, Faith simply stands there, trembling in silence.

Taking this chance to strike, the Shredding Reptile fires its head at Faith; widely opening its jaw to crunch the frightened prospect.

"Dustdevil!" Cast Yuuna.

A strong whirlwind erupts from beneath the ghoulish lizard, forcing its head upwards and disrupting its advance right before reaching the target. Max darts in, grabs Faith, and carries her out of harm's way. He puts her down by Pilet, crouching down to her level and looking into her eyes.

"You have to snap out of it. This nightmare is *very* real. Either you accept it and help, or we may very well perish."

Faith just continues to stare blindly into space, unreceptive to Max's words. Max turns to Yuuna.

"Have you ever seen her like this before?"

"No, Faith is the bravest person I've ever met! She's been scared of ghosts for the past few years... but I've always taken it as a joke! I don't understand what could make her just shut down like this!"

As Yuuna's Dustdevil cast begins to peeter out, the Kekehio Shriidah sets its sights on the group of prospects huddled against the wall. The smaller Kekehio begin to crawl out of their coffin homes. Yuuna backpedals to her teammates at the sight of the impending swarm.

"What do we do Max?! There's too many of 'em!"

Max stands up, pacing towards the middle of the room.

"What are you doing?!" Said Yuuna. "That thing will tear your head off!"

Max motions a hand out to his side, signaling Yuuna to stand down.

"Be still. A beast like this will *feast* on your fear."

Max walks right up to the Kekehio Shriidah, folding his arms in contempt, lifting his chin high in the air and furrowing his brow. The Kekehio meets his gaze, coming dangerously close with a menacing look in his eye. Yuuna covers the top of her head with her hands in frustration. Watching panicked as the group of small Kekehio begin to close in on them, she turns to her sister in desperation.

"Sis! Snap out of it! We need you!!" She screamed, tears beginning to flow down her cheeks.

Faith slowly turns to her sister, her face expressionlessly somber. Pale as a specter, she looks around; seeing the devilish undead eyes of the surrounding Necrocast mini-lizards. Again, these eyes send shivers through her skin. She looks to Max, in his face off with the Kekehio.

Just then, the shredding reptile lets loose a mighty roar into Max's face, spewing small amounts of putrid spittle onto his cheek. The beast's boisterous scream sends Faith into an uncontrolled panic, as she rips her tome from her satchel and casts "Oaaknilifo" around her and Pilet. Multiple rows of thick, oaken logs sprout forth from the ground at a 45-degree angle, forming a small, protective tent around the two of them. Yuuna pounds on the wooden prison, stomping her feet in protest.

"So you're just gonna leave us here like this?! Are you serious?!"

The Kekehio Shriidah continues its savage howl in the face of the bold prospect. But the proud Sanda warrior doesn't bat an eye at the intimidation tactic of the ancient reptile; standing firmly rooted in his staunch stance. His eyes narrow in scorn.

"I see." He said. "Then it's war you want..." Max takes five paces backward, keeping his eyes locked on his foe. "Then, it's a war you will get."

He takes a crouching posture, the blade of his left hand facing the ground with his right fist curled at his hip. The yellow gem encrusted into his chest plate begins to emit a white aura, triggering an organic, writhing reaction throughout his armor.

"MK 2, Release!"

His yellow gem shines radiantly throughout the dim chamber, as a rush of gunmetal gray chords erupt from beneath it. The chords cover Max's body, detailing themselves to the contour of his musculature. Electricity surges wildly in between the flexible, metal fibers of the protective suit.

Such fibers form a fiendish, intimidating helmet over Max's skull. His eyes shine a brilliant golden hue, as his voice reverberates with a devilish bass.

"You will regret your foolish decision." Said the transforming Sanda warrior.

Yuuna marvels at the sight of the illustrious transformation, shielding her eyes from the dust kicked up by Max's powerful aura.

"Oh, I forgot you could do that. Well that helps a bit..."

Suddenly, a set of piercing shrieks can be heard. Yuuna turns at the cry of a small Kekehio Shriidah, lunging at her from behind and snapping at her with its saw-like teeth.

"*Gasp* Get away!" She exclaimed, holding her arm out to protect her.

Her Guardian Mist cast automatically activates, instinctively protecting herself with her greatest defense. The pressurized aura covering her body stops the Kekehio from being able to bite down. In response, the remaining mini-Kekehio take an aggressive posture, covering their bodies in a crimson aura. They begin to curl themselves into compact balls and start rolling around like pill bugs on their rows of sharp spines. The rolling reptiles ride up the mounds of dirt like earthen ramps, aiming for the Wind and Star caster with deadly precision.

"Agh!!"

A Kekehio manages to scrape across Yuuna's back, its sharp, aura-enhanced spines somehow able to penetrate her auric defenses. Blood drips down her back, staining Yuuna's white blouse a deep red. She casts "Kitestream '' and takes to the air to avoid the rolling assault.

"Max, be careful! These are *mythical* creatures, they can use auracast!"

"What?! Auracast is a sacred gift from the Mighty Serpent Dragon to humankind! No other beast that walks Giganus can willingly access its power! They... they lack the organ to cultivate it!"

"Yeah, keep believing that line of crap they're feeding you in Hachidori. My parents were archeologists, they knew their shit." Yuuna pelts an incoming mini-Shriidah with a bolt of compressed air from her palms. "*Mythical* creatures were really adaptive, they evolved their bodies to cultivate aura just like ours! They have the organ too! Don't be surprised if that big guy has an easy time cutting into your fancy armor." She barrel rolls mid-flight, her evasive maneuvers narrowly eluding the saw-like onslaught of several more undead reptiles. "Like I said before, that thing will *literally* tear your head off!"

Max stands before the Shredding Reptile, hand firmly gripping his drawing sword. The beast leaps into the air, curling itself into a ball like its fellow lizards and rolling swiftly towards the Sanda warrior.

"Tch." Max scoffs. He takes note of the balled-up, defensive posture of the beast and reaches instead for his dueling sword. "This won't be over so quickly."

The Sierro's Secret

Beneath the wooden shelter formed by Faith's Oaaknilifo spires, the elder Sierro weeps and sobs dolefully. A river of tears streams down her face, dripping onto Pilet in his slumber. Mucous flows from her nostrils, as they flare out wide like a frightened rabbit. The ghoulish eyes of the Kekehio haunt the halls of her mind. As she rocks herself back and forth, Faith holds her head in her hands tightly, reliving a chilling memory...

In the dead of night, a fiendish fog sees itself creeping across the burial ground of Devin and Lina Sierro. Faith Sierro; clutching a black book with tattered binding and auric symbols across the front, appears before the final resting place of her parents. She kneels down, patting the soft dirt gently with her palm.

"I, I miss you guys. I want you back. It's just been so hard without you..."

Faith reaches behind her, lifting a metal shovel from the freshly cut grass. She stands up, driving the shovel into the soft dirt of the burial ground.

"Yuuna's at a friend's house... I just need to see you one last time. I think I figured out how. I just... have questions."

An hour or so goes by, the dirt of the graves has been thoroughly dug out, revealing two cherrywood coffins lined with gold trim. Faith drops down into the left pit, removing the lid to her father's coffin. She sees the decrepit face of Devin, hands crossed over his chest in a frozen posture. Breaking into tears, she begins to pray over the corpse.

"Please, please God. Please let this work. I don't know what else to do!"

She crawls out of the pit, now dropping down to the coffin of her

54

mother. Faith removes the coffin cover, revealing Lina in a similar posture to her husband. Unable to contain herself, Faith sobs woefully over the decaying woman.

"Mom! I miss you! Why! Why did you have to go so soon!!"

Taking a moment to collect herself, Faith climbs out of Lina's pit. She reaches for the old black book, lifting it from the grass and sifting through the pages.

"I know, I'm not supposed to... But I can bring you back! I found a way, I swear!! We can be one big, happy family again and you can teach me everything there is to know about the secrets of the ancient world! We'll find the hidden city of Lapis Lazuli together. And we'll go down in history as the most famous archeologists to ever live, and we'll do it together! Just like we always wanted!"

Faith stops on a page somewhere towards the middle, tracing her finger along the Rok-Senn lettering.

"Ahah, yes! Here it is."

The young auracaster holds out her right palm, reading a verse from the cryptic tome.

"Krohh dediia ahn misettio." She casts.

The book begins to emanate a foul odor, sending a chill shivering down her spine. As Faith exhales, her breath forms a dark mist, creeping through the night air and reaching into the mouths of the deceased.

"Brishbrisha, Kaidda!" She continues.

The dark mist takes an arcane glow, filling the lungs of the corpses with a mysterious aura. The earth starts to shake, as the bodies of Lina and Devin begin to quake and quiver. Their muscles begin to shift and spasm, as fingers and wrists begin to bend and twist.

Faith gasps in glee.

"I did it!"

The eyes of the deceased open wide, revealing a blood-red glowing hue. The two hauntingly exit their coffins, arms held out lifelessly toward their daughter. Their mouths agape and expressionless, Lina and Devin begin to shuffle laboredly toward Faith.

"Mom, Dad? Wait. Wait a second. Are, are you there?!"

Lina takes a swipe at Faith, narrowly missing with her rotted fingernails.

Faith backsteps hesitantly, tripping over her shovel in a panic. She falls to the ground, looking up in horror at the undead nightmare she's created.

Her father trips on his own feet, grabbing at her ankle and trying to pull her toward him. As he claws at her legs, Faith begins to kick and struggle.

"Dad, no! Please! It's me, Faith! I'm your daughter! I... I love you!"

Devin begins to crawl up to Faith's knees, raising a hand to scratch at her face. In a panic, Faith balls her hand into a fist and cultivates a cerulean aura.

"Release!" She cries, unclenching her fist and sending the aura flying towards her parents.

Immediately, the two turn to dust, leaving behind a faint auric glow as their remains blow away in the wind. Frightened, yet puzzled at the outcome, Faith dives into the ashes. She grasps what's left of her parents in her quivering hands, watching as the ash and dust falls to the ground beneath her fingers.

"Wait... What?! No! Where did their bodies go!?"

She leaps for the black tome, rummaging through until she comes to a page towards the end. Suddenly, she freezes. Her eyes open wide as can be, as her jaw quivers unrelentingly. Her finger stops on a single line as she translates it to Kettlenian.

"These and any Necrocast techniques are an abomination, and hereby forbidden in the name of the Great, King Sage Bacara. The souls of the departed brought back in this way are forever damned to burn in the world below the world, never again to rest in paradise."

The tome drops to the floor, the echo of its leather hide thumping the ground can be heard throughout the dead of night. Faith drops to her knees, staring blankly into the ashes. Suddenly, she releases a blood-curdling shriek, piercing the silence like a jagged knife through the cryptic fog...

Back to the present, a faint buzzing can be heard vibrating through Pilet's pocket. The white Dragonfly Seeker begins to wriggle its way out, popping itself free with its tiny mechanical forelegs. It takes flight, struggling to maneuver in the small area between the wall and Faith's Oaaknilifo. Watching through the Seeker's eyes, the Hired Blades board of executives begins to converse.

"Sir, it looks like we got The Hidden Blades Dragonfly Seeker back online." Said one executive, turning his chair toward the Chairman.

Chairman Yang finishes pouring himself a coffee and walks to his seat at the head of the table.

"What the hell happened to it in the first place? I walk away for five minutes, and the next thing I know I'm in the dark on my favorite prospect!"

"I'm sorry sir, he was being attacked by a morph swarm. The Seeker kept flying into his face while he ran around really fast. It looked like he just got fed up and shoved it in his pocket."

"Hah! I love this kid! Such spunk! Such angst! Reminds me of myself when I was his age." Yang takes a sip of his coffee. "Now, what's the status report?"

"Your guess is as good as mine. Here, take a look."

The executive scrolls through his laptop, switching the focus on the room's primary monitor to The Hidden Blades' Seeker. The board looks on, seeing what little they can from within the small, dark fortress of trees.

"What is this?" Said Yang. "It's dim as the womb in there! Activate the night vision."

The executive does as Yang says, as the monitor reveals Faith crying uncontrollably in the darkness. The Chairman tilts his head in befuddlement. Gliding by the sobbing Sierro, The Dragonfly Seeker finds a tight crawl space in between two logs and wriggles out of the Oaken wedge.

The night vision switches back to normal as the battle scene unfolds before their eyes. Yang immediately recognizes the ghoulish, Necrocasted fiends. He pushes himself back from his seat in shock, resting his forearms onto his thighs and leaning in for a better look.

"My oh my..." Said The Chairman. "*That's* not supposed to be there." He folds one of his massive legs over the other in a relaxed posture, lifting his mug to take another sip. "Get me on the line with Scott, we have to talk."

"Yes sir!" Said another executive, sending a call through to Scott Diliger's Chatch.

Proctor of the auracast portion of the Hired Blades exam, and storied archeologist in his own right; Scott Diliger is a renowned authority on Rok-Senn culture.

As Scott picks up the line, his screen is displayed on the main monitor for the board to see. He brushes his medium length, brown hair from his face, displaying a triangular tattoo with a "3" in the center on his palms. He fixes the collar of his maroon button up, clearly trying to spruce up for the officials.

"You rang, Mr. Chairman?" He said.

"Scott, I've got some questions." Said Chairman Yang, folding his arms contemplatively. "And I hope to God you've got answers."

Max and Yuuna V.S. The Shredding Reptiles

Back at the chamber of the undead reptiles, Max and Yuuna continue their heated battle. The large Kekehio Shriidah rips across the floor at high speed, tearing up the ground beneath the saw-like power of its sharp spines. As it approaches Max, the Sanda warrior draws his dueling Lacerate and blocks the creature head-on.

A loud, high-pitched series of clanging sounds emanates from Max's blade, as sparks fly from the spine of the Kekehio like a rogue buzz saw. The shredding reptile continues its rotating assault, forcing the Sanda warrior stumbling back towards the wall behind him.

"Agh! I- will not bow to you!"

The advancing Kekehio's gyrating force pushes Max's back to the wall, as he presses his free palm into the back of his blade for much-needed support. As the reptile's spines draw closer to his face, Max finds his footing, pushing off of the wall and knocking back the shredding reptile just far enough for him to evade. In that moment, he leaps away on a sharp angle; parrying the Kekehio with his Lacerate as it recovers its momentum.

With a clang and a mighty crash, the Kekehio smashes into the wall; sending limestone and debris flying through the air. Pulling itself free from the wall, the Kekehio curls into a ball and launches itself once more at the Hachidorinese warrior. But Max plants his feet and swings the backside of his blade at the beast, swatting it into the air like a massive baseball.

"How's that for a strike, demon?!" The swordsman snaps.

As a small Kekehio nearly catches up to Yuuna mid-flight, Max's strike sends the larger spinning reptile crashing into it, shredding the mini-undead in half with ease. Flying by, Yuuna turns to see the mini Kekehio torn to shreds right before reaching her.

"Phew!" She exclaimed, wiping her brow of anxious sweat. "Thanks Max! That last one almost turned me into shredded lettuce, woah!"

Yuuna dips and barrel rolls in the air, narrowly avoiding a collision with another mini Kekehio. She turns to face the spinning foes and casts "Starshot", flicking a compressed projectile of light at them.

The Starshot whizzes by the trailing group of mini Kekehio and hits the floor behind them with a bang, exploding into a brilliant light show.

"Damn! Slippery little bastards!" She snorts.

Max channels aura into his Lacerate.

"Just keep the small ones busy, I will deal with the big one."

Max holds his blade aloft, pointing the tip skyward. As the blade begins to cultivate golden aura, the yellow stripe across his helmeted head begins to flash brilliantly.

I'll need to suppress this, lest the whole pyramid might come down on us..." He grips his Lacerate tightly. "Zen'no... Divide!"

He swiftly swipes his blade downward, sending a mighty wall of lightning aura slicing into whatever it meets. The lightning wall roars with the fury of ten thousand bolts, all concentrated into one precise slash through the air. With an almighty flash that could light the whole pyramid, his secret technique hits three small Kekehio and the Large one head-on.

But, as the blinding lights start to calm, the Sanda warrior sees the fearsome reptiles with merely a line of missing scales where the Zen'no Divide struck.

"What?! How can anything survive the Divide?! Pulled punches or not; at thirty percent, most *anything* finds itself parted with its appendages!"

The small Kekehio hit by the strike are rendered paralyzed by the electric aura, but the main reptile shakes off the technique and continues his rolling assault towards Yuuna. It leaps into the air, curling into a ball and attempting to batter the younger Sierro.

"Nope!" She exclaimed, clasping her hands and pointing her palms toward the beast. "Autumn stream!" She casts.

A jetstream of wind blasts the Kekehio Shriidah mid-flight, but the auric spines saw through the wind like soft butter. The Shriidah closes in on Yuuna in an instant, forcing her to take evasive action at the very last moment.

"Aagh!!" She cried, as the spines of the Shriidah shred into her right pectoral.

She falls to the ground, crashing into a pile of sand and rolling across the floor; leaving a trail of blood in her wake.

"Yuuna!!" Exclaims Max, rushing to her aid.

As Yuuna tries to get up, she finds herself unable to move her right arm. Her hand trembles, as she groans in agony at the pain of the gruesome injury. Shaking her head awake, she reaches to her side and ruffles through her bag anxiously.

Both the small and large Kekehio Shriidah shriek eagerly in unison. The group of smaller undead reptiles curl into balls, rushing towards the fallen Yuuna. Meanwhile, the large Shriidah reptile takes a rooted posture and starts to cultivate a crimson aura all throughout its body. The aura begins to form a glowing bubble in its throat, emanating an arcane heat. It begins to cough and hock, like a cat with a bad hairball. Flaming drool begins to drip from the reptile's mouth, riddling the floor with drops of arcane fire.

Suddenly, with a ghoulish howl; the Kekehio Shriidah lets loose a wicked stream of brilliant flame, white-hot with an azure tint. The flame shoots forth from its mouth like a gust of wind, headed straight for the crippled Sierro sister.

"Holy shit!" Cries the Wind and Starcaster, rummaging through her satchel at a frantic pace.

As the flame draws near, and the barrage of small Kekehio approaches, Yuuna finally grasps what she's looking for. She pulls a red jasper stone from her bag, clutching it to her chest with haste. As she holds the stone tightly, the blinding glare of the flame forces her teary eyes shut.

With her eyes closed, she feels the heat of the beast's flame radiating near her, yet she remains un-singed. Yuuna opens her eyes to see Max Quinn with his back to the flame, standing before her with arms spread out protectively.

"M, Max?..." She uttered.

"Uuuurrraaaaaggghhh!!!"

Max cries out in pain, his arms and legs shudder with the agony of the searing flames onslaught.

The red jasper begins to glow, its vibrant aura creeping out from between Yuuna's fingers. The stone's aura seals her wounds, restitching and regenerating tissue at a rapid rate. The color starts to return to her face, as she begins to come to. She gasps in fright.

"Max! No!"

The Kekehio Shriidah's fiery breath finally halts, As Max collapses to his knees. Following this is the sound of the tumbling mini Kekehio, echoing throughout the chamber as they close in on the prospects. Shaking in pain and breathing heavily, Max lifts his sword to his face and lets loose a mighty battle cry.

"Grrraaaaaahhh!!"

He gains a second wind, spinning on his knees to face the Kekehio and cultivating aura into his Lacerate. With his back facing Yuuna, she is now able to see the vicious wounds suffered by the flaming breath of the beast. Lengthy burns cover his mid to upper back, as the charred fibers of his armor begin to regenerate and pour healing aura onto the wounds. The fibers begin to interweave themselves and stitch over the injured tissue, covering the vulnerable region like nothing had happened.

"Bolster!" He casts, as his Lacerate becomes engulfed in yellow energy.

He stands to one foot, keeping his other knee grounded for stability, and holds his Lacerate by his ear like a baseball bat. As two mini Kekehio draw near, they bounce into the air and descend onto Max with their saw-like assault. But Max swiftly bats both Kekehio away with the back of his blade, the aura enhanced Lacerate sending them flying towards the back of the room with haste.

One of these mini Kekehio buzzes over the back of its larger counterpart, skimming some of the titans scales off in the process. Max gasps for air, seething in pain.

"Max, are you alright?" Said Yuuna. "Your armor... Did it fully heal you?"

Max nods his head no.

"Ok then, wait one second." Yuuna goes into her bag, pulling out a pink stone. "This Rose Quartz will heal any burn with the right auric frequency! Here, open your armor up for a sec."

Breathing heavily, Max concentrates and pulls his shoulder blades forward, relaxing the stitching in his armor to release. The armor on his back begins to rescind, revealing his ravaged back.

"Ugh, Max..." Her lip quivers, a sympathetic furrow in her brow. "Thank you for saving me. This'll make you feel way better, I promise."

She clasps the Rose Quartz and releases its latent aura, sending a wave of pink energy rushing over Max's body. In an instant, the massive burns covering Max begin to fade away. Not even a scar is left across his back, as the Sanda warrior stands to his feet.

"I feel... Amazing. Yuuna, how?"

"Crystals can do all sorts of cool things Max! Like here, remember this?"

Yuuna grasps her red jasper crystal, channeling aura through the rough-cut gem and pouring it over Max. The Sanda warrior becomes engulfed in scarlet energy, as his muscles begin to pulsate with a newfound, hulking strength and vigor. This same technique was used during their brutal bout with Scott Diliger, in the auracast exam.

"Thank you Yuuna, I feel like the power of a granite-horned ox is rushing through my veins." He picks up his Lacerate, training the blade on his mighty, scaled adversary across the way. "And *you!* You and I have unfinished business."

Sensing the aura of Yuuna's crystal, the Kekehio Shriidah furrows its brow, brandishing the red jasper stone embedded in its forehead. Much like Yuuna's, the red jasper releases a strengthening aura into the beast. The Shriidah's muscle mass increases, its veins begin to pulsate and bulge along its long scaly neck.

"Holy crap, does this thing ever run out of tricks?!" Said Yuuna.

"Let's hope not." Replied Max. "The last thing I want is to get bored." He stalks his foe, slowly making his way across the chamber. "Yes, that's it, give me everything you've got. Come at me... *come at me!*"

Max rushes toward the Kekehio with his blade in tow, tucked by his waist. The mini Kekehio begin to roll by and come at him from lateral angles, but Max swats and batters them away with ease. As he closes in on the main Shriidah, his foe lashes out at him with its tail, narrowly missing Max as he ducks and rolls beneath. At the end of his roll, Max emerges behind the Shriidah, loosing a vicious rising slash from a crouched position.

"Hah!"

Max's aura-enhanced Lacerate scrapes across the sturdy scales of the Shredding Reptile, sending a wave of vibrant sparks flying into the air. Unscathed, the Shriidah whips its head behind it in response. The horns of the beast clang off of Max's Lacerate as he parries the blow reflexively. Next, the Shriidah stands on its hind legs, towering over the stalwart prospect.

It wails at Max, flailing its arms wildly and whipping its head straight down towards the swordsman. Max leaps to the left, missing the lashing attack by mere inches. Smashing its own chin into the ground, the Shriidah scrapes its head along the floor, hoping to sweep the legs of the nimble prospect. But Max was too quick, hopping and flipping over the beast with ease. Max lets loose a spinning, flipping slash with his Lacerate, as an arcane blade of electrifying aura flies airborne from his blade.

The electric aura blade bounces effortlessly off of the Shriidah's scales, slicing into the stone floor below. Max lands five feet from the Shriidah, dashing away to gain some ground.

"Is this beast made from damn Lacerate steel?! How can it withstand these attacks?!"

"It's *Mythical* Max! *Mythical!* To the Rok-Senn these were so rare, some thought they didn't even exist!"

"Yes ok I get it! Do you have any *constructive* advice?" Replied Max, while swiftly firing an electric slash wave at his opponent.

Yuuna looks around inquisitively. She notices the smaller Kekehio, shredded in half by its larger counterpart earlier. She then turns to examine the main Shriidah, taking note of the line of shredded scales from Max's deflective parry. Finally, Yuuna sees the sarcophagi littered throughout the room and hatches an idea.

"Max, you're a swordsman right? Iron sharpens iron! Look at the row of missing scales across its back, use its friends against it!"

Max takes note of the chink in the Shrridah's armor, grinning and nodding to his ally.

"Now this I can work with."

The Shriidah curls itself into a ball and fires itself at Max in a flash. But Max pivots on his heel and blocks the assault of the beast in response, heaving as he sends the bulky Shriidah flying across the room.

With a heavy thwack, the Shriidah smashes forcefully into the wall. The smaller reptiles respond to this by launching themselves in compact, whirling projectiles at the Hachidori warrior. Max continues to smack and batter them away, aiming his strikes at the large one but missing by inches. Both the large and small Kekehio begin circling him, like tires fallen off a speeding car.

"You underestimate the might of the Sanda tribe."

A mini Kekehio rolls swiftly towards Max from behind, narrowly missing as he sidesteps nimbly out of harm's way. Another mini dashes out, barely whiffing by the Sanda swordsman. But as it passes, a third Kekehio hidden in its shadow smashes into Max's chest. The sharp, curved spines of the reptile shred into Max's armor.

"Ugh!" Exclaims Max in pain. "Shit, good move."

Sensing the difficulty of Max's battle, Yuuna takes a moment to ponder their options. She remembers the selenite crystal that she picked up in the mines outside of the village Giduh.

"Selenite repels evil..." She thought. *"Well, worth a shot."* Yuuna draws the selenite from her satchel. She pours aura into the clear crystal, aiming it at the main Shriidah. As the Selenite begins to glow with her arcane energy, she fires a shot of pure aura from the sharp tip of the stone.

The auric bullet hits the Shriidah on its shoulder as the massive lizard rolls by Max. It stops itself, raising one of its brows in confusion and looking around for what tapped it, before curling itself back into a ball and continuing its rolling attack.

"What?!" Said Yuuna, smacking the Selenite on her palm in frustration. "Damn thing doesn't work! It's supposed to repel evil, what's more evil than *Necrocast*?"

The black onyx in her bag begins to emit its signature black fog.

"Hahahaha, stupid girl! You know nothing about Necrocast! Just like those clueless do-gooders that wrote the book on it."

Yuuna pauses, contemplating what to do next.

"Max!" She cried. "Give me two minutes, think you can hold them off till then?"

Max blocks the rolling assault of the main Shriidah, immediately parrying and deflecting two mini reptiles.

"I don't see what difference it makes, I've been doing that this whole time!"

"Tch, well *fine* then. I'll be right back."

A Deal with The Devil

Yuuna takes to the air, flying as high as she can before her Kitestream reaches its height threshold. She clutches the black onyx from her bag, holding it to her chest and closing her eyes meditatively.

Within the confines of her mind, she meets with the soul of Besmith, the mighty ancient Necrocaster trapped within the stone. The two sit across from each other on red leather, teakwood armchairs. Surrounded by pitch black, with nothing but a hanging lamp lighting the radius around them.

"Hey, look buddy." Said Yuuna. "I don't know what's going on here but a little bit of *helpful* information would be nice. I know you want my body, and if these hungry zombie lizards eat me, you'll be shit outta luck."

Besmith crosses his legs, looking eerily at the young prospect with his dark-ringed eyes. His tight, matted braids fall past his shoulders, riddled with the bones of fallen foes twined within each braid. His woolen jacket stained with dried blood, covers what appears to be countless scars across his arms and torso. He raises his filthy hands to his chin, his jagged, unkempt fingernails stroking his long braided beard.

"I need *you*. I don't need the swordsman, or your sister, *or the really* stupid one who never shuts up. I could stop those Shredding Reptiles with the snap of my fingers, but do I really need to? Make me an offer I can't refuse."

Yuuna slams her fists into the armrests of the chair, firing a fierce glare at Besmith.

"Idiot! If we die you'll be stuck here when this pyramid goes back in the ground! Do you want to go back to being a relic?!"

"Again, I need *you*! If you let me take over, I can stop them from hurting you. *But*, If you don't you'll die, and I know you're too scared to let that happen. Now *you tell me* why I should be saving the others."

"Ugh." Replied Yuuna. "Look, what do you want from me? Do you want me to just *let you* have my body permanently? Because that's just not gonna happen."

"The dragon sorcerer." Said Besmith.

"... What?"

"The dragon sorcerer, the one who brings the dragons back to life. He can create bodies from bones, yes?"

"Oh... the Fossil creature guy? The *scientist* you mean? Dude, those are dinosaurs, not dragons. God you're old."

"They look like dragons to me, I don't know of these "Dinosaurs" to which you speak. Anyway, I want a new body. Your marksman friend with the stupid green hat has connections, he seems to be well known in your world. Tell him to find this "Dinosaur" sorcerer and make me a new body, one with *your* blood."

"Ew what?! Why *mine* you creep?!"

"Shut up stupid girl! You're lucky, you were born with a strong auric liver, as was I in my time. By now my body has long since decayed, and I don't remember where I was when I was imprisoned within this accursed stone. *Your* aura is naturally very strong, I want yours."

"Well, what about Pilet's? He like, never *ever* runs out of aura! And he can do amazing things like teleport and regenerate without even trying!"

"Yuck! His blood?! That boy is tainted! I... I can't remember why, but something about him... Those eyes..." Besmith flares his nostrils, his heart starts to pound in his chest as he breaks into a cold sweat. "I want nothing to do with that, *abomination*. That being said, *your blood*. Or death. You choose."

Yuuna cringes, looking away from the dark auracaster before standing up and extending her hand to Besmith.

"Ugh, FINE. Deal! Now take care of these damned lizards!"

Besmith seals the bargain with a handshake. He grins ominously.

"If you say so..."

Back on the ground, Max struggles to hold his own against the onslaught of the ancient reptiles. He manages to grab a mini Shriidah by the tail, swinging it around and smashing its spines into the others. The spines flake scale after scale off of the vicious lizards, causing them to circle him with newfound caution.

"Aha! Not so fearsome now are we?!"

Just then, the Shriidah he's holding flails and manages to escape his grasp, balling itself up and shredding into his armor on the way out.

"Gaah! You, slippery brat!"

The large Shriidah takes this opportunity to barrel into Max, sending him flying into the tight fortress of oak encapsulating Faith and Pilet.

"Oof!" Max lets out a wheeze on impact.

The clamoring sound of Max thumping against the barrier snaps Faith out of her stupor and wakes Pilet from his slumber.

"Nggh, whah?" Said Pilet, wearily wiping his eyes. "Where am I? Why... why's it so dark in here?"

Faith snaps at the thumping sound and falls back onto Pilet's stomach in surprise. Pilet groans in pain as his still very sore abdomen is crushed by the elder Sierro.

"Ow you dipshit, get off! Oh that hurts! Why does that hurt so bad?!"

Max turns his head at the sound of Pilet's cries.

"Pilet? Quick! Get out here!"

At the call of his ally, the infrared sound of Pilet's Dragonflies echoes within the oaks. In a flash, Pilet filets the oaken fortress with a dazzling display of quick knifesmanship. The trees are diced in an instant as Pilet bursts through, leaping high into the sky. At the height of his jump, Pilet sees Yuuna meditating in the air, wrapped in a vortex of dark aura.

"Yo!" He exclaimed, receiving no response from his ally. "Ok then..." He said, beginning his descent to the ground.

He lands stoically in front of Max, as bits of charred, sliced wood fall from the sky before him. Pilet sees the torn and shredded chords of Max's armor, restitching themselves meticulously.

"The hell happened to you?" He said.

Max points behind him in response.

"That."

Pilet turns around, seeing their ghoulish reptilian foe for the first time. The Kekehio Shriidah takes a deep breath cultivating its crimson aura for an arcane blast. Pilet's jaw drops. He rubs his eyes vigorously, squinting in disbelief.

"What in God-damned Giganus is that?!"

"Ah, shit..." Said Max. "Move!"

Max pushes Pilet out of the way, narrowly escaping the fiery breath of the Kekehio Shriidah. The flame keeps going, headed straight for Faith as she finally comes to. Pilet and Max look on in horror.

"Faith get out of the damn way!" Exclaims Pilet.

Faith's eyes widen as she witnesses the brilliant flame closing in on her. But just as the white-hot blaze nears the tip of her nose, it vanishes, as the Kekehio Shriidah and its miniature companions halt their advance. They stand in place, staring blankly as if awaiting a command.

"..."

"Dude." Pilet whispered to Max. "You think it's waiting for her to move too?"

Max glares at the reptiles, mysteriously frozen in place.

"That would not be my first guess, but at this rate what do I know..."

Befuddled, Pilet shrugs his shoulders.

"Welp, works for me. Fleetfoot!" He cast, bolting towards the main Shriidah in the blink of an eye. With wicked speed, Pilet unleashes an onslaught of lightning-fast slashes and stabs onto the beast. Sparks fly, creating a vivid light show across the back of the Kekehio that makes the dark chamber look like mid-day.

"Eat metal!!" Cried the King Killer.

With an unrelenting pace, Pilet continues his barrage of blades along the hide of the mythical creature. The Kekehio Shriidah just stands there, looking completely unphased by the attacks of the fiery prospect. Not a scale on its body has a single scratch on it from his assault.

"Are you kidding me?! Die!"

He drives the hot blades straight down onto the beast, creating fountains of brilliant sparks pouring out. Still, the King Killer finds no success in his efforts, mildly blinding himself in the process. Staggered by the light of his own attack, he covers his eyes and darts back to Max, gliding across the floor in one fluid motion.

"*Pant* Pant* *Pant*" Pilet gasps for air in exhaustion. He looks down at his Dragonfly knives, now chipped and worn from his mindless tirade. "Crap! How hard *is* this thing?! Even the big scorpion had a few scrapes and dents put on it by these. But I've never seen something that my knives couldn't even scratch!"

Max glances at his Lacerate in disdain.

"I share the sentiment..."

Just then, Yuuna drops down from the sky, enveloped in a dark aura. Her hands bear auric orbs of pure dark purple, as she waves them before the stiffened reptiles.

"Yuuna?" Said Max. "Took you a while there, everything alright?"

"Shut up, jock." Said Yuuna, her voice raspy as the desert.

"Oh, ok..." Replied Max in shock.

Pilet holds back the desire to laugh, taking his turn at addressing their colleague.

"Yo Yuuna, what's with the new shade? What happened to the platinum aura, don't you know purple is *my* thing?"

"I said silence, freak!" She replied.

"..."

Pilet takes off his tank top and throws his knives to the ground marching toward Yuuna and pointing his finger in a peeved rage.

"Oh *hell* no! *I ain't* the one! If there were a toilet here your *head* would be getting shoved in it! You hear me?!"

Max holds him back, grabbing him from behind while Pilet flails wildly in protest.

"Get off me! I don't take shit from nobody! Minego Mayhem, Minego Mayhem!" Said Pilet, forming two downward "M's" with his hands.

"Oh not this nonsense again, cut it out you fool! Can't you see something is amiss here? *That's* not Yuuna! It's her boisterous friend from the fist-fighting exam. Remember?" He looks at Yuuna with contempt. "The *loser* trapped in the black stone?"

Yuuna looks back at Max with nostrils flared.

"Do you *really* need that one?" Said Besmith in Yuuna's body.

A voice rings through his head.

"Just cool it, you were being kind of a dick first anyway. Kill the lizards and let's be done with it, ok?!"

"Hmmph, fine."

Besmith clenches his fists, flicking his finger and sending one of the smaller Kekehio flying towards Max in a curled ball. Right before making impact, the Kekehio opens itself up and slams into Max with its underbelly, sending the both of them soaring across the room in an instant. Whizzing by Pilet's ear, the King Killer drops to the ground in laughter.

"Hahahaha! He sure told you, *banana* braids! Baaahaha!!"

"Tch, idiots." Said Besmith, shaking his head in disgust. "Now if I could just find the right auric frequency..." He waves his hands before the beasts, the dark purple aura swirling between his fingers. "Oh? That's it! Well, that was... far simpler than it should have been..." Besmith balls his fists tightly, cultivating whirling stores of purple aura in between his fingers. "These are tough to find, what a waste of a Mythical... Release!" He cast, sending a shockwave of dark purple aura pulsating throughout the room.

In an instant, each of the Kekehio Shriidah disappears, fading into grainy piles of ash on the ground. Max brushes the mound of ash off of his chest and stands to his feet, cracking his back for relief. He walks back over to Pilet and Besmith, sheathing his longsword and releasing his Sanda MK2 armor. As Max approaches, he looks back to Faith, waving her over.

"Whatever you feared is no more, the least you could do is join us."

Hesitant, Faith nods and stands to her feet. Her legs wobble in fright, as she makes her way over to the group in the center of the chamber.

"So, I take it we should be thanking *you*?" Said Max, eyeballing Besmith with contempt.

"Thank your stupid friend. If it were up to me, that Shriidah would have torn you all to shreds by now. Consider yourselves lucky, you *survived* an encounter with a mythical creature. Not an easy task, I'll give you that. But *just so you know,* you never could have won. Don't go letting this go to your head, useless swine."

Max folds his arms and grins.

"Hah! I had those overgrown iguanas on the ropes."

Besmith rolls his eyes.

"Sure... Are we done now? Yes? Good. Have a nice life, failures." Besmith snaps his fingers.

Yuuna's body lifelessly drops to the ground with a thud.

"Oops!" Said Pilet, trying to catch her at the last second.

The Wind and Starcaster opens her eyes, as Pilet and Max help her up off of the ground.

"Ugh, that dick. But anyway... Yay! We did it!"

"No Yuuna, *you* did it." Said Max. "Without your pretentious friend, I don't know how much more of that we could have taken. Great work!"

"Oh, *now* you say that, huh? You were singin' a different tune earlier, but you're welcome just the same."

Max holds his hands up in surrender. He mutters under his breath.

"Well at the time it was true..."

Suddenly, a large auric rune begins to glow in the center of the room. A twenty-foot radius of the ground around it begins to levitate, rising slowly but surely to a now-open door near the ceiling.

"Guys, that must be the way to the third floor!" Exclaimed Yuuna. "Hurry, hop on!"

Max and Pilet rush to the platform, while Faith continues to stand there in silence. Yuuna walks over to her, arms folded in contempt, and smacks her across the face.

"Wake up!" She shouts. "The zombies are gone now. I don't know what about Necrocast makes you so scared, but we have to go now and I need you! So wake up and let's go already!!"

Startled, Faith shakes her head awake and nods to her sister.

"You're, you're right. I'm sorry. Let's go."

Faith takes Yuuna's hand, as Yuuna flies the two up onto the rising platform. Faith takes a seat over by Max.

"Hey, I'm sorry-"

"Save the apologies." He interrupts. "I'm going to tell you right now. I had every intention of taking this exam alone for this very reason. The last thing I want is to fail my father and my country because of someone else's fear and lack of conviction."

Faith grows silent, bowing her head in shame. Max continues.

"However..." He puts a hand on her shoulder. "There is no more an honorable death than dying for the life of a comrade. Whatever the problem, I don't need to know. Just make sure it doesn't happen again, deal?"

He holds out a fist to Faith. Faith finally begins to crack out of her shell, as a subtle smile creeps out of her lips. She bumps fists with Max.

"Deal. Thanks, I needed that. I'm here now. Let's get this show on the road."

A Rush of Madness

The platform slowly rises up to a single door at the height of the ceiling, a balcony of sorts extends from the wall for entrants to stand on. As the platform reaches the edge of the balcony, The Hidden Blades step onto it with care. They look into the dark corridor beyond the open door, slowly, one by one entering in silence.

As the last to enter, Faith jumps in surprise as the door abruptly and noisily slams shut behind them.

"Shit!" She yelped, holding her chest in shock. "Seriously?! This place is a constant heart attack!"

Suddenly, an auric rune begins to glow across the front of the door, as a loud rumble begins to echo throughout the halls.

"Woah, hey, woah!" Exclaimed Pilet. "Is that an earthquake?! Or maybe this place is about to blow! Come on now we just walked in the door, give us a break!"

"Wait." Said Yuuna, holding out her hand and touching the wall. "Is this... moving?" She holds her fingertips extended from her palm, as the wall slowly creeps to meet said palm with unyielding force. "Holy shit! The wall is closing in!"

"What?! Tah hell with this!" Exclaimed Pilet, drawing his Dragonfly knives and attempting to drive them into the recently shut door.

The auric rune glows again as the knives make contact, protecting the wall with a blue energy barrier. The barrier absorbs the force of the knives, sending an electrical shockwave blasting the four prospects several feet down the hall.

Max lands on top of the heap, his buttocks on top of Faith's head. She lets out a muffled cry of frustration as Pilet forces his head out from the bottom of the pile. Max looks down at the King Killer with disdain.

"Any more *bright* ideas?" He said.

"*Wheeze* Tch. Yeah, one more." Pilet replied. "Run!!"

"Fleetfoot!" They cast in unison.

The soles of each member's feet glow with an auric shade. The panicked prospects scatter in all different directions, smacking face-first into the walls of the labyrinth-like corridors and tripping over their own feet in a rush.

"Shit!" Shouted Pilet. "Where are you guys!? Where am I?"

"This place is a madhouse!" Exclaimed Max, attempting to cut through the dense, encroaching walls. "This is futile, we need a plan! Follow my voice and meet me here!"

Hurriedly, the three find themselves back to Max, the chamber close to half the width it was at the start.

Yuuna, hit me and Pilet with your jasper stone. Pilet, use your gorilla strength to help me hold back the walls. Maybe if we can hold them back in one spot, the rest of the labyrinth will halt until we can no longer stop it."

Yuuna and Pilet do as he says. The King Killer draws from the power of the Wurm gorilla of Chamboree Mountain to which he owes his name, growing exceedingly muscular and covered in purple fur. Yuuna digs through her bag, yanking her jasper crystal and pouring a bolstering aura into her comrades. Finally, the enhanced Sanda warrior and the hairy King Killer do their best to halt the advance of the walls.

"Grrraaaaahh!!" They cry, whilst pouring forth every ounce of strength they have into holding back the ancient trap.

The two succeed, as the encroaching walls begin to slow almost to a halt. But as the pulsating muscles of the two hulking brutes give in to the pressure, they hear the low rumble begin again.

"Aagh!! Shit!" Exclaimed Pilet. "It's slowing down, but it's not stopping! Faith! Plant some damn trees!"

"On it." replied Faith, opening her tome and swiftly shuffling through the pages. "Oaaknilifo!" She cast, driving her palms into the ground. Rows upon rows of trees sprout up alongside the walls, adding additional support to the muscular duo. But even the many trees are no match for the pressure of the relentless narrowing chamber, as they begin to snap and crack loudly.

"What the hell!" Exclaimed Faith. "These walls are ridiculous!"

"*Huff* *Puff* At least, we're slowing it down." Said Pilet, grunting while pressing the walls apart. "Keep planting! And Yuuna, look for a way out!"

"Right!" She replied, darting down the halls as fast as she could.

The young Wind and Starcaster bolts down each hall nervously, hoping to find something more than the inevitable dead end. But dead ends are *all* that she sees, spotting no sign of escape from the hellish maze. Turn after turn, the younger Sierro is met with disappointment and roadblocks, unsure if she is even running in circles.

Back at the maze's first hall, Max and Pilet struggle to hold on.

"Gaaaah!! Yuunaaa!!" Cried Pilet in agony, his muscles burning with lactic acid.

"You need to hurry!!" Exclaimed Max. "I- don't know if we can hold out much longer!!"

Around the corner, Faith struggles to keep up with the snapping of her auric trees. She casts them in the form of wedges propped up against the corner of the walls, lines them in tight rows, she even starts to cast them horizontally across from one wall to the next. Nothing can halt the press of the creeping walls.

"Damn it! How many trees do I need to cast for this nightmare to stop? I swear these walls have killed more trees than a forest fire!!"

Finally, as Yuuna hurries past what appears to be a small hole in the wall, she stops and backtracks. As she peers into the hole, she sees another chamber, unaffected by the advance of the killer walls. Inside is a wide-open ramp, leading to what appears to be the next level of the pyramid. Yuuna gasps.

"The exit! Ok ok ok, Mom and Dad used to talk about this. This is a fake wall with an auric rune lock. I just have to find the right panel aaand-"

Yuuna carefully feels around, cultivating aura in her palms and pressing firmly into each tile. She presses into one near the top that keeps the auric imprint of her hand, activating an auric rune at the center of the tile. The wall begins to recede, opening the way to the exit.

"That's it! I released it!!" She exclaims. "But, how am I going to retrace my steps?!" She takes a moment to ponder, slapping her side in frustration. Her hand hits her bag, as the sound of her many crystals shifts and rattles throughout. "Hmmm... Aw man, I'm sorry my babies."

She begins to hurry back, activating and carefully placing one of her crystals at the center of each hallway. The glow of the activated crystals lights the way back to the exit, as she zips and zooms down the halls. Hurriedly, she turns a corner and accidentally bumps into her sister.

"Gaaah lookout!!" She cried, flying at a breakneck pace toward Faith.

"Oh my God!!" Cried Faith in horror, as her sister trips and spears her in the stomach with her head.

The two roll across the floor like speeding tumbleweeds in a sandstorm, as Yuuna lands with her buttocks directly on top of Faith's face.

"Why does this keep happening to me!" Exclaimed Faith, holding her stomach and wincing. "Max skips showers and you don't use soap, I don't know what's worse!"

"What?! How dare you! I use soaps, they're just all-natural."

"They're bullshit!" Faith replied, curling into a ball as Yuuna stands to her feet.

"Meh, have fun with psoriasis and cancer then." Said Yuuna.

"Now's not the time Yuuna! Where's the exit!"

"Oh, right! This way!"

The sisters turn the corner and meet with Max and Pilet, who by this point are up to their elbows pressed against the wall.

"Guys! Follow my crystals!" Said Yuuna.

The Hidden Blades do as she says, nimbly darting and dashing down the halls of the corridor. Hall after hall, they see the glow of the activated crystals light their way to freedom. Twisting and turning, as the walls become so short that they end up strafing sideways while sucking in their stomachs for space. Finally, they reach the exit. Faith and Yuuna tumble out, sprawling out onto the floor. but Max finds himself caught in between the walls, his chest pressed up against them with crushing force.

"Ggggaaaaaaaaggghh!!" He cries in agony.

"Max!" Shouts Faith, as she and Yuuna scramble to their feet to assist him. They pull with all their might, wiggling his armor just enough to yank him from the clutches of death. The three fall to the ground, shaking their heads in disbelief.

"I can't believe we made it out of there." Said Faith. "I'm gonna be totally honest sis, I thought you got lost and we were doomed."

"Oh yee of little faith, pun intended." Replied Yuuna. "The *real* victims here are my crystals, my precious babies!" Yuuna dramatically throws herself to the floor. "Whyy, oh whyyy! The horror! You've all been smooshed!!"

Faith and Max look at each other in derision.

"Get used to this." She said to Max. "Most of them were $10 aurem at a thrift store, and she's convinced each one was destined to find her."

Yuuna pauses her dramatic woes for a moment.

"Wait... Where's Pilet?" She said.

"..."

"Oh shit! Pilet!!" Said Faith. "Did *he* get lost again?!"

"How could he?!" Replied Max. "It was so simple, just follow the glowing stones!"

"Ahem." A voice from behind them coughs.

The three turn to see Pilet in his Fever Point, his gorilla form now completely deflated and back to normal. He holds the lot of Yuuna's crystals in the bottom of his tank top like a fabric bowl. As he releases his Fever Point technique, the deep violet glow of his aura dissipates into thin air.

"Yo, you dropped something." He said, a subtle grin across his face.

"Oh my God Pilet!!" Cried Yuuna, tackling him to the ground and kissing him relentlessly on the forehead. She presses his cheeks together, talking to him like a baby. "You're my favorite, you're my new favorite! Yes you are!"

Pilet pulls away from her, fixing his shirt and wiping the dust off his pants.

"Chill Yuuna chill! And here, take this too." Pilet pulls an amethyst crystal from his pocket and hands it to her. "Hold onto your shit ok? Found this in my pillow, it gave me a serious headache."

"No way! You had this the whole time?! She's my absolute favorite! I thought I lost her!!"

Pilet turns to Faith.

"'*She?*' It's a rock..."

"Just go with it." Faith replied. "She's saved our asses a few times today, if she wants the rock to be a girl then it's a girl alright?"

Pilet shakes his head.

"Weirdos."

The Nine Elements

The Hidden Blades continue up the ramp to the next level, finding the way to be long and very steep. After a few minutes of walking, they find themselves at the entrance of the pyramid's fourth level. Two wide double doors stand before them. Adorned with 9 jewels in a circular pattern, with one large, clear crystal in the center. Rok-Senn runic language covers the doors from top to bottom. Faith walks up to the door and begins to read aloud.

"Congratulations mighty thief, enjoy your lavish horde. Let all who enter here beware, the gateway to our Lord." Faith tilts her head contemplatively. "Gateway to our Lord? How very intriguing..."

"Yeah yeah, but how do you open it?" Replied Pilet.

"I'm getting to that hold on! Sheesh." Faith cultivates aura into her hand, shining the glow onto each jewel for a better view. "See this pattern of colorful gems? Each color represents one of the nine elemental types of aura." She traces the wall with her fingertips, continuing to read to herself. "It looks like this is what's called a "nine-element lock", you have to unlock it in a particular combination."

"The artistry of The Rok-Senn was truly praiseworthy." Said Max.

"Wasn't it?" Replied Faith. "Now the Rok-Senn discovered the elements in a specific order, and it's in that order that these must be activated. Luckily, they're placed in the right order, counterclockwise to begin with." She begins to point at each stone, identifying them in order. "Red, Blue, Yellow. These are Fire, Water, and Lightning. Max knows all about that last one."

Max folds his arms and grins, nodding in agreement.

"Then we have Brown and Green here, that's Earth and Nature. Nature meaning, you know, plants and such. Oh, here's a fun one!" She looks back at Yuuna with a grin. "Now class, we have White and Purple. Any guesses as to what these are?"

Yuuna smiles mischievously and flexes her muscles.

"Wind and Star!" She exclaimed.

"Very good Yuuna! You get a smiley face sticker!"

Faith pulls out a sticker from her satchel and puts it on Yuuna's forehead. Yuuna smiles in delight.

"Wah- hey that's bullshit!" Said Pilet. "There's stickers now?! I want one! She's cheating, she already knows this stuff..."

"Every class has its clown I suppose." Replied Max.

Faith laughs, continuing her lesson.

"This Black color represents "Dark Matter" or Darkness for short, one of the last elements recognized by The Rok-Senn people. It's used in a number of interesting techniques, many of which are very taboo." Faith points to Yuuna's bag. "Besmith, that jerkface from the black onyx, was a master of this element. It's instrumental in the use of *Gulp* Necrocast... Moving on-"

Faith reaches up to the final colored stone. "Now this one is very interesting, this silvery or *metal* color represents *just that*, "Metal". Metal was the final element recognized by The Rok-Senn, so late in fact that it was discovered at a time close to their extinction. It was considered to be in the category of earth, until they realized its ability to conduct electricity as well as aura. Since the Rok-Senn were so focused on nature and auracast, their technology was very primitive, consisting primarily of stone tools and weaponry until around their last century. It wasn't until a very skilled soldier and auracaster discovered metal's potential that The Rok-Senn decided its worth in the elemental wheel."

Pilet looks at the silvery stone inquisitively. He pulls the chromium necklace from his back pocket and holds it aloft.

"That looks kinda like this, doesn't it?" He said.

Surprised, Max, Faith, and Yuuna stare at Pilet with raised eyebrows.

"Where did you get that!?" Said Faith.

"I found it." Replied Pilet.

"I- ok..." Faith clasps her hands together and takes a deep breath in frustration. "*Where* did you find that though?"

"Over some dead guy, in a secret room behind a wall. It was on an eagle's head. The thing turns my Hollowpoints into metal cannonballs when I wear it, It's pretty freaking awesome actually."

"..."

"Pilet... what the hell?" Said Yuuna. "You discovered an ancient secret! And you're acting like it's a gum wrapper you found on the floor..."

"Yeah well, whatever. Finders keepers that's all I know. I'm not telling the board *shit* about this bad boy."

The Dragonfly Seeker camera comes floating by. The four of them look into the eyes of the curious mechanical bug. Pilet hangs his head in defeat.

"Damn it..."

"Alright, well anyway." Faith holds out her pointer finger, focusing intently on the tip. "Skarrya." She cast, as a 4-inch blade of Flame aura protrudes from her fingertip.

"You can do that without the book?" Said Max.

"It takes a lot of concentration, but this is about as much as I can muster on my own." She replied. Faith gently taps the Fire stone with the tip of her knife, retracting the blade as the gem glows a brilliant scarlet hue. "Next up, Frisio!" Faith shoots a small burst of icy aura at the Water stone, prompting the same reaction. "Ice and water have different words in their language, but they're categorized as the same thing. Now Max, if you'd please do the honors."

Max cultivates a bit of aura between his pointer finger and his thumb, creating a small, arcane electrical current. He walks up to the yellow gem and tazes it, activating the Lightning stone.

"Perfect!" Said Faith. "Back to me."

She holds her arm out and casts, "Gilazia Shida." The outside of Faith's forearm becomes covered in crystalline glass, to which she taps on the Earth stone to activate it. Once the brown gem is lit, she casts "Oaaknilifo", causing a branch to form out of the palm of her hand. She taps the Nature stone, giving it a beautiful, emerald auric gleam. Faith turns to Yuuna.

"Wind and Star girl, you're up!"

Yuuna cracks her knuckles, walking up to the double doors with her chest puffed out.

"You're gonna get it now, wall. You done messed up!" She takes a deep breath. "Autumnn-" On the exhale she yells, "Burst!" shooting a compressed ball of air from her mouth.

The blast activates the white, Wind stone, but sends Yuuna tumbling down the ramp a few feet, knocking Pilet over in the process.

"Ow! Say it, don't spray it psycho!" He said, gaining his footing and helping her up.

"Thanks Pilet!" She said. "Ok, time for round two."

Yuuna cultivates vibrant green aura into her fingertips, compressing it into a tightly clenched fist. When she opens her hand, a brilliant ball of light the size of a coin emerges. Yuuna holds the light up close to the purple gem. With an arcane *ding* the Star stone is lit.

"Nice, now..." Faith rubs her hands together vigorously. "I hate this auracast, but here goes." She holds her hands out towards the Darkness stone. "Brishbrisha, Kaidda!" She casts, sending a small, ominous black fog creeping into the black gem. The Dark Matter gem activates.

Yuuna glares at Faith suspiciously, witnessing her use of the dark incantation.

"I've never seen you use that cast before sis..." Said Yuuna. "Looks a *whole lot* like something Besmith would use..."

"Yeah well, it's good to have diversity. Right? I mean, how else would we be able to get through situations like this?"

Unconvinced, Yuuna drops the subject.

"Right..."

Faith walks over to the Metal stone.

"So we have a bit of a predicament here." She holds up her tome and waves it to the others. "Most of what I know came from this book, which was written by an ancient Warrior of The Rok-Senn. Problem is, he wrote it before Metal was discovered as an element, so there aren't really any Metal casts I could draw from here. Sis, I know *you* don't have any Metal casts, and I'm assuming you don't have any either Max?"

Max shakes his head.

"The Sanda are born from lightning, to lightning we stay true. Metal is for cutting, not casting."

"Fair enough, well that leaves Pilet!" Faith points to his chromium necklace. "It's honestly a blessing you found this thing, otherwise we'd all be shit outta luck right now. Why don't you use a Metal cast from that?"

Pilet shrugs his shoulders.

"Sure, why not." He replied, pulling the necklace over his head.

The chromium stone begins to glow, lending a silver hue to the aura surrounding Pilet. His eyes glow a metallic shine, as he begins to create a small, metal-laden Hollowpoint. Pilet concentrates, hardening the metal inside the Hollowpoint and releasing the cast, catching the marble-sized metal ball in his palm.

"Ow damn, that's hot as hell!" He exclaimed, dropping the ball to the floor.

The metal ball starts to roll down the ramp swiftly, as Pilet bolts after it.

"Shit shit shit!

Yuuna, Faith, and Max laugh boisterously at their teammate's misfortune.

"Shut up!" He retorts, tripping and rolling down the ramp.

"Oh my Goddd Pilet! Learn to walk!" Said Yuuna.

"How does the fastest one here have two left feet?!" Said Faith, rolling on the ground in laughter.

Max simply facepalms, covering his laughter in his hand.

Pilet eventually grabs the metal marble, trudging back up the ramp begrudgingly. As he approaches his team, he looks at them in disdain.

"Not another word." He said, giving them all a stern look.

He holds the metal ball aloft to the silvery jewel, prompting a metallic shine to emerge. Finally, with all stones activated, the large clear crystal in the center begins to shine.

"What now?" Said Pilet. "The big clear one's not doing anything."

"Well, why don't you try hitting it with a Hollowpoint?" Said Faith.

"... You want me to blast it?" He replied.

"No no, don't *blast* it. But maybe pelt it with a little one. I forgot to mention, that clear crystal is quartz, and it represents a Neutral or "Pure", aura. Auracasts like Callous, Fleetfoot, and Mend, they're all neutral casts. Without an elemental property, Neutral casts are a lot easier to master. Hollowpoint is Neutral too, so it should do the trick!"

"Oh, that makes sense! Alright here goes."

Pilet holds out his right palm, reinforcing his arm at the elbow with his left hand. He creates another auric marble, this time of pure Hollowpoint energy. As he concentrates on the Hollowpoint, the dust starts to whip up beneath him from the pressurized aura surrounding the fiery prospect. He looks at his fellow teammates, remembering the many escapades, battles, and adventures leading up to this point.

"Look guys, standing on the other side of this door is the finish line. We get in there and it's home-free. I just... I just want you punks to know that no matter where we all end up," Pilet fights to hold back tears. "just know that we'll always be friends alright!"

Yuuna immediately begins to cry, running to Pilet and hugging him around the waistline from behind.

"I'm gonna miss you Pilet!! Keep in touch! You better not drop us like you did that village girl ok?!"

"I, what?! Shutup Yuuna!"

Faith puts a hand on Pilet's shoulder. She flashes him a warm smile.

"Always, no matter what."

Pilet nods soberly in response. Suddenly, Max Bear hugs the three of them together from behind. The pressure of his crushing grip makes them collectively wheeze.

"I've said it before and I'll say it again. A friend of The Sanda is a friend for life. We are forever linked on the branches of time!"

Pilet groans in pain at the mighty squeeze.

"Ow you dickhead loosen up!"

Max grins, tightening his grip on his three allies.

"What was that? I couldn't hear you Pilet."

Struggling to squirm free, Pilet loses focus and begins to charge more aura into his Hollowpoint. Turning around to bark more profanity at Max, he fails to notice the size of his arcane projectile increasing exponentially. Gasping for air as she's squeezed intensely, Faith sees the Hollowpoint changing but struggles to verbalize her concern.

"*Wheeze* Pilet! *Pant* *Wheeze* It's too, *Gasp* strong! I *Wheeze* said not to, *Pant* blast it!!"

Yuuna's face, tucked tightly underneath Pilet's armpit in the bear hug, barely manages to see the plight in action. She tries to speak, but can only let out a muffled cry with her mouth plastered across Pilet's side.

"Mmpphhh!!" She wails.

After unloading an unholy string of profanity at his Hachidorinese teammate, Pilet turns back around and sees the enormous, three-foot-wide orb of aura he's created.

"Oh, shit!!" Exclaims Pilet, attempting to downsize his massive weapon. "It's too damn big! I can't bring it down!!" He struggles to hold onto the giant auric sphere. "I, I gotta let it go!! "I can't hold on any longer!!"

"No!!" Cried all four of them in unison.

Pilet releases the Hollowpoint into the clear crystal, as The Hidden Blades all grit their teeth in panic. But the crystal immediately absorbs the auric sphere like a sponge, as it and the 9 surrounding crystals suddenly lose their arcane glow. The Hidden Blades silently observe the now dimmed crystal grid in shock.

"......................"

Faith shouts obnoxiously in Pilet's ear.

"YA BROKE IT-"

But in the blink of an eye, all ten crystals suddenly explode into a powerful shockwave of aura mid-sentence; blasting the four prospects and sending them flying down the inclined hall.

"Aaaaaahh!!" They cry, tumbling and rolling uncontrollably.

Max draws an M6 Gash from behind his waist, burrowing the blade into the ground to regain his footing. Yuuna casts Autumn Stream and sends a powerful turbine of wind down the hall, stopping her in mid-air as she falls safely to the ground. As Faith reaches for her tome and begins sifting through the pages, she's abruptly whacked in the face by an airborne Pilet's buttocks. Muffled by her allies clumsy behind, she cries out in rage as they fly down the corridor.

"Fffffmmmmm!!"

As the two hit the ground and start to tumble and roll, they both cast "Fleetfoot" and nimbly regain their footing, swiftly darting back up the hall to the locked door.

Max and Yuuna get there first, gazing intently as the gems shine brilliantly as ever with a newfound aura. Each surrounding crystal sends a thin, vibrant stream of energy flowing directly into the clear center gem. The aura streams match the beautiful colors of the gems they originate from, creating a diverse palette that lights the corridor like the stars in the night sky. Pilet arrives next, followed by Faith who immediately push-kicks him in the back.

"Watch where you put your ass!" She exclaimed, sending Pilet flying into the pulsating crystal grid.

"Aaaagh!!" Cried Pilet, as he's zapped and frozen by the yellow and blue crystals. "Yyyyoouu bbbitchh!!"

He falls to the ground, seizing and curling his fingers in pain. Yuuna and Max look down at Pilet, then back at Faith with concern.

"He'll be fine." She said.

As the vibrant, aura-infused door continues to glow, the runic Rok-Senn inscriptions across it begin to glow as well. The lettering shines a majestic golden hue, as the clear crystal in the center begins to rotate. Slowly but surely, the arcane door slides open, revealing the final chamber of the mirage pyramid. As Pilet stands to his feet and brushes off the dust of the ancient floor; a sharp, feminine voice can be heard behind the group.

"I told you the bitch with the book could open the door."

The Hidden Blades turn around, instantly drawing their weapons and taking to fighting stances. They see the assassin twins of The Reaper Elite, emerging from the shadows cast by the wall mounted torches.

The twins; Asger and Dabria, in matching assassin's garbs with thin cloth covering their lower faces. Asger's garb is a stark turquoise, his naturally teal hair gel-flipped at the front. Dabria, in a maroon garb, with a long, three-stranded braid of her natural scarlet hair.

Asger drags Lazlow "The Gavel" up with him from the limestone ground, while Dabria rises arm in arm with Arturo of the Fubuki tribe of Hachidori. Lazlow, platinum blonde, bulky and muscular in frame; he's covered head to toe in the fearsome "Alabaster armor" of the Kettlenian Elite. Arturo bears two blue stripes in his cornrowed hair, bearing the same lamellar armor as Max, but with a cobalt blue trim, and a blue gem in the chestplate.

As the two teams engage in a staredown, Dabria continues.

"Like I said, even *these clowns* are capable of getting past that childish collapsing maze." Dabria looks at Arturo and Lazlow. "But we wouldn't have to wait if either of you *idiots* had some degree of auracast diversity."

Vrrr

Just then, the infrared cry of Pilet's knives echoes throughout the hall, as he points them intently toward the rival team.

"What are *you* doing here?... Looking to square up for round two? Or are you gonna run away again, like a *punk*."

Lazlow draws his massive, mechanized kite shield, which parts down the middle to reveal the powerful ARK tri-cannon hidden within.

"Please, that fight got boring and you know it. You and your little butter knives aren't worth my time." Lazlow begins to rev the gatling barrel of the tri-cannon. "But if you *really* want, I could end your miserable life right here and now. Free of charge..."

The Final Chamber

"Stop." Asger thrusts his arm across Lazlow's chest plate in protest. "We're not here to fight, that portion of the exam's already passed. We have a mission, remember? Eyes on the prize."

Lazlow scoffs at Asger, as he releases the gatling trigger within his shield. As the massive barrel of the menacing weapon begins to slow, he glares at Pilet in contempt.

"Luckiest day of your life."

Asger raises his hands in a submissive gesture.

"Look, we both have the same goal. We need to get in that room just as much as you do, and we're all part of the same organization. It just doesn't make sense to fight at the finish line."

"Why should we believe *you* of all people!" Shouts Yuuna. "Last time you said something like that you ended up putting a knife in my sister!" Yuuna cultivates aura into her left hand. "I swear to God I'll make you pay."

"Tch." Dabria scoffs. "*Your* funeral, girl." She turns to Asger. "That's what you get for being soft, brother. Next time, finish the job."

Arturo reaches for his Shred longsword, as Max reaches for his Lacerate. The serrated edge of Arturo's Shred, a stark difference to the plain edge of the Lacerate.

"I'm going to enjoy this." Said Arturo.

"The only thing you're going to enjoy is the moment your soul leaves this world, ending the pain I'm about to inflict on you." Replied Max.

Tension rises, as the clashing candidates menacingly clutch their weapons. The Hachidorinese warriors grill each other with heated disdain, while the two hot-headed Emissaries exchange middle fingers and profanities. Yuuna stares down Asger and Dabria with the intensity of an enraged lion, her nostrils flare as she chokes back tears of anger. Faith stands there, holding her tome open with her free hand cultivating aura.

"You know what..." She said, with a look of contemplation written across her face.

Faith closes the tome and dissipates her stored aura. Her sister turns to her, perplexed at Faith's actions.

"What are you doing? You're not going to abandon us again are you?!"

Faith puts a hand on her sister's shoulder.

"Relax. I've got this." She turns to Asger. "Look, I'm gonna be honest dude, I don't trust a single word coming out of your mouth. I honestly can't, and if I did I would be a damn fool."

"I... Well, that's fair..." He replied.

"But I want to." Faith continued. Asger's eyebrows raise in a surprised manner. "I would love for nothing more than to walk through those doors right now without a problem, grab my damn treasure, and get out of this dusty pyramid. It's been a long day, and I'm exhausted. So I'll tell you what. I know how to re-lock this door instantly, it wouldn't be hard *at all*. You let us go in first, we grab the goods and leave, and *then* you psychos can take your turn. *But-*" Faith draws aura into her free hand. "If any of you try anything funny, I will immediately lock you out, *without* hesitation. Is that fair?"

Members of the Reaper Elite look to Lazlow for approval. Lazlow hocks up a loogie and spits over his shoulder.

"You're smart. Cowardly, but smart." He nods to his team. "Alright, but I'm sick of this dark, dank pyramid too. You got five minutes. After that I'm kicking the shit out of all of you, don't think that door will stop me."

"But it literally did..." Muttered Arturo. "I watched you try to punch it and get zapped across the hall..."

"Shutup! Whispered Lazlow. *"It's a front, dumbass!"*

Faith nods to their rivals, holding her aura-glowing hand aloft.

"Fair enough. Alright guys, let's get this artifact and get out of here."

Faith leads The Hidden Blades into the final chamber, as Pilet and Lazlow exchange mocking faces before separating. As they turn away, Yunna flashes her sister a confused look.

"You can remotely shut a 9-element lock?" She said. "Since when was *that* a thing?"

"Shhh" Faith hushes her sister. "Since *I said* it is." She whispered. "A good *bluff* can be more powerful than any auracast sis, remember that."

"Ooooohh." Replied Yuuna, as she grins and nods her head.

They venture into the final chamber of the Mirage Pyramid, glaring in awe of the spectacular wonders left before them. Golden-hilted swords with colorful, gem-encrusted scabbards hang decoratively across the walls. Silver-headed spears adorned with eagle feathers line weapon racks made from mesquite wood around the room. Hundreds of gold and silver coins lay scattered across the floor in uneven piles, mixed with bronze cutlery and fine jewelry. Two doors on adjacent walls lie slid open, a clear sign that The Hidden Blades are not the first to reach the finish.

The only wall without a door showcases a lavishly adorned silver sarcophagus, lined with gold, lapis lazuli, jade, and garnet. The face of the finely furnished casket displays the scowl of a noble wolf, with two emeralds for eyes, and rubies for teeth. Above the lupine sarcophagus, mounted onto the center of the wall, sits a 2-foot-tall tablet made of pure gold.

The precious tablet displays the image of a mighty Serpent Dragon, glaring ominously into the room. The lengthy, serpentine body of the ancient reptile coils itself into a figure-eight pattern in the background. Its hypermuscular, scaly arms clutch shining spheres of pure aura in each, three-fingered hand. Lightning strikes down from the sky above it, bathing the dragon in a radiant shower of fulmination.

As the group walks through the embellished chamber, they reach a simple, folding table in the middle of the room. Miscellaneous, precious artifacts from within the room have been strewn across, hand-picked by the exam proctors for passing candidates. Faith approaches first, lifting a golden chalice with rubies and sapphires encrusted around the rim.

"My God." She said. "Sis, could you imagine getting sloshed on Itedonian rose wine with one of these?" She tosses it to her sister.

Yuuna shrieks as she catches the ancient cup with care.

"Yuck." She said, wiping the dust inside with her finger. "I mean, I'd wash it first, but that's one way to drink like a Queen!"

Max is drawn to a finely crafted dagger, adorned with sapphires within the hilt. The sapphires are meticulously acid-etched with Rok-Senn runic language.

"What a stunning piece of handiwork." He said. "Hey Pilet, you like knives right? You must see this fearsome piece." Max turns around, seeing Pilet staring intently into the Serpent Dragon tablet. "Oh, the attention span on *this* one..."

The hair on the back of Pilet's neck stands erect, as his skin begins to clam incessantly. His nostrils flare, as his eyes begin to take to an arcane glow. Flashes of lightning and the blood-curdling screams of hundreds of people echo throughout the halls of his mind. He breaks into a cold sweat, as the fiery prospect finds himself locked into an undying gaze with the fierce golden image.

"Why am I so scared, so scared of you?..." He thought. He shakes his head and slaps himself mercilessly. *"Wake up dude! We're finally finished. I'm gonna do it, I'm gonna be a Hired blade!!"* Pilet collects himself and approaches the artifact table with the rest of his team.

"Finally tired of gawking at Braaga?" Said Faith.

"Who?" Replied Pilet.

"Braaga De Anihalaa, or I should say, "Braaga The Annihilator". The almighty God of the Serpent Dragons, and destroyer of time. He's kind of a big deal."

"Oh... Yeah I knew that. Well whatever, so what are you guys thinking of picking here?"

"Well Max wanted this dagger." Said Yuuna. "And I can't blame him, it's so pretty!"

"It *would* be a nice addition to my nightstand." Said Max. "However I cannot be so selfish, I'm not the only one here looking for an ancient souvenir."

"It's fine Max, take it." Replied Faith. "Our parents accumulated enough priceless trash, we grew up in a house full of it."

"Pilet?" Said Max. "What about you?"

Pilet draws the chromium necklace from under his shirt.

"I'm good dude, knock yourself out."

"Fair enough." He replied, placing the ancient knife into a bag at his side. "Now let's get out of here."

"Wait." Said Yuuna, fiddling with her Chatch and running over to the Wolf sarcophagus. "Whoever this is must have been super important. I'm taking a selfie before we go." She poses by the head of the sarcophagus and smiles brightly. "Say cheese Mister old fancy-pants!"

With a click and a flash, the Chatch snaps a photo of Yuuna beside the ancient coffin.

"Rest in peace man!" She said, pacing back to her teammates.

Faith shakes her head, smiling in amusement at her sister's antics. She spots a red button on the end of the table.

"I'm guessing this is our way out?" She said, pressing the button curiously.

Just then, the sound of stone scraping against itself echoes throughout the chamber. A door starts to shift open in the ceiling, revealing the setting sun of the Devil's Tongue desert piercing through the darkness. A rolled-up ladder unfurls itself from the lip of the opening, as a familiar voice calls out to The Hidden Blades.

"Well, it certainly took you lot long enough!"

Pilet scratches his chin.

"Is that..."

Faxion pops his head out from the lip of the opening, grinning and tipping his hat to the gang.

"Hurry up now, we don't have all day!" He said.

"Fax!" Exclaimed Yuuna. "Thank God, I guess we're finally done with this mess!"

Faith hops up onto the swinging ladder. She struggles for a moment to find her balance as the ladder sways to and fro.

"Damn thing, it's just like gym class all over again."

Faith reaches the top, as Faxion offers her a hand and pulls her over the lip. She sees that Faxion is standing upon a flying gondola, positioning the head right above the pyramid's opening. The narrow high-tech gondola is kept aloft by a series of powerful thrusters, meticulously lined beneath it.

"Always traveling in style aren't you Fax." She said.

"Hah, yes. Well, you know me." He replied with a grin.

The others soon make their way up and out of the opening, taking their seats on the flying gondola. The thrusters below begin to intensify with the added weight of The Hidden Blades, blasting dust and sand off of the pyramid's surface. They begin their descent towards the sands below, passing Lazlow The Enforcer, the father of the Reaper Elite's Emissary on their way down. Faxion tips his hat to them.

"Guess yours came in last this year, huh? It was probably just too easy for them, they were taking a leisurely stroll through the pyramid I'm sure."

Lazlow Sr. simply scoffs, as he continues upward on a gondola of his own. Faxion turns to the group, giddy with excitement for their achievement.

"Well my God, you've done it! You're all as good as Licensed Hired

Blades now! We'll just have to prepare the ceremony, but congratulations folks!" Faxion pulls a bottle of champagne from his jacket, along with a set of plastic cups. "Here's to health, success, and many more hangovers. Pilet, you do the honors." Faxion tosses the bottle to Pilet.

Pilet catches it with finesse scanning the bottle up and down excitedly.

"Oh shit Fax, this is the good stuff!"

"No penny is to be spared on my team." He replied.

Yuuna gently tugs at the hem of Faxion's pants pocket.

"Hey Fax?" She said.

He turns to her, a curious glint in his eye.

"Why, yes love? What can I do for you."

"Just, remind me later," She brandishes the black onyx stone housing Besmith. "I've gotta talk to you about something. It's about the FC science guy. The one who brings fossils back to life."

"Aah, Dr. Nashorn?" He replied. "A right, *genius* that man is. What of him?"

"Well, I made a deal with a, erm... friend. Just, let's talk later. Wouldn't want to spoil the moment."

Faxion flashes her a warm smile, patting her gently on the back.

"But of course, no spoiled moments here lass."

Just then, Pilet draws a Dragonfly knife and pops the champagne bottle's cork with ease, sending a spray of champagne all over Faith's face.

"Aaaagh! You idiot!" She exclaims, covering herself from the alcoholic onslaught.

"Hahahahaha!" He chortled. "Underage or not, *I'm* gonna drink and *you're* just gonna have to deal with it!"

As Pilet continues to rain champagne all over Faith, she loses her patience and tackles him. As the two begin to tussle and roll across the gondola, the narrow flying vehicle begins to shake and shift violently. Faxion, Yuuna, and Max fall over and almost fall out.

"Woah now!" Exclaimed Faxion. "Let's play nice, there's no need to rock the boat-"

Faxion is interrupted by the continued vicious rocking, sending him flying out of the gondola. He holds on to the lip with one hand while holding his fedora in the other.

"This is fine, everything is fine." He said, clinging to the vessel for dear life.

"Would you fools calm down!" Yelled Max, stomping his feet in protest. "At this rate we're going to-"

Max is sporadically flung from the gondola mid-sentence. As he tumbles down the slanted wall of the pyramid, he lets loose a string of profanity.

"Damn you! Damn you all! I'm so sick of this shit! Aaahh!!"

Faxion waves to Max as he tumbles down the pyramid.

"Bye Max! Remember to tuck and roll at the end now, wouldn't want to injure your spine."

"Fax do something!" Exclaimed Yuuna.

"Oh I can't possibly, I'm having far too much fun." He replied.

Yuuna leaps from the gondola and casts "Kitestream", taking flight as she rushes after the tumbling swordsman.

Suddenly, Pilet and Faith roll out of the vessel in their wild tussle. They tip the gondola completely over, colliding with Faxion as the three begin to fall down the pyramid with haste.

"Aaaaggh!" Shouts Pilet and Faith.

"Woohoo!" Exclaims Faxion. "Oh what it's like to feel young again!!!"

Just as Yuuna catches up to Max and grasps his arm, the others ram into them from behind, creating a landslide of clumsily falling Blades.

"Ow what the hell!" Exclaims Yuuna, as Faith's head rams the small of her back mid-flight.

The Hidden Blades continue to uncontrollably roll down the pyramid, smacking their faces and backs against the jagged edges of the limestone brick. Finally, they reach the bottom, piling on top of each other like a stack of overfilled trash bags. Faxion is the only one who lands gracefully, as he tucks and rolls with great finesse over the pile. He ends with a back handspring and sticks the landing, giving a celebratory bow to his sponsored candidates covered in sand.

Faxion turns to see the other victorious candidates, as well as the attending proctors, sponsors, and other Hired Blades staring at them. It appears that the Mystic Marauders, The Funk Munkeys, and the lone archeologist Bhujanga Garuda, are the only candidates to have successfully emerged from the ancient ruin. He exchanges passing glances with Toste, giving him a wink and a grinning nod. Toste laughs and shakes his head.

"Some things never change."

"A rough translation? Morph..."

The crowd erupts into laughter and applause for The Hidden Blades, as they collect themselves and brush the sand from their backs and shoulders. The group looks at each other, smiling and laughing in response.

"Woooo!" Exclaimed Yuuna. "We did it!"

"After all this, it almost feels surreal." Said Max, grunting while cracking his back. "I can't believe it, I have finally brought honor to my tribe."

Faith gives Pilet the stink eye, as Pilet shrugs his shoulders and smiles wide.

"Sorry?" He said with a high-pitched voice.

Faith punches him in the arm.

"Ow." He yelps in response.

She wrings out the champagne from her hair and grins.

"That's what you get, jerk."

Suddenly they hear a loud metal clunking from above. The flying gondola starts crashing down the pyramid's side, tumbling and rolling straight for the Hidden Blades.

"Aaaaaah!" They cry in unison, ducking in surprise.

But a soft, swift, clink can be heard, just as the metal vessel comes close to smashing into them. Miraculously, the gondola splits in half at the center. Cut clean in two, the separate pieces thud and roll past the startled candidates. Embedded into the wall bears the singed mark of a slashing aura bolt, similar to those demonstrated by Max.

"You have to be more alert, son. The Sanda yield to no one, let alone a renegade dingy."

The group looks up to see Kenzo Quinn, sheathing his Drawing sword and affixing it back to his magnetic belt. Max bows in reverence.

"I'm sorry Father, it won't happen again." He replied.

Kenzo gives him a stern look, which after a brief pause morphs into an elated smile. He lets loose a bellowing laugh, as he runs over to Max and gives him a relentless Bear hug.

"You did it boy! You made it! The Sanda Clan will rejoice on this night!"

"*Urp* Thank you father, *Wheeze* I told you I would not disappoint." Max said, as his father crushes his ribs.

Scott Diliger and Caffo Gilwick approach The Hidden Blades, offering them each a congratulatory handshake.

Caffo Gilwick, staunch and stern head proctor for this year's Blades exam; sports a pair of faded blue jeans, black boots, and a plain white tee with the sleeves rolled up to his shoulders. His dirty blonde hair is slicked back with grease, with a navy headband holding it back. A pair of thick, high-tech vambraces, cufflinks of sorts, wrap around either of his wrists; with a Chatch screen in the middle of each. He holds his usual black leather jacket folded over his shoulder, an unbearable wear in the desert heat. His face, serious and fatigued, with a very subtle hint of benevolence.

"Congratulations on a job well done." Said Caffo. "We watched the whole thing from our Chatches, you guys really went through hell in there."

"Yeah, seriously!" Said Scott. "Pilet, that fight with the tree was badass. What an observant way to capitalize on its weak point. And Max, the way you stared down that Necrocasted Shriidah was legendary. Everyone here got chills!

"Thanks man, all in a day's work." Replied Pilet.

Max offers Scott a humble bow.

"I appreciate the compliment. You heard my father, The Sanda yield to no one."

Speaking of The Shriidah..." He looks to Caffo, as the two turn to Faith and Yuuna.

"We have some questions about that encounter, and the two of you are quite possibly the only ones with a decent answer." Said Caffo.

"Welp, I know how this goes." Said Pilet. "Here comes a conversation about some shit I don't know anything about. Catch me later dudes, I'm grabbing a beer."

"I too will leave you to it." Replied Max.

Max and Pilet make their exit to the drink coolers, leaving the Proctors with the Sierro sisters. Caffo continues.

"When we initially scouted this pyramid, we hadn't taken the route you three did, so no one had encountered that Necrocasted behemoth. But I'm sure with the knowledge you two have, you understand why it would be strange to see that there..."

Faith's eyes grow blank with fear, as she fights the urge to relive the horrid memories of the event. She shakes her head, remaining attentive to the conversation at hand.

"Uh, yeah. Yes, it *was* strange." She looks at Yuuna. "I'm not proud of how I handled it either..."

Yuuna puts a hand on her shoulder and flashes her a warm smile. Scott continues to deliberate.

"Well listen, this isn't a "Bully Faith" circle." Said Scott. "We've all wet our pants from some of the things we've seen on the field at some point, just ask Caffo." He glances back at Caffo with a deviant smile.

"It was *one* time..." He replied.

Scott smirks and chuckles to himself.

"Anyway, the bottom line is we need your help on this. *You're* the experts here, especially with the Necrocast extraordinaire around your neck little lady." He points to Yuuna.

Yuuna grasps the black onyx on her necklace.

"You mean this guy? *Ugh*, he never shuts up." She replied.

"Piss off!" Said Besmith telepathically to Yuuna.

"Well, we're going to have a meeting tomorrow after the festivities." Said Caffo. "Your first official order of business as a Licensed Hired Blade is to attend and give us your insight into today's events."

"We would be honored." Replied Faith. "" as a Licenced Hired Blade" God that sounds good."

Caffo folds his arms and grins.

"Glad to hear it. Just be prepared, on a hard enough mission you *might just* get tired of hearing that..."

Pilet and Max separate. Max returns to his father, as Pilet approaches Benny the aircraft pilot, Toste, and Faxion in a huddle by the coolers. Pilet sneaks behind Toste, drawing his gifted parrying dagger and holding it to Toste's neck from behind.

"Checkmate," Pilet said. "gotta be aware of your surroundings man... Ow!" Pilet feels the pinch of a hidden dagger in Toste's sleeve against his ribs, as Toste uses his free hand to grab Pilet's arm and throw him like a bag of ice onto the sand.

"*Oof*" Grunts Pilet as he hits the ground.

Toste turns to the fiery Blade.

"As you should be aware of yours." He replied with a mischievous smirk.

Pilet picks himself up, dusting the sand off of his buttocks.

"Shit, one of these days I'll get your ass..."

They all share a laugh, taking a swig of their assorted beverages.

"You know kid, it's gonna be sweet learning swordsmanship from this guy." Said Benny. "He's easily one of the deadliest men with a blade this side of Kettlena."

"*Learning?*" Replied Pilet.

"Pilet, I've had the pleasure of working out a deal with Toste." Said Faxion. "He's going to meet with us periodically to teach you the way of the sword, or in your case the knife."

"*Get* the hell outta here. Toste, you're gonna come chill with us?"

Toste laughs as he picks up the parrying dagger Pilet dropped.

"Hah! In a manner of speaking, there will be much *chilling* to be had. Whether it be in an ice bath to soothe the aches of our training sessions remains to be seen." He tosses Pilet his parrying dagger. "Here's a lesson for you, don't let go of your weapon. It could cost you your life."

"Oh.. You mean like this?" Pilet sheaths the blade and chucks the hard metal hilt at Toste's foot.

"Ow!" Exclaimed Toste, holding his foot in pain as he tackles Pilet to the ground.

The two engage in a playful scuffle, as Faxion and Benny cheer them on from the side.

As the sun begins to set, The Reaper Elite emerge from atop The Mirage Pyramid. They board Lazlow Sr.'s flying gondola, as the final group slowly descends to the desert sands. As they do, a particularly bright shine glints off of Lazlow Jr.'s armor. Caffo Gilwick grows suspicious of the blinding shine as he gathers the other proctors in concern.

"Do you see what I'm seeing?" He said. "What the hell is that big shining thing? They were *only* supposed to take what was left on the artifact table!"

Benny scratches his head.

"Relax Caffo. I mean, even if the kid grabbed something on the side, can't you just slap him on the wrist and put it back?"

"Shit, it doesn't work like that Benny." Replied Caffo. "We carefully chose pieces that we knew weren't booby-trapped. If you just go around grabbing shit, you might end up setting off something big. And they were in the *Throne room*, Lord knows what kind of traps the Rok-Senn could have set for them."

"I mean, it looks like they got out relatively unscathed." Said Scott. "At the very least they either got lucky and grabbed something that *wasn't loaded,* or they survived whatever came at them. Ugh, great. I just hope the Throne room isn't full of poison gas or Morphs now. I'll have to clean that up later..."

The Reaper Elite reach the bottom of the pyramid and step off of their vessel. Lazlow Jr. is the last to dismount, carrying the golden tablet of Braaga The Annihilator proudly over his shoulder. Upon seeing this, Caffo Gilwick immediately throws a cup of coffee he was drinking to the ground in a heated rage.

"Are you kidding me!" He screams. Caffo marches towards Lazlow Jr., getting in his face and pointing incessantly at the tablet. "Who told you to take that you peabrain!! You were *explicitly told* to take *nothing but what was on the table!!*"

Lazlow Jr. laughs.

"Hah! Pssh, I do what I want, dickhead. Besides, now I'm a Licensed Hired Blade too, so we're on the same level. By the way, if you keep yelling at me like that, I'm going to rip out your voice box and put it in a squeaky toy."

Lazlow Jr. brushes off the triggered proctor, bumping him in the shoulder as he forces his way past.

Enraged, Caffo grabs Lazlow by his massive arm to pull him back.

"Where do you think you're going!!-"

In an instant, Lazlow Jr. swings the golden tablet at the angered proctor with the force of a speeding hover car.

But the seasoned Blade nimbly ducks the strike, scurrying behind the hulking Kettlenian Elite in a flash. Caffo kicks into the back of Lazlow's Knee, forcing him to the ground. Lazlow plants his free hand on the floor, bracing himself to avoid falling face-first. He turns and swings his forearm wildly at Caffo, but the blind strike is swiftly blocked, as Caffo snakes his arm across Lazlow's neck. Caffo begins to work in a rear naked choke, as Lazlow Jr. fights to grasp at Caffo's hands.

"Still think we're on the same level you spoiled brat!?" Exclaimed Caffo, as he began to tighten his squeeze around the young Blade's neck.

The rest of the crowd begins to converge around the scuffle, curiously watching the dispute taking place. Lazlow drops the golden tablet, beginning to cough and choke from the pressure around his throat. Suddenly, A massive backfist comes straight for Caffo's face from behind, as he releases the hold on Lazlow Jr. just in time to block the surprise technique.

He cups his ear with his hand, raising his elbow to cover his face. As the backfist lands on his forearm, the force of the blow sends him flying back. Caffo slides across the sand, planting his feet to stop himself from crashing into the crowd. He lowers his guard to the sight of Lazlow Sr., standing in front of him in a menacing posture.

"I'm The Enforcer here, not you." Said Lazlow Sr. "I'll handle the boy, you stay in your Goddamn lane Caffo."

Caffo brushes his face in frustration. He stands to his feet, fixing his mechanized cufflinks.

"Tell your son to follow orders, we're not lawless here." Lazlow points at the golden tablet, now strewn across the floor. "You see *that?* He's not supposed to touch that! He could have gotten himself and his team killed in there, and he could have cost all of us our lives too. The most dangerous traps are set at the end of any ruin. He's lucky nothing happened!"

As Caffo says this, an ominous rumbling begins to sound throughout the desert. The earth starts to shake, causing the sand to shift below their feet. Dark clouds suddenly begin to form above the evening sky, blocking out the light of the setting sun.

"That's... peculiar..." Said Faxion. "It's not due to rain in Devil's Tongue anytime soon." He turns to Scott. "Does this look right to you?"

"No, no it doesn't..." Scott replied. "These look like... *Arcane* clouds..."

"I thought so too..." Said Faxion.

A massive, auric rune begins to glow crimson across the face of the pyramid, as spectators all gasp in shock. Faith's jaw drops, as she points to the symbol in fright.

"That's, no. No it can't be. There's just no way."

"What?" Said Pilet. "What's wrong? Hey, I've seen that one before." Pilet turns and looks at Puerto and the Mystic marauders across the way. "That symbol was on the big tree that tried to kill us, right? What does that word even mean?"

Puerto is unable to answer, in awe of what transpires before him.

In a flash, a wicked bolt of blood-red auric lightning shoots forth from the clouds of darkness; firing upon the top of the Mirage Pyramid. The charge of the arcane bolt causes the rune across the front to glow with a new, blinding intensity. The sands begin to quake at a much stronger rate, causing the tables and chairs surrounding the Cool Oasis to fall over.

Suddenly, Bhujanga Garuda appears from behind Pilet. The only exam candidate to test solo; he's an archeologist prodigy of Scott Diliger, and a terrifying auracaster in his own right. A tan skinned man of average build, he sports a green, plaid shirt and beige, fitted khakis. His hair is dark brown, short around the sides with some length to the top. He bears a wire-wrapped, black and white crystal around his neck; which begins glowing as he strides calmly by Pilet.

Bhujanga begins conjuring his signature technique; "The Emerald Flame", in both of his hands. A mystical, green fire rushes forth from his palms, engulfing either fist with arcane flame. He takes a ready stance in front of the crowd of worried onlookers. He answers the question that Puerto could not.

"A rough translation?" Says Bhujanga, cultivating a luminous, emerald-green fireball in between his hands. "Morph....."

CHAPTER

THREE

Round One; Gateway of the Damned

The boardroom of The Hired Blades Association. Chairman Yang and his associates watch as the events at The Mirage Pyramid begin to unfold. After seeing the scuffle between his appointed Head Proctor and Lazlow The Gavel, he curiously strokes his beard.

"Chairman, this kind of behavior is simply unacceptable." Said a board member across the table from Chairman Yang. "The boy just completely disregarded the regulations set in place by his superior! He *must* be punished, else we risk future candidates displaying this spirit of lawlessness within our ranks!"

Chairman Yang simply watches, observing as Lazlow Sr. breaks up the action and begins to scold Caffo. Deep in thought, he squints to get a better look, as the earth starts to quake on the monitor.

"What is this?" He said, confused by the sudden shifting of the screen. "Is our internet down again? I told you lot to log your Chatches off of the damn wifi! Now look at what you did!"

"Sir, the wifi is fully functional at the moment." Said Chairman Yang's technical assistant, tapping away at his laptop keyboard. "I believe what we are seeing is live in Devil's Tongue."

"Oh... Fair enough." He replied. "What a curious event..."

The boardroom continues to watch, as the ghoulish glow of the massive auric rune spans across the Pyramid face. Chairman Yang shakes his head in bewilderment, as he again begins to stroke his beard observantly. As the scarlet bolt of lightning strikes the tip of the ancient structure, Yang sits back and postures up in surprise. He glances at his arm, scanning the multitude of auric tattoos strewn across his tanned skin. Staring intensely at a tattoo of a Wolf, its eyes an emerald green and its teeth and maw red from the blood of a fresh kill. Chairman Yang draws his attention back to his peers.

"Get the Mayor of Titanus on the phone immediately, and prepare The Crimson Pagoda. We need to set a course for The Cool Oasis, ASAP."

"Sir, your private airship?..." Said his assistant. "But there are many vessels more capable of making it to the Oasis in record time."

"*I said* to prepare The Pagoda, did I not?! Do not question my methods! And send out an emergency response notice to all Blades currently in the Capital. Now go! There's no time to waste!"

"Of course sir." Said his assistant, as he hurriedly paces down the halls, phoning away at his Chatch.

Back in the Devil's Tongue Desert, The party of Proctors and Exam candidates brace for the mysterious trouble that lies ahead. As members of the crowd reach for their weapons in anticipation, Lazlow Sr. approaches his son with a look of disdain.

"Boy, is it true you were not to take this?" He said, lifting the golden tablet off of the sand.

Lazlow Jr. pauses and looks at the ground, a shameful glint in his eyes.

"Yes sir..." He said.

Lazlow Sr. brushes his face in his palm in frustration. He stares intently at his son for a moment, before smacking him across the face with his massive, calloused hand. The mighty thwack of Sr.'s blow whips his son's head to the side, as his eyes wince in pain. He gazes past his father, unable to look him in the eye.

"You made this mess." Said Lazlow The Vice. "Whatever madness is about to ensue, you are to take care of, *yourself.* Am I understood?"

Lazlow Jr. nods in response, hanging his head in shame.

"Good, now as for you..." Said Sr., turning to Caffo Gilwick. "You want to be Enforcer so bad? Here!" He tosses the golden tablet at Caffo's feet. "Help the boy clean up whatever mess he's made. I'll have nothing to do with it, this happened on *your* watch."

Caffo stands in silence, as do the rest of the attending Blades. A look of pure disgust plastered across the proctor's face. Lazlow turns to Ingemar, Aslaug, and Bernardo; the parents of The Reaper Elite, and motions them to follow his lead.

"Let's leave this horrid place before I get a damned heat stroke." Lazlow then yells toward the cockpit of his light aircraft. "Pilot! Let's get going, fire up the engine!"

Ingemar and Aslaug Trygve approach Asger and Dabria. Ingemar folds his arms and tilts his chin high in the air, looking down at his lethally trained children; while his wife Aslaug takes a timid posture, crossing her hands in front of her and swaying from side to side. The father speaks.

"You two had better *steal* the show." He said, pointing his rough-skinned, untrimmed fingernail in their direction. His sun-aged, wrinkle-ridden face, mixed with a multitude of miscellaneous scars tell a tale of the violent hardship that the man has faced. The bags beneath his eyes speak on the sleepless nights spent stalking prey in the name of the Clan Trygve. "*Don't* make me lose face. You understand?"

His scarlet and teal-garbed assassin children nod their heads in acknowledgment, trying carefully not to anger the fierce head of the Trygve Clan. Asger sees his mother, Aslaug, and offers her a wave of his hand with a timidity that matches her own.

"Bye Mom." Said Asger. "I lov-"

As the teal assassin offers up a heartfelt goodbye, his father flashes him a stern, sharp glare. Asger's sister punches him stiffly in the arm.

"What did father say about public displays of affection?!" She murmured. *"Get it together, idiot!"*

He prostrates himself, stiffening his lips and offering a light bow to his parents. Dabria follows suit.

"Goodbye, Mother and Father." Said Asger. "We will take care of matters here, in the name of the Trygve Clan..."

Ingemar flashes a wicked grin, nodding to his son in approval. Aslaug sighs, shooting her son an affectionate stare, speaking volumes to him without uttering a word. She smiles.

"In the name of the Trygve, indeed." Said Aslaug. "Do your very best-"

"Return victorious, or dead." interrupts Ingemar. He turns around, pacing methodically towards Lazlow Sr.'s aircraft. He motions his wife to follow. "Now Aslaug, we go."

She flashes her children a humble smile, before mounting the aircraft with her husband. Bernardo Schimo too can be seen leaving the presence of his son, Arturo. The Fubuki tribesmen of the island Hachidori offer each other a quick bow.

"I'll leave this desert a winter wasteland." Said Arturo, patting the sheathed swords along his hip.

His father Brenardo chuckles and cracks his knuckles in response.

"I'd expect no less. Give 'em frozen-hell son. Don't let those *Sanda* show us up!"

As Bernardo Schimo boards the light aircraft, the vessel's engine begins to rev loudly. A moment later, the ship takes off into the darkened sky, leaving a steady stream of exhaust in its wake.

"God-damn coward." Said Kenzo, gripping his Lacerates tightly in disdain. "I would never dream that the Enforcer to such a fearsome organization would be so ignorant to his own cause."

"Hah!" Laughs Faxion, putting a hand on Kenzo's shoulder. "Surely a man in your position understands the corruption of politics. Those with whom power is given may choose how and when to use it, at their own leisure..."

The God of the Sands Approaches

The earth continues to quake, as the symbol across the Pyramid face becomes brighter and brighter with every passing moment. Suddenly, the top of The Mirage Pyramid begins to change shape, as the limestone bricks forming the massive structure begin to shift and slide apart. A complex series of compartmentalized parts emerge from within, as the pyramid starts to rapidly rearange before the baffled eyes of the Hired Blades Association.

Immense arms sprout forth, and hands emerge from within these arms. Gigantic legs begin to form, and from them just as gargantuan feet come to shape. The head of the ghoulish figure appears from within, as the bulkiest part of the pyramid shapes into a torso of incredible length and width. The God-like figure of the ancient world begins to stand to its mighty feet, as the thunderous sound of its creaking joints echoes throughout miles of sand and stone.

The titanic ancient Morph stands high above the desert sky, its head engulfed in the dark clouds that dropped arcane lightning upon it. As the gigantic structure towers over the sands, a devilish pair of verdant eyes gaze eerily upon the attending Blades below, peeking from within the clouds of darkness.

"Sweet Lord." Said Faith, her gaze set upon the eerie sight of the ancient behemoth. "Then it really is true..." Her lips quiver, as a hand covers her mouth to hide her fright. "God only knows how much blood was spilled to create a morph this size..."

"Caffo..." Said Faxion. "Have you ever led a squadron against a foe of this magnitude?"

"No." Caffo replied. "I can't say that I have..."

Faxion gives Caffo a warm look of concern.

"I know you're the appointed head of this year's exam, but if you'd like, you may pass leadership to me for the time being. The choice is completely up to you."

Caffo pauses for a moment, staring at the immense fortitude of the ancient foe before them.

"Alright." He replied. "I think that would be best. If there's anyone who can handle a mess like this... it's The Deadeye of the HBA." He nods to Faxion as the two shake hands. "And thank you..."

"My pleasure." He replied. Faxion paces to the front of the group, turning to face the crowd with folded arms. He stomps his feet, demanding the attention of onlookers. "Now listen up!" He bellowed. "As of this moment, you are all recognized as officially Licensed Hired Blades. You've all shown the skill required to face the mightiest of opposition that walks Giganus, and it's at this moment that these skills will be put to the test!" Faxion points behind him to the pyramid Morph. "Your first mission as

Licensed Hired Blades is to stop this menace from advancing any further! If the titan were to reach the Capital city it could spell catastrophic disaster."

The pyramid Morph begins to walk toward the group from afar. Its massive stone legs shake the earth with every slow and methodical step that it takes. Lazlow the Gavel grows impatient with the Veteran Blade's briefing and crouches in a runner's position.

"My mess, my problem..." He states.

Faxion looks at him with a soft gaze of disapproval.

"Suit yourself." He says with shrugged shoulders.

"Springboard!" Lazlow casts.

With a deafening boom, a massive cloud of sand kicks up; as the hot-headed Gavel propels himself across the desert at top speed in one, fearsome bound. He draws his shield, bolstering it at his shoulder for a mighty tackle to the leg of the marching titan.

But as he nears his target, the Morph braces itself, pulling its rear leg back before kicking Lazlow, mid-flight, like a soccer ball straight back to where he came from.

Lazlow zooms past the Blades, wildly crashing along the ground and smashing into a huge mound of sand in the distance. As he swiftly tumbles by, Faxion simply smiles at the brash, young Blade.

"Welp, you can't knock his spirit." He said.

Pilet shakes his head free of his incredulous thoughts, finally accepting the horror before him. He mutters to Faith.

"Tell that to the giant sand robot..."

A serious glaze sweeps across Faxion's face, as he turns once more to the group.

"As I was saying. I'd be hard pressed to say that all of us will see the light of day again, but that is a sacrifice you have all signed on for!" Faxion readies his Arcane Pierce and hoists it over his shoulder. "Steel yourselves Blades! And defend your Capital!"

Faxion fires a plasma shot into the air, as the Hired Blades collectively release a mighty war cry. All attendees draw their weapons, cast "Fleetfoot" and charge towards the Massive Morph, screaming as they traverse the desert sands with haste. But just as they start to near its limestone hide, the Morph releases a powerful shockwave of aura, blasting its pursuers back across the dunes.

"Oh shit!" Exclaimed Lukah of The Funk Munkeys, as he whizzes toward Pilet, smashing into him and Yuuna before the three of them land in a dogpile at the foot of a high sand dune.

"Aggh, dude get off me!" Exclaimed Pilet, wriggling out from beneath the mohawked Funk Munkey.

Yuuna wheezes as the air escapes her lungs.

"My bad, my bad." Said Lukah, offering the two a hand up.

The shockwave sends a barrage of sand rushing in its wake, headed straight for the three. Lukah holds his microphone to his mouth and starts to rap.

~"*Beat it Sandman best respect what I'm tellin' ya, I'm a whirlwind you're a breeze when I'm fellin' ya.*"~

As Lukah raps into the mic, aura begins to cultivate into the very bottom of the handle. At the end of his sentence, an auric bolt fires from the end of the microphone into the sand, as a mighty whirlwind emerges right in front of them. The whirlwind envelops the incoming sand and protects the trio from harm. Pilet and Yuuna gaze on in amusement.

"Woah!!" Gasped Yuuna. "You, that's... You can rap auracast? That's a thing now?!"

"Damn!" Exclaimed Pilet, holding his head in astonishment. "Tch, remind me not to buy tickets in the front row..."

As the rest of the Blades are sent flying back in miscellaneous directions, the Morph begins to raise its open palms to its chest. The palms face each other, as a green aura begins to pour forth from the massive rune across its chest, forming a ball between its hands. The titan then mechanically rotates at the hip to face the Cool Oasis with its auric bolt. Having landed side by side from the shockwave, Caffo and Scott brush the sand off of their backs and turn to each other in bewilderment. Scott speaks.

"Wait, that looks like..."

With a clamoring boom, the Morph fires the auric projectile into the Oasis, causing a massive splash of water into the surrounding area. The titanic Morph then drops its arms lifelessly, hunching over and freezing in place as the rune across its chest begins to dim.

As the swishing surface of the water begins to settle, pillars of vibrant green light start to emerge from within the depths, shining brightly beneath the dark sky of the thick overcast. Yet again, the ground begins to tremble.

Small ripples turn into mighty waves within the wide Oasis, as mysterious bones begin to float to the top.

"An... an aura break? How?!" Exclaimed Caffo.

Having been flung near the shore of the Oasis, Faxion and Bhujanga rise to their feet.

"What in heaven's name..." Said Faxion.

"Heaven has nothing to do with this, Mr. Deadeye." Replied Bhujanga Garuda, readying his Emerald Flame. "I've seen this in ancient scrolls. Prepare yourself, we're about to have some unwanted guests."

The bones begin to come together, as auric binding forms shining, arcane cartilage between their joints. Hordes of skeletons begin to emerge, making their way onto the sands. Suddenly Scott Diliger appears behind Bhujanga and Faxion, flipping over them and amassing a collection of aquatic cannonballs around him with aura.

"Nope, not today!" He said, as he begins to fire the cannonballs into the skeletons at will. "You all can go *right* back to hell!"

With each skeleton felled in this way, three more emerge in its place. Faxion holds his eagle tattoo aloft. He turns to Scott.

"You're thinking too small-scale my friend." Faxion then looks to Bhujanga and smiles. "Give me a hand would you?"

"My pleasure." Replied Bhujanga with a nod.

"Nubibus Autem Oleum!" Cast Faxion, as a yellow bolt of aura fires from within his tattoo into the air.

Nimbostratus clouds begin forming directly over the oasis, as they start to rain immense amounts of gasoline into the water. Immediately, Bhujanga leaps into the air, cultivates a massive emerald fireball, and fires it into the Oasis in a blaze.

The Oasis lights ablaze with the spectacle of thick, verdant fire. The emerald light of the burning body of water illuminates miles of desert darkness. But even this proves to be but a farce, as the otherworldly skeletons begin to emerge from the burning depths, seemingly unaffected by the Emerald flame. Now covered head to boney-toe in green fire, they continue their march towards the shore. They begin drawing ancient axes and short swords from holsters around their waists, pointing them towards the auracasting trio with a deviant glint in their eyes. The stench of their burning leather coats and trousers fills the air.

Bhujanga and Faxion glare at the undead army, agape at the devilish sight before them. Scott approaches, cultivating cerulean claws of pure aura. He fires them off like homing missiles at the first wave of skeletons to reach the shore, exploding on impact and blowing them to smithereens before they can gain ground.

"Any more bright ideas between you two?" He retorts.

Faxion grimaces and reaches for his Stinger pistol, as Bhujanga charges another fireball.

"Welp, pick a side and start firing." Replied Bhujanga. "Last one to die wins. But keep a tally, just in case we actually live..."

Scott laughs and fires off another set of missile claws.

"Sounds good to me!" He replied.

Faxion draws his Stinger, unloading a clip of plasma bullets into the first wave of skeletons. As the fiends fall back into the depths of The Cool Oasis, a volley of lead and plasma rushes past Faxions ear, into the next set of skeletons. He turns around to see The Mystic Marauders, Benny, Dex, and Dustin with their weapons drawn. Steam and smoke billows from the barrels of their weapons, as Dustin speaks.

"Don't steal all the kills this time, Deadeye. Save some for us."

"Ha!" He replied, taking off his hat and motioning towards the skeletons with a bow. "Have at it then."

Regroup!

Not far away, Danba The Witchdoctor, Clint, and Svenn watch the events at the Oasis taking place.

"Damn brotha." Said Danba. He turns to Clint. "I thought I seen alotta shit in my lifetime, but this takes the cake! Quick, get the amps! I'll ready the stage. Looks like we gonna put on a show..."

"You got it boss!" Replied Clint. "Svenn, let's get the goods!"

Svenn flips his hair out of his eyes and nods, as the two scurry off to their teams light aircraft with haste.

"Faxion!" Exclaimed Caffo. "I got a message from the Chairman, reinforcements will arrive within the hour." He points to the massive Rok-Senn Morph. "Until then, what do we do about *that?!*"

Faxion looks up at the titanic structure, as the light of its rune begins to cultivate aura from the air around it, gradually increasing in brightness. The Morph starts to posture up, standing tall and pulling its shoulders back into place. It looks down at the scattered group of Hired Blades with its ethereal, glowing eyes. A subtle look of concern flashes across Faxion's face. He turns to his would-be firing squad at the Oasis.

"Puerto." Said Faxion.

The Man 'O War dispatches a skeleton with his Pilum beam rifle, before looking over his shoulder inquisitively.

"What's up."

"Have your team focus their fire on this side of the shoreline. Keep the enemy from getting too close to the sand."

"Roger that." Replied Puerto.

"Dex and Dustin, you two back the Mystic Marauders from a distance. Pick off any you see creeping past them."

"Affirmative." Replied Dex.

Dustin mutters under his breath to Dex.

"I hope to God the big one doesn't trip and fall on us again..."

Faxion turns to Benny.

"You my friend, take to the skies and rain hell on these tasteless insurgents. Tell the other pilots to do the same."

"Thought you'd never ask!" Replied Benny, holtering his Stinger and casting "Fleetfoot".

He bolts across the sands toward his ship, light aircraft No.7.

"Scott, Bhujanga, I need you two with me. Leave these guys to the gunners." Faxion glares at the devilish eyes of The pyramid Morph. "We've a much bigger fish to worry about."

Scott and Bhujanga nod their heads, as the three cast "Fleetfoot" and dash off, back towards Caffo.

As Benny reaches his aircraft, he begins skidding past the open hatch door, struggling to control the speed of his Fleetfoot. He rushes to the on board radio, pulling it to his face and clicking the intercom.

"Calling all pilots, calling all pilots! This is Pilot No.7. Who else is left on this Godforsaken sandbox?!"

Another pilot immediately responds.

"Pilot No.3 here, just got back into my ship after that sand blast from the big man. Gonna have to unload some gear for the Funk Munkeys right quick and then I'll be ready to fly."

"Pilot No.5 present and ready. Looks like the Reaper's pilot ran off with The Enforcer a second ago. The rest kinda flew away earlier when their passengers died in the pyramid.

"Pilot No.2, en route to the scene of the fight. I left for Giduh right before the madness ensued to refuel. The Chairman sent out a mass message to any Blades between Devil's Tongue and Grand Titanus. More help should be on the way ASAP."

Benny wipes his face in his palms in frustration.

"Damn, just us then. Alright blokes, let's get to work! Faxion The Deadeye has taken over as Head of command, as his Pilot I'll work as top wing of this mission."

A unanimous "Roger that." comes from the remaining pilots.

"Let's take to the skies and start to blast these suckers." Said Benny. "No.3 and No.5, give the group by the Oasis some cover fire. I'll handle the big man. No.2, give me a hand when you get here."

"Copy that, over and out." They reply.

Benny hangs up his radio, takes a seat in the cockpit and prepares for takeoff.

"*Sigh*. Fax I sure hope you know what we're dealing with here. Because I sure don't..."

The remainder of present Hired Blades answer a call by Caffo on their Chatches, soon meeting the head proctor with haste. Pilet, Yuuna and Lukah arrive first. Then The Reaper Elite, followed by Toste, and Rexmere; who is the Martial Arts Exam Proctor. Faith, Max, and Kenzo appear at the same time as Faxion, Bhujanga, and Scott. Caffo walks over to Faxion.

"Is this everyone?" He said with a raised eyebrow.

"I believe so?" Replied Faxion. He starts counting the present Blades. "Or... No. Someone's missing."

"Nah hold up, where's my boys at?!" Interrupts Lukah.

Suddenly, the sound of bass guitar strumming can be heard in the distance. A twenty-or-so-foot wide tree stump with massive, foliage covered wings flies through the air. A golden, glowing pair of hollow eyes, and the fiendish grin of a wooden-fanged mouth reveal themselves across the stump's front, as it lands abruptly beside the group. Atop the flattened platform of the stump, the missing trio brandish their instruments. Clint and Svenn begin playing a mellow tune on their guitars, as wispy aura begins to surround them with every strum of the strings.

"Don't forget about *us,* ya know?" Said Clint.

"Lukah, where's your dumb head been at?" Said Danba, as he begins lightly tapping on a cymbal, attached to a drumset covered in auric runes.

Faxion and Caffo turn and look at each other with a bewildered, yet amused grin.

"Ah hell yeah! Let's party!" Exclaimed Lukah, as the stump holds its branch covered wing out for him to step on. He leaps from the wing onto the platform and pulls the chrome mic from his back pocket. "You fools are up for a treat! This show's on us!"

"Hah!" laughs Toste, drawing the rapier from his hip. "What a breath of fresh air you four are."

"Alright everyone, listen closely." Said Faxion.

He huddles everyone into a tight circle and draws out a detailed plan in the sand; all the while the titan of a Morph begins slowly marching toward the band of mighty mercenaries. The sounds of plasma and gunfire can be heard in the distance, as The Mystic Marauders and the Marksmanship proctors continue to hold the waves of undead fiends at bay.

Suddenly, Faxion's group separates from the circle, readying themselves for battle. Rexmere and Toste bolt off to the Oasis to lend a hand. Scott fiddles with his Chatch, pressing a button on the touchscreen that causes a laserbeam to draw two long, beaded necklaces of pure quarts into existence from seemingly nowhere.

"What?" Exclaimed Pilet. "How, how did you do that?!"

"Ha!" He responds. "Don't worry about that *now.*" He looks at Yuuna, tossing her a set of quartz beads; and wrapping the other set around his wrist like a bracelet. Here kid, take this. I've been charging these bad boys with aura for *years*! Let's have a blast!"

"Wow, thanks Scott!" Yuuna replied, pulling the necklace over her head. "Now, are you ready?"

He nods, as they both clasp their hands in a prayer posture. The two begin breathing deeply and slowly, meditating on the aura infused jewelry.

The quartz starts glowing, as storehouses of energy begin flowing within the two casters. Scott looks over to Bhujanga.

"Knowing you, you're not going to need one of these. Right? Tough guy?"

The bottoms of Bhujanga's shoes begin emanating Emerald flame, as he flares his nostrils and exhales fire.

"You know I don't." He replied. "Now are we going to smash this thing or what?"

"Kitestream!" Cast Yuuna, as she flies off towards the Titanic Morph.

"Well that answers that!" Said Scott, as he and Bhujanga dart off after their flying companion.

A Masterclass in Auracast; Pride of The Wind and Star

As Yuuna draws near the pyramid Morph, she begins to soar higher than she ever has before. The breeze flows by her face, as she takes a deep, strong inhale.

"This much aura, I've never had so much flowing through me before. It's... incredible."

Yuuna claps her hands, cultivating platinum aura in between her palms. She rises high into the air, almost nearing the height of the mighty structure's face. She points her palms directly at the eyes of the fiend, releasing an intense amount of stored aura toward its face. The Wind and Starcaster screams at the top of her lungs.

"Scatterstar!!!"

A barrage of huge, vibrant auric stars fly forth from her palms, viciously battering the face of the Morph.

The Titan raises its hands in an attempt to block the onslaught of the relentless Starcaster, staggering back blindly in the process.

Suddenly, the sound of light aircraft No.7 can be heard racing up behind Yuuna. The barrels of three blasters extend from hidden compartments across the front of the aircraft, as Benny releases a volley of laser fire onto their foe.

The Morph swings its massive fist at the ship to thwart the offense of the flying Ace, swatting at Benny with a pestered fury.

But the skills of the Veteran Dogfighter shine, as Benny swiftly barrel rolls through the sky, skimming just inches past the blow. Benny scoffs at the Titan.

"You gotta do better than that if you wanna best me! These are my skies!"

Suddenly, Scott Diliger darts behind the Morph, drawing azure aura into his hands before plunging them deep into the sand.

"Cryo-Lake!" He casts.

A thick sheet of slippery ice forms around the Morph, spanning the size of two football fields. As the titanic foe continues to stagger blindly backward, Bhujanga skates nimbly across the ice, his arcane flame mystically blending with the thick ice for a smooth glide. Charging two powerful fireballs in between his clenched fists, he skates between the legs of the Morph; releasing his charged blasts at the ankles of either leg.

Both fireballs make contact, each creating an ear-splitting explosion as they hit. The impact of the blasts trips up the Morph, causing it to stumble onto the ice floor and fall flat on its back with a mighty thud.

The ice breaks with the landing of the heavy foe, and as it does so, Scott begins to flourish his hands and manipulate the scores of ice around the Morph. He melts the ice into water, before drenching the Morph and tightly clenching his fists. The veins begin to bulge from the learned aquacasters forehead, as he pours forth immense amounts of both focus and effort into his technique. Scott cries out, with an uncharacteristic ferocity in his eyes that could send a pride of lions reeling in fear.

"Cryo... Casket!! Grraahh!!"

His clenched fists and forearms pulsate with fatigue, as the thoroughly soaked Morph's massive body is gradually rendered frozen solid by the efforts of the aquacaster.

Yuuna flies by again, another concentrated handful of aura clenched within her grasp. She's met by Bhujanga, who propels himself into the air beside her with powerful jets of Emerald Flame. Bhujanga rubs his howlite necklace; a white stone that allows his Emerald Flame to bond with other elements at will. Activating the stone's latent aura, and with a fistful of flame, he yells to Yuuna, "Now!". Yuuna nods, pointing her palms skyward.

Stars begin to form in the sky above them, as Bhujanga tosses Emerald bolts of flame at each one. This emerald aura meshes with the stars and begins to blend together, forming immense, intensely hot green and platinum suns in the sky. With every muscle in her body shaking profusely under the weight of the powerful aura, Yuuna screams at the top of her lungs.

"Solar-storm!!"

She releases the barrage of suns down onto their foe; as each destructive projectile begins to fall like a shooting star, leaving a trail of light and flame in the sky. As the suns descend, Scott's legs begin trembling under the fatigue of his techniques. Bhujanga skates by, hoisting Scott over his shoulder and releasing a jetstream of flame from his free hand behind them, propelling them away from the killzone with great haste.

"Thanks for the lift." Said Scott, struggling to hold onto his colleague.

As the mighty suns make impact on the titanic Morph, Yuuna continues to push them down onto her foe. She presses her curled fingers down toward the Morph, directing the auric suns with great force down onto the target. Every fiber of her being begins to tire as she fights to send a heavenly bombardment of punishment onto the enemy. Muscle fibers throughout her body begin to rip and tear under the immense pressure of the fearsome cast. Her skin reddens, as steam begins billowing from her feverish pores.

Still she fights on, pressing every ounce of will that she has into the oppressive onslaught of auric heat. A sight to make the Wind and Star Tribe proud.

As the platinum-green suns crash down onto the Morph, they explode into a fiery orb of flame and light, enveloping the frozen fiend in its entirety. The others look on in awe of the display of power and heart in Yuuna.

"Faith…" Said Max.

"Yes?" She replied, choking back tears.

"Your sister, she is as fearsome as they come."

"Yes she is, Max. Yes she is…"

Faxion fixes his hat and smiles. His eyes glue themselves to the scene. It's as if he's viewing a masterful pastel painting being drawn right before his eyes; a picture of perfect destruction so elegant, it could be hung from the world's finest museums.

"I knew she could do it. Good show lass..."

As the smoke begins to clear, and the light of the falling suns fades into dark once more; the massive Morph lies on the ground with the frontal portion of its body completely crumpled. With every ounce of aura drained from her body, Yuuna slowly fades out of consciousness, as she begins to plummet to the earth.

"Oh no..." Thought Bhujanga, as he witnesses the falling of the wind and starcaster.

He puts Scott down by the others, before blasting off to catch her with both hands shooting flame behind him. He picks up speed, gradually getting closer and closer to the target. But as he approaches the falling Yuuna, he senses that he will fail to cover the distance in time. As beads of sweat start to pour from his brow, the Emerald flamecaster puts everything he can at once into a mighty burst of blame behind him, hoping that the force of the explosion will propel him to her in time. But even with his fiery boost, Bhujanga watches as Yuuna begins to fall hopelessly to the ground before him.

"Shit, I'm not gonna make it!"

Benny takes note of Yuuna's plight as well, firing his thrusters to try to meet the unconscious Blade in the skies.

"Hang on kid! I gotcha!" He exclaimed.

As he draws near, he tries to engage a grappling claw function built into the ship. But as he presses the button to deploy, the claw jams, rendering the ace pilot unable to do much more than watch as Yuuna continues her descent.

"What? I thought I had that fixed?! I, I'm firing that mechanic!"

The arc of Yuuna's fall sends her plummeting towards the top of a particularly high sand dune, as Bhujanga races to slide up the dune like a ramp. He gets closer and closer to the top, his nostrils flare as he fights to reach his falling ally. Right as she comes several feet from impact, Bhujanga realizes that he cannot reach her in time.

"No!!"

But suddenly, as Yuuna's body is just about to hit the sand, she vanishes in a violet haze. Bhujanga races through the haze but a half-second later, as he's sent flying into the air at the height of the sand dune like a ski ramp.

Soaring through the sky, he sees a violet figure, teleporting from place to place until finally slowing to crash into a pile of sand.

"Is that?..."

The Emerald Flamecaster lands several yards from the figure, as he walks over to investigate.

"Uugh, crap." Groans the violet figure. "Yuuna, are you getting heavy or what?"

Bhujanga releases a sigh of relief at the familiar voice. He approaches to see Pilet, with his Fever Point engaged, lying beneath a sleeping Yuuna. Pilet stands to his feet and cracks his back, grimacing in pain.

"God damn, what a rough landing." Said Pilet. "Oh, what's up dude. I hung back for a second to see if you'd catch her... But hey! You gave it a solid go. Nice hustle."

Bhujanga grins, he shakes his head in disbelief.

"You *hung back*? Now that's speed."

Pilet smiles from ear to ear, dusting the sand off of his pants.

"Don't you know by now?" His smirk, a picture of perfect confidence. "Ha! I'm the fastest thing on Giganus..."

The War of Devil's Tongue

The two carry Yuuna back to the others, as she slumbers under a tent of trees created by Faith's tome. While conversing on the events that just transpired, a shout can be heard coming from the Oasis.

"Faxion!" Exclaimed Puerto. "There's too many of them, they just don't stop coming! We're getting pushed back here!"

Rexmere and Toste, having come to the aid of the firing squad at the Oasis, now find themselves locked in close quarters combat with hordes of skeletons that have begun to overrun the others. Pilots No.3 and No.5 drop cover fire while flying in circles above the Oasis. The group begins to retreat, giving up ground to the army of skeletons as they begin to come ashore.

Puerto invokes the auric jellyfish tattoo on the back of his hand, as he casts "Azure colony!" in their direction. A school of hundreds of auric jellyfish appear around the skeletons as they make their advance, blowing any who dare touch them to smithereens. This however, only proves to slow the advance of the horde; as more and more make their way through the ranks of cobalt jellies.

"Hmm." Ponders Faxion, scratching his chin while watching the scene unfold.

He lifts his Arcane Pierce, aiming the sight towards Puerto.

"I...-the hell are you doing dude?!" Said Puerto in confusion.

Shhzapp

Faxion pulls the trigger, firing a wicked bolt of plasma past Puerto's ear. The bolt burns a hole in the forehead of a massive skeleton behind him, releasing the aura used to reanimate the fiend as it collapses to the ground. Puerto ducks in shock, covering the top of his head in his hands and rolling out of harm's way.

"Sorry about that!" Said Faxion. "Gotta keep watch of your surroundings! Now, fall back and bring the fight to us!"

Puerto looks at Faxion with a contemptuous glare, before picking his Pilum beam rifle up off of the ground.

"So, *that's* where the King Killer gets it from..."

Puerto signals the group to retreat, as they converge into a huddle of marksmen and women marching backwards. Rexmere and Toste pick off any skeletons who get too close, speedily kicking, punching and slashing the opposition to pieces. Cornelius retracts his forearm cannons, in favor of his back-mounted shield and a Papercut longsword.

"Die you unholy scum!" He exclaims, laying waste to dozens of skeletons in his path in a flurry of slashes and stabs. He turns to his comrades. "Get the lead out! I'll hold 'em off!"

"Don't have to tell me twice, big guy." Replied Wendy, laying down cover fire from atop her flying disc.

As the Oasis squad regroups with the others, the hordes of skeletons begin to surround the weary Hired Blades. As this is happening, the sound of shifting sands can be heard in the distance. All in attendance are drawn to the scene of the ravaged Rok-Senn Morph. The disfigured chest of the Morph reveals the glowing rune that once gave it life, pulsating with great fervor. Sand mystically begins to converge in the air above the Morph, as it shockingly begins to reform the structure of the massive titan in great detail.

"You've got to be kidding me..." Said Faith, facepalming in frustration. "After everything my sister just went through?!"

The massive Morph begins to hinge at the hip, sitting up and glaring at the Hired Blades with ghoulish contempt. Its glowing green eyes pierce the darkness like a ray of hate.

"You know, I picture hell to be like this..." Said Asger, clutching the handle of the sword over his shoulder. " Are you guys sure we all didn't die somewhere along the way?"

The frightening sight drives the Hired Blades to steel themselves, each preparing for what may very well be their final stand.

Faxion draws his infrared spear in one hand, holding his lethal Stinger pistol in the other.

The Reaper Elite prepare themselves for combat, as The Funk Munkeys tune and strum their deadly instruments.

Caffo pulls a belt of bullets from within his jacket pocket, affixing it around his left vambrace. He then draws another belt, lined with colorful crystals, and attaches that to his right in a similar fashion.

Max and Kenzo stand side by side, clutching the handles of their drawing swords and training their gaze on the nearest foe.

Faith turns the page on her tome, casting "Gilazia Shiidah", as she becomes covered in shards of crystalline armor.

As Pilet draws his dragonflies, the infrared buzz fills the air with a devilish humm.

Bhujanga and Scott ready arcane water and fire for the bout ahead, staring off into the vast number of the undead before them.

"Our abilities are better suited with space to move." Exclaimed Faxion. "Spread out!" He points to the small fortified tent of trees housing Yuuna. "Anyone in trouble regroup here, otherwise... *Charge!*"

They each break off into the fray, taking on any and all in their way.

Rexmere bolts and darts across the battlefield, utilizing Kinetic-Chain; a technique created to launch aura infused punches and kicks into his foes. The braided ends of his cornrowed hair whip back and forth, as he launches a barrage of crimson, aura-infused kicks at the bony foes before him. Wearing only black and gold trunks and fingerless fighting gloves, the freeing apparel allows the fighting proctor an uncanny agility. After demolishing a gaggle of ghouls, he stands stoically over the skeletal pile; brandishing the tattoo of a bloodied panther across his back with pride.

"Been a while since I got to see some action." He said, kicking a severed skull quite far from the pile. "And I thought this year was gonna be a dull one."

Caffo Gilwick leaps into the air over Rexmere, pointing his left arm towards a wave of skeletons as his vambrace begins to fire off hundreds of bullets into the undead crowd like a machine gun.

"Not on my watch." Replied Caffo, landing in a forward roll before the martial arts proctor. "Unfortunately nothing is ever dull when I'm in charge, whether I'd like it or not..."

Asger and Dabria melt into their shadows, pulling hordes of skeletons into the sand by their ankles to immobilize them; as Lazlow Jr. and Arturo lay waste to the struggling corpses.

As the fierce battle ensues, the flying tree stump carrying the Funk Munkeys and their equipment drops into the fray with a massive thud, crushing many skeletons beneath it.

-THUMthumthumthumthumthumthumthum THUMthumthumthum thumthumthumthum

GrEerEErEEEEEEEEEEEEEEEEEEERRR

Tsssss Boomchickapap BoomBoomchickapap-

The sound of electric guitars squealing fills the air, followed by the boisterous clanging of a cymbal and drums. Surrounding ghouls are drawn to the music, inquisitively peeking their heads towards the mighty oaken stump. As the fiends gather together, Lukah lifts his chrome microphone to his lips.

-"Check, check, one two check.

The Munkeys touchin' down best be showin' some respect.

Bout to hitch'ya like a missile so ya better hit the deck,

but ya moved too slow now you went and broke ya neck!"-

Lukah raps smoothly into the mic, the speed of his lyricism cultivating aura into the air around him. Suddenly, the butt end of the microphone siphons the surrounding aura and fires it back out in the form of a torpedo-like projectile.

With a hefty boom and an ear-spillting crash, scores of skeletons are blasted away; as a shockwave sends their remains flying into the desert sands. Clint and Danba prepare a chrome mic to their faces, joining in song with Lukah; as Svenn shoots a fierce, mute glare to the undead army.

~WHO tears down-the lords of-the land~
~THE MUNKEYS!~
~And WHO breaks-the will of-the man?~
~THE MUNKEYS!~
~ Gonna hit ya like a TRUCK
tell ya man he's outta LUCK
till we the only other killas on the sand~
~THE MUNKEYS~

With every chant of "*The Munkeys*", a powerful pulsewave of aura is sent out around the auric performers, pressing back the enemy. The music continues to cultivate visible aura around the Funk Munkeys, providing them with boundless amounts at their disposal.

~Dunk dunk-ah dunk dunk-ah dunk dunk-ah dunkdunk~

Svenn's bass begins to draw the loose energy into a soundhole, filling the strings with vibrant color. The energy transforms into teal waves of aura, launching itself from an opening at the tip of the bass headstock and zooming across the battlefield. The teal waves scatter, finding members of The Hired Blades and shooting into the top of their heads like smoke returning to a burning candle. As Faxion drives his infrared spear into the sternum of an unlucky skeleton, the Veteran Blade is struck by the energy.

"Oh my..." He said, feeling the aura surge through his body. He looks at a cut across his forearm, as it begins to seal itself with alarming speed. "What a boost! And this, this rush of energy..." He turns to an approaching group of foes and fires off several powerful "Hollowpoint" casts at them, crumbling the opposition with ease. "I knew those boys had *something* special up their sleeves..."

The rest of the Blades hoot and cheer for the Funk Munkeys; while utilizing their gifted, bolstering aura to further punish their foes.

In the distance, Pilet casts "Fleetfoot", speedily dispatching a dozen skeletons in the blink of an eye. However, the quick-footed prospect stumbles on the severed shin of his fallen foe, tripping face-first into a sand dune.

"Aah!" He exclaimed, right before eating a mouthful of sand.

While attempting to remove his head from the dune, a large skeleton with a double-edged battle axe rears its ancient head. The ghoul lifts its weapon, readying a lethal strike onto the Fiery prospect. Pilet pulls himself free just in time to see the massive edge of the battle axe coming down toward his skull. But just as it's about to make contact, a familiar voice can be heard casting "Springboard!" from afar.

Like the speeding bolt of a crossbow, Toste comes lunging across the sand with his rapier trained on the foe. Skewering the oversized undead warrior in an instant, he presses it back effortlessly with the kinetic force of his advance.

The battleaxe crashes blade first into the sand, narrowly missing Pilet's face by inches.

Speechless at the near death encounter, Pilet looks up at Toste in awe. Toste simply wipes the debris off of his blade, standing atop a pile of bones that was previously the axe wielder. He turns to Pilet.

"Get a move on, boy. Can't make a proper Blade out of a corpse, can we?"

Shaking his head awake, Pilet grins and lifts his Dragonfly knives from the sand.

"Nah, I don't suppose we can." He replied. "But don't let that get to your head, pretzel brow. I was just warmin' up!"

With a scoff, Toste casts "Springboard" again, blasting off into a crowd of skeletons and shish-kebabing several in his path mercilessly.

"Tch, showoff." Said Pilet, as he rushes back into the fray with reckless abandon.

With each of the scattered Blades holding their own across the battlefield, the mighty pyramid Morph continues to advance on the opposition. It holds out its gigantic arms, spreading its fingers out wide towards the HBA forces as a large opening reveals itself within its palms. Like an arcane portal to the inside of the menace, the borders of the opening glow with jade aura. Suddenly; scores of small, beetle-like Rok-Senn Morphs, much like the ones responsible for gutting Pilet, erupt from inside. They take to the skies, their wings fill the air with an ominous buzz as they ravenously rush towards the direction of the resisting party.

As this occurs, Caffo fells a line of skeletons standing before Faxion in an instant; dashing past the debris to reach the Veteran Blade. As his machine gun gauntlet runs out of ammo, the head Proctor fiddles with the screen on his Vambrace and fires some form of 3D printing laser into the sand; creating another belt of bullets from thin air. As he retrieves the belt and begins to reload, Caffo points his left, crystal covered Vambrace towards an impending enemy. He flicks the revolver-like belt to the setting with a green stone. As this stone begins to glow, his palm takes to a brilliant jade, before firing a green Hollowpoint with a shining seed-like energy in the middle at the enemy.

The impact of the projectile knocks the foe down, as powerful vines sprout from the shining seed and render it immobile. The vines constrict the skeleton with powerful, crushing force, shattering it into powder with ease. Caffo turns to Faxion and points to the flying Morph foes in the sky.

"What are we going to do about *that?*"

Faxion fires a barrage of bullets into several skeletons with his Stinger.

"Have faith Caffo, *we too* have friends in high places." He replied, pointing skywards. He pulls his Chatch to his face. "Now's as good a time as any, empty the payload."

"Roger that." Replied Benny, as four light aircrafts come flying overhead.

The aircrafts converge in a cone before the flying insurgents, revealing a large missile docked at the bottom of each vessel.

"Alright boys!" Said Benny over the intercom. "Let 'em have it!"

A unanimous "Roger." is heard, before each of the aircrafts releases its payload on the enemy. The missiles fly true, striking into the waves of beetle Morphs and creating intensely large explosions in the process. The blasts startle surrounding camels far in the distance, as they run from the intense light of the assault. Limestone and mortar fall from the sky in cinders, giving the appearance of a rain of fire and stone to the battling onlookers.

"Direct hit! We got those bastards!" Shouted one pilot.

But as the smoke clears, dozens of Morphs continue to pour out of the titan in waves.

"Crap!" Exclaimed another pilot. "How many of these oversized mosquitoes are there?!"

"Get yourselves together, double back and get ready for a dogfight." Said Benny, as the flight crew circles round and sets their sights on the flying foes.

Faxion turns to Caffo with a look of concern.

"I'll be frank, I'm not certain of how we can best this foe, Caffo." He throws a spinning kick to an approaching skeleton, knocking it down as he drives the tip of his spear into its skull. "These foes are weak, but nigh *endless*. And our flying foes seem to share the same quality. This, gigantic monstrosity of the ancient world took one of the most powerful techniques we could have thrown at it in stride, and came back like a God damned mummy. We may be nearing the time for a tactical retreat."

Caffo fires a set of four more green Hollowpoints into a wave of skeletons; creating a massive tumbleweed of entangling vines around them, before the green gem shatters inside the gauntlet.

"Shit, another one out of juice." He said, ejecting the shattered stone from the chamber. "If we retreat, God knows what will come of this place. The Morph might continue until it reaches the nearest town and wreaks catastrophic destruction. The last thing I want to see on the morning news is a giant pile of rocks stomping flat Giduh or Helena."

"Very well." Replied Faxion. "We'll hold them off the very best we can then. But at the rate these things are emerging, I'd give us 20 minutes *tops* before we're overrun. Touch base with Scott STAT, we need any info we can get on what this thing is or how to beat it."

"Sounds like a plan." Said Caffo, mowing down another group of skeletons with a hail of bullets, before bolting off towards the learned archeologist."

Faxion turns and sees Faith by the tree tent containing her sister, hacking and slashing with her Skarrya blade alongside the Sanda swordsmen. Blocked by a thick cluster of skeletons, Faxion leaps into the air and lands atop the head of a bony foe. Like a frog to lilypads, He proceeds to swiftly hop across the skeletons shoulders, making his way to the elder Sierro with haste.

"Excuse me. Pardon me. Ooh my apologies madam, what a lovely occipital protuberance you have! Allow me to borrow your collarbone if you will."

Faith sees this taking place and taps Max on the shoulder.

"Are you seeing this?"

Max rubs his eyes in disbelief.

"What an interesting man, the secret techniques of a seasoned Blade must be vast and-" He's interrupted by the cold grasp of a fallen skeleton on his ankle, only to slice it into six pieces in a flash. "expansive..."

Faxion approaches Faith, Max, and Kenzo, nimbly backflipping into the air before landing smack dab in the middle of them.

"Well well well!" Said Kenzo, slicing three skeletons in half in the blink of an eye before resheathing his drawing sword. "What took you so long, Master Blade?"

"Oh you know, just sniffing the daisies, taking in the sights and making friends! It's not every day you get to speak to the dead in such a casual manner." A skeleton swings a hatchet at Faxion haphazardly. He side steps out of danger before smashing its skull with the butt end of his spear. "Stop it now, I *just said* we were casual. You're going to embarrass me in front of the popular kids." Faxion steps on the skull, shattering it to pieces. He looks up at Faith with a more serious gaze. "My friend, I've two very important questions for you." He points to the Pyramid Morph with the tip of his spear. "*What* is that... And can we defeat it?..."

FOUR

Round Two, Champion of the Desert

Soaring over the forests of Miantha, the Crimson Pagoda races towards the Devil's Tongue Desert with haste. The four story vessel glides over the sharp pines, its many thrusters carrying it across the skies in a blazing flash. Reclined on a couch in the main level's lobby, The Chairman converses with the mayor of Grand Titanus City on a large wall mounted monitor. Arms folded with a look of chagrin, the Mayor vigorously wipes his face with his palms in frustration.

"So you're telling me you want to deploy the city's *main defense* force for this rescue mission of yours?" Said the Mayor. "The Hired Blades started this mess. *Your people* uncovered this ancient menace, and now you want to duplete Grand Titanus' resources and leave us vulnerable to fix it? And for what, a dozen or so of your members? I just don't understand, why didn't The Hired Blades have this whole test planned out and accounted for?!"

Chairman Yang sips his tea, placing the cup down and looking up at the Mayor with a serious glare.

"Mayor Dupree, now is not the time for assigning blame. No one could have predicted the outcome of this year's exam. But, what *is* certain is that if we don't stop that Morph from reaching the capital, it's going to cause *unfathomable* damage. Do you want to be the man in charge when that happens? I can imagine the headlines right now; "Mayor John Dupree's folly let's titanic monster of the ancient world run amok in the city streets.". Has a nice ring to it, doesn't it?"

"OK ok. Lord knows I'm doing God awful in the polls of late. So, fine then. I'll have the Strikeforce deployed, just send me the coordinates."

Chairman Yang takes another swig, hiding a smirk behind his cup.

"Thank you Mayor, always a pleasure working with you."

"Oh can it, Yang! Typical of The Hired Blades to think you can operate on your own rules. Separation of Blade and State was the stupidest idea in history!"

Click

Chairman Yang hangs up on the Mayor.

"Hmmph, pretentious prick. Can't believe I voted for him."

As The Crimson Pagoda races across the skies, The Blades continue to do battle with their undead enemy. The Funk Munkeys take the center of the battlefield, playing an intense, blood-pumping tune of rock and roll. The music continues to blast away countless foes while aiding their fellow Blades with healing aura. Toste nimbly lunges across the battlefield, "Springboarding" to and fro and skewering skeleton after skeleton with his trusted rapier. As the Pyramid Morph closes in on the Hired Blades, it lifts its foot high above the Reaper Elite in an attempt to stomp them out.

As Arturo pulls the serrated edge of his Shred longsword from an enemy skull, he looks up; graced by the sight of the titans foot beginning to fall towards him.

"Oh damn!" He exclaimed. He turns to his team members nearby. "Laz! We gotta move!"

As Lazlow finishes tearing three skeletons in half with his bare hands, he notices the shadow of the fiend above.

In a swift, mighty crash; the titanic leg of the Morph makes impact with the ground, shaking the desert floor and shifting the sands of the nearby dunes. The loud crash of the monster's stomp sends chills through the bones of surrounding Desert life, sending flocks of buzzards flying off into the darkened sky in retreat. As waves of sand rush forth from the impact, Lazlow Jr. blasts away from the scene with his Hachidorinese ally hoisted over his shoulder. Asger and Dabria take up the rear, shadow gliding just inches away from the oncoming sand wave.

This sand wave picks up speed, rushing toward Faxion, Max, Kenzo, and Faith. Faith notices the oncoming sand and shouts a warning.

"*Gasp* Lookout!"

Kenzo takes a combative posture, slowly gripping his Drawing Lacerate and facing the massive wave with a meditative look across his brow. He channels aura into his palm, as the space between his clenched fists begins to glow.

In a flash, Kenzo draws his Lacerate and fires an immense, slicing blade of auric wind into the sand wave, creating a huge divide that passes over him, Max, and Faxion safely. Faith attempts to reach the gap in the sand, but just barely finds herself swept up into the wave and strewn violently across the desert like a rag doll.

"Aaaaahh!" Cried Faith, all the while being tumbled and thrown across the scorching sand.

As the winds die down, Faith finds herself strewn far from her allies. She shakes the sand from her hair, gripping her head as the desert floor won't stop spinning. Groaning, Faith comes to at the sound of explosions erupting several yards away.

"Ugh, where did I just end up?" She thought. *"And what the hell is that sound?"*

Still dazed and nauseous from the tumble in the sand, she crawls along the ground to a mound of stone before her. She climbs the rocks, hoping to see the origin of the intense sound. Peeking over the highest point, Faith rubs her eyes in surprise at the sight of Bhujanga Garuda, effortlessly scorching droves of skeletons with his Emerald Flame. Blasting the undead fiends with relentless fireballs and intensely hot cyclones of verdant fire, she notes the unamused look plastered across his face.

"Tch, boring." He scoffs, shooting a rain of flaming darts down from the sky above. "Your ranks are vast, but not endless. Eventually my flame will outlast the lot of you. Unfortunately for you, it's not *my time.*"

As he says this, a skeleton in the distance hurls a jagged-edged hatchet through the air from behind him. What happens next causes Faith to gasp in shock.

The hatchet strikes Bhujanga in the base of the skull, burrowing deep into his brain matter. The Emerald Flamecaster drops lifeless to the ground, a final fireball popping forth from his lifeless palm into the air.

Wide-eyed and shocked, Faith's hand covers her dropped jaw in horror. She slinks down behind the stone, silently reveling in the weight of what she's just witnessed.

"No... Bhujanga..."

The skeletons begin to collect themselves, picking up their blown off arms and legs and reattaching them firmly into their sockets. A moment of silence ensues, as the skeletons stand directionless without a target to stalk. Still covering her mouth in sheer stupor, Faith's supporting hand slips on a pebble beneath her palm, sending a handful of small stones tumbling down the rock formation.

"Agh! Oh no!" She thought, as the stones clack together breaking the eerie silence.

The skeletons turn toward the sound, beginning to curiously hobble towards the rock formation. Faith nervously reaches for her tome, slowly flipping open the top of her satchel and sliding her hand inside. The haunting image of the marching skeletons begins to send flashbacks through her mind of the graveyard behind her forest home. A chill runs down her spine, as the hair on the back of her neck begins to stand erect.

Just then, a curious fizzing can be heard. The sound of a fire beginning to furiously crackle diverts the undead hordes' attention. Faith's eyes light up, turning towards the sound while remaining hidden behind the stone. The body of Bhujanga begins to burn bright with Emerald Flame, as he starts to crumple to ash almost instantly.

"What the hell?..."

As the ash begins to pile, the Emerald Flame floats above it, forming the image of a mighty eagle with three heads. The middle head is of a classic eagle, whilst the two peripheral heads form vicious, angered looking snakes. Suddenly, the three headed eagle begins to morph into the silhouette of a man. Sprouting arms and hands from the snakes, the legs and feet of the eagle become humanoid as the eagle's head molds itself to the man's cranium.

In a brilliant flash of light, the Emerald Flame bursts forth from the figure, sending a shockwave that knocks back the surrounding skeletons. The flash blinds Faith for but a moment, as she turns away and covers her wincing eyes. As the light dies down, she curiously turns back to the scene. Standing in the place of the flaming eagle is Bhujanga, grasping the very hatchet that took his life but moments ago.

"What? How is he alive?!" She thought.

He skims the edge of the blade with his thumb.

"Hmm. Impressive. To think I was done in by such a shoddy weapon." He points his fingers like a gun at the skeleton who killed him. "Ignis Saggita." He casts, as a bolt of verdant flame shoots forth like an arrow from his fingertips, piercing through the fiends skull with ease. "I wish I knew your name in life warrior, to think you would have the luck to take mine after death. But as I said before, I'll say again. It's not *my time.*" Bhujanga stares at an engraving on the hatchet. ""Nezzha", so that was your name. I think I'll keep this on my wall, to honor your achievement."

Bhujanga puts the hatchet in a leather holster inside his shirt, nuzzling it in between the handle of a Stinger pistol. He then lifts his hands skyward, cultivating green aura into his palms and clenching them into closed fists. Emerald Flame creeps out from between his fingers, as he cries out to the horde of undead assailants.

"I've had enough of you! *Karmic-*"

"Shit, this doesn't look good." Thought Faith. *"This guy can handle himself, I'm out of here!"* "Fleetfoot!" She casts, darting away from the scene.

Bhujanga slams his fist to the ground.

"Dive-bomb!"

Intense explosions of Emerald Flame pillars begin to erupt from beneath the sand all around Bhujanga, blowing the surrounding skeletons to smithereens. As shattered bones and ancient weapons fly through the air, Faith narrowly escapes the encroaching firestorm, sprinting with arcane swiftness back in Faxion's direction.

"Good Lord! This guy is insanely strong!" She said. *"And he should be dead... What happened back there?...."*

The Star that Shines Brightest

Springboarding across the battlefield with nimble grace, Toste continues to skewer and slice hordes of skeletons with ease. Leaving a trail of mangled bones in his wake, the swift prince of Menanois dives into the fray against a congested wave of the undead. Relentlessly lashing his foes with unbridled speed, he lets loose the signature barrage of his people, "The Star of Menanois" into the enemy crowd.

A six-sided-star pattern created by Toste's vicious swordplay parts his foes' limbs from their bodies; as a whirlwind of hands, arms, and skulls fly deftly overhead.

"The Brilliant Star of Menanois will be victorious this day!" He exclaimed, laying waste to all in his path.

Rexmere bashes and batters his own foes not too far off, sending a flurry of kicks into a group of several ghouls that stand before him. Taking a brief pause in between enemies to admire the work of his colleague from Menanois, he notices a skeleton about to close in on Caffo Gilwick from behind. Rexmere wastes no time, leaping over a sand dune between them and firing an explosive, aura-infused kick into the fiend in a single bound.

As the sneaky skeleton is swiftly reduced to a pile of debris, Caffo turns to his ally in surprise.

"Thanks for the hand, Rex." He said. "Hell of a job this exam turned out to be. If they'd have told me I was going to be fighting a Goddamn army, I'd have brought the *big* guns."

"Don't mention it." Replied Rexmere, as he punches the head off of a skeleton like a tee ball. "Get a load of the Sword Prince over there, I guess someone had a balanced breakfast this morning. At the rate he's going, there won't be any left for the rest of us."

Caffo peers over at the sight of Toste, decimating crowds of foes with his rapier.

"That's why we keep him around, isn't it." He said. "When it comes to pure skill and mastery of the sword, there aren't too many this side of Kettlena that can stack up to The Star of Menanois-"

As he speaks, a gust of violet wind rushes overhead; mowing through the surrounding skeletons as Caffo and Rexmere duck down in surprise.

"Shit! What the hell was that?" Exclaimed Rexmere.

The violet wind continues on its path, zipping and zigzagging across the sand and slicing countless undead into bits in the process. The wind halts itself at Toste's side, as Pilet steps out of a violet cloud with his Dragonfly knives trained on their foes.

"That, *damned* King Killer!" Said Caffo, collecting himself from the sand. "This year's candidates are going to be the death of me, I know it..."

Brandishing his Dragonflies, Pilet grins at Toste with a competitive glare.

"Hey punk." He said.

Toste meets him with a contemptuous side-eye and a grin. Pilet continues.

"First one to a thousand wins. But try not to pull a hammy, I know you're getting up there in years."

"Ha!" Laughs Toste. "Eat my dust, boy!"

Toste shoves Pilet to the ground jestfully and leaps into the fray, sending severed limbs flying through the air.

"Hey! You ass!" Exclaims Pilet grinning ear to ear. He brushes himself off and follows suit, vanishing into the crowd of skeleton warriors. "Oh you're *toast* now!"

The two perform a beautiful dance of death; slashing, slicing, and dicing countless unfortunate foes with effortless finesse and swiftness. Piles of bones begin to litter the desert ground, as the duo of furious Blades glide across the battlefield with ruthless precision. Pilet flourishes his knives with the speed of a buzz saw, laying waste to hordes of enemies and mincing them into a fine powder. Toste ping-pongs back and forth within the ranks of the undead; piercing and slashing them to bits while narrowly evading the poorly timed swipes of their swords, axes, and knives.

As they traverse the raging sands, the combative swords prince and the fiery prospect pass by Faxion in the heat of their advance. Jovially, Pilet swats the tip of Faxion's hat over his face before darting off, back into the fray.

"Oh my." Said Faxion, fixing his hat before shooting an advancing ghoul in the face. "Glad to see *someone* is having fun."

The severed top half of a skeleton warrior grasps at Faxion's ankle, tripping him at an awkward angle. The agility of the Veteran Blade kicks in, as he breaks into a backwards somersault before standing to his feet, ending up back-to-back with Kenzo Quinn.

"He's not the only one!" Replied the Sanda Chief. "These Hired Blade parties are a real riot! This is the most fun I've seen in years!" Kenzo rips into a huge skeleton with his Lacerate, turning to his son in glee. "What say *you* boy?!"

Max Quinn sends a herd of undead flying in a whirling display of swordsmanship.

"It *is* a glorious opportunity for combat, Father." Max replied, pouring electrifying aura into his Lacerate before stabbing into an oncoming skeleton. "I relish the opportunity to be here."

"Just the same, stay frosty my friends." Said Faxion. "I have a feeling this battle is far from over…"

Pilet and Toste continue their tirade through the ranks of the undead, passing between the massive legs of the titanic ancient Morph. As the Pyramid Morph attempts to swat away at the pestering of Benny and the fighter pilot Blades, it takes note of the speeding duo dashing by. Seeing the violet hue of Pilet's Fever Point, the Morph's eyes suddenly take to a crimson glow, affixing themselves to Pilet in a menacing glare. The Pyramid Morph ignores the blasters of the fighter pilots, as a massive opening appears in its chest and begins to take the shape of a mighty cannon. Suddenly, the auric rune across the behemoth's chest reappears directly above the cannon, shining vividly in the darkened sky.

With an ominous whirring noise, the cannon begins to glow an evil green, as the sound of auric-storehouses charging within begins to ring throughout the desert. Over by the Oasis, The Mystic Marauders and the Marksmanship proctors take note of the sight.

"Woah!" Exclaims Wendy, flying over the water on her hovering platform. Her line of sight allows her to see the weapon first. "What the hell is that green thing?! Puerto, you'd better take a look at this…"

Puerto and the rest turn to see the ancient weapon in action.

"Holy shit!" He replied. "Cornelius, are you seeing this?! Please, tell me that's not what I think it is."

Cornelius drops his massive shield at the sight of the mighty cannon of the ancient world, His jaw nearly unhinged in shock.

"It, it looks like… an Arcane Eraser?…" He replied. Cornelius looks down at his transforming gauntlets. "Is *that* where we got the Eraser from?…"

Dex and Dustin empty a clip of laser fire into an oncoming wave of skeletons before turning around at the whirring mechanical screech of the cannon.

"Hoh, oh God. We better get paid extra for this." Said Dex.

"We gotta survive first to get paid." Said Dustin. He lights a cigarette and takes a long drag. "And I gotta be honest, at this rate I don't see that happening..."

Toste and Pilet, ignorant of the mighty weapon charging behind them, continue to fend off hordes of skeletons in their pursuit of competition. But as a foe grasps at Toste's shoulder, the sword prince does a 180 degree slash to part the fiend's hand from its body, thus drawing his attention directly to the Morph's attack. The Prince of Menanois glances at the cannon for a moment, turning back and witnessing the horrific scene unfold. He sees the Morph's menacing glare affixed intently on Pilet; as the boy darts back and forth between enemies, his back unwittingly turned to the titan.

"Boy! Behind you-" Toste tries to warn him, but is swiftly interrupted by a swarm of skeletons rushing him from behind.

The morphing cannon draws the eyes of the rest of the attending Blades; as Scott, Rexmere, Caffo, Faith, Bhujanga, and The Reaper Elite rally to Faxion. As the weapon charges, Faxion looks on in worry at his pupil in the distance. He lets out a holler of warning.

"Pilet! You have to move!!"

But Pilet fails to hear him, focused intently on keeping tally of the foes he's extinguished.

"452, 453, 454, I'm totally gonna blow Toste out of the water!" Thought Pilet.

"We have to get him!" Cried Faith. "He can't hear us! I don't know if he can take a blast from, well... whatever that is! Even with Fever Point!"

Faxion grabs her by the arm before she can rush out to her ally.

"You can't, I'm sorry but it's too dangerous." Faxion replied.

"We have to do *something!*" Exclaimed Max. "The fool is going to get himself incinerated!"

Faxion looks back in horror, unable to come to a clear decision. A vision plays in his mind of a young Hired Blade. His short hair is jet black, with fine stubble like sandpaper across his face. He sports a black tee with the logo of the PF1 Grand Prix across the chest, and a pair of camouflage fatigues. Slung over his shoulder is the same, dark blue Arcane Pierce that the Deadeye is known for. After just rescuing a group of children from a burning building, the Blade duo rally the kids to safety. Faxion puts the smallest of them down on the bed of a nearby pickup truck with his siblings, when suddenly a scream is heard from within the blaze.

"I thought that was all of them?!" Said Faxion.

"Apparently not." Said the young Blade.

"Wait, where's my brother?" Said a young girl in the group. "Where's my little brother?!"

Faxion and his ally turn anxiously to the scene. The young Hired Blade tosses his Arcane Pierce on the bed of the truck and begins to make for the building, but Faxion grasps him by the shoulder in protest.

"Wait, there's no time! That building's structure is nearly crumbling by now, it's unsafe to go in there!"

The young Blade gives Faxion a playful grin.

"Come on, have a little faith in me." The Blade puts a hand on Faxions shoulder in response. "After all, I learned from the best."

After a brief pause, Faxion shakes his head in disapproval.

"Just hurry up then, you've not got much time." He replied.

Smiling ear to ear, the young man bolts off into the burning building. A moment later, a small boy comes running out of the building as fast as he can, coughing and gagging on smoke.

"*Cough* The guy! The guy who *wheeze* helped me! He's stuck!!" Cried the boy.

Without a moment to spare, Faxion darts toward the building.

But mid-sprint, he's interrupted; by the entire blazing building collapsing on itself in an instant. A massive pyre shoots forth from the plummeting structure, as the heat of the blaze waves over the skin of all in attendance. The kids scream and cry in fear of the wreckage, balling themselves together at the base of the pickup bed. Faxion drops to his knees, staring at the wreckage in front of him with a blank, expressionless look on his face. The glow of the roaring flames reflects off of his eyes, as he stares into the pyre with silent dread.

"*Fax...*"

A subtle voice is heard in the depths of his mind.

"*Fax... Fax... Fax...*"

Suddenly, the glow in his eye shifts from the scarlet flames of the building, to the vibrant jade aura charging within the titanic Pyramid Morph's cannon. Faith and Max are in his face, waving their hands frantically.

"Fax!" Exclaims Faith. "Wake up! What do we do?!"

Faxion shakes his head, snapping out of his trance. After a brief pause, he mutters under his breath.

"Fleetfoot."

Confused, Max turns to Faith inquisitively.

"What? What did he say?"

But before he can get his response, Faxion sprints off towards Pilet; kicking up a whirlwind of sand into Max and Faith's faces in the process.

"*Pffft* *Spew* What the hell?!" Exclaims Max.

"Fax wait!" Said Faith, shading her eyes with her forearms from the sand. "Wait for us!"

In a mad dash to the fiery prospect, the Veteran Blade launches flying kicks and fires energy bullets from his Stinger pistol at the intercepting skeletons. He draws his Papercut and begins to hack and slash at any foes between him and his prodigy, sending fingers, forearms and skulls flying through the air. His heart races like a speeding hovercar, as the tension forces him to break into a cold sweat.

Finally, the cannon has reached its peak charge. With an incredible, booming burst; a mighty, jade beam of pure aura fires from the mouth of the massive cannon, swallowing the sky between Pilet and the Morph. The intense booming sound of the firing cannon finally snaps Pilet out of his competitive haze. He turns around at the sound of the beam, his eyes widening at the sight of the unprecedented onslaught before him.

But as the beam travels toward him at a staggering pace, he feels the push of a full body tackle from behind, sending him flying abruptly out of harm's way. A long, thin object flies past his ear, as he turns while still airborne to see the source of the push.

He spots Toste, standing where he stood but an instant ago.

The force of Toste's own shove stops his momentum dead in its tracks, as the Titan's auric beam swallows the fierce Prince of Menanois like a massive python of light. He gives Pilet one final smile while his body begins to incinerate in the harsh heat of the blast.

"An honorable end, Father. I return to you with one for our family."

A split second that felt like an eternity goes by, as Pilet reaches out in desperation for his burning friend. He's forced to watch as he's pushed away from the scene, flying into Faxion as the two end up tumbling into the sand.

The beam continues to wreak havoc across the desert for a moment, burning massive lines of sand into divides of blown glass; before finally beginning to peter itself out, returning the darkness to the sky once more. As the beam starts to power down, the Pyramid Morph hangs its head and arms in a drained posture, like a fallen God of limestone towering above the desert dunes once more.

"..........."

Having landed atop Faxion in a dogpile on the sand, Pilet picks himself up, crawling lifelessly to the ashes of his fallen comrade. Quivering in emotion, he scoops the remains of the fallen Prince in his hands, holding them to his face as he begins to shed tears of frustration.

"Toste........." He said. "Get up. Get up!" Pilet begins sobbing uncontrollably. "What about round two? *What about round two*!?"

"Lad..." Said Faxion, with a somber glaze across his eyes.

Shink

The sound of Caffo Gilwick drawing a Papercut longsword from his pocket cuts the silence.

Vrrrrr

The blades' infrared buzz fills the air, as its scarlet glow forms a beacon in the darkness. He thrusts the Papercut into the ground, slicing through the sand with a gritty fizz. Scott and Rexmere give each other a nod, drawing their Papercuts and following the actions of their comrade. Before long, all attending Blades begin to pass their standard issue Papercuts through the sand, forming a ghoulish buzz that puts even the skeletons at bay for a moment. Even Kenzo draws one of his Lacerates, holding the sword to his chest in a humble gesture of respect.

Faith and Max catch up to Faxion, stopping themselves before The Veteran Blade with an inquisitive look in their eye. He pulls out a Papercut and ejects the blade from the handle.

"Do as I do..." Said Faxion, as he drives the Papercut into the sand like the others.

Max and Faith draw theirs in response, pushing the infrared blades into the ground. Max then draws a Lacerate and follows the actions of his father. As they do this, the trio look to Pilet in remorse.

"Pilet..." Said Faith.

The fiery prospect continues to weep into the pile of ash in his hands. He cries out in agony, burying his face in his forearms to shield his disheveled appearance from the others. His team looks on in chagrin, unequipped to console their partner in his unstable state.

"A warrior of true virtue, he was..." Said Max.

Stunned and devoid of emotion, Pilet proceeds to sit in the sand in silence. His eyes, blank and expressionless. Faith takes a step toward her disheartened ally, but is halted by Faxion's forearm.

"Wait, give him a moment." He said. "It's his first fallen brother. I've been there, he's going to need some time."

"I know..." Replied Faith. "I feel terrible... But, he can't just sit there in the middle of a battlefield, can he?"

Suddenly, the whites of Pilet's eyes take to a pitch black, his iris forming a devilish maroon. A dark, burgundy cocoon of aura sweeps around Pilet. The aura wraps and entwines around the boy from Chamboree, forming an arcane, egg-like barrier around him. Faxion's brow rises in confusion, as Faith and Max step back in shock.

"What is *that?!*" Said Faith. "I've never seen anything like it in my life!"

"I... What, what kind of trickery is this Faxion??" Said Max. "Is he to morph into a giant Flare Pheasant?!"

Faxion draws his Stinger, pulling back the chamber and readying his sights at the surrounding skeletal soldiers.

"I, I don't know... There's clearly much more to the boy that we don't understand. But whatever it is, I will stay with him." He peers back somberly at Pilet's egg of stark, darkness. "He will have his time to grieve."

Faith looks at Pilet, sighing and turning a page in her tome.

"Fine. Skarrya!" She casts. Her two-edged blade of pure flame aura cuts the darkness like a blazing lanturn. "Well then, so will I!"

Faith and Faxion turn to Max curiously. He gives them both a serious glare, nodding his head in agreement. The Sanda swordsman places a hand on his drawing Lacerate and takes a defensive, crouching posture.

"Need you even ask?"

The Terrifying Trio

Before long, the skeletons begin to surround the Hired blade's forces, backing them all into a wide circle around Pilet. The Blades do their best to avoid being cornered, unleashing every trick, technique, and weapon in their respective arsenals on their endless foes.

Dunya and her mirage copies dance across the battlefield, her traditional Itedonian dance leaving flaming footprints in the sand that blow unsuspecting foes to smithereens.

Cornelius equips his infrared battleaxe, standing back to back with Lazlow and his ferocious Ark tri-cannon. The two Kettlenian Elite proceed to sweep hordes of ghouls off their feet and create piles upon piles of shattered bone behind them.

The Funk Munkeys land their flying, tree stump of a stage beside Pilet, blasting away waves of oncoming enemies with the aura enhanced soundwaves of their instruments.

A skeleton hurls a spear at Wendy, knocking her flying disc out from beneath her and forcing her to fire at her foes from the ground. She groups with Dex, Dustin, and Puerto, as the four fire away at the enemy with everything they've got.

Scott and Bhujanga take on waves of skeletons with their arcane prowess, as fearsome waves and hellish blazes roar across the battlefield with vicious fervor.

A rogue skeleton chucks its dagger at Faith from behind, as she turns just in time to see the ancient weapon headed straight for her throat.

Suddenly, a teal figure erupts from Faith's cast shadow on the ground, deftly swiping the dagger away in mid air. The figure is revealed to be Asger, as he pours electric aura into his straight sword and dispatches the foe with ease. Stunned, Faith looks at him with a confused, slightly confrontational glare. He simply nods his head to her and takes a fighting stance against the oncoming enemy.

A tense moment of silence occurs between them as they await the creeping enemy to advance. Asger digs his feet into the ground, bracing his blade against his forearm and charging the blade with teal lightning. Faith summons a small cloud of arcane cold into her hand, preparing to blast the nearest foe.

"I'm sorry..." Said Asger, his voice full of shame and regret. "About the whole, hanging and stabbing thing. I told you, I *hate* killing..."

Faith scoffs.

"Tch, yuck. You remind me of my sister." She replied. "Don't apologize. You did what you had to do. You did what we're here for, and you won fair and square." She chuckles. "I'm honestly lucky you hesitated. If I were you, I would've killed me *sooner.*"

Asger grins, as the tension eases between them.

"Yeah, you remind me of *my* sister too. Just a touch less psychotic."

"Frisio!!" Faith casts, freezing a wave of oncoming skeletons solid with a wicked cone of frost.

"Oh, no one is as crazy as *her.*" She replied. "That one is a special case, I applaud your patience..."

As the army of the undead continues to press forward, the Hired Blades are forced into a smaller and smaller circle. Before long they find each other too close for comfort, as their movements become hampered by their close proximity to each other. Cornelius backs up into his colleagues while back-fisting a group of foes. Bhujanga accidentally singes the back of Lazlow's neck with his Emerald Flame.

"Yeowch! Watch it, dickhead!" Lazlow barked.

"Shit." Thought Bhujanga. *"This is why I tested alone, I can't fight how I'd like here..."*

Caffo returns to Faxion, as the two begin to mow down the enemy to give them some space.

"Max!" Said Faxion. "Can you and your father buy us a moment?"

The Hachidorinese warrior turns to the Veteran Blade and nods his head.

"I'll do as I can." He replied. "But be swift, at this rate we may be greeting our ancestors within the hour."

"Do not gripe, boy!" Hollered Kenzo, lobbing the heads off of a group of skeletons. "This is what the Sanda were born and bred for!"

Faxion turns to Caffo for answers.

"So what news have you from Scott? Something handy I hope?"

"Not much unfortunately." Caffo replied. "He said that normally a Rok-Senn Morph loses its aura when the rune is destroyed, but clearly your Wind and Star casting girl did *just that* when she dropped a damn meteor shower on it. But when the Morph's rune reappeared out of thin air and reconstructed it, all bets were off. The only other option he brought up was to re-trigger whatever catalyst brought the Morph to life, kind of like a "reset" button."

Faxion ponders for a moment.

"The catalyst... So the golden tablet, no?" He said. "We would have to return the tablet to it, correct?"

"Look." Replied Caffo, pointing in the distance beyond the Pyramid Morph. A glimmer in the sand reveals the golden tablet stolen by Lazlow Jr.. "The thing walked right past it, if it was after the tablet it would have taken it and calmed down. And there's no way to return it to the room at the top, it's not even a pyramid anymore. I'm not even sure where everything that was inside of it went, because when it was half destroyed it looked like it was made purely of solid stone and sand."

"You're right." Said Faxion, scratching his head in confusion. "What manner of wild castery is at work here?..."

As the two converse, the pyramid Morph comes back to life, slowly swaying its arms and drawing itself into an erect posture. It begins to draw aura from the atmosphere yet again, cultivating another deadly beam to eradicate the opposition.

Electrifying a wave of skeletons with his auric tendrils, Puerto is one of the first to notice the Morph's return.

"Shit!" He exclaimed, leaping over a pile of freshly charred bones and landing before Cornelius. "Bad news, take a look at that."

Cornelius diverts his gaze towards the Pyramid Morph, beholding the titan in action.

"Oh no..." He replied. "Does the endurance of this monster know no end?" He clangs the massive vambraces attached to his forearm together. *"I might have to use it again. But how much juice have I got left?..."* He thought.

Rexmere fires a barrage of lightning fast punches at the opposition in a mad dash, clearing a path for him towards Faxion and Caffo.

"What are we going to do about *that?*" Said Rexmere, digging his feet into the sand to halt the momentum of his assault.

"Oh my..." Replied Faxion, taking note of the circular formation the Hired Blades have been gradually forced into. "They're intelligent, the bastards are boxing us into the line of fire. It seems as though escape is not an option."

"Good!" Replied Kenzo, strutting towards the frontline in the direction of the Morph's aim. "No more talk of this, *escape* nonsense. The Sanda are not track stars, we do not run!"

Kenzo takes a martial posture, crouching and pointing the blade of his palm to the ground. White aura begins to cultivate around the 4th degree Sanda master, pulsating from the yellow gem across his chestplate. The air pressure shifts directly around him, as auric lightning begins to crackle from the gem and scorch the sands around the warrior.

"Father..." Said Max. "What are you thinking..."

"This is the pride of The Sanda!" He replied. "I will not be remembered as a coward!" His armor begins to wriggle and writhe organically. "MK 2! Release!!"

Powerful electric aura starts to surge around Kenzo, as gunmetal gray metal fibers erupt from his yellow gem. The fibers cover his face and cornrowed hair, leaving the silhouette of the four golden stripes pulsating across his skull. As the fibers vigorously cover the Hachidorinese warrior's body, lightning and thunder begin to crackle across the sky. While Kenzo's hand begins to creep towards the handle of his drawing Lacerate, Cornelius draws near, his Arcane Eraser cannon fully formed and molded to his forearms.

"I like your spirit, old soldier." Said Cornelius. "Let me stand beside you!"

He sets the Arcane Eraser's sturdy tripod to the ground, beginning to charge aura into the chamber from every fiber of his massive being.

Just then, the sound of scorching flames echoes by. Bhujanga appears, charring the skull of a felled undead warrior in his palm. He crushes it in his hands, releasing the powdered skull onto the ground like black sand from an hourglass.

"I guess it can't be helped." He said. Bhujanga clenches his fists, pumping his hands with aura as verdant flames begin to erupt from between his fingers. "I'll join in. Hope you two can keep up..."

The Hired Blades in attendance are drawn to the scene, watching intently as Bhujanga, Kenzo, and Cornelius stand firm in the face of their titanic foe. The fierce trio charge their techniques, cultivating intense, pulsating aura around them and drawing it into their weapon of choice. All the while the Pyramid Morph's cannon starts to overflow with green aura, pooling to the brim as though ready to burst like a water balloon.

"Get ready boys!" Shouts Kenzo. "Looks like it's set to blow!" His hand clenching the handle of his Drawing Lacerate, golden aura begins to shine from the blade within. A bewitching glow emanates from the four golden stripes atop his head, palpitating to match the beating of his heart.

Cornelius takes a knee, stabilizing the mighty cannon on its thick, built-in tripod. The massive barrel begins to hum ominously, rotating slowly with a gradually increasing speed. Azure aura starts to peek out from within, lighting the darkness around the hulking Kettlenian Elite.

Bhujanga drives his feet into the sand, holding his verdant, glowing fists out in front of him. His hands catch ablaze, Emerald Flame creeping up to his shoulders in a wicked pyre. A small, floating fireball emerges from the shoulder flames, fluttering up to Bhujanga inquisitively like a firefly in the night. He nods his head to the floating blaze.

"It's time." He said.

The fireball flickers brightly with glee, floating up and down as if to reply with a nod of its own. It returns to Bhujanga's arm for a brief moment, before emerging with several more lively fireballs, dancing around Bhujanga with excitement.

"Calm down now, this is serious. You see that big thing there?" He points to the Pyramid Morph. "Kill it."

The flames unanimously flicker with elation, snapping and popping in the night sky.

Caffo turns to Faxion with a concerned look across his brow.

"This is it." He said. "If they don't manage this, there's not much else to be done."

Faxion puts a hand on Caffo's shoulder.

"Relax proctor." He replied. "Take in the sights. We have the pride of the Kettlenian Elite here, standing beside a War Chief of the legendary Sanda, and well... Whatever that young protégé of yours is. This is not a sight you're likely to see more than once in a lifetime."

"I just hope it's not the last sight I have to see." Said Caffo.

"We've done our duty, lad. Protected the innocent and what-not."

Faxion tips his hat. "While I don't wish for it, I wouldn't complain if it was."

Behind him, Pilet's auric egg pulsates eerily like a cardiac rhythm.

Finally, the green aura of The Pyramid Morph reaches its breaking point, as the ancient titan unleashes a mighty cannon of intensely hot, verdant energy upon the Hired Blades. With an unholy light that pierces the heavens, the intense beam of destructive aura fires straight for the frontline trio. Cornelius hollers in protest.

"Eradicate your ancestor! My... *Arcane Eraser*!!"

The 8 foot wide beam of pure aura blasts forth from Cornelius' Arcane Eraser, blowing whirlwinds of sand behind him from the sheer force of the blast. The Eraser's beam soars through the sky, its aim true for the Morph's projectile.

Instantly, the roaring, mighty beams collide in an immense clash of light; struggling back and forth for dominance.

Bhujanga releases his fists, revealing a small emerald light fluttering in the air between his palms. Suddenly, the light grows to the size of a basketball, as the Emerald Flamecaster clasps it between his hands. The school of floating fireballs around him immediately increases in size, each one liken to a small car.

"It's now or never!" He drives his fingers into the scorching orb. "*Karmic... Death Parade*!!"

The massive fireballs rush forth in rapid succession, meeting the Morph's beam of destruction with a fearsome, explosive power of their own. As one fireball leaves Bhujanga's side, another is immediately formed to replace it, flying swiftly into the fray and combusting into the mix of combative light. The rapid firing barrage of fireballs aids Cornelius' Eraser, both working in unison against the Morph.

Suddenly, the four stripes atop Kenzo's head glow with an immensely powerful shine. The Sanda War Chief prepares to draw upon the foe.

"Take heed my son! The power of the Sanda!!" He grips his sword tightly. "Go forth! *Zen'no Divide*!!"

In the blink of an eye, Kenzo draws and resheathes his Lacerate four times in rapid succession. With each slash, the Sanda Master fires a bolt of immense, continuous lightning that vertically swallows the horizon. The four flashes of lightning illuminate the night sky as if it were the middle of the day. They meet head on with the Pyramid Morphs destructive beam, gradually beginning to slice through the beam as it struggles against its two other opposing forces.

Together, the three warriors begin to gain the upper hand on the Morph's beam, as the ancient weapon begins to slowly recede with the intensity of the struggle. Light flashes, flame dances through the air, intense heat waves flow throughout the Desert Devil's Tongue. Camels, Giduh monsters, and salamanders across the vast landscape run for cover in fear of the powerful force. Birds from every corner of the land fly away, even as far as the forests of Miantha beyond the desert sands. Curious children in the desert villages run to their windows, wiping their eyes in disbelief at the mighty light of the arcane showdown.

In the distance, a fleet of HBA airships led by The Crimson Pagoda speeds towards the scene. Chairman Yang stands upon the balcony of his airship, arms folded, with a glimmer of excitement in his eye.

"This year's crop is something special..." He turns to his pilot. "Let's move, move, move! Blades are fighting for their lives out there!!"

Kenzo, Bhujanga, and Cornelius pour every ounce of aura they have left into their techniques, screaming at the tops of their lungs with the pain of aurically dupleted muscle spasm.

"Grrraaaaaaaahhhhh!!!" The three casters release a unanimous battlecry.

The Pyramid Morph continues to pump aura from within, pushing back the efforts of its opponents.

As vicious sands begin to whip up behind the three casters, Scott raises his arm into the air.

"Killzone." He casts, bringing a protective dome of aura over the rest of the Hired Blades.

The sound of the wind's relentless assault on the auric dome drowns out all but the ominous humm of the arcane duel taking place several feet away. The sand continues to batter the "Killzone" cast, completely blocking the view of anything occurring before the eyes of The Hired Blades. The bystanders standby in silence, unable to act to help their combatant comrades on the other side of the barrier.

Suddenly, an ear shattering explosion is heard just outside the dome, as even the sand is blown away by an immeasurable force.

And just like that, a gentle calm befalls the desert, as the wind begins to slow to a mild breeze. Finally, the dust begins to settle, revealing the outcome of the combatants' last stand...

Rampage of the Chimera

Cornelius lay face down in the sand, immobilized and seemingly unconscious from the exertion of his Arcane Eraser's full power.

Kenzo kneels onto one knee, his Lacerate driven into the sand to support him from collapse. Breathing heavily, his MK2 Sanda armor begins to recede into the gem encrusted in his chestplate.

Bhujanga stands tall, his arms folded in contempt as he wipes the dust from his shoulder.

"Hmmph." He scoffs. "Is that all? *Mighty* Pyramid?"

The Pyramid Morph stands in a hunched position, its arms dangling lifelessly with the cannon protruding from its chest completely destroyed. The scores of surrounding skeletons lay blown off into the distance, slowly picking their twisted and mangled bodies up from the sands.

Seeing this, Scott Diliger drops his "Killzone" cast, rushing to the downed Kettlenian Elite's side. He casts "Mend", emitting healing aura from his palms onto the collapsed warrior. He checks Cornelius' pulse tentatively, hoping for some sort of activity within his veins.

"......................................"

Thump...............................*Thump*..............................*Thump*

"Phew." Scott releases a sigh of relief. He holds a thumbs up to the crowd. "He's good."

The Blades let out a thunderous roar of applause, firing shots into the air at will. Scott puts a hand on his slumbering comrades shoulder. "Good job, soldier."

"*Pant* Wait, it's not over." Said Kenzo, struggling for breath. "Pause your celebrations, the battle is not yet won."

"Scott." Said Bhujanga, glaring off toward the distant, towering, ancient God of the desert. Scott's attention is drawn to the Emerald Flamecaster. "We've seen this before, the thing's just going to take a breather and come back swinging. You know running out of aura's not a problem for me, but

I can't muster enough firepower at once to stop that cannon on my own. And the three of us were *barely* able to compete just now. All we did was stop it from reaching you."

Scott looks back into the distance. He takes note of the waves of undead, slowly advancing towards The Hired Blades forces once again. The veteran caster turns to Faxion.

"*Sigh* Welp, any ideas?"

Faxion turns to see the exhausted faces of his allies, covered with sweat and sand. Lavished, head to toe in miscellaneous cuts, scrapes and bruises, a glint of unmistakable determination still burns within the tired eyes of each Blade. The Deadeye ponders for a moment, cycling through possibilities and plans of attack in his head.

With a series of faint, "thuds", a reverberating sound is heard. Faxion turns towards the others in confusion. He spots Pilet's auric cocoon, pulsating with small waves of energy.

The thudding sound continues, as the eerie cocoon sends small waves of burgundy energy lashing out. Suddenly, a thin crack looses at the top of the arcane egg. A thick, dark aura pours forth, beginning to circle menacingly around it. Then, more cracks appear at the top, creating an opening as the dark aura begins siphoning itself inside. The mysterious egg quickly quadruples in size, leaving onlookers in awe and bewilderment.

Lazlow Jr. scratches his head in confusion.

"What the hell's wrong with King Killer now?" He said.

"Shhh fool." Replied Dabria. "You're distracting me, I want to see the *freak* come out to play."

"..."

Suddenly, the auric cocoon surrounding Pilet explodes, releasing highly pressurized dark aura and blowing a gust of devilish wind onto the crowd.

The wind rushes past Faxion, almost blowing off his hat before the Veteran Blade reflexively catches it.

"What the hell is this boy?..." Thought Faxion.

The cocoon shatters entirely, as a huge, bronze pincer begins to emerge from the dark cloud left behind. With this, an intense, ominous wail can be heard coming from within. A pair of massive, muscular, bronze-armored legs step out of the darkness; and two giant, bronze pincers begin clawing away at the cloud, revealing a pair of glowing, deep-red eyes from within. Finally, the creature grows weary of the dark cloud surrounding it. It cries out with a devilish screech, sending a shockwave that blows away the dark aura in an instant.

The crowd gasps, at the reveal of a twelve-foot tall, armored titan standing before them. Covered head to toe in the bronze exoskeleton of Kuweha the scorpion; the beast boasts the violet fur of the Gorilla that attacked Chamboree, peeking out from within the armor's joints. Its face, adorned with two fright-inducing pincers, and a helmet of pure bronze with a horn-like stinger protruding from the front. As the beast screams, its gorilla-like lower jaw splits into two halves that spew a noxious fluid from its mouth. Dozens of small stingers miscellaneously jut out from every part of its body like a hellish porcupine. Two massive, powerful pincers adorn either hand of the beast. A long, spiked tail with razor sharp edges along the sides peeks out from behind, brandishing an imposing stinger at the tip.

"That's... *Pilet*?!" Said Faith in shock.

"Get back!" Exclaimed Faxion, as the creature turns to the crowd menacingly.

It whips its tail around in an instant, whizzing its lethal stinger right by Faxion's face as he swiftly and evasively back-bends onto all fours.

"Are you in there lad?!" Hollered Faxion. "You need to fight this! This is not you!"

But his words fall on deaf ears, as the creature sets its sights on The Pyramid Morph. The image of Toste being eviscerated by the Behemoth's auric beam plays through its mind, as it cries out in anguish.

The morbid cry forces everyone to cover their ears in pain, while the sound triggers a reaction from the sleeping Morph.

It opens its eyes, immediately targeting the wailing creature with the same scarlet irises that once tracked Pilet with murderous intent. The Morph itself lets out a primal sound, shaking the desert sands beneath it. It winds up, sending its massive forearm flying towards the creature.

"Move move move!!" Shouts Caffo to the others.

The Hired Blades dart away from the scene, leaving the transformed Pilet to deal with his aggravated foe.

As the arm of the Morph approaches Pilet, it is immediately sliced

146

in half like butter by the longer top pincer of the ferocious monster. The beast leaps towards the Morph with blinding speed, running up its massive arm and slicing away at it with his tail on the way up. But as Pilet closes the distance to the Morph's face, auric runes begin to glow along the sand titan's arm, exploding like mines as Pilet unwittingly steps onto them.

The beast leaps high into the air just in time to evade the hidden blasts. As he soars through the sky before the face of the Morph, every sharp spine along his body begins to cultivate a dark, coagulated-blood red aura.

He cries out, spinning his body wildly as the stored aura within each spine manifests into a dark red Hollowpoint. The dark orbs of pure aura fly out recklessly into every direction, exploding viciously wherever they land. Many of the Hollowpoints whiz by Pilet's comrades, narrowly missing the Hired Blades as they struggle against their many skeletal foes.

"Ey ey! Heads up!" Exclaimed Danba, as a rogue Hollowpoint flies straight towards him.

The drummer charges aura into his wooden drumstick, creating a yellow dagger of energy. He slashes the Hollowpoint in half, mid-flight; dissipating the reckless projectile before it can harm him and his musical allies. Lukah pauses his arcane lyricism at the sight.

"Damn! King Killer's gotta watch it!" Exclaimed Lukah. "I've had folks throw tomatoes during a show, but this is some *next level* bullshit!"

The dark-Hollowpoints batter the Pyramid Morph, leaving dents and leaking sand all over the ancient titan. The beast lands atop the Morph's other arm, hunching over and brandishing the wicked stinger atop his mighty tail. The stinger itself begins to cultivate aura, lending to a large orb of dark red energy like a massive Hollowpoint appearing at the tip. With a whiz and a mighty crash, Pilet fires the immense projectile at his foe with a wicked smile; sending it soaring through the air at top speeds before pounding into the face of the Pyramid Morph with immeasurable force.

As the projectile explodes on impact, the Pyramid Morph staggers back with the force of the blow. Suddenly spears of sand erupt from the arm of the Morph, stabbing into the beast where he stands.

Pilet cries out, as the spears burrow into the space between his armor, piercing joints and boring through flesh. He swiftly breaks the spears in half with his pincers, freeing himself from the bothersome weapons and savagely roaring at the Pyramid Morph in anger. As the wounds between his joints begin to heal at an alarming rate, the beast dashes with blinding speed up and down the body of the titanic foe. He slashes, slices, and dices away at the hide of the Pyramid Morph; severing fingers, cutting away at the knees, even slashing off the ears of his immense enemy with ease.

Unable to keep up with the barrage of slashes from the raging beast, the Morph hopelessly swipes and swats at itself in hopes of catching its speedy foe. As its joints are diced to bits by Pilet's ballistic onslaught, the Pyramid Morph helplessly falls to one knee. Turning his attention to the head of the Pyramid Morph, the raging beast begins to swipe away at the neck of his foe. But as the Morph lifts its hands to its neck in defense of a beheading, the sand-titan's arms are swiftly parted from its body at the shoulder. An instant later, the severed head of the Morph strikes the ground, just before its mighty arms do; followed by the lifeless body of the ancient titan, sending waves of wind and sand rushing throughout the desert floor.

The impact of the falling limbs sends a terrifying shockwave throughout Devil's Tongue, as the booming sound can be heard from miles upon miles away.

As the beast lands atop the parted head of the Morph, he lets loose a savage roar of victory. The Hired Blades scattered throughout the battlefield let out an ecstatic cheer, as they watch the titan of the ancient world fall to its demise.

Turn the Tides! The King of the Mercenaries

"Son of a bitch..." Said Caffo Gilwick to Rexmere. "He did it. I don't know how, I don't even know what he is to be honest, but the kid *actually* did it."

Rexmere fires a roundhouse kick to the head of an oncoming skeleton warrior, sending its skull flying off into one of its brethren in the distance like a speeding softball.

"This is one hell of an exam huh?" Rexmere replied. "I might just retire after this shit, assuming the boss pays us what this damn job was worth."

Suddenly, a water-whip lashes through a group of skeletons as they draw near the two exam proctors; revealing Scott Diliger, as he steps over the piles of bones.

"Don't get your hopes up fellas..." He said, pointing to the lifeless Morph in the distance.

In an image of pure dread, the immense auric rune that gave life to the Pyramid Morph again takes shape in the darkened sky. Its verdant glow gives rise to an eerie sense of impending doom in the pit of Caffo's stomach.

"You can't be serious!" Caffo exclaimed, tossing his Stinger pistol to the ground in frustration. "I mean, it looked dead! How in the name of the Serpent Dragons do you kill this thing?!"

Just then, the fearsome beast responsible for bringing the Pyramid Morph to its knees begins to cough incessantly. A cloud of dark red aura looms over the beast, surrounding it before shrinking its contents back to the size of a man. Suddenly, this cloud dissipates; revealing Pilet, coughing and gagging up blood and fluid uncontrollably. His white tank top stained entirely red, the boy struggles to breathe as he chokes on his own blood. His eyes peel back into his skull, revealing swollen, aggravated veins and blood vessels where the whites of his eyes should be.

"Pilet!" Cried Faith, hastily dashing toward her ally.

"Right behind you." Said Max, following in pursuit.

The fallen body parts of the Pyramid Morph begin to turn to piles of sand that start to fly towards the auric rune in the sky, forming the body of the ancient titan once more. The head to which Pilet pridefully stood atop begins to shift as well, carrying the struggling King Killer into the air with it. As Faith and Max sprint as fast as they can towards Pilet, the boy is swept up by an unseen speeding force before he can be whisked any higher into the air. The dashing duo plant their feet to a stop in confusion.

"What?!" Said Max. "Where did he go? Has he awoken already?!"

They scan the desert floor for a moment before seeing Faxion, holding Pilet in his arms not but a few yards off.

"Fax!" Exclaimed Faith, as she and Max dash to the Veteran Blade with haste. "Is... Is he ok?"

Without answering, Faxion holds Pilet's face to his ear to hear for a breath. He places him swiftly but gently onto the floor before applying chest compressions in a rhythmic pattern.

"He's not breathing." Said Faxion, a stone cold look cemented upon his face.

A moment of silence incurs before he shouts at the two fresh Blades. "Cast Mend! Now!"

Max and Faith both jump, startled by the octave of the otherwise docile Veteran. They immediately cast "Mend", sending healing aura into the chest cavity of their fallen comrade. Faxion continues his chest compressions, as the three begin to sweat profusely with the anticipation of the next few moments. They fall silent, the sound of the shifting sands forming the massive titan behind them haunts the trio as they try to focus on the dire task at hand.

Coughing and gagging, Pilet suddenly coughs up and spits coagulated blood onto the face of Faxion; who, completely unphased, closes his eyes and continues chest compressions. Just then, they hear a faint wheeze escape Pilet's lungs. Faxion stops his compressions and casts "Mend", joining the others in their healing endeavor. Max and Faith silently look at each other, then back to Faxion. Faxion stops, he puts his ear to Pilet's chest again.

"......................................"

ThudThud

He looks back up to Faith and Max. With a subtle grin, he pulls the brim of his fedora down to hide his watery eyes.

"Glad to have you back, Lad." He said. "Glad to have you back..."

Scott, Caffo, and Rexmere approach The Hidden Blades, harnessing aura in preparation for battle.

"You can pause your celebrations, Fax." Said Rexmere. He cracks his knuckles one by one; as a crimson, bolstering aura begins to pour into each finger joint. " The party's not over yet."

A mighty shadow casts over the trio; as Faxion, Max, and Faith turn around to the sight of the nearly re-formed Pyramid Morph. At the same time, the sound of crackling and popping can be heard in the distance; as the ghoulish skeletal remains of the Rok-Senn army begin to pull themselves together once more. Tired, battered, and bruised, the candidates and proctors plant their feet in the sand; preparing for a final stand against their unrelenting foe.

"Scott..." Said Caffo. "Things are looking pretty grim here. Please tell me you have some semblance of an idea as to what to do."

"I, I wish I did." Replied Scott. "I have a faint idea of what's going on, but absolutely no clue of how to stop it. We're gonna need a miracle at this point..."

As the skeletons recompose themselves, they begin their steady march back towards the Hired Blades forces. Simultaneously, the Pyramid Morph comes to a full reformation, as its haunting eyes take to a green auric hue. The Morph looks down at the Blades in front of it, curiously eyeing Pilet in the group. Those green eyes warp to a sinister scarlet once more; as the titan raises its massive fist, preparing to fire a devastating right cross straight towards them.

"Max, take Pilet out of here!" Exclaimed Faxion.

"Right!" The Hachidorinese swordsman replied, hoisting his comrade over his shoulder and bolting towards the others.

The eagle tattoo on Faxion's arm begins to glow intensely, as he directs it towards the massive oncoming fist of the Morph. A colorful combination of yellow, violet, green, red and blue aura begins to swirl vigorously around the Veteran Blade's forearm, pouring into the tattoo and accumulating at the palm of his hand.

"I never thought I'd have to use it..." Said Faxion, aiming his palm towards the immense, imposing structure.

"Faxion..." Said Scott, recognizing the technique instantly. "Are you sure you want to do this?"

Faxion turns somberly to his colleague. He gives him a nod and a subtle grin.

"We can't let it end like this now, can we?" Faxion Replied, a glint of contented glee in his eye. "Just in case, take care of my little bean sprouts, mate. They'll make fine Blades some day."

Scott nods in silence.

"Wait, what is he talking about?!" Said Faith, with a look of stark concern. "Fax, what are you doing? What is that?!"

The Massive Morph lets loose a mighty roar, firing its fist towards the Veteran Blade like the asteroid that killed the prehistoric Fossil creatures.

"Take care of your sister, lass." Replied Faxion. "Oh, and your parents..." The Veteran Blade flashes Faith a smile of sincerity. "they forgive you."

A surprised and stunned look appears upon Faith's face, rendering her speechless and daft.

The auric tattoo upon his forearm drains the energy from all of the muscles in Faxion's body, rendering it hard for him to stand. The contour of his face begins to sink in, as his tissues and sinews dehydrate at a rapid pace. The adenosine triphosphate that fueled the cells of his body, mixed with the vibrant aura cultivated within the tattoo; forms a large, colorful arrowhead beginning to protrude from his palm. Faxion takes to a knee in exhaustion, bolstering his arm with his free hand and aiming true for the verdant rune across the titans chest. He takes a deep breath, struggling to mutter a string of words.

"About time I joined you, boy..."

As he steels himself and readies his aim, the subtle sound of thruster fire can be heard not far off.

"Huh?..." Said Rexmere, turning towards the oncoming sound. Suddenly, he smiles with excitement at what he sees. "Well shit, you might want to hold off on that cast, Fax."

Approaching from the skies behind is the personal, pagoda-styled airship of Chairman Yang, The Crimson Pagoda; with the Chairman literally standing atop the roof. Behind the Crimson Pagoda, a lengthy fleet of accompanying airships can be seen closely in-tow.

"It's about Goddamn time!" Exclaimed Caffo.

The Chairman brandishes his crimson crystal necklace, nearly identical to Pilet's chrome stone, tightly grasping the crystal for a moment to activate its latent aura. The crystal shines bright enough to emulate a crimson star across the desert sky, even blinding Benny and the other fighter pilots for a brief moment.

"Oh hell!" Exclaimed Benny, while shielding his eyes with his forearm. "Chief, take it easy with the light show!"

The Chairman crouches down, positioning himself like a football player about to explode into a dash. Suddenly, the crimson stone begins enshrouding Chairman Yang with energy, as his body bursts into a wickedly hot flame.

"Springboard." He casts.

In an instant; the Chairman's flame-shrouded, hulking body blasts off of the airship at an alarming speed; headed straight for the oncoming fist of the Rok-Senn Morph. The force of his "Springboard" leap tips over The Crimson Pagoda mid-flight, as the pilot struggles to retain balance.

"Ahhhh! This is why I hate driving for him!" Exclaimed the pilot, anxiously clutching the steering wheel.

The Chairman soars across the sky, leaving a crackling streak of vibrant flame trailing behind him. As the head Blade nears the coming fist of his foe, he tucks his head into his shoulder, bracing for impact.

With an almighty crash, the blazing Master Mercenary collides with the titan of sand in a devastating, full-body tackle; causing the Morph's fist to explode and shatter into bits on impact. Shards of the Morph's fist mixed with flickers of flame rain down like a shower of sparks onto the desert floor, sending a sigh of relief wheezing out of the collective mouths of Faxion and the others. Faxion rescinds the arrowhead of his powerful, lastish-effort auracast, reabsorbing the aura and nutrients used to charge it. His face regains its full, healthy contour, as the Veteran Blade collapses in exhaustion.

"Not a moment too late, sir..." He mumbles.

The force of the collision sends Chairman Yang soaring backwards, as he lands nimbly onto the roof of The Crimson Pagoda once more. The Pyramid Morph is sent staggering back by the recoil of its punch, planting its feet firmly in the sand before it can topple over.

The Ancient titan lets loose a mighty roar towards the Chairman, acknowledging the new challenger. Chairman Yang shakes his head in protest, before channeling his focus into the tattoo of a green-eyed, bloody-mawed wolf on his right forearm. The tattoo begins to glow a verdant hue, as a scarlet aura culminates within the Chairman's palm.

"At ease ancient guardian. Today, I give you no quarry." He raises his arm skyward. A dense, dark cloud begins to form above the head of the Pyramid Morph. "Now... heed the order of your Commander! *Return to your post!!*"

The Chairman clenches his fist tightly, squeezing the cultivated aura within his palm like a balloon ready to burst. The dark cloud in the sky fills with red aura, crackling and flashing profusely. Suddenly, a series of ferocious, scarlet lightning bolts crash upon the crown of the massive Pyramid Morph. A barrage of intense crackles and bangs are heard, with the onslaught of this arcane force of nature.

As the Scarlet lightning pours down upon the ancient titan, the color begins to slowly fade from the Morph's ghoulish eyes. The auric rune appears across its chest yet again, engulfing the Morph in a mystical emerald aura. Suddenly, the Pyramid Morph crouches down and sits humbly to the ground, the impact of its immense body sending a shockwave throughout the desert floor. Hugging its knees in a fetal position, the Morphs' curled body begins to shift and change; slowly but surely transforming itself into the immense pyramid that arose from beneath the ground many hours ago.

Tired from the throes of combat, the exam candidates and proctors glance in awe of the shocking metamorphosis. Mouths agape and brows raised in surprise, they fire celebratory shots into the air, crying out in victory.

"He did it! He really, seriously did it!" Exclaimed Dex, unloading a clip of plasma from his Pilum beam rifle into the sky.

"Wow, we legitimately didn't end up dead." Said Asger, turning to Dabria with subtle, piqued excitement. "Good thing too, or father would have probably killed us."

"Speak for yourself brother!" Replied Dabria. "No way in hell would this ragtag pile of bones be the death of me!" She fires a barrage of flaming throwing daggers into a group of skeletons, their wicked heat burning the ghouls to cinders on contact.

Scott turns to Bhujanga with a subtle grin on his face. Bhujanga returns with a grin of his own and a nod, tossing a ball of Emerald Flame into the sky. At the height of its ascent, the flame bursts into a collection of smaller fireballs like a celebratory light show, each of which incinerating an unlucky skeletal warrior as they fall to the earth.

Having dropped Pilet's unconscious body off by Yuuna, Max returns to Faxion.

"The Pyramid has returned to its docile state, but what of this endless army before us?" Said Max.

Faxion ponders for a moment, before looking up towards the Chairman standing atop The Crimson Pagoda. He points up toward the fearsome mercenary King.

"My young friend, I think *he* may have the answer to your question..."

The FC Strikeforce

Gazing down at the army of the undead before him from his seat in the sky, The Chairman strokes his beard inquisitively.

"An enemy force of this magnitude." He draws his Chatch to his face, speaking into the device with elastic bands mounted onto his massive wrists. "Killer Cera, do you think the Strikeforce can help me clear a path to scramble the Blades?"

A raspy, charismatic voice speaks back to him.

"It'd be our pleasure, Chairman. Have your forces steer clear once we're down there, things tend to get a bit messy."

The Chairman grins, gazing at the scores of undead soldiers marching below.

"I was hoping as such..."

Suddenly, the largest of airships approaches at the front of the fleet. The hull, gunmetal gray with reinforced steel beams running a checkered pattern all across.

"Release the Ptero-Trio; Missile Mike, Tina Beam, Clyde, You're up." Said the raspy voice.

The on-ramp to the ship bursts open, as three colorful pterodactyls fly out with the swiftness of a speeding bullet. They immediately dive bomb towards a dense cluster of skeletal soldiers, abruptly halting their descent some 30 feet from the ground to a brisk glide.

Missile Mike, scales blood-red in color, with a body covered in small mechanical hatches that open to reveal hidden missiles, the largest of which protruding from his back like a rocket. He fires a barrage of said missiles down upon the crowd of skeletons with reckless abandon, decimating whole squadrons of ghouls with relative ease.

As the smoke clears from the heated barrage, many more skeletons who were missed or not hit square begin to stand to their feet; but as they do so, a second pterodactyl approaches with haste. Tina Beam; light blue scaled, with the barrels of beam rifles protruding from the tip of her beak, fingers and toes as well as two larger beam rifles sprouting from her wings. The flying Fossil creature points her wings towards a row of rogue skeletons, as azure beam projectiles fire out in rapid succession. With vicious precision, the bullets of pure plasma strike true; felling each target and leaving piles of charred bone in her wake.

The third pterodactyl, Clyde, sweeps up the rear; sporting a vibrant yellow coat of scales and a bandolier of assorted grenades over his shoulder. As he soars over the remaining foes, he deploys small grenades and plasma bombs from mechanical openings in his palms and feet.

The myriad of plasma and incendiary grenades fall to the ground, leveling the remaining skeletons to piles of fine ash.

The dust clears from the airborne assault, leaving a sizable open space of sand devoid of the skeletal foes. The immense airship of the FC Strikeforce hovers above the clearing, as a platform carrying three Fossil creatures begins to lower to the ground. One FC; A stegosaurus, copper in color with two rows of bladed, infrared spines protruding from its back. Alongside it stands an ill-tempered looking ankylosaurus. Jet black scales, with a long, crimson-glowing stripe running along either of its sides; the armored beast impatiently tamps the studs of its heavy, clubbed tail into the lowering platform. Standing before the two is a triceratops, his scales a vibrant shade of purple, with flame-like orange streaks across his sides. A blue vizor built into his face covers his eyes, with a little red light pacing back and forth inside. Two large, high-tech laser cannons with a paint job matching his scales affix to his shoulders. He clicks his tongue, engaging the infrared function on the dense, swordlike horns jutting from his forehead and nose. The triceratops speaks.

"It's game time boys. The Chairman needs us to clear a path for the Blades to advance."

"About Goddamn time." Grunts the Ankylosaurus. "I been waiting to blow off some steam for ages! I wanna rough 'em up, let's get down there already!"

"Easy, Boom." Replied the Stegosaurus, with a calm, tranquil demeanor. "A reckless FC is a dead one, we must proceed with caution. Right Chief?"

"That's correct, Twister." Said the Triceratops. "Just don't go blowing any of the Blades' heads off, alright? And the next time I tell you to stop, you'd better listen Boom. You answer to Killer Cera as long as you're with The Strikeforce. Otherwise you're welcome to return to Prehistoria, good luck answering to the king once you get there..."

"Hmph." Grunts Boom. "Ta hell with the king! And the lot of those *deserters* he took with him. Independence for FC's my ass, that prick just *had* to ruin a good thing and start shit with the humans. They paid us good aurem to knock some insurgent skulls! Now we gotta follow all these damned *rules,* and for less pay too..."

The platform finally lowers to ground level, thudding to the desert floor. Killer Cera takes the first step onto the blazing sand.

"That's enough lip, soldier up and let's go. Strikeforce, engage!"

The three FC's bolt off towards the dense sea of armed skeletons, a glint of pure adrenaline shines across each of their faces.

"Break!" Shouts Killer Cera, as they near the frontlines.

Twister and Boom branch off to either side, rushing into the fray as they pummel and trample skeletons in their wake.

Suddenly, Twister's eyes begin to glaze over in an orange hue. The glowing infrared spines atop his back begin to fire out into the crowd, effortlessly slicing through the opposition like flying chef's knives to a cluster of ripe fruit.

The whirring infrared spines proceed to whiz through the air like remote controlled planes of death; as Twister rocks back and forth with a meditative gloss across his face. As they reap through countless skeletons with their super heated edges, the infrared spines begin to whirl in a circle around the stegosaurus like a tornado of blazing steel. The spines pick up speed, letting off a wicked wind and an ominous hum; as they tear through the opposition with unrelenting velocity.

"Return to your slumber, oh ancient ones." Hummed Twister.

Some 100 yards away, Boom tramples scores of foes in his wake. With a single swing of his mighty studded tail, the ankylosaurus effortlessly sends entire waves of skeletons soaring through the air. Each time his club makes contact, the glowing crimson stripes along his body begin to slowly fill with radiating energy.

His herculean tail bludgeons hordes of foes, bashing away at the bony insurgents and knocking them into the air like tee balls. Suddenly, the glowing lines across Boom's body completely fill, releasing a blood-red flash of brilliant light.

"Finally!" Exclaimed Boom. "Now, *you're all gonna get it!!*"

The studs on his clubbed-tail begin to glow crimson, as the vicious ankylosaurus raises said tail in a defensive posture.

"Have fun in hell!!"

Boom violently smashes his tail into the ground, causing an explosion that swallows up a thirty foot radius around him. Swords, axes, knives and bones go flying across the desert. Waves of sand rush forth, engulfing approaching groups of skeleton warriors like the rising tide of the ocean. After the shockwave thoroughly ravages the surrounding area, the smoke finally clears; revealing Boom using his glowing tail to continue smashing further skeletons with explosive strikes.

"Now it's a god-damn party!" He cries out, decimating whole hordes with ease.

Meanwhile, Killer Cera draws near his foes with haste.

As he rushes the frontlines, the laser cannons atop his shoulders train themselves on the skeletal insurgents before him. A vibrant, violet laser beam bursts forth from either cannon, sweeping across the frontline and instantly reducing the first few waves to dust. The bionically enhanced triceratops rears its infrared horns at the enemy forces, charging vigorously into the fray and shish kebabing anything unlucky enough to be in front of him. Dashing through the ranks of the undead, Killer Cera emerges on the opposite side of the army. His blue visor locks onto the countless skeletons before him, as missile silos open from behind the bony plate surrounding his skull. Suddenly dozens of missiles rush forth from the triceratops' frills in succession, instantly bombarding the enemy in a hellish blaze of heavy firepower.

In the skies above Killer Cera, The Ptero Trio relishes at the sight of their commander's carnage.

"That's why he's the boss..." Said Missile Mike, gliding over the desert sky.

Having cleared a sizable path of skeletal warriors, Killer Cera audibly engages a headset hidden behind his bony cranial plate.

"Headset engage." Said Killer Cera. The headset responds to his voice with a soft "plink" sound. "Alright, send in the Saber Nychus', and let the Blades know that the battlefield is primed and ready for their arrival."

"Roger roger." Replied a voice from within the Strikeforce's airship.

Finally, the airship of the FC Strikeforce lands squarely to the ground.

The massive hatch door opens, as dozens of brilliantly feathered, raptor-esk Deinonychus rush out into the fray.

Already dangerous hunters, with a vicious sickle shaped talon on either hind foot; the Saber-Nychus is a more modern adaptation of the ferocious killers. These FC's sport hidden blades within the feathers of their mohawk, forearms, and tail, and retractable bladed claws within their fingers.

The Saber Nychus pounce onto the frontline, tearing and shredding away at the skeletal opposition with ruthless vigor. The roars and snarls of the advancing Fossil creatures fill the air, as does the sound of snapping and crunching bone.

Standing atop The Crimson Pagoda, Chairman Yang surveys the scene in place. Arms folded, with a subtle grin of glee across his bearded maw. He speaks into his Chatch.

"It's time, scramble the Blades."

"...You're just like him."

The hatch doors of the surrounding HBA airships fly open, as scores of Licensed Hired Blades dash out in a frenzied storm. Many of the deadly mercenaries fall deftly to the ground before the ships even land; with the power of Fleetfoot, nimbly darting off into the fray with Infrared swords, knives, and axes in hand. Others wait but a moment before the shutter doors reach the ground, marching out onto the sand. The Blade infantry draw beam rifles, pistols, gatling guns, missile launchers, and all manner of heavy weaponry; raining a brilliant barrage of lead and laserbeams across the battlefield. Many Hired Blades begin to tap into their auracast; hurling massive arcane boulders, roaring auric fireballs, and vibrant bolts of lightning into dense clusters of insurgent skeletal soldiers. A ferocious warcry rings throughout the desert, as one Hired Blade shouts an order.

"Push through! Get to the candidates!"

Off in the distance toward the slumbering pyramid, the exam proctors and candidates become tightly surrounded. Protecting the tent of trees housing an unconscious Cornelius, Yuuna, and Pilet; the group struggles to fend off the onslaught of the undead. Wounded and tired, covered in blood and sweat, the layers of "Callous" armor have been gradually peeled from their hides. Yet the weary exam group continues to swing away at the encroaching enemy.

Tearing through the ranks of several enemy skeletons with her Skarrya blade, Faith dashes from behind her felled foes and dodge-rolls toward Faxion and Max. She points her blade toward the fleet of allied airships in the distance.

"Are they even going to get here in time?!" She exclaimed. "It's like... an ocean of *deadly calcium* out here!"

Faxion gazes off toward Chairman Yang.

"Oh yee of little... Faith." He grins. Faith does not appear amused. Faxion continues. "The presence of the man standing upon that vessel is an *omen* to our enemies." He puts a hand on her shoulder. "You're not likely to see what happens *next,* more than once in your lifetime."

Looking down on the vast waves of skeletal fiends between the exam group and his own forces, the Chairman realizes the dangerous plight of his stranded allies. He curiously peers down toward the many tattoos covering his body. His inner right forearm bears the image of a golden bull. On the back of his left hand, he gazes at the tattoo of a flaming bush. He then peeks at the meat of his right bicep, showcasing a mighty ship, traversing a harsh storm at sea.

"Hmph, guess I'll have to get my hands dirty after all. These'll probably do the trick."

He takes a deep breath, exhaling slowly and methodically. Suddenly, every single auric tattoo scattered across the Master Blade's immense body begins to glow. The inks shine with a vivid, white light; leaving only the silhouette of the Chairman's gigantic physique to be seen.

"Compact!" cast Chairman Yang.

Just then, his silhouette begins to drastically shrink. His swollen muscles slim and shorten, as his vascular arms, legs, and midsection, tone with chiseled definition. Made of an incredibly flexible woven material, the Chairman's white tank top and navy slacks shrink to fit his newfound physique. As the light of the tattoos dims, waves of heat begin radiating from the pores of Yang's reddened skin.

Catching a glance of Yang's transformation, Faith inquisitively taps Faxion on the shoulder.

"Did, did he just do what I think he did?"

Faxion grins and nods.

"Look at you, how *impressive* your wells of knowledge are."

"What *did* he do?!" Inquires Max. "Where did the rest of the man go? Would he not have been of more use before?"

"Patience, my friend. Patience." Said Faxion.

Cloaked in his newfound physique, Chairman Yang takes a step off of the Crimson Pagoda, plummeting calmly towards the sand. As the slimmed Master Blade hurdles toward the ground, he forms a fist and cocks it back, winding up towards a cluster of skeletons below.

A mighty crash rings out, as Yang slams his fist into the desert floor; pummeling the whole cluster of foes with the seismic force of his blow. Vast waves of sand fly forth from the point of his descent, showcasing the might of the vetted warrior.

Before the dust can clear, The Chairman bursts forth from a sand cloud at incredible speed. Ping-ponging across the battlefield at a pace rivaling even Pilet's; Yang begins to decimate scores of the undead with nothing but his fists and kicks. Bones fly through the air, raining down on friend and foe alike. Tibias, femurs, humerus', and jawbones downpour in a shocking display of martial power.

"An absolute monster he is." Said Kenzo, as he rips through several skeletons with his Lacerate. He turns to Faxion. "The leader of your tribe is truly worthy of his title, a rare occurrence these days."

"I must say, I wouldn't be here if he wasn't." Replied Faxion.

Chairman Yang continues his assault, plowing through countless foes on his way toward Faxion and the exam group. In an attempt to stop him, many skeletons converge in front of Yang, forming a heavily congested mass before the Master Blade. He halts on a dime, shaking his head in disapproval.

"How unfortunate."

Raising his fist skyward, the golden bull on his forearm begins intensely glowing. He crouches and drives his fingers into the ground like a spear, pumping a golden brown aura into the sand.

A moment later, the ground begins to shake; as a mighty fissure forms between Chairman Yang and the examinees. The desert opens up, swallowing countless undead as the sands shift and quake below their feet.

But, as the Chairman focuses on the foes ahead, more surround him from either side. He stands to his feet, cultivating aura within the palms of his hands. The flaming bush on his left hand, and the storm-driven ship of his right bicep begin to glow, as Yang points his palms outward. Crimson aura begins to amass at the bush, whilst the ship takes to a violet sheen.

In an instant, massive balls of entangled vines barrel forth from his left hand; sparking to a brilliant flame and toppling scores of the undead. His right palm releases the violet aura, firing an intense, rushing windstream infused with wicked violet lighting at the enemy forces.

"His power..." Said Faith, her jaw hung in awe of the Master Blade. "A normal man would have collapsed from the burden of those auric tattoos."

"Lass, that man quit being *normal* many years ago..." Faxion replied.

The fearsome, flaming tumbleweeds and intense blast of storming winds wreak havoc on the unsuspecting skeletons; leaving mounds of ash and dust on one side of Yang, and heaping piles of charred bone on the other. As the surrounding enemy forces are quelled, Chairman Yang drives his fingers into the sand once more; sealing the mighty quaking fissure around its unfortunate victims. This halts the seismic shifting of the desert floor.

Now with a sizable, skeleton-free gap between Yang and the exam candidates; The Chairman bolts towards them with blinding swiftness. As he draws near, the speeding elder mercenary decimates the crowds of skeletons surrounding them in a vicious storm of pugilism. A gust of sand whips up, as he comes to a screeching halt before his subordinates. He stands before Faxion of the Deadeye and Caffo Gilwick, arms folded contemptuously, with a serious look in his eye. Standing atop a mound of bone and rusted swords, The Master Blade speaks.

"I thought I had the exam covered this year under your watchful eye, Caffo. Am I to believe my decision was mistaken?"

Wide-eyed, with beads of nervous sweat forming across his forehead, Caffo struggles for words. Fortunately for the head Exam proctor, Faxion intervenes.

"Be easy on him sir, it was *I* who took the reins of this situation as it began to unfold. I pulled rank."

The Chairman's serious glare shifts to Faxion, as the battle-fatigued Deadeye staggers from the ground to his feet.

"So I'm to believe this whole mess is your fault then?" Yang replied.

Faxion and Caffo hesitantly look at each other, as Caffo shrugs his shoulders to Faxion in speechless chagrin. The Veteran Blade searches for words.

"I..."

"Good!" Yang interrupts. "This is the most God-damned fun I've had in decades! You'll have to be rewarded accordingly."

Caffo's jaw drops, as his head hangs off his shoulders in shock. Taking a brisk, tension-relieving sigh; Faxion tips his hat to the head exam proctor, fighting back a deviant smirk. Caffo merely stares holes into Faxion's soul in response.

"I *do* aim to please, sir." Said The Deadeye.

The Chairman turns his attention to the surrounding, would-be Blades in attendance.

"*Well*, what a crop we have here! Representing everywhere from Hachidori to Itedonia, and beyond. And even some of our nation's *finest* Elites in the Alabaster armor among you. How very exciting this year's commencement ceremony will be!" Curiously, he scans the group once more. "I say, where's our sword Prince? Was he not taking part in this year's exam?"

The troupe keeps to a resounding silence, generally unsure of what to say. Some look towards Lazlow with a contemptuous side-eyed glare. Others glance down at the sand timidly. Finally, Caffo speaks up.

"He fell, in the line of duty sir..."

The stark silence follows his statement. The distant roar of Fossil creatures, and the clanging of metal from the battling Blades and skeletal soldiers acts like white noise; further drawing the company into a sense of impending dread. The Chairman spots some of the group's Papercut longswords, still dug into the sand in reverence of the fallen Prince.

"Oh, I see..." Replied Yang. He crinkles his nose, rubbing his face vigorously in an emotional stupor. "That's a shame. Not many a Blade could give me a good spar with the sword, not like the Star of Menanois. I'll notify his family myself..." Yang glances back at the slumbering pyramid. "Now, *who* is responsible for awakening that ancient behemoth?"

Caffo flares his nostrils in contempt.

"It was your Enforcer's son, sir." He said pointing to Lazlow. "He took an unauthorized artifact from the top-most chamber, somehow triggering that God-forsaken trap on us all. And-"

"*And?!* So what?!" Howls Lazlow, cutting through the crowd to the front. He tosses his shield and sword to the ground, furiously pointing his finger in Caffo's face. "I don't give a *shit* what I take. If it's there, and I want it, I take it!" He looks at Chairman Yang with a glare of pure venom, walking dangerously close to the Master Blade. The muscle-bound Kettlenian Elite towers over the compressed form of the Chairman. "My father says I can do whatever I want! Even *you* can't stop me, and you know it! You old shithead."

A silent tension engulfs those in attendance, as even the other Reaper Elites hold their breath at the words of the brazen Gavel. Suddenly, Yang cuts the tension, planting his fist across Lazlow's jawline with blinding speed.

"Oof!" Grunts Lazlow.

The feisty Kettlenian Elite is instantly sent flying far across the sand; his hefty body tumbling uncontrollably at a dizzying velocity. He soon crashes into a high dune, sending an avalanche of sand falling upon him. After a moment, the buried young candidate bursts forth, holding his sore jaw in lament. Dazed from the blow, he scans the desert floor in confusion.

"Wwhat, what the hell happened?..."

Before Lazlow can finish the thought, The Chairman appears before him out of thin air.

Wasting no time, Yang rips a wicked uppercut under the chin of the young Elite, sending him soaring into the sky. Lazlow flies high into the air, the silhouette of his massive, muscular frame floating bewitchingly before the full moon. Yang dashes into the air just above Lazlow, spinning vertically like a buzzsaw before whipping a vicious dropkick upon the crown of the youth's skull.

With unforgiving force, the young Elite is sent crashing back down into the dune; as sand and desert stone lifts high into the air on impact. The Chairman follows him down swiftly, lifting the massive Elite by the throat with one hand and punching him far across the sand once more. He proceeds with this pattern, knocking the disrespectful youngster up and down Devil's Tongue in a harsh display of force.

After several moments of this relentless barrage, Lazlow's body flops along the ground before coming to a full stop.

"Hnguhh..." Groans Lazlow, pushing himself laboredly off of the ground to his knees. Rivers of dark, crimson blood flow down his nostrils, running off his lips onto the ground. *Phtooew* "Ugh." He hocks a bloody loogie, grimacing in pain as he cracks his lower back into place. As he looks ahead, Lazlow spots the golden tablet from atop the Pyramid on the ground before him. *"That, damn thing..."* He thought.

Just then, Yang crashes down before him, forming a crater of sand with the force of the landing. He slowly paces toward the rowdy young Elite; a terrifying, predatory gleam in his eyes. As Yang approaches, the Master Blade starts growing back to his normal size, dwarfing even Lazlow's brawny frame. He stops right in front of the boy, raising his massive fist to deliver a finishing blow. But, just as the Chairman is about to strike, the young warrior looks down in defeat. Misty eyed, his crystal clear tears begin to mix with the blood all over his face. Breathing heavily, with a disheartened expression, Lazlow mutters under his breath.

"I knew it."

Yang halts his blow, curious of the boy's message. Lazlow continues.

"...You're *just* like him."

A silence befalls the two of them. Nearby, the subtle electrical buzz of hovering terrariums fills the air with an eerie tranquility. Finally, the Chairman drops his fist onto the boy.

Thud

But instead of a strike, the disheartened young man is met with a rhythmic, gentle rub to the top of his head.

"Ha! Crazy kid..." Said the Master Blade.

Yang turns around, picks up the golden tablet, and casts "Springboard"; blasting off toward the exam group in a flash.

The wind rustles between the sands, pushing debris and scattered bone to and fro. In silence, devoid of emotion or thought; the battered son of Kettlena sits there on his knees, staring blankly into space...

The Cryptic Duel

The Chairman approaches the destination of his arcane lunge. As he draws near Caffo, he plants his feet firmly into the sand, whipping a thick cloud up onto the exam group.

Some sand billows into the faces of the Mystic Marauders, as Puerto and Wendy are berated by the Chairman's brake.

"*Cough* *Gag* *Cough*"

"*What* the *hell!*" Exclaimed Wendy, wiping the sand from her eyes. "I don't know what was worse, little guy or *big* guy!"

"*Cough* *Spew* Shh, *shutup!*" Replied Puerto, spitting clumps of sand. "He's *right there*. I'm not pulling him off if he hears you!"

As the dust clears, Chairman Yang exits what's left of the cloud and approaches Caffo with the tablet. With Cornelius down, The Chairman now towers over everyone there in his burly form.

"Here you go son." He said, tossing it into Caffo's arms without warning.

Upon catching it, Caffo is immediately pulled to the ground by the weight of the solid gold artifact.

"Oh, wha-shit!" Caffo is quickly pummelled by the golden brick. "This thing's heavy! *Ouch*, my arm's stuck under!"

Several of the exam candidates chuckle at the plight of the head proctor, while Arturo, Asger, and Dabria peer off in Lazlow's direction. The Fubuki swordsman facepalms, shaking his head in disapproval.

"Man, Laz is such an idiot."

"...Think he's alright?" Said Asger. "If the guy didn't have such a thick head, I'd fear he'd have brain damage. I mean, that was one *savage* beating."

"Eh, he got what he deserved." Replied Dabria. "The fool's mouth wrote a check he couldn't cash. It'll be *his* fault if he's eating out of a straw for a few weeks."

Faxion and Kenzo help Caffo up, each lugging a side of the hefty golden tablet skyward.

"Your martial talent is exceptional, Master Blade." Said Kenzo, as he lifts his end of the tablet. "I'd expect no less from a man of your position and rank."

Chairman Yang's right fist begins to tremble, as he hides it within his left.

"I spent too much time in that form." He thought while glancing towards Lazlow Jr. *"Oh, how youth is wasted on the young."*

"Thank you, Sanda Chief!" Yang replied. "You must know a thing or two of smashing skulls yourself."

The two grin and nod to each other, as Faxion accidentally trips and drops the tablet on Caffo's big toe.

"Urp, gaah!" Caffo writes in pain.

"Oops! Sorry lad, let's fix that right up." Said Faxion.

"No! No no." Replied Caffo, trying to remain calm. "You've done enough today, Deadeye. Thank you kindly."

Chairman Yang draws his Chatch to his face. He mutters into the device; "Bring it in for a landing. And take the wounded inside."

Moments later, a small airship touches down beside them. Several medics with gurneys march out, lifting a sleeping Pilet and Yuuna and ferrying them onto the vessel. Two of them try hopelessly to lift Cornelius, only to be toppled over by his immense, brolic weight. They return with a mechanical gurney that barely manages to hoist the slumbering Elite. As the three unconscious candidates are taken aboard, the Chairman continues.

"All of you here have done enough to earn your badge today, there's no need for you to continue the fight." He motions to the Blades and Fossil creatures doing battle in the distance. "Those who you see here are more than equipped for the foe at hand. I'd understand if everyone wants to hop on that ship and head back to the capital. That offer extends to my officers as well."

After a brief pause, Man O' War Puerto turns to Danba the Witchdoctor.

"My crew's free for the afternoon, what about you?"

"I don't have nowhere to be, brotha." Danba replied. He looks at The Funk Munkeys. "You all busy?"

Clint and Svenn simply shake their heads "no", while Lukah picks up the mic.

"Hell nah."

The "shinging" sound of a sword leaving its scabbard is heard.

"We're always down for a scrap." Said Arturo, as he pulls the dueling sword from his hip. The serrated edge of his M8 Shred gently rips at the scabbards lip on its way out.

The proctors look at one another for approval, before silently nodding in agreement.

"What about you, tough guy?" Scott said with a smirk, patting Bhujanga on the back.

The Emerald Flamecaster cultivates a small fireball in his hand, before clenching his fist tightly around it.

"These *weak* things bore me. But if you insist, I'll stick around."

Faxion and Kenzo look to Faith and Max.

"Welp, what do you say?" Said Faxion.

Max clenches his drawing Lacerate, his grip indenting in the wrapped leather. He turns to Faith and nods, as the Elder Sierro pulls the tome from her satchel.

"This test isn't over yet." She replied. "Let's finish it."

Faxion grins. He stands before the exam group, his arms folded in a relaxed, yet authoritative posture.

"I believe you have your answer, sir."

"Heh." Chuckles Chairman Yang. "Hope you know what you're getting into." He fiddles with his Chatch, as a state of the art program begins to draw Chairman Yang's weapons into the sand. A huge, sawed-off plasma shotgun appears. Alongside it lies a massive, double-edged, infrared battleax; with half the handle chopped off for single handed use. Yang lifts his weapons, activating the infrared function on the ax and powering up the plasma shotgun.

Vrrrr

Both weapons release an ominous hum throughout the air.

"Blades! Draw arms and fall in line!" Yang barks. He points his sawed-off at the immense waves of undead soldiers, at war with the Strikeforce and Blade reinforcements. Twisting a notch on the gun with his thumb, he pulls the trigger; firing an explosive projectile at the enemy.

The neon-green plasma shot erupts into an immense fiery explosion on impact, leveling dozens of skeletons in an instant. In awe, Dex nudges Dustin with his elbow.

"That's some serious distance for a sawed-off..."

The Chairman cries out.

"Now! Engage!!"

The exam group unleashes a unanimous warcry, as they dash towards their foes with haste. Rushing the enemy forces from behind, they sandwich the skeletal soldiers between the FC Strikeforce and The Hired Blades reinforcements. Twister's flying, infrared spines whiz past the Funk Munkeys and straight through their foes; as Svenn and Clint strum flamethrowing guitar notes onto the enemy crowd. Dunya vigorously performs the flare Pheasant dance of the Itedonians; leaving flaming, explosive footprints throughout the desert floor. Puerto draws his Papercut, as he assists Max and Kenzo in ruthlessly cutting a path of chopped bones towards the Hired Blades main forces.

"Stand back!" Exclaims Puerto, as he raises his auric jellyfish tattoo aloft. *"Nematostorm!"*

A barrage of azure, electrically-charged aura tendrils rush forth from his palm; whipping and frying the enemy forces before them with ease.

The path to the Blades is finally cleared, as the battered candidates rush through under cover fire of plasma, laser, and lead. The roaring praise and joyous cheers of The Hired Blades drowns out the sound of metal clashing for a moment, as the exam group is welcomed into their new mercenary family. Together, the collective Hired Blades stand firm against the waves of oncoming undead. Planting their feet in the sand, with infrared weapons drawn and guns trained on their foe, they rush the skeleton army head on. A unanimous war cry rings throughout the desert, as hot metal collides with weathered bone.

Hired Blades from Hatchidori draw their Lacerates, Shreds, and all manner of foreign sword against their foe; riddling the sand with cleanly sliced appendages. Kettlenian Elites wield their mechanized, morphing weaponry; massive shields with protruding machine guns, warhammers with grenade launchers housed within, infrared halberds that fire plasma beams from the butt end of the polearm.

Itedonians, Zardenians, Menanois warriors, and many more peoples from all over the world make up the Hired Blades forces; forming a diverse cast of deadly warriors leveling the sands of Devil's Tongue.

But... as the battle continues, the Hired Blades soon realize how outgunned they truly are. With every skeleton felled, two more take its place; crawling hauntingly from the depths of the Cool Oasis. Chairman Yang battles his way towards Caffo Gilwick, cutting down scores of foes with his immense infrared battleax.

"They just keep coming, we've got to do something about that Oasis!" He said.

"We tried." Replied Caffo. "There's some form of powerful auracast at work, it prevents us from even freezing the damn thing solid."

"Well then we've got to disrupt the cast that's bringing them to life! We can't keep fighting them back at the rate they're spawning."

Overhearing the conversation from behind, Faxion draws near. He glares down at the golden tablet, then back at the Mirage Pyramid.

"Disrupt the auracast..." He thought. He taps away on the touchscreen of his Chatch, drawing it to his face. "Benny, I could use a ride."

"Roger that, Fax." Replied Benny, as his light aircraft soars through the skies toward the Veteran Blade's location.

Faxion hoists the golden tablet over his shoulder and beckons to The Chairman.

"Sir."

"What is it Fax?" Yang replied.

"I've got an idea, would it be too much to ask for a quick lift?"

As he says this, Benny arrives in the air above. The fighter pilot releases his hatch door with haste.

"Hurry up Fax we don't got all day!"

The Chairman quickly puts two and two together, requiring little explanation. He lowers his ax like a platform for the Veteran Blade.

"That looks heavy, you sure you can handle it?" Said Yang with a subtle grin.

"I'll manage." Replied Faxion with the same.

He leaps onto the infrared weapon, a foot landing on the flat of either ax head. The Chairman then fires Faxion effortlessly into the air, as the Veteran Blade flies into the awaiting aircraft with incredible velocity.

"Aaah!" Cries Faxion, as he's flung far quicker than he had hoped.

With heavy tablet in hand, Faxion slams into the roof of the aircraft and bounces off of the floor. The vessel shakes from the force of impact, giving Benny quite the fright in the process.

"Holy shit!" Benny yells in surprise. "C'mon boss, easy on the merchandise!"

The Chairman chuckles, twirling his ax jovially.

"Guess I got a tad too excited. Anyway, on with it now! Time is of the essence!"

"Wait!" Exclaims Caffo. He draws a small black device with a red button atop it from his jacket, tossing it aloft to Faxion. "You're gonna need it."

Faxion shakes his head to clear the cobwebs. He catches the device just as he comes to, giving Caffo a nod of acknowledgement before pointing to the Mirage Pyramid.

"I need to get to the top, STAT!" He said to Benny.

"Roger that." Benny replied. "Buckle up buddy, this ride is going to be a bumpy one.

Benny blasts off towards the Mirage Pyramid, thrusters firing at 100% across the desert skies. In an instant, the spirited fighter pilot clears the distance and arrives at his destination. Floating just feet above the Pyramid's peak, Benny opens the hatch door.

"You know, if you muck this up we're all gonna die." Said Benny with a mischievous smirk.

"Meh, I've been there before." Faxion replied, fighting to lift the heavy tablet over his shoulder. "That's where I do my best work.

"Yeah, if it were anyone else saying that I wouldn't believe them. Just be careful in there, we ain't young men anymore."

"Ha! Speak for yourself!" Laughs Faxion.

He dives from the aircraft, falling straight for the pyramid. Drawing Caffo's device from his pocket, he swiftly presses the red button. The shutter door for candidates to exit the top chamber slides open, revealing a stark darkness within. As Faxion continues to fall from the sky, he laments his current position.

"Oh my, I hadn't quite thought this part through..."

With a heavy crash, he falls to the ground within; the golden tablet protectively nuzzled between his arms. On impact, dust flies throughout the chamber, enshrouding the room in a cloudy mist. The red button flies out of Faxion's grasp from the fall, clacking along the ground and abruptly shutting the door above him. The Veteran Blade stands to his feet, cracking his back in disdain.

"*Cough* Ugh, *I am* getting old." He brushes the dust off his shoulder, reveling in the pitch blackness around him. He pats himself down, curiously checking his many pockets for the door switch. "Now where did that damn thing go?... Oh well, no matter." He holds his fist aloft, as the eagle tattoo of his forearm shines for a moment. "Rutilans." He cast.

His clenched fist takes to a brilliant blue glow. Eerie silhouettes of the hand's metacarpal bones can be seen through the translucent flesh of his fist. The arcane glow begins to light the whole room, as Faxion scans his surroundings curiously. Slowly waving his spectral hand to and fro, the Veteran Blade makes out what appears to be the wolf-faced sarcophagus from earlier. Above it, he spots what appears to be a wall mounted holster for a portrait of sorts. He holds the golden tablet aloft, eyeballing what seems to be a perfect measurement for the portrait holster.

"That's it, this must have come from there." He thought.

As he approaches the wall in question, Faxion takes note of the silver sarcophagus resting before it. With the top portion shifted open, the contents of the sarcophagus appear to be completely empty. Having never seen this room before, Faxion remains ignorant to the significance of this discovery.

"Wow, they took the body too? That's a big no no, the expedition team's really getting brave these days."

He stumbles over a pile of coins on the ground, nearly dropping the golden tablet. Catching himself by holding the edge of the open sarcophagus, he curiously continues to scan his surroundings. Lavish jewelry, fine ornamental weaponry and priceless antique furniture line the walls of the regal chamber. But just as his gaze begins to turn towards the far right side of the room, Faxion sees something curious out of the corner of his eye. Nuzzled between the spear racks on the wall, his peripheral vision picks up what seems to be a mysterious figure lying in wait. But as his eyes draw to the figure, the auric glow of his hands peeters out, leaving the Veteran Blade in darkness once more. He looks at his hand puzzledly.

"Well, that's not right..." He thought. He raises his fist, casting "Rutilans." once more.

The arcane glow returns to his hand, as Faxion swiftly turns to get a better look at the eerie figure. But shockingly there was nothing there, just an empty corner with a few spears leaning against it. The Veteran Blade shakes his head perplexedly.

"These eyes of mine, I must be getting older than I thought..."

Faxion goes back to the tablet's holster, lifting the heavy artifact to return it to its resting place. But just as he's about to snap the tablet back in, the glow of his hand abruptly goes out again. Surrounded by darkness once more, the puzzled look across Faxion's face begins to morph to one of silent concern. Unable to see the attachments for the tablets holster, he places the heavy artifact gently onto the ground.

"Callous." He cast, patting his chest to activate the auric armor.

But as just quickly as the auric armor begins to surround his body does it fade away into nothing, leaving Faxion defenseless. He seals his eyes tightly shut for a moment, taking a deep breath while cultivating aura. Suddenly, a heatless, azure flame overtakes both of his eyeballs. Faxion quickly starts to scan the room with his new, flame-covered eyes. But as quickly as he begins the search, the flames upon his eyes peeter out; leaving him stupified once more. A moment of silence goes by, as the Veteran Blade quickly realizes that he is not alone.

Shink *Vrrr*

The sound of Faxion's Papercut longsword extending from its hilt along with its infrared hum cuts the silence. The glow of the blades' superheated edge lights but a small perimeter around him, as he lies in wait for his foe.

"............."

"Agh!" Cries Faxion, as a mysterious blade cuts a slice into his calf.

He swings his Papercut swiftly behind him, hitting only air as the threat is nowhere to be seen. Faxion stands there, listening for some form of sound to retaliate to.

"...................."

"Ngggh!!" The Veteran Blade struggles to bite his tongue, as he's cut twice more in what feels like a single, deft swipe. Once in the shoulder, another across his mid-back.

Faxion swiftly releases a spinning slash all around him in response, yet again failing to strike a target. For a moment he stands awestruck, unable to comprehend the nimble silence of his foe. He glances at his weapon, peering contemplatively into the infrared glow of the edge. He listens to the blade's low hum, unable to make out any other sounds throughout the room. Nodding his head in acceptance, Faxion disengages the Papercut's infrared function. The glow of the blade's edge and its ominous hum are snuffed out, leaving a sharp, yet far less dangerous weapon in the hands of the Veteran. Faxion comes to his knees, breathing in and out, slowly and methodically.

ThumpThumpThumpThump *ThumpThumpThumpThump*

The rapid sound of his heartbeat rings in his ears. He continues his breathing technique.

ThumpThump *ThumpThump*

His heart begins to slow, as his blood pressure begins to descend.

Thump *Thump*

Slowly, his heart rate begins to decelerate to almost a stand still, as a silence as true as before he arrived returns to the chamber. As though time itself stands still; every entity throughout the room is locked in a silent, motionless pose. Whether it be ancient artifact, the golden tablet, the Veteran Blade, or the mysterious challenger, all remain still in the presence of the ominous silence.

That is until, they are not.

Suddenly, a sharp clang can be heard; followed by a heavy thud to the limestone floor...

The War is Decided

Meanwhile, the Hired Blades' forces and the FC Strikeforce continue to do battle with the skeleton army, slowly but surely becoming too surrounded for comfort. Engulfed in a sea of undead warriors, the allied forces begin to fight more drastically. Releasing immense, costly auracast techniques and massive barrages of missiles, plasma bullets and gunfire, they begin to steadily duplete their stores of ammunition and aura.

"Where the hell is Fax?!" Exclaims Chairman Yang. "We can't hold off these things forever!"

Caffo Gilwick fires a flying kick into a large skeleton, sending it barreling into several behind it and toppling them like a bowling ball. He follows up the kick with a Hollowpoint cast powered by a blue crystal on his vambrace, which freezes the lot of them in a glacier of crystalline ice on impact.

"Something's not right. It shouldn't have taken him this long to put back the tablet." Caffo peers up at the top of the Mirage Pyramid. "But he's one of our best. If something's giving *him* a problem, then I'm worried."

Kenzo cuts through a wave of skeletons with a lightning infused, slashing bolt of aura.

"Have you no faith in your ally?!" Said Kenzo. "If not for long, I know this man. If there is something in his way, I can assure you he will not hesitate to cut it down!"

Just as Kenzo finishes speaking, the skeletal army surrounding the allied forces begins to come crumbling apart. The glowing, arcane binding holding their articulating joints together begins to vanish, as each and every skeleton releases an astral cloud of what could only be described as a fleeing soul from the crown of their skulls. Waves and waves of the undead fall in an instant, as the sands of Devil's Tongue become visible once more.

"Is it... Is it over?" Said Max, still clutching cautiously to his Lacerate.

The Blades and Fossil creatures lie still for a moment, warily holding their weapons close.

".."

Suddenly, the topmost chamber of the Mirage Pyramid swings open; as a wounded Faxion waves back and forth at Benny from inside.

"Shit!" Exclaimed Benny. "Took you long enough! I was beginning to get worried!"

Holding his side in pain, Faxion simply smiles back at his friend. He looks back at the open sarcophagus for a moment. The bandaged corpse of an ancient warrior, draped in a dark cloak lies strewn across the foot of the ancient coffin. A bladed scepter with a purple stone affixed to the top lies clutched hauntingly in its left hand. Above the sarcophagus, the golden tablet showcasing the Serpent Dragon sits in its rightful place once more. Faxion glances up at his partner.

"I could use another lift." Said Faxion, grimacing in pain.

"Oh you're hurt... one ride comin' right up!"

As Benny ferries his wounded ally across the skies, the thunderous cheer of the allied forces drowns out the desert. Hired Blades fire brilliant shots of plasma into the air from their primed beam rifles. Twister the stegosaurus sends infrared spines soaring through the sky, the superheated edges creating a wicked whirlwind of light. Puerto holds his glowing jellyfish tattoo aloft, as dozens of auric jellies shoot forth from his hand. The bright, iridescent parade of invertebrates marches through the sky, bewitching onlookers in awe before exploding in a glorious burst of light.

As the exuberant crowd continues its thunderous cheers, Benny's ship zooms by, preparing for a landing by the Chairman. The landing gear to the light aircraft juts out from beneath, as the vessel slows to a near stop hovering just above the desert floor. The aircraft lands, ever so gently onto the sand. As the hatch door opens, Benny begins to walk out; a wounded Faxion's arm draped over his shoulder for support. Faxion's free hand hovers over his side, casting "Mend" while delivering healing aura to the bleeding injury. Yang quickly takes note of the Veteran's curious condition.

"The *hell* happened to you?" He said, lifting an eyebrow in confusion.

"It's a long story sir." Faxion replied. "But rest assured, I look *far* better than the other guy."

Yang grins, nodding his head in approval.

"You Goddamn better! Or I might regret what I do next!" Yang lifts his Chatch to his face. "Bring down the Pagoda."

"Right away sir." A voice replies.

As several Hired Blades come to Faxion's aid with healing auracast, his exam companions cut through the roaring crowd to greet him.

"Faxion!" Said Max, as he, Faith, and Kenzo begin to peer out from within a cluster of dancing Saber Nychus. "We were wondering where you went, I had feared some foul ghoul had gotten the better of you upon these cursed sands."

"Shit Fax, you look bad!" Exclaimed Faith. She shooes the medics away. "Thanks, but stand aside. I've got it from here, ok?" Faith opens her tome, pointing her palm toward her wounded ally.

"Praudah Ngroo Vripii!" She casts.

A small, verdant portal of aura opens up within Faith's palm; as long, salve laden green leaves protrude from within. They wrap and entwine Faxion's injuries, creating a cooling sensation everywhere they land.

"They're coated with medicine, that should help you feel better real quick." Said Faith.

Feeling the cooling sensation, Faxions eyes light up.

"Oh my! Well then, I think I quite like this." Faxion tips his hat. "Thank you kindly young lady."

Faith gives Faxion a hug, but soon notices a tinge of purple ooze beginning to secrete from the outside of the leaf wrap.

"Woah Fax, you were poisoned? The leaves, they draw out venom. Who the *hell* did this to you?!"

"It was, a *mummy* of sorts, in the Pyramid's royal chamber." He replied. "The bastard was good too. Sneaky, with an aura-canceling scepter."

"Aura-canceling scepter?" She replied. "No way... That sounds like-"

"Those skills, and such intellect!" Kenzo interjects. "What an impressive young woman your friend is, son. And beautiful too! You'd better not let her distract you on your path to greatness."

Max' face grimaces in discomfort.

"Father, don't make things weird in front of my friends...."

Faith overhears their exchange.

"Uhh... Thanks?" Replied Faith awkwardly.

"Now, there's something in which I've been meaning to do..." Said Kenzo. He turns to Chairman Yang inquisitively. "Master Blade, I overheard that this year's candidates have essentially completed their exam duties, and are now considered Licensed Hired Blades. Is this true?"

Chairman Yang spits some blood from a blow suffered during the battle.

"True as the moon hanging over this desert, swordsman." He replied. "After the shit these kids have seen today, I'd be a whole-fool not to pass 'em. This year's crop is truly something special. I'm excited to see where they go from here."

"Fair enough." Replied Kenzo. He walks up to Max, putting a hand on his shoulder. "Kneel boy."

"I... Father..."

"I said kneel!" Kenzo repeats. "Today, we do this right!"

Max's lip begins to quiver, as he chokes to hold back tears. But the young swordsman composes himself, steeling his face and clearing his throat assertively.

"Of course, father." Said Max, as he takes to one knee.

Some of the Hired Blades begin to take note of the scene unfolding, as those from Hatchidori all kneel in respect. In the crowd, both blue and yellow haired members of the Sanda and Fubuki clan bow in reverence. Several swordsmen adorned with red, green, and purple stripes kneel as well, none above a third degree in rank.

Faith whispers to Faxion.

"What's going on?"

"Something that probably should have happened long ago." Said Faxion, with an unconcealable smile strewn across his face.

The Sanda Chief starts to vigorously rub his hands together, the friction beginning to generate visible heat waves from between his palms.

"Shoshin!" Casts Kenzo.

Suddenly, a blinding golden aura bursts forth from the Sanda master's right hand. The vibrant energy wraps and entwines mystically around his forearm, glowing with the intensity of a dying star. He clenches his fist, as the golden light begins to amass and cultivate between his fingers.

"From this point forth," The stored aura converges at the pad of his thumb, as Kenzo presses it against the hairline of one of his son's black cornrows. "I declare you a second degree warrior, of the House of Sanda."

The color of Max's cornrow instantly transforms from a matte black, to a stark blonde; as the braid of hair releases a blinding flash across the night sky.

The Hatchidorinese Hired Blades let out a unanimous howl, as they release brilliant, colorful flashes of aura from their own braids in response. The night sky becomes saturated in a captivating lightshow, dazzling the war-torn audience with breathtaking beauty.

"Hey." A voice beckons to Max from behind.

Shedding tears of pure bliss, the young Sanda looks back at the individual in question. Arturo of the Reaper Elite stands before him, hands rested on the hilt of his M8 Shred swords. Alarmed, Max springs to his feet and wipes the tears from his face. His hand hovers over the hilt of his Drawing Lacerate, ready to strike at the slightest provocation. The Fubuki swordsman's serious glare slowly morphs into a softer grin.

"Congratulations." Said Arturo, taking a bow to his Hatchidorinese colleague. "You definitely *fight* like a two stripe. I'd say it's about time you got more color in your hair."

Shocked, Max glances back at his father. Arms folded in a strong posture, Kenzo gives his son a slight nod of approval. Max then looks back at Arturo, with a subtle smile peeking from his stalwart face. The young Sanda bows in response.

"Thank you." He replied. "Our battle was the highlight of my exam."

"Heh." Scoffed Arturo. "A battle that's far from over. Stay on top of your game Sanda, I'll be waiting for round two."

Max's grin widens.

"You as well, or next time my Zen'no Divide will *surely* part you in half."

As the young warriors finish speaking, The Chairman's ship approaches, hovering above the group. The Crimson Pagoda draws near.

"Coming in for a landing sir." Said the ships pilot over the Chairman's chatch.

"Copy that." Replied Yang. He turns to the crowd of Blades before him. "What are all you staring at? Clear a space for the man!"

Various Hired Blades make way for the immense aircraft, packing their equipment and making their way back to their own vessels. The turbines of the Pagoda release pressurized air towards the ground, sending waves of sand flying as it slowly descends. With a revving vroom, the vessel finally grounds itself; the pistons of the hangar door beginning to release. The Chairman draws a key from his back pocket, firmly handing it to Faxion.

"For your exemplary work, Deadeye." He said. "Keep it up, we need more killers like yourself within our ranks. As my premier talent scout, I hope that this vessel will more than suffice to house you on your travels."

Astounded, Faxion is left dumbfounded by the generosity of his superior.

"I... Sir..." Said Faxion in stupor.

Just then, a much larger and grandiose airship arrives from behind. Another Pagoda styled ship, this one gold in color with silver lined tiles atop the roofs of each level. The Chairman continues to speak.

"Besides, this old heap is taking up too much space in my garage. My *new* ship has all the bells and whistles this one lacked!"

Max whispers to Faith.

"So, it's a hand me down?" He said.

"Are you surprised..." She replied, facepalming in awe of the Chairman's exchange.

With a subtle smile, Faxion takes the key and grasps it to his chest.

"I'll forever cherish your generosity, sir." He said.

Chairman Yang grins and nods to his subordinate.

"She's a good ship, treat her right and she'll take you to the ends of Giganus and back without a hitch."

As the moon begins to rise above the sands of The Devil's Tongue Desert, the ranks of the Hired Blades Association begin to rescind to their various airships. The Chairman and several executive Blades on hand meet with the FC Strikeforce, debriefing the mighty Fossil creatures on the exploits of the mission. Most of the exam proctors and candidates hitch a ride back to Grand Titanus on the Selena Marie, while Faxion invites Kenzo, Faith, and Max onto his newly acquired Crimson Pagoda. As a specialized clean up crew begins attending to the remnants of the battlefield; the battle-weary members of The Hired Blades Association nurse their wounds, while soaring leisurely over the night sky.

Peering through a window of the Crimson Pagoda, Faith stares intently at the ghastly Mirage Pyramid in the distance. Faxion approaches from behind.

"Everything alright?" He said.

"I just wonder how Yuuna is doing, and Pilet..."

Sigh "Yes, the boy needs to learn to better control his gift. He'll be out for a while, but we both know he'll make a full recovery. And as for your sister? I wouldn't worry." Faxion rests his hand on Faith's shoulder. "She comes from a strong family, and she's only *begun* to tap into her incredible potential. The two are more than worthy of the moniker of "Licensed Hired Blade."."

Faith smiles, sighing in relief..

"Yeah, I guess you're right." She glares back at the Pyramid, nudging towards it with her chin. "And what about that thing? Of everything I know about the Rok-Senn, nothing seems to point back to *that* abomination. It just doesn't make sense."

"Welcome to the world of the mercenary." Replied Faxion. "You'll see a *whole lot* of that."

"A lot of what?" Questioned Faith.

"Things that don't make sense. Some of these things are nice! They couldn't hurt a fly. But sometimes these, *nonsensical* things are not so nice.

You know the kind, the ones that prey on the weak. The kind who take from the uninitiated, from those who cannot defend themselves."

"I do, I know that kind all too well." Faith replied.

"Just remember. *Understanding* these things? That's not your job. We have people for that, and of course you can help them if you'd like. But *your* job is to make sure these, *misunderstood* things do no harm, by any means necessary. And to that effect, I'd say that today you accomplished that mission quite effectively."

Faith offers Faxion a warm smile, before the two lean out over the ship's open window; surveying the starry night's sky.

The Crimson Pagoda soars over the desert, making its way towards the bustling city streets of Kettlena's sleepless capital. Following closely, The Selena Marie and various aircrafts ferry Hired Blades towards HQ; forming a scenic fleet across the sky. Weary Blades, young and old let their heads hit the pillow; earning a good night's rest from the throes of combat. And just as such sleeps the ancient weapon. The sands of Devil's Tongue whip against the Mirage Pyramid; as the titanic Morph slumbers, awaiting the call of its master once more...

CHAPTER

FIVE

Class of 2117

The bustling halls of Grand Titanus General Hospital. Lined with disheveled gurneys, dying potted plants and wet floor signs. Overworked and understaffed; the various doctors and nurses pace back and forth, attending to the wounded Blades of the battle at Devil's Tongue. It was the crack of dawn when a weary Faxion checked out of his hospital bed. Lethargically rubbing his eyes, he takes a sip of the freshly brewed coffee nestled between his cold fingers.

"*Yawn* God, I hope this stuff kicks in soon."

He makes his way down each crowded corridor, bumping various shoulders and struggling not to spill his piping cup of joe. As he turns a corner, the Deadeye runs into Puerto; Emissary to the Mystic Marauders. The Man O' War quickly spots him, grasping his shoulder inquisitively.

"Hey, is it me? Or is this place a damn maze?" Said Puerto.

Faxion chuckles.

"Ha! Yes, it is quite large." Faxion grips his nose. "And being full of sweaty, battle-weary Blades certainly doesn't help. I'm guessing you're headed to the same place, Puerto?"

"Yeah, I was hoping you knew the way. I've been walking around for half an hour! These nurses are so stressed out none of them seem to know where they are."

"Well you're in luck, follow me and I'll show you the way." Said Faxion, motioning for Puerto to accompany him.

The two Hired Blades trek the halls for several minutes more, before arriving at a wooden door with a glass window across the front. Inside they see the slumbering King Killer, strewn across the hospital bed in an awkward position.

"Does he always sleep like that? It can't be good for his back..." Said Puerto, a concerned, slightly condescending look in his eye.

"Afraid so. *Eh*, the boy's young. He'll learn when he starts to wake up feeling like a pretzel."

Faxion twists open the doorknob, as the two quietly stroll into the room. Pilet sleeps beside a curtain, blocking off several other beds in the room. Faxion gives him a shake, hoping to wake the sleeping youth.

Snoring and grumbling, Pilet's eyelids don't so much as budge. Faxion shakes him again, this time with a bit more vigor. But to no avail, as the Fiery Prospect continues to snooze incessantly.

"Hey man, you're shaking him pretty hard..." Said Puerto. "I think he's probably *wasted* from that crazy transforming thing he did yesterday. Why don't you just leave him til later?"

"Nonsense!" Faxion replied with a grin. He draws a Papercut from his hip, pressing the trigger to eject the blade from the hilt.

A short, single-sectioned blade, this one only the size of a dagger. The infrared edge begins to heat, as Faxion gently presses against Pilet's left butt-cheek.

Puerto watches in terror, grimacing at the sight.

"What a psycho... Glad I'm not the King Killer." He thought.

Tsssss

As the flat of the Papercut dagger lightly sears the flesh of Pilet's glutes, his eyes begin to slowly flutter open.

"Hnnng, so tired..." He mumbled.

"..."

After a moment, the pain begins to set in. Pilet's eyes widen in shock, as he leaps from his bed onto the white, tiled hospital floor.

"Gah!!" He exclaimed, grasping his rump in fright. "What the hell! I'm on fire!"

"Shhhhhshshshsh, hush." Said Faxion, rescinding the blade. "I only took a little off the top. You'll be fine! We could use it for a sandwich later or something..."

"Like hell! What's wrong with you?!" Pilet spots Puerto propped against the wall. "And you couldn't stop him dude?! You *useless* prick!"

"Wha- hey! Don't look at *me!*" Puerto shrugs his shoulders. "You guys have a weird thing going on, leave me out of it..."

Pilet takes a seat on the hospital bed, struggling to keep the singed butt cheek hanging off the edge.

"God damn it. Now I can't sit right. Wait..." Pilet scans his surroundings. "Uh, am I in the hospital?"

"Grand Titanus General." Said Faxion. "Listen, we need to talk about your... let's say, "unique skills". They have, with no exaggeration, "put you in the hospital"."

"They did?" Pilet replied. "I mean... I don't even know how I got here Fax. Last thing I remember I was kicking ass with Toste. We were racing to see who could get the most kills and then-"

The blinding light of the Pyramid Morphs cannon plays through Pilet's memory, as he watches the jade beam swallow up his stalwart friend once again.

"No..."

Pilet's lips quiver, as he covers his mouth with his clenched fist to hide the pain. His eyes well up with tears, instantly forming rivers that flow down rosey cheeks.

"What did I do... Please Fax, tell me it was a dream." Cries Pilet.

Faxion and Puerto fall silent, looking at the floor in lament.

"I just, there's no way man. He's gotta be hiding behind this curtain right?! It's a joke, it has to be!"

Pilet's violet eyes begin to shine with a menacing glow, the corneas red with exhaustion and rage.

"Stop that!" Hollered Faxion.

The shout of the otherwise docile Blade shocks Pilet, as the glow in his eyes begins to fade. Faxion wipes his face in frustration.

"Look, *that* is going to solve absolutely nothing! What part of "Ace in the hole" do you not understand lad? You're invoking the Fever Point every time you so much as stub your toe! If you keep this up, the very technique that is meant to protect you is going to put you in the grave!!" Faxion takes a breath, sitting beside Pilet on the hospital bed. "*Sigh* Look, Toste is dead. *Dead.*"

Pilet bites his lip in frustration. The gut wrenching reality of the situation begins to sink in, as his stomach churns in lament. Faxion continues.

"Accept it, understand it, and move on. I know he was your first loss, your first fallen brother in arms. I'm not asking you not to *feel,* but you cannot be swallowed by emotion every time you lose a companion. To do so will render you useless on the battlefield!" Faxion puts his arm around Pilet in compassion, giving him a gentle shake as Pilet wipes his tears. "This is the path that you've chosen Lad, you *must* get a hold of yourself. If you listen to anything I say *for once,* let it be this!"

The room falls silent for a moment, as Pilet heartily weeps for his fallen comrade.

"This is getting really awkward..." Thought Puerto. *"If the kid's gonna bust out into tears every time someone dies in the line of fire, the poor sap's going to have a short career."*

After a moment of silence, Puerto chimes in.

"Hey, King Killer."

Cleaning his face with his grimey, white tank top, Pilet turns his attention to the Man O' War.

"Yeah... what's up." He replied in a hoarse, raspy voice.

"Sorry, but... Shut the hell up."

"......"

Unsure of how to reply, Pilet simply glares at Puerto. The Man O' War continues.

"Look man, I've lost dozens of friends in the heart of a fight. Back in Port Lyso, Goddamn Pirates used to raid the harbor every *month.* Hell, my old man was one of 'em."

Faxion's eyebrows subtly lift in surprise.

"These bloodthirsty mongrels would show up at the end of the month, demanding their share for "allowing" the ships to pass through for trade. And if the people of Port Lyso didn't have enough, the pirates would just trash the dock and steal whatever they wanted! Ships, cargo, even women! My mom was taken captive. Shitty as it is, that's how I came to be."

Pilet looks to Faxion, as they both gulp at the somber realization. Puerto grits his teeth.

"They brought her back after they had their fun... And nine months later I was born, and raised into that constant hell. The village people suffered like this for *years,* scared to call for help, scared to stir the pot and fight back for fear of death. Those pricks wouldn't even let them leave town."

Puerto draws the Stinger from his hip, brandishing the barrel of the pistol with fervor.

"Until one day, they stopped giving a shit. They scrounged up all the cash they could, paid it to a vicious Hired Blade, and fought alongside him to take a stand. I was nine years old. That Hired Blade tore *right* through most of those pirates, but tons of the villagers got wasted in the process..." Puerto clenches his fist in rage. "My uncles, cousins, even some of my *best* friends. Their tombstones all share a space along those bloodied shores. Port Lyso will never forget the day *The Blade* came to town. He ultimately refused to accept the money, instead asking for a small hut on the cape. Then he retired to Port Lyso, spending his days teaching us the ways of warfare."

"This Blade you speak of." Interjects Faxion. "Based on your title, I assume you're referring to Vincent, "The Man of War"?"

"I am." Replied Puerto, symbolically raising the hand with the jellyfish tattoo to his face. "Look, sorry I'm getting off track. The bottom line is that you're probably going to bury even *more* friends before you end up in the ground yourself, Pilet. Honestly, get used to it."

Prrrt

The mild sound of flatulence fills the air, as the trio begins to smell the aftermath of a wicked fart.

"Shit!" Exclaimed Puerto. He violently tosses a nearby empty vase into the curtain behind Pilet. "And I'm going to bury *you* much sooner, Cornelius!"

The vase knocks down the curtain; revealing Cornelius and Yuuna, reclined on each of their hospital beds spanning the rest of the room.

186

"Yuck dude!" Yells Yuuna. "I said not to make a sound, and it was just getting good too! Where the hell did that come from?!"

"I'm sorry, I'm sorry!" Replied Cornelius. "You see I've been holding that in for the past hour! My protein shakes are delectable, if not infamous for disaster!"

Puerto pulls a package of candy bars from his back pocket, tossing them at Conrelius' face.

"Well I came to bring you your favorite candy, jackass. Watch your bowels, I hope I don't end up paying for it later!" He Exclaimed.

Cough *Cough* "Oh crap." Said Pilet, covering his face in his forearm. "How long have you two been spying on us?!"

Faxion simply pinches his nose and turns to Yuuna and Cornelius.

"Oh why hello!" He said with a nasally voice. "Glad to see you're both healthy and well. You both did a bang-up job in the desert!"

"Why thank you kind sir!" Replied Cornelius. "Apologies for the foul stench of my morning glory."

"Foul is right!" Said Yuuna. "Oh, and hi Fax!" Yuuna dashes for Faxion, clenching him in a loving hug. "Glad to hear you're alright too. I heard you got hurt in the battle!"

"Oh it was nothing, nothing more than a "papercut" really! Bahahaha!" Faxion dangles the hilt of his Papercut longsword from his fingers.

"......"

"Yeahh." Said Pilet. "Well, alright Fax, I get it. I gotta stop using Fever Point for a bit. And I gotta *start* using my head, not losing it. But..." Pilet hangs his head. "Toste..." He looks to Faxion. "When... does the pain stop?"

Faxion takes off his fedora, holding it in his hands and fidgeting anxiously with the inseam. He glances at his pupil.

"I'll let you know when I find out, Lad." He places the hat on Pilet's head. "I'll let you know when I find out..."

Red Sky at Night

The group recounts the events of yesterday, reveling in the thrill and the agony of their experiences. After some time; they exit the hospital room, checking themselves out at the busy reception. The group disperses as they leave the bustling hospital, each preparing themselves for the first mandatory event of their graduation. "The Funeral of The Fallen". Pilet and Faxion trek through the hectic streets of Grand Titanus City, heading back to their hotel rooms in The Free Enterprise. As they arrive at the 35 floor skyscraper of a condo, Pilet gets a message on his Chatch.

"Hey idiot, don't be late." - Faith.

"Tch. Some things never change, huh."

Pilet replies with an emoji of a middle finger, as he and Faxion walk through the doors of The Free Enterprise. Moments later, Pilet is rummaging through his closet for a reasonable suit to wear.

"God, it's only been a few days. How did it get so dusty in here?"

As Pilet pokes and prods through his hung clothing; he pats down his denim jacket, causing the worn knife his childhood friend James had gifted him to fall to the ground.

"Yikes! Damn thing almost stabbed me in the toe. Good thing it didn't, or according to Fax I'd be in Fever Point right now..."

He lifts the dagger to his face, examining the chipped and worn edges. A rush of warm childhood memories floods Pilet's mind, as he recounts endless afternoons hunting snakes with James in the wetlands of Chamboree. He takes a deep breath.

Sigh "That doofus. I wonder how he's doing."

After a moment's pause, Pilet returns to his denim jacket curiously. He digs through the inner pocket, sifting through old candies and loose aurem bills until he ultimately finds what he is looking for. He draws Nivia's letter from within the jacket, folded into a small, neat square. Nivia, a young woman from Chamboree, and good friend to Pilet; had handed him a letter upon his departure. A wonderful letter, with lots of encouraging words and sentiments; and a bold proclamation of her love for the Fiery Prospect.

Unfurling the letter and reading it over once more, Pilet feels a warm pressing in his stomach. His chest becomes heavy, as the boy from Chamboree folds it back into a small square. He recounts his conversation with Yuuna, in the fishmarket of the village Gidah.

"I just want to wait until I pass this test. I want to go back home as a Licensed Hired Blade before I talk to anybody from Chamboree. Until I've

got that badge, I'm just not doing it. I haven't talked to my grandpa or my grandma or my best friend OR the woman who loves me. I'm not ready yet, I'm not... I'm not good enough yet!"

Pilet holds the letter in his hand, staring at it with a glare that could melt the hull of The Selena Marie.

"I... I still don't have that badge yet." Thought Pilet. *But I passed, I'm basically a Licensed Blade, right? I should be good enough now. So why do I feel like I'm not? And, when will I feel like I am?..."*

Riddled with self doubt, the young Blade shuffles haphazardly to his expansive apartment window. The view at the 32nd floor gives him a clear sight of the city's skyline. He gazes at the scarlet evening sky, lost in the beauty of the maroon clouds dancing before the setting sun.

Pilet cracks open the window, lifting it up as he leans outside for a better view. He sniffs the crisp air, far above the pollutant smog of the passing hovercars.

"Red sky at night, sailor's delight. Just like Grandpa used to always say. With the air pressure changing, tomorrow should be beautiful."

He looks at the letter in his hand, sighing heavily before holding it out over the open window. The breeze blows the opened letter to and fro in Pilet's grasp, as if struggling to free itself from his loosening grip.

"But... Can tomorrow possibly be beautiful without you?..."

"Well then, let's talk about it."

Several hours later, Pilet and Faxion arrive at an immense funeral home, four times the size of a traditional one. Faxion pulls up in a sleek, black SUV with a bulky frame. His signature vehicle; The Rhino. The tires to the vehicle lay folded horizontally into the underside, as each one propels the car inches off the ground via hover technology. Faxion drives into the closest spot he can find, nestled far too close to a verdant green car with custom flame decals near his passenger side. Pilet sees the lack of space he has to exit the vehicle, shaking his head at Faxion and giving him a disdainful glare.

"Really?" Said Pilet. "I'll swing this door wide open and wreck this dude's paint job, you *know* me. You *know* I've got no problem with that."

Faxion giggles.

"That's Bhujanga's, I'll tell him you did it." He said with a devilish grin.

Pilet's eyes light up. He recounts the time when Bhujanga handed him and Faith the bag of HBA dog tags, taken off of countless other candidates by sheer force.

He gulps, staring at Faxion for a moment with pure contempt. Faxion exits the vehicle from his side, forcing Pilet to crawl over the center console and out through the driver's side as well.

"Dick." Muttered Pilet.

Faxion tips his hat to him, as they make their way towards the funeral hall. Approaching the huge, decorative mahogany doors, Faxion and Pilet flash their ID's to security guards outside. The guards take the ID's, scan a handheld tablet and flash the two a thumbs up, one of whom stating "You're on the list, good to go."

They then proceed through the front door and down a long hall embellished with all manner of colorful flowers in expensive looking vases.

"Damn, they have security for this?" Said Pilet. "It's just a funeral, do things get *that* bad?"

"Ooh you'll see, you will see..." Faxion replied.

The two come upon a set of heavy double doors at the end of the hall. Pushing the doors open, Pilet is greeted with the sight of many clamoring, boisterous crowds of people. Rows of seats fill the immense room, as many disgruntled funeral goers occupy them while conversing about the event. In front of the massive room sits a podium on a stage, with a very large screen mounted across the wall. The screen depicts old photos of deceased exam candidates, arm in arm with their families and loved ones. As Pilet and Faxion cut through the crowd to find their seats, they begin to overhear the grief stricken conversations of their peers.

"Brandon, my little boy!" One funeral goer said, rocking a crying baby in her arms. "I told him not to do this exam, I told him to just be a fisherman like his father! He was only 19. Why? Why didn't I stop him?!"

"It's the God damned media!" Exclaimed another disgruntled patron. "They make this nonsensical violence look like it's brave *hero* work, convincing the young people it's all sunshine and rainbows. But it's not! I always knew the Hired Blades were a bullshit organization. They're in the business of taking people from their families!"

Continuing to pass through the boisterous crowd, Pilet begins to hold his head down in unease.

"Wow, I... I never really thought about the candidates who died along the way like that." Said Pilet. "I figured they knew the risks, and whatever happens, happens. I guess this is why I never told Grandma and Grandpa about, well, what could *happen*..."

"You're not the only one." Said Faxion, pointing over his shoulder to a man shouting in the distance.

"Where is my daughter!!" Hollered the angry man. "She said she was going to the city take a test for a damn job! Now I get a letter that she was "lost in the line of duty." or whatever the hell that means! Where is she!?"

Security guards come to the angered patrons side, holding him back while trying to explain the situation.

"I guess not everyone's family would have been 100% supportive had they known." Said Faxion, taking a seat in the second row.

Pilet cringes at the realization. He takes a seat beside his mentor, gazing at the commemorative slideshow before him. Suddenly, he feels a meaty, firm grip on his shoulder from behind.

"I'm glad to see you've recovered from your tirade Pilet." Said a voice behind him.

Pilet turns to see Max, with Faith and Yuuna right behind him.

"Dude!" Exclaimed Pilet. "Long time no see! *I'm glad* you didn't turn into skeleton food while I was taking a nap."

Faith smacks Pilet in the back of the head with her book.

"Ow!" He cried.

"That's for being an idiot." She said. "Try not to scare us like that anymore alright?"

"Grr, I'll give your ass something to be scared about." He muttered, rubbing his smarting head.

Yuuna nudges Faxion out of the seat on the edge of the row.

"Faaax!" She said. "Let me sit there! What if I suddenly have to pee?"

"I, what?" He replied. "How often does that happen to you?"

"It doesn't." Said Faith. "She's just trying to get the edge seat so she can make a dash to the refreshments when they come out. *Right* sis?"

".... Hush." Yuuna replied.

Taking their seats, They are soon greeted by the sight of Bhujanga Garuda and Scott Diliger, sitting right before them in the front row.

"Yo." Said Pilet, tapping Bhujanga on the shoulder. "Listen, I know we're not supposed to talk about this here but uh... How many of these guys did you put in those caskets?"

Wide eyed, the rest of the group scolds Pilet for his boldness.

"None." Replied Bhujanga. "I beat the brakes off of the candidates who gave me their dog tags, but they did so willingly. I'm not in the business of taking lives unless it's absolutely necessary."

Stunned by the realization; Max, Faith, and Yuuna fall silent. Scott turns to Faxion and begins to whisper.

"Hey Fax, your friend's not very nice."

"I know." Faxion whispers back. "Isn't it great?"

The two giggle to themselves, as an executive of the Hired Blades public relations department takes to the podium.

"Good evening ladies and gentlemen." He said.

Members of the crowd look on with contempt and disdain for the executive. He continues.

"On this night we honor the valiant efforts of the brave candidates who undertook this year's exam. We take a look at the accomplishments, the many victories and beautiful memories that these courageous warriors shared in life."

Members of the audience begin to interject.

"Guess they didn't accomplish *enough* huh?"

"Why don't you make this stupid test a little safer, dickwad!"

"Ahem." The executive clears his throat, tugging the collar of his dress shirt to air out his sweating chest. "Right, well... If you'd take a look at the screen, you'll see a wonderful, touching moment between-"

He's interrupted again.

"Shove that beautiful moment right up your ass!" Said an angered funeral goer. "This half-assed funeral isn't going to give me my brother back!"

Pilet whispers to Faxion.

"Psst, Fax. This is cringy, why do they even put these people through this? The city's just gonna pay for all of their separate funerals right?"

"It's a mandatory event." Faxion replied. "A bit of a spiteful move on the city's part. The Mayor hates The Hired Blades, and he hates having to shlep out the funds to cover the candidates funerals every exam. So the deceased's families have to attend this wretched funeral in order to qualify for compensation, and to have a separate funeral covered by Grand Titanus."

Pilet puts on a disgusted face.

"What a piece of shit! No wonder everyone here is so pissed off..."

Members of the audience begin to stand to their feet, booing incessantly whilst throwing water bottles and assorted food items at the PR executive on the stand. Stuttering and shaking, the executive mumbles to himself.

"God I hate this job..." He beckons to the audience yet again. "Listen I'm sure we are all very shaken by this tragedy, I'd ask that you all find your seats and pay your respects to those who have fallen."

The crowd becomes increasingly rowdy, as security Blades start to form a line in the front.

"Should we intervene?" Said Max, turning to Faxion.

Faxion shakes his head no.

"That's why *they're* here. Besides, this happens every time! They'll calm down, sit for the show and leave with their checks. Just relax Max."

"Yeah but, they're really getting into it." Said Faith. "Oh shit!"

Suddenly, an angered civilian picks up his chair and tosses it over the security Blades, cracking the PR executive head on. He falls to the ground, holding his head as vibrant blood begins to pour down from a gash on his hairline. The security Blades immediately restrain the assailant, pressing him to the ground whilst locking his arm behind him at a painful leverage.

"Stop now, civilian!" Hollers the security Blade. "Do not force me to use drastic measures!" The Blade reaches for his Papercut, pulling the hilt from his belt without releasing the blade. The assailant begins to cry, shouting profanities at the security Blade atop him.

"Get your hands off of me you bastard! You killed my son, you piece of shit!!"

The sight of the restrained man triggers more members of the audience to take a brazen stand. They march toward the security Blades, causing the Blades to draw their Stinger pistols and point them at the audience. The security Blades begin to shout orders at the aggressive attendees.

"Yield!"

"Stop your advance!"

"Do not force me to use drastic measures!"

All the same things they are taught to say, unable to communicate in a heartfelt or honest way. But the crowd keeps coming, as the exams graduating candidates stand to their feet in the assorted front few rows.

"What can we do?!" Says Wendy of the Mystic Marauders. "I mean, these aren't Wurm lizards or those ruin Morphs. These are like, people! Can't we get in trouble for hurting them?"

"I'd say stay back honey." Replied Dunya. "This isn't our problem, the last thing we need is to lose our licenses before we even get them."

"Why do we even have to be here?" Said Lazlow Jr. "We won, didn't we? We're alive, and these losers are dead. So what, now we have to sit around and "honor" they're failure? And you wonder why all these hopeless poor bastards are mad?"

"He's got a point." Said Arturo. "You all don't want to admit it, but everyone we're here for accomplished absolutely nothing in the exams before they died. I'd be mighty peeved too if I was forced to sit and watch this shitshow."

Suddenly, a civilian draws a 9mm pistol from inside his jacket. With tears in his eyes, he aims it at the PR executive on the stand.

"How did he get that in here?!" Exclaimed Yuuna. "They frisked most of the people who came inside!"

Turning his head at the unanimous gasp of the crowd; Faxion hears the buzz of an infrared weapon beside him, followed by a faint whisper.

"Fleetfoot."

He turns back to see Pilet missing; as Max, Faith, and Yuuna look to him in surprise.

"Oh no, where is he..." Said Max.

Suddenly the sound of clanging metal rings through the room, as the unruly audience falls silent for a moment. Pilet stands before the gun wielding civilian, a single Dragonfly longknife pointed at his face. Suddenly, the barrel of the pistol falls to the ground, having been sliced clean through by the Fiery prospect's scorching hot blade. The civilian drops the minced pistol, holding his hands in the air in defeat. He wipes the tears from his face, giving Pilet a glare of pure contempt and hatred.

"Crap, we should go stop him." Said Faith.

But as she proceeds down the aisle, Faxion stops her from advancing.

"Just wait, let's watch." He said.

Feeling the energy of the civilians glare like a silent language to his soul, Pilet deactivates the infrared glow of his Dragonfly. He lowers his weapon, looking back at the civilian with a subtly somber glance.

"You're hurting, aren't you." He said.

Without responding, the civilian simply nods his head.

"Yeah, I get that." Pilet continues. "One of mine died here too. Who are you here for?"

Sniffle "Tina, her name was Tina." Said the civilian. "She was my fiance."

"Damn, I'm sorry to hear that." Replied Pilet. "Did you guys know how dangerous this test was?"

"Yeah, we did. We just, no. We knew what could happen."

"Doesn't make it any easier though, right?" Said Pilet.

The civilian looks up to Pilet, visibly surprised.

"No! No it doesn't! And no one else is talking about that!" He said.

Pilet sheathes his Dragonfly inside his suit jacket.

"Well then, let's talk about it." Replied Pilet, as he turns around and walks down the aisle.

He walks past a security Blade, who puts an arm out to stop him.

"Back to your seat candidate." Said The security Blade.

"Dude, really?" Replied Pilet. "Give me like, five minutes. Then if you want we can throw down. And by the way, I'm not a candidate any more." He walks by. "I'm a Hired Blade, and I'm saving *your* ass."

Pilet walks behind the podium, taking off his tie and tossing it to the PR executive.

"Tie that around your head, you're leaking everywhere man."

"Thanks." Replied the executive. He mutters under his breath as he walks away. "I swear I'm never working this bullshit event ever again."

Pilet then draws one of his Dragonflies once more, viciously stabbing it into the podium. The sudden thrust causes the crowd to gasp in shock.

"Yo." Said Pilet, now addressing the silenced crowd. "So everyone's here because they lost somebody they loved, right? Yeah, that sucks. You're all probably sad because you didn't want them to do this, to try to live a life so full of danger and shit all of the time."

Several members of the crowd begin to talk amongst themselves, nodding their head in approval.

"You can say it, you didn't want them to take the Blades exam." He said with a sarcastic glaze. "*But,* guess what... they did it anyway. And you know why?"

Audience members fall silent.

"Because being a Hired Blade is the best damn job in the world! If that's what you *want to do.* And I guarantee you that if you turned back time and tried to get them to stop a hundred more times, you're probably still gonna fail! Look, what do you do for work dude?" Pilet points at a random civilian.

"Uh, I'm a truck driver." He replied.

"Great!" Said Pilet. "I mean that... kinda sucks! To *me,* but to you that might be the coolest job ever!" Pilet chuckles, shrugging his shoulders. "And if it's not, then work towards doing some cooler shit some day! Look, the bottom line is that everyone you people lost probably spent the last moments of their life doing *exactly* what they wanted to. Which is fighting for a better tomorrow! The Hired Blades were born to protect, and to defend the weak. And that's not always easy, sometimes you get hurt." Pilet grits his teeth, clenching his fist in frustration. "My friend lost his life. I watched it happen without... without being able to do a single thing to stop it." Pilet's lips quiver, his eyes tear up as they begin to glow their signature violet.

"Don't stop now boy." Muttered Faxion. "Keep it together..."

Pilet takes a deep breath, the audience now seeing the visceral emotion in the boy from Chamboree. He composes himself, halting the Fever Point in its tracks.

"Look, I took the exam your loved ones took, and I passed." A glint of raw emotion twinkles in his eyes. "I can promise you that I'll live on to honor their hopes and dreams."

Members of the audience begin to cry, pulling handkerchiefs from their pockets to clear their faces.

"Every time you see a Hired Blade, I want you to see who you lost in them. Because that's who they are, and who they wanted to be!"

The silence in the room is unparalleled, as Pilet steps down from the podium and approaches the gunman once more.

"I hope that helped, I'm sure your fiance would have made an amazing Blade."

He nods his head, crying profusely and running into Pilet's arms.

"She would have, I know she would have. Thank you."

Pilet tries not to visibly cringe at the grown man crying into his chest. *"Poor guy. But man, this got weird fast..."* He thought.

The crowd begins to cheer at the sight, giving Pilet a round of applause before taking to their seats. Pilet leaves the man and returns to his seat as well, where his peers give him a shocked expression.

"What?" He said. "*Someone* had to tell them what's up. I spit the truth, yo."

"Aaand just like that, you ruined it." Said Faith. "Also, I think that guy blew his nose on you or something."

Faith points toward Pilet's chest, where a fresh puddle of mucous lies right below his handkerchief pocket.

"Oh shit! Are you kidding me?!" Exclaimed Pilet.

The group laughs as Pilet proceeds to remove his jacket and throw it in the trash. Faxion puts an arm around his pupil.

"Stop being weird man." Said Pilet.

Faxion grins, giving Pilet a noogie.

"Good job lad. Good job."

The evening proceeds famously well, as members of the audience laugh, cry, and converse with each other. They honor the memory of their fallen loved ones, praising the Hired Blades for their service. As the different slides and videos go by, Toste's segment begins. The group looks at Pilet, who composes himself surprisingly well throughout. But as photos of the legendary swordsman play across the screen, Pilet sees one of Toste arm in arm with a woman, with a young boy standing beneath him. He then hears a woman sobbing across the room, drying her tears with her blouse. The woman, unmistakably the same as in the photo, with the same young boy sitting beside her.

"Fax, is that... his family?" Said Pilet.

Faxion nods his head.

"Would you like to be introduced?" Faxion replied.

"I... after. Let's wait til after."

The events of the night conclude, as weary audience members head home to rest their weeping eyes. As Toste's family exits the funeral hall and proceed to the parking lot, Pilet and Faxion approach from behind.

"Joline!" Said Faxion, beckoning to the woman.

The woman turns around, her brunette, curly hair bouncing in the wind. The young boy, his hair the same shade with a buzz cut, and a red and white striped shirt. Maybe no older than 2, he stands puzzledly, holding his mothers hand whilst wiping the late hours fatigue from his face. At the sight of Faxion, Joline smiles and wipes her tears.

"Faxion, how've you been?" She said.

Faxion simply hugs her, as she breaks down; proceeding to cry into his arms.

"I'm sorry, I was there, I could have done better." He replied.

She separates herself.

"No, don't say that. He knew what he was getting into. You did everything you could and more. I saw the videos of that monstrosity in the desert. I'm, *I'm proud* of my husband for having defended us from *that*." She sees Pilet. *Gasp* "And who is this?"

Unsure of what to say, Pilet simply waves at her. Joline beckons him over.

"Oh come here. Is this Pilet? Are you the new friend?" She said, embracing Pilet in a tight hug.

"I, yeah..." Said Pilet. "Listen, your husband was... He was just awesome." Pilet pulls the parrying dagger gifted to him by Toste from a holster behind him. "He gave me this, but... I don't fight like him." He looks down at the little boy. "But I'm sure he will. Is it ok if I..."

"Aw, are you sure?" Replied Joline. "It was a gift to you, I'm sure there was some meaning behind it if *he* thought it would serve you. Honestly, thank you. But you should hold onto it."

Pilet looks at the boy, who quietly gazes up at him in confusion.

"Does he know?" Said Faxion.

"He doesn't understand yet, I think we'll keep it that way for now." Replied Joline. "In time he'll come to understand, and I'm sure he'll be swinging those damn swords around just like his father in no time."

The boy grasps at Pilet's pant leg, lightly tugging while smiling at him. A tear comes to Joline's eye.

"It means he wants you to carry him." She said.

Pilet shoots her a curious look.

"Is that ok?" He replied.

"Of course! Please I'm sure he'd love it, both of them would..."

Pilet smiles at the child, hoisting him up and making funny faces. The boy giggles, shaking his legs in glee. Pilet tries to hide the tears forming in his eyes.

"This kid is too cute, and he's got *his* eyes, right?" He said, turning to Faxion.

Faxion smiles and nods.

"He sure does. I'm sure one day he'll have his courage too."

Joline holds back tears.

"Well look, let's exchange contact information and keep in touch guys!" She said. "I'm sure the house of Menanois could be of some use to you in the future, and maybe we could use your help too."

"That'd be great, Joline." Said Pilet. "And anything I can do, just let me know."

The two converse for several minutes more, exchanging Chatch numbers before parting ways. As Pilet and Faxion head back to the Rhino, they reflect on the events of the evening.

"You know, it's crazy Fax." Said Pilet.

"What is?" Faxion replied.

"I can't imagine what life would be like for my grandparents if I died during the exam." Pilet pauses, staring into the night sky. "It never really hit me until now. But if this job is as difficult as they say, I guess I'd better start to imagine that more..."

"That's the last thing you should be worried about lad." Replied Faxion. "Live life to the fullest, while you're alive. Worry about being dead once you get there, and not a moment sooner..."

The two make their way back to The Free Enterprise, parting ways at the 32nd floor for their respective rooms. As Pilet's head hits the pillow, he recounts the events of the evening with a heavy heart.

"Being a Hired Blade is some heavy shit, I just hope I can keep up with the others at the pace this job goes..." He thinks of his grandparents, worrying

for a moment about the possibility of his demise. *"I don't give a shit about dying... I just can't imagine leaving them alone like that. Not after everything they've done for me, and my Mom..."* His eyes become increasingly heavy, slowly drooping shut under the weight of the day's mental fatigue. *"She'd want more from me, she'd want me to be the best I can be."* *Yawn* *And I know I can be the best, the best Blade there ever was..."*

Pilet's eyes flutter laboredly for a moment, fighting sleep. He makes out the image of his mother in the corner of the room. A surreal, teal silhouette of the woman who birthed him sitting crossed-legged on the cafe chair. She gives him an innocent, warm smile and waves. Pilet's eyes flutter open and shut one last time, before falling into a deep slumber.

"I'll be the best for you. I promise..."

The fiery prospect from Chamboree drifts off to sleep, as dreams of adventures soon to come fill his wandering mind.

Debriefing; More Questions than Answers

The moon and the stars dance over the night sky, until the warm rays of the sun signal for the celestial bodies to make way for the dawn. Across Grand Titanus city, the crisp morning air travels through the windows of HBA headquarters' boardroom. Filled with members of Grand Titanus legislative committee, board members of the HBA, and several other important Hired Blades; the bustling boardroom houses one of the largest debriefings to date.

Chairman Yang paces back and forth at the head of the boardroom, his massive legs quaking the floor beneath him with every step he takes. Staring contemplatively into space; he suddenly pauses, reaching into his back pocket and pulling out a cigar. Yang places the cigar in his mouth, clamping it lightly with his teeth as he presses his crimson gem necklace against the lighting end. Slowly, the gem begins to glow and radiate heat.

Tsss

As if possessed by mystical embers, the arcane gem instantly singes the tip of the cigar. The Chairman takes a long, meditative drag, before puffing a cloud out towards the attendees. He speaks.

"After the events of the most recent Licensing exam, it's come to our attention that there's more to the Rok-Senn people than we thought we knew. While this should come to the surprise of no one, considering how rich in culture they are; it does expose to us a very important new finding in their history. To explain in detail our findings; I invite expert archeologist and one of our own Hired Blades, Scott Diliger. Take it away Scott."

Scott rises from his seat, nodding to Chairman Yang in acknowledgment as he moves to the head of the table.

"Thank you sir." Said Scott. "Good evening ladies and gents. So we've got a serious new finding on our hands here, several actually." Scott turns on a massive monitor spanning most of the front wall. As the screen comes to life, an image of the war-torn sands of Devil's Tongue displays in vivid detail. Multitudes of fallen skeletal warriors lay scattered across the scorching dunes.

"The first point of interest is that due to these findings, the Rok-Senn people have now been shown to employ ritualistic human sacrifice. Up until this point, all evidence that we've found on them had suggested they honored human life above all else. That is to say, no tribe would ever dare to kill another human in order to power any auracast. However, we've deduced that *all* of the skeletons that were reanimated had been sacrificed so that their collective blood could power the auric rune of this newly minted, *Mega-Morph.*" Scott scratches his head in confusion.

"This is unprecedented in their culture, as The Rok-Senn were religiously obliged to protect life at all costs! Excluding the bold participants of the treasure trials, but more on that later. The second thing of note here is the sheer magnitude of the weapon they've created, utilizing said sacrifice of course." Scott presses a button on the monitor's remote. The image changes from the army of skeletons to that of the Mega-Morph, preparing to fire its massive auric cannon.

"This shot was taken by a Dragonfly Seeker camera during the battle. An auric Morph *so large and powerful* that the Chairman himself had to come down to stop it, and *even then* he was only able to "turn off" the ancient titan. I can't think of a single enemy so vast or powerful that the Rok-Senn needed to sacrifice hundreds of lives to create such a super weapon."

Mayor John Dupree interjects, standing to his feet in contempt.

"And what if this ancient monster decides to awaken again? The fact is that at any moment this *behemoth* may re-activate and run amok across the desert, possibly even traveling as far as Grand Titanus!

Sigh "This is true." Said Scott. "Unfortunately, the Morph now lies dormant; submerged once more beneath the sands at the heart of Devil's Tongue. Look, clearly there's many factors about this situation that don't lie well with us. We need to analyze both what we know about the Rok-Senn so far, and what we've learned from this most recent encounter." Scott motions towards the center of the long table, pointing at Faith as she scribbles away at a notepad. "With me I've brought Faith Sierro, an expert in the culture and language of the Rok-Senn people. She's been a huge help in deciphering the meaning of this fiasco. Faith, any thoughts?"

"Yes, thank you Scott." Said Faith, putting away her notepad. "The Rok-Senn people were indefinitely known for their love and reverence for human life. While they were a competitive people, who went to war more than once historically; they would never kill unnecessarily. They were also known for their great skill in auracast. Many of our nation's "Kettlenian Standardized Auracast" come directly from inscriptions found within the many ruins scattered throughout Kettlena." Faith pauses, folding her arms contemplatively.

"Yesterday showed us a side of their behavior that we've never seen before; in the sacrificial offering of countless tribesmen and women. These sacrificed people were subsequently reanimated to battle us, which seems to have been part of this ancient trap set for some... *mysterious enemy*." Faith bites her lip, clenching her fist in lament.

"Now keep in mind, bringing life to the dead in such a way is labeled under "Necrocast", which was heavily forbidden by the Rok-Senn people. It has also been noted that the skeletal remains of these people match that of several *different* tribes of Rok-Senn. This is a startling find, as the various sub-tribes of the Rok-Senn have never shown signs to unite for anything. This combination of behaviors is *extremely* unlike them, and to be honest I'm still struggling with comprehending the motives behind it..."

"Thank you Faith." Scott replies. "Now, what we know is that the Rok-Senn were *excellent* trap setters. They were so good at setting traps that catching animals for both food and sport became too easy for them, thus leading to the creation of Rok-Senn treasure trials."

Scott fiddles with the monitor's remote, displaying images of several different ancient ruins shown in succession.

"As you can see here, the Rok-Senn were no slouches in the creation of complicated structures of great magnitude. Many of these were completely *laced* with deadly auric traps, easily triggered under the right conditions. The different tribes of Rok-Senn would create their own deadly trials, and invite rival tribes to attempt to solve them; promising great riches at the heart of the trial. Now, these treasure trials became the pride and joy of all Rok-Senn people, it basically became their most celebrated sport. And with our analysis of the Mirage Pyramid, we believe that it was set up in a manner similar to a treasure trial, but on a much grander scale than most."

Caffo Gilwick interrupts, wiping his face with his hand in befuddled frustration.

"Scott, all this background info is great. But *my* question is, what sets this thing apart from the rest? I know from the fight that it transforms and raises an army of the dead, so that's pretty different in itself. But what about what's inside? You're telling me that there's nothing that even *hints* toward the potential meaning to this nonsensical Pyramid?"

"Right, straight and to the point then." Replied Scott. "Well for one, most of the chambers of any treasure trial held some form of formidable enemy for the trials participants, but nothing completely out of the ordinary. A swarm of small Morph's, or maybe a single large and powerful one, that kind of stuff. But the chambers of The *Mirage Pyramid* held foes far greater and stranger than most. Hell, one chamber even had several Necrocasted "Kekkehio Shriidah"; an ancient, auracasting reptile so rare and powerful it was thought to be a myth. And in the top chamber, we found this..." The next image displays the ghoulish, bandaged corpse that did battle with Faxion strewn across the floor.

"Krohhsio, or "The bringer of Death"." Said Scott. "The mummified remains of the Rok-Senn Chieftain's most beloved bodyguard. A terrifyingly efficient assassin with an auracast-canceling scepter. He seemed to have been reanimated when the golden tablet was taken from its post." Scott grins. "Fortunately, it looks like our resident Deadeye was there to welcome him to the 22nd century."

Scott nudges his chin towards Faxion, as The Veteran Blade reclines in his chair towards the back of the room. He winks at his archeologist ally, tipping his hat in a friendly gesture.

"All in a day's work lads." Said Faxion.

Scott continues.

"Now the layout of the top chamber suggests that this was the final resting place of The Rok-Senn Chieftain. Bacara, the Mighty Sage." Scott changes the image to that of the sarcophagus, beside the wall mounted golden tablet. "Now we've been here for a while and I know you're all getting restless so I'll make this brief."

"Finally." mutters Mayor Dupree.

"Bacara was King of the Rok-Senn." Said Scott. "Both their wisest and most powerful auracaster by far. Atop the sarcophagus, the emerald wolf with ruby teeth has historically been used to represent Bacara throughout all of Rok-Senn culture. It's unknown as to whether he had passed away before or after the tombs being built, but for whatever reason his body was not placed inside his own coffin. Krohhsio's body was placed there instead, most likely as a trap for whomever would steal the tablet. Now the location of Bacara's final resting place has remained one of the biggest mysteries of Rok-Senn culture to date, and based on a hidden tomb found by one of this year's candidates, there's evidence that his body is still hidden within the pyramid." Scott points to the golden tablet mounted on the wall.

"Finally, the most important part. This tablet is a piece of history that has only been alluded to, but until the events of the Hired Blade exam we had no idea what we were looking at, *or* its significance." Scott outlines the Serpent Dragon along the tablet with his finger. "This Serpent Dragon represents "Braaga de Annihala" or "Braaga the Annihilator" in native Kettlenian. Lord of the all mighty Serpent Dragon race, Braaga has been the focal point of Rok-Senn religion throughout history. The all-powerful creator of auracast as we know it, Braaga has been said to travel between the spiritual realm and Giganus via the golden tablet, like a gateway..."

Shocked eyebrows raise throughout the room.

"He who possesses the tablet is said to have access to unlimited stores of aura, as well as complete and total mastery of all auracast techniques; past, present, and future. Needless to say, this isn't your average slab of gold."

One of Grand Titanus' legislative committee members raises her hand. Scott points to her.

"Yes?" He said.

"Mister Diliger." She said. "If this tablet is as powerful as you say, why doesn't The Chairman himself or another learned auracaster simply use its prowess to completely destroy the auric rune powering the pyramid?"

"And why would we leave such a dangerous piece of history mounted on a pyramid wall?" Retorts another committee member. "Couldn't some other powerful auracaster wreak havoc if it falls into the wrong hands?"

Chairman Yang Interjects.

"Because no one knows how to work the damn thing! There's no manual, not even a single historical account of *someone* from their time successfully using it for anything! Hieroglyphs just tell the tale of what it *can* do, but nothing of what it *has* done. If we were to try to futz around with it, we could cause catastrophic events to occur for the sake of curiosity." Yang takes a drag of his cigar. "And as fun as that sounds, I'm not willing to risk the safety of more of my Blades in order to do so."

Several Hired Blades in the room let out a sigh of relief. Scott switches to the next slide of images. Hired Blades, stationed around the perimeter of the Cool Oasis.

"Look, the Pyramid has sunken itself back beneath the desert." Said Scott. "It's safely being guarded by a band of Blades round the clock. The most important next step to take here is to continue searching for information to explain these new findings. I have a strong feeling that there's more than meets the eye to the circumstances of this year's Blades exam. Are there any more questions?"

The room falls silent, as the audience struggles to comprehend the new information they've been given.

"Alright then." Said Scott. "Thank you all for attending, that concludes today's debriefing."

Disgruntled and unnerved, the attendees begin to leave their seats and make for the door. As Faxion starts to see his way out, Scott and Chairman Yang beckon him over. Faith follows suit.

"Fax." Said Chairman Yang. He holds up the metallic, chromium necklace Pilet found in the Mirage Pyramid. "I want you to give this to that crazy kid from Chamboree."

"Oh?" Faxion replied, taking the chromium crystal. "May I ask sir, what is this?"

"Oh that's... Pilet's necklace, right?" Said Faith, recognizing the metallic gem.

"That's right." Said Chairman Yang. "The boy discovered this in the tomb of a very special ancient auracaster. Our medics found it on him when they picked him up in Devil's Tongue. We considered holding onto this for safekeeping, but I think it's in better hands with him."

"They change the nature of your inner aura." Said Scott. "There's about ten in total, scattered throughout the world. One for each element on the elemental wheel, and then one for pure aura. That one there's the Metal element, so it's gonna change any auracast Pilet uses into a metal type without having to learn metalcast. That crystal's location has been wracking the brains of archeologists for *years*. Leave it to Pilet to discover it by taking a piss where he's not supposed to..."

Chairman Yang proceeds to remove the crimson stone from around his neck. "While we're at it, give him this too." He slaps the crimson crystal into Faxion's hand.

Scott looks at Yang in shock.

"Chairman..."

"I have faith in the kid, Scott." Said Yang. "It takes months of training to make one if these work, and I watched him use one the moment he put it around his neck. The Key Crystals need a good home."

"Key crystals..." Thought Faith. *"Where have I heard of that before?..."*

Faxion takes the two crystals from Chairman Yang, nestling them away into the inner pocket of his olive overcoat.

"I'm sure he'll put these to good use sir." Said Faxion.

"I'd hope so, I'm gonna miss the little firecracker." Yang replied. "That one's fire, so watch out when he uses it."

Faxion and Faith anxiously glance at each other.

"Oh, wonderful..." Replied Faxion.

"I really wish he hadn't given you that..." Muttered Faith.

The four part ways, as Faxion and Faith head down the stairs and out of HBA headquarters. As they pass through the courtyard, Faxion holds the two Key crystals up to the sun. The glint of the sun's rays shimmer beautifully off of the metal and fire stones.

"So, what's so important about these stones?" Said Faxion.

Faith scrolls through her digital notes on the screen of her Chatch.

"You know, I'm not sure." Said Faith." I've read about them somewhere, I guess I'd have to go home and scan through my texts to find out more. Or I guess I could ask Scott."

"Why didn't you ask him *just* now?"

"Uhh... I was too embarrassed." Replied Faith, her cheeks beginning to blush. "I mean, I didn't want to seem like I didn't know anything."

Faxion looks at Faith with a subtle smirk.

"Ha! Hahahaha!" Faxion laughs hysterically.

"Hey! Shut up!" Exclaims Faith, her face turning beet red.

Faxion puts an arm around her shoulder.

"Aw lass. You've got storehouses of knowledge. Of this I'm sure he's certain."

"Yeah well, whatever..."

The two continue towards the parking lot, arriving at Faxion's Rhino. They plop down onto the seats of the bulky SUV, as Faxion twists the key in the ignition and pulls the shifter into drive. The wheels fold in, rotors within the center of the hub caps begin to propel the vehicle off the ground. Exiting the parking lot and beginning their trek through the bustling city streets, The Rhino effortlessly glides inches above the pavement like a paper airplane, flung from a window.

The PF1; Grand Prix

After some time, Faxion and Faith reach a massive colosseum with navy blue walls. Burgundy spires erect from between each level, giving the structure a cactus like appearance. From the spires, the flags of the planet Giganus' many countries hang, flapping proudly in the gentle breeze. Faith and Faxion exit the vehicle, making their way into the vast colosseum with anxious excitement.

The roar of the bustling crowds drowns out their thoughts, as they burst through the double doors of the entrance.

"Tickets please."

A doorman greets them with a gesture for their admission. Faith hands over two tickets to the doorman, as he stamps them with red ink.

"Ah, V.I.P. seating for the Hired Blades graduation ceremony! What luck you both have. I'm guessing a relative made the grade?"

Faith grins.

"Well, you're not wrong."

The doorman hands them back the tickets.

"Head through the corridor, down the hall and to your left. Your seats are front and center, smack dab in the middle of the action. The PF1 Grand Prix is going on right now, if you're quick you might catch the tail end of the two Dinos fighting for the belt! No pun intended."

"Thank you kindly." Said Faxion, tipping his hat to the doorman.

Faxion and Faith continue down the hall. Miscellaneous popcorn buckets and empty soda cans riddle the corners of the floor. They turn a corner, peeking through another set of doors and entering the stands. They're immediately met with the roaring cheers of the crowd, battering their eardrums with a startling intensity. As they look to their right, they're greeted by the sight of two Pachycephalosaurus; doing battle in the middle of an arena.

One Pach fighter; scales light blue, with a gunmetal gray cranial dome. The second Fossil creature sports black ankle braces, covered in radiant yellow scales which are now tinged orange with the hue of blood. Faxion and Faith glance up at the animated banner above the cage.

"PF1 Grand Prix: Middleweight Title fight. Stinger Logan V.S. Dunn the Matador."

Faxion points to the Yellow Pach fighter.

"That's Dunn, I helped train him! Glad to see him employing absolutely none of my teachings..."

Faith shakes her head in shock.

"Wait, you trained a famous Pach fighter? I don't know too much about this sport, but I know the yellow one. Dunn's the flashy knockout artist that keeps winning with barely a scratch on him right?"

"That's right!" Replied Faxion. "Although today, it looks like he has yet to wake up and smell the coffee. Seems to be he's getting whooped by the reigning champ in Stinger Logan. The blue fighter has a solid style with strong basics, the antithesis of any fancy knockout artist."

Suddenly, the two are interrupted by an empty water bottle bouncing off of Faxion's hat. Puzzled, they look in the direction of the weightless projectile; seeing Pilet, Yuuna, Max, and Kenzo yelling in the stands.

"Hey! Down in front!" Shouts Pilet. "Hurry and get your ass over here! You're blocking my view!"

Faith shakes her head in disdain.

"Oh Lord, why am I not surprised."

Faxion taps her on the shoulder.

"You go on ahead, I've a quick matter to deal with."

Faith peers at one of the many monitors throughout the colosseum, seeing the open scoring of the fight. She notices Faxion's fighter lagging severely behind.

"Oh boy." She said. "Just try not to start any trouble would ya?"

"Ha!" Chuckles Faxion. "Oh you know me. I wouldn't dream of it!"

As Faith heads over to Pilet and the others, she turns around for a moment to see where Faxion is going. Not to her surprise, The Deadeye has effortlessly vanished into the crowd.

"What's he up to now..." She thought.

Faith takes her seat by her sister, laboredly stepping over mounds of fallen popcorn and candy wrappers.

"Sis, where've you been?!" Exclaimed Yuuna. "You missed all the fun here! I didn't know watching Fossil creatures fight like this would be so awesome!" Yuuna shouts out towards the cage. "Yeah! Kick his ass!! Wait, what if they're girls? Kick *her* ass? Oh I don't know, but this is amazing!!".

"Glad to see you back, spell sister." Said Max. "How did the debriefing go?"

Faith furiously wipes down her seat with a disinfectant wipe from her purse.

"Ugh it's so gross here!" She sits down, crossing her legs in a relaxed posture. "It went as good as it could I guess. Scott had me present in front of the city's political team, and the Mayor! Which was *super* stressful... But I think I did alright." She pulls a water bottle from her bag and takes a swig.

Gulp gulp "Yup. I've been a nervous wreck ever since. Hope I left a good impression on the city council..."

Suddenly, Pilet chucks a handful of popcorn at Faith's head.

"Oh would you quit your whining?!" He exclaimed. "You're such a know-it-all that I'm sure it reflected in your *presentation* or whatever. Besides, if they all left alive it means you didn't *bore* them to death with your long-ass explanations. So at least you did something right."

Faith lunges for Pilet's popcorn, as the two tussle for control over the butter-laden snack.

"You got this shit in my hair you prick!" She hissed.

"Hey! Beat it you soulless ginger!" Pilet replied. "Get your own! I gotta save this to throw at the big blue asshole in the cage!!"

With a loud crack and a thud, the sound of Stinger Logan, smashing Dunn the Matador in the face with his skull dome rings throughout the stadium.

"Ooooohh!" Jeers the crowd.

Pilet yanks the popcorn from Faith's grasp, persisting to toss handfuls incessantly into the crowd below. He cups his hand to his face and shouts.

"Get the lard out of your ass!! C'mon ya big yellow son of a bitch! Where's the finesse?!"

The crowd roars in excitement, as the voice of the ringside announcer takes over the stadium.

"Yeeowch!!" Exclaims the announcer. "Looks like more of the same here in round 6 of this 7 round title fight! Stinger Logan is continuing to dominate with precise, accurate skull strikes to The Matador. Dunn's usual antics and playful banter have seen him no luck in this match. It *looks* like he came to play, while Logan came to fight!"

Stinger Logan roots himself in a strong stance, prepping his neck for a moment before firing off a barrage of short skull strikes. Taking a deep breath to recoup from his last blow, Dunn attempts evasive head movement to survive the relentless surge of strikes.

Managing to evade the first few, The Matador soon finds the scales along his side cracked and dented from the continued barrage. The relentless pace of his foe brings Dunn to his knees, as the exhausted Fossil creature doubles over in pain.

"Ugh, prick!" He exclaims in agony.

Stinger Logan tries to capitalize on the fallen Pach fighter, leaping back and lowering his head for a full-force skull bash. He scrapes his skull base along the floor to guide the weapon to the grounded foe. Dust and sand clouds follow suit as he viciously trails along the ground.

But at the very last moment Dunn manages to roll out of harm's way, his beak coming inches from the rigid tip of the blue Pach fighters skull. Standing to his feet, Dunn dances around on his hind legs to taunt the ruthless champion.

But the seasoned Champion simply scoffs at The Matador, tucking his chin and marching toward him with careful aggression.

"Shit, this guy's a tough nut to crack." Thought Dunn. *"He won't let his guard down an inch. There's just no opening to strike..."*

As Logan marches forward, Dunn backs up into the electric fence surrounding the arena.

"Agh!" Exclaims Dunn, as his tail grazes the live chain links. "Oof!" Dunn then hits the ground, as Logan fires a sharp, ramming headbutt into his chin.

Just as Logan stands atop him and readies for a finishing sequence, the bell signaling the end of the round goes off.

"Hmmf." Logan scoffs. "Saved by the bell..."

The blue Pach Fighter nonchalantly struts away, as Dunn struggles to get up to his feet.

The Matador spits some blood onto the sand, staggering back to his corner in pain. Two Pachycephalosaurus enter the cage from his side. Mortimer the Enforcer, clad in his usual green scales; and another, covered in gray with blood red-colored streaks going down his side body. The streaked Fossil creature carries a stool in his mouth towards the exhausted fighter, beckoning Dunn to take a seat.

"Ugh, this blows." Grunts Dunn, as he plops lifelessly into the metal stool. He looks up at the streaked Fossil creature with a disheartened glaze over his face. *Sigh* "Coach Nick, what do I gotta do?"

Mortimer snaps at his colleague.

"Well for one thing, you gotta stop being a bitch!" He exclaimed. "You always run! Always dance around and look cute! But this guys a heat seeking missile and he's coming right for you!"

Coach Nick nudges Mortimer away from Dunn.

"Enough, Mortimer. This isn't your fight, it's his." He looks back to Dunn. "I've given you the best advice I can, young Pach. But you never listen. At this rate you're going to throw your chances at reaching the top away, in favor of your own fighting style." He looks down at the sidelines, spotting Faxion standing right outside the cage. Faxion winks at the FC coach.

"May I?" Asks Faxion.

Coach Nick nods his head.

"Of course! You know you're always welcome in our corner."

Faxion grins, casting "Fleetfoot" and effortlessly leaping over the fence. He gracefully soars through the air, backflipping at the height of his jump before landing smoothly in front of Dunn. The exhausted Pach Fighter jumps in surprise.

"Gah!" Dunn exclaimed. "Oh, Fax? Where the hell did you come from?!"

The referee walks towards Faxion in an authoritative manner, as Nick stands before him in protest.

"He's with us, his name is on the coaching list." Said Nick.

"Fair enough." Replied the Ref. "But make it snappy, the next round's about to start."

As the Ref walks away, Faxion begins massaging Dunn's legs.

"How are the ankles doing?" He said.

"Ugh, tired. But not bad." Replied Dunn. "This guy won't budge an inch. He just keeps comin' forward, and he won't commit to any of his strikes!" Dunn hocks a bloody loogie to the side. "The guy's got a rock solid defense, I just can't seem to catch him off guard."

"Yes I see that." Replied Faxion. "Your opponent has a strong root, and a cautious disposition. Ha! Quite the opposite of yourself."

"Yeah, so what?" Retorts Dunn. "All I need is one good opening, and this tail's going to send him back to the Cretaceous period."

"Maybe..." Faxion chuckles. "But that opening is *never* going to come the way *you're* fighting."

"So what the hell am I supposed to do?" Dunn replied.

"Well, even the highest, most solid tree is only as strong as its roots." Faxion glances at Dunn's calloused, muscular tail. "Most Pach Fighters rely on that thick skull of theirs to batter their opponents, but not you. That battle hardened tail is responsible for more K.O.'s than any other in the division. But Logan's defense has proven too solid for a good strike to the head."

"Ok... How does this help?" Retorts Dunn impatiently.

"Maybe you should chop down the tree?" Faxion replied. "Have you ever considered how important those legs are to his style? Taking an ax to that powerful root of his might do you some good..."

Just then, the bell rings for the final round, as the Referee returns.

"Alright thats it, everyone out of the cage for the next round." He said.

Faxion finishes massaging Dunn's ankles, giving him two thumbs up before exiting with Mortimer and Nick.

"Good luck!" He says while walking out of the cage.

A new look of determination in his face, Dunn glares at his opponent across the arena.

"Chop down the tree..."

As Faxion exits the cage, Nick inquires about his encounter with Dunn.

"What did you tell him?" Said Nick.

Faxion grins.

"I gave him the tree analogy." He said.

Coach Nick snorts contemptibly.

"Well at least he listens to *somebody*, I told him that in the first damn round..."

Mortimer taps Faxion with his tail.

"Glad you came, Fax. Let's hope he took a fraction of what you said seriously."

"Ha!" Laughs Faxion. "Eh, even if he doesn't. It was worth a shot, no?"

Faxion bids farewell, finally heading towards his seat with The Hidden Blades. He sits beside Kenzo, as the 4th degree Sanda Master glares at him befuddled.

"You know these beasts?" Said Kenzo.

"Oh yeah, we go waaay back!" Replied Faxion, reclining in his seat in a relaxed posture.

Max, Faith, and Yuuna all stare at The Veteran Blade; completely flabbergasted by his actions.

"You wanna tell us what you were doing in there Fax?!" Exclaims Yuuna. "Like, are we just gonna ignore you hopping into the cage and talking to an FC cage fighter in the middle of a freaking pay-per-view?! That just happened, right?!"

"Incredible!" Said Max. "The respect you must have amongst these mighty creatures is astounding. I am truly glad to have met such a renowned warrior."

Faxion pretends to blush in embarrassment.

"Oh stop now, I'm but a humble mercenary hungry to share my skills."

An empty bucket of popcorn bops Faxion over the head. Pilet stands on the other side of the group with his arms folded in contempt.

"Hmmph, showoff." Pilet mocks Faxion in a nasally voice. "I'm but a humble mercenary" yada yada yada, blah blah blah. Ya think you're so cool..."

Faith giggles and whispers to Yuuna.

"I think Pilet's jealous."

"I heard that!" Pilet retorts.

"Oh Lad!" Said Faxion. "That reminds me..." Faxion pulls the flame and metal Keycrystals given to him by the Chairman out of his coat, holding them aloft before Pilet. "Chairman Yang sends his regards, may you use these with great care and discernment."

He hands them to Pilet, as the fiery prospect gazes at the gleaming stones in wonder.

"Oh, I remember this one but..." He glances at the Fire Keycrystal. "There were more?"

Faxion grins.

"It's a long story, but for now let's just enjoy the show." He points to the cage, a contented look on his face.

"Ooooh!" The crowd cheers.

"Huh?" Said Pilet, as the group turns their attention to the cage.

The announcer gives his play-by-play.

"Incredible, Dunn The Matador has taken up an inventive new strategy. He's fiercely whipping at Stinger Logan's legs with that formidable tail of his! Could this be what that strange man who pole vaulted into the cage told him to do?!"

In the cage, Dunn proceeds to deftly dodge at the rapid strikes of his foe. Dipping and ducking at odd angles, The Matador manages to take dextrous swipes at Stinger's legs with each evasive maneuver.

"Nnnngh!" Stinger Logan writhes in pain as his feet are struck. He begins noticeably shaking his throbbing legs out in discomfort.

Logan continues his approach, ducking his head down and attempting a volley of short and powerful skull strikes to his foe. But Dunn proves to be too deft, nimbly bolting out of his line of sight before answering with vicious tail whips to Logan's feet and ankles once more.

"Aggh!" Exclaims Logan in agony. "Screw you!"

Stinger Logan lowers his head, lunging forward with reckless abandon as his legs begin to quiver.

"Ha." Dunn chuckles to himself. "Now we're fightin' *my* fight."

Dunn easily escapes Logan's desperate attack, as he follows up with a powerful tail swipe to the Champ's face.

"Aaaaaah!!" The crowd roars in shock and awe.

Mortimer reels at the sight of the attack. Coach Nick laughs, as he turns to his prodigy.

"You've seen the other end of that tail far too many times I take it."

Mortimer snorts.

"Tch, more than I'd like to admit..."

The onslaught continues in the arena, as Dunn continues to batter his foe with level changing techniques. A low tail swipe here, and quick skull bash to the ribs there, a high tail swipe to the face on occasion. The crowd simply loses their mind at the astounding turn of events. The round continues as the two Pach Fighters play what looks like a brutal game of cat and mouse, with the mouse taking the lead.

Suddenly, Dunn lands a powerful, lunging skull bash into Logan's chest; sending the frantic Champion reeling back into the electric fence.

"Aaaaagh!" Exclaims Logan in agony, as the electric fence proceeds to relentlessly shock him up the spine.

Every muscle in his body begins to lock up, as he draws the last of his energy to look up towards his opponent. Suddenly, as if time began to slow throughout the arena, a thin shadow passes over Logan's face. The shadow begins to widen in size, as Logan's eyes peer to his left at the source of the shadow. An airborne Dunn, at least three feet off of the ground; spins and contorts his body toward his foe. Logan's eyes turn back to see the shadow belonging to the calloused, battle hardened tail of The Matador headed straight for his nose. Weary and fatigued, he closes his eyes in fright of the impending blow.

With a brutally loud smack, Dunn's tail makes direct contact; delivering crushing force to the bridge of Logan's beak. A moment later, the Champion falls lifelessly to the ground, as The Matador stands stoically above his downed foe.

Silence befalls the room for a split second. Not even the sound of spectators chewing popcorn can be heard, as most mouths hang open in shock.

"............."

A slow clap immediately erupts into thunderous applause, as the crowd shouts and hollers in elation for the yellow, blood soaked Fossil creature. The Referee dashes by, pushing Dunn away from Logan before waving his hands in a fight-ending gesture.

"Fight's over, fight's over!" He exclaimed.

"Woooooo!!" The crowd goes wild.

The vicious knockout replays itself on the various monitors scattered throughout the colosseum. Visions of The Matador, nimbly soaring through the air like a one ton acrobat adorn the stadium walls.

"That's it folks!" Exclaims the announcer. "We have a new PF1 Middleweight Champion!! Snatching the belt off of a very dangerous foe in Stinger Logan, Dunn The Matador has cemented himself as the undisputed king of the 900lb cage!!"

The president of The PF1 Grand Prix enters the cage, wrapping the Championship belt around Dunn's waist and exiting once more. Elated at the presence of the new belt, Dunn lets out a bellowing cry that shakes the colosseum goers to their core.

"Goooooouuuugghh!!"

"Exceptional!" Exclaimed Kenzo. "To see a creature of that size display such fine control of itself mid-flight, what a sight to behold! Wouldn't you say boy?!"

"I agree father." Max replied. "To have snatched victory from the jaws of certain defeat like that, the resilience and mental fortitude required must-"

Hell yeah Dunn!! Ya damn near took his head off with that one!!" Shouts Pilet at the top of his lungs.

Max winces, covering his ears from the extreme pitch of his colleague.

"Holy Serpent Dragon is there no mute button on this God damned ignorant fool!" Exclaims Max in frustration. Enraged, he turns to Pilet and hollers. "Shout in my ear like that again and I'll send you to the great Cloud Viper nest in the sky!"

Pilet goes silent.

"..."

"Sheesh Max, relax." Said Pilet. "I was just cheering on my friend. You really gotta get a handle on those emotions there buddy."

Faith and Yuuna struggle to hold in their laughter, snorting and giggling to the side.

"... You bother me." Said Max, taking his seat to continue watching Dunn's victory speech.

The announcer walks into the cage with a microphone, approaching Dunn as Mortimer and Coach Nick gather in support.

"It was an amazing performance here tonight!" Said The announcer. "You started out this fight having a really hard time with your opponent. Up until the very end he seemed to have the jump on you, could you walk us through the strategy that saw you pull the upset of the year here tonight?"

Dunn draws himself close to the Mic.

"Yes sir, I'd like to thank my coaching staff and teammates for getting ready for this fight, without them there's no way I would be here today. And a special thanks goes out to a good friend of mine, that crazy son of a bitch who hopped in the cage and his waterboy."

Pilet's eyes furrow in confused protest.

"Waterboy?!"

Faxion breaks out into laughter.

Dunn continues.

"He's a slick Hired Blade and the reason The Crasher Kings were able to make it in this town. And his understudy Pilet is graduating today as a Blade too."

"Understudy?!" Exclaims Pilet.

His peers break out into uncontrollable laughter.

Dunn nods his head towards Faxion.

"Get your asses in here!" He said with a grin.

Faxion and Pilet glance at each other, smiling ear to ear.

"Fleetfoot!" They both cast, as they dash past the crowd and into the cage in an instant.

The crowd explodes into applause for the two Hired Blades, as Pilet leaps on top of Dunn's head like a prehistoric steed.

"Hell of a scrap, ya big yellow bastard!" Exclaimed Pilet.

Him and Dunn share a fistbump, as the arena roars in joyous celebration.

Final March of the Prospects

Within the hour, the audience for the PF1 Grand Prix finds themselves out of the Colosseum, whilst the cleanup crew begins to start set-up for The HBA commencement ceremony. Suddenly, the sand and stone covered Pach Fighting arena begins to mechanically sink into the ground. A completely automated floor system swaps the fighting grounds for a completely blank stage with a podium. The colosseum crew begins carrying chairs onto the stage, aligning them in a neat, single file order. Before long, friends and family of the graduates begin filtering in through the double doors. All the while, Pilet and the other graduates prepare themselves to march on the stage in a back dressing room.

Unlike one's usual graduation attire, The Hired Blades Association's robes come with a blank, leather lanyard sewn into the left side of the chest. The silken robes vary in color, based on the team of the graduate wearing it.

Like a black and white cookie, The Funk Munkeys sport a half black, half blue robe with the colors split directly down the middle. The Mystic Marauders wear robes a distinct, Navy hue, with a tasteful gold trim. To no one's surprise, Bhujanga dons a vivid emerald robe, the threaded pattern of an orange ball of flame plastered across his chest. The Reaper Elite, clad in blood red robes with white trim, with a white threaded pattern of a scythe looming over their right shoulder.

Finally, Pilet and The Hidden Blades walk into the dressing room. With one side of fitting rooms dedicated to the woman and another the men, the crew parts in two. Faith and Yuuna enter their side, passing by

Dabria of The Reaper Elite on the way. She gives the arcane sisters a crass glare, before looking the other way in contempt.

"Hmmph, bitch." Muttered Yuuna. "Man, I'd like to go another round with that one..."

"Relax sis." Said Faith. "We made the grade, that's what counts. Speaking of, I wonder what horrible color Pilet made our robes."

"Wait, Pilet picked them?" Yuuna scratches her head.

"Yeah. He's the emissary, remember?" Faith replied.

"Oh Lord, whose bright idea was that?! God I hope he didn't pick some fugly shade of poop brown..."

Max and Pilet take a step into the men's fitting room. Each one a row of small, 5 by 6 foot rooms with a curtain in front. As they step into the rooms adjacent each other, Pilet finds his robe in a neatly wrapped plastic package first.

"Max you're gonna love this, dude." Said Pilet, ripping and tearing into the package with delight. "I picked the coolest color *and* pattern imaginable. All those other bitches are gonna be so jealous."

Max sees his own on the bench, lifting it to his chest and drawing an M6 Gash dagger from his backside. He skillfully slices through the top of the bag with a smooth, clean cut, reaching his fingers inside.

"Yes well I'd hope so Pilet. This robe will be a visual representation of each and every trial we went through to get to this point and-"

As Max pulls the robe from the bag, he immediately falls silent.

"....."

While unholstering his Dragonfly longknives, Pilet becomes puzzled at the sudden silence.

"Uhh, you were saying?"

Suddenly, Max's electrified Gash stabs through the thick cedar wall of Pilet's fitting room, piercing the hanging glass mirror and frightening Pilet something fierce.

"GAAAH!!!" Exclaimed Pilet. "What in God's name is wrong with you pineapple head?!" He exclaimed. "What, they don't freaking knock where you're from?!"

Max effortlessly slashes a massive hole into the fitting room wall, slicing the mirror clean in half and stepping into Pilet's room with robe in hand.

"What is this, Pilet?!" Max exclaims.

He holds up the robe; a violet hue liken to the color of Pilet's eyes, with the embroidered pattern of a pair of Dragonfly longknives sewn across the chest.

"Is everything a joke to you?! How does this represent us as a unit?! It only has stuff related to *you* on it!!"

Pilet scans Max's robe in confusion.

"Wait, did you get mine?" Pilet grabs the robe from his own package. He pulls it out, revealing a pattern of the same design. "Wait no, this one is mine. So did they send you a copy of mine?"

Taking a moment to breathe, Max facepalms in frustration.

"Pilet, you were tasked with picking a robe for The Hidden Blades. Not for yourself..."

"Ohhhh... Alright." Replied Pilet.

He stands to his feet, throwing his robe over his tank top and looking in the half of the mirror not destroyed by Max's tirade.

"I mean, it's still a pretty fly robe. I wouldn't worry about it. Heh, I'd be more worried about the cost of that wall."

Pilet walks away, strutting in his new robe like a peacock.

Max shakes his head in disdain, looking at the carnage he let loose on the fitting room wall.

".....One hell of a clean cut though. Father would be proud, I hope..."

Just then, the Sierro sisters come crashing through the men's fitting room doors.

"Pilet what gives?!" Shouts Yuuna.

"Doofus!! What kind of team robe is this?!" Hollers Faith.

Max hears the sound of the Sierro sisters tearing into Pilet. He smiles, chuckling to himself.

"Never a dull moment."

Outside, the festivities begin for the HBA graduation commencement ceremony. Flamecasting Blades breathe fire into the air, dazzling the crowd with brilliant streams of pyre. Starcasters fire vibrant auric stars into the sky, as the mechanized ceiling of the Colosseum begins to open up to the clear blue skies over Grand Titanus City. Martial artists march out onto the stage, performing furious forms and techniques with glowing infrared weaponry. In the midst of the festivities, Chairman Yang walks out onto the podium with a microphone in hand.

"Good afternoon citizens of Grand Titanus!" He exclaims.

The crowd cheers for the fearsome Blade Master.

"We have come here today to celebrate the success of our newest batch of exam candidates. No, our newest *Licensed* Hired Blades!"

"Wooooo!!" The crowd roars in excitement.

"These proud warriors have completed every task necessary to call themselves one of our own. They've braved vicious monsters, ancient weapons, and titanic behemoths; and they've done so with both strength and finesse. As per usual, I'd like to take this moment to honor our founding fathers. I invite today's firing squad to come forth for our traditional "Ode to the five generals.""

A group of five Hired Blades with Pilum beam rifles march onto the stage in a single file line. They stop before Chairman Yang, saluting the Chairman before turning to face the crowd.

"It is tradition to fire off five shots in remembrance of the founding five Hired Blades. The Five generals risked their lives defending President Rodney Petersin, on the night of his infamous Grand Titanus Address. All but the Blade's creator, General Gregory Galant, fell in battle that night. But the President emerged unscathed, and the treacherous plot of the enemy was foiled in their efforts!"

Chairman Yang clears his throat.

"Ahem, gentlemen!"

The firing squad stomps their feet.

"For General Johnathan Packerd."

The first Blade fires a shot into the air, the brilliant azure beam dashes through the sky at breakneck speeds.

"For General Mathew Blanc."

The second shot rings true.

"For General Timothy Locke."

The third shot is fired.

"For General Malachi Smith."

The fourth shot is released.

"For General Gregory Galant."

The fifth shot rips through the sky.

"And finally, for President Rodney Petersin."

All five Hired Blades aim their Pilum beam rifles into the sky. The five unanimously pull the trigger, as each one fires a brilliant blast of plasma into the sky. The beams rip a hole through a white fluffy cloud, leaving the imprint of the Generals in their wake.

The audience goes nuts, jeering and clapping at the visceral display of honor for the founders. Chairman Yang nods to the firing squad, as they bow to the crowd and march off into the halls of the Colosseum. Yang lifts the mic to his face.

"In honoring the old, we now honor the new. It is time to welcome our gaggle of new Blades, fresh from the fight!" He scans a sheet of paper in his hand.

"First up, a musical quartet with a fearsome disposition. Guided by their wise and loyal emissary, Danba the Witchdoctor. I give you; The Funk Munkeys!"

The audience claps and whistles.

Danba, Lukah, Svenn, and Clint all enter through the colosseum corridors. The rowdy band members jeer and shout playfully at the crowd, as many of their groupies chant "F.U.N.K." in jubilee. The Funk Munkeys make their way to the stage, taking a seat in the second row.

"Next up." Said Chairman Yang. "Frightfully effective in the thick of a fight, a cohesive unit second to none on the battlefield. Directed by Puerto, the "Man O' War". Here are; The Mystic Marauders!"

Puerto leads his team from the corridor into the colosseum. Falling in line are Wendy, Dunya, and Cornelius. Subsequently, the graduation robe appears far too small for Cornelius, as he walks out with it tied around his neck like a cape.

A mix of applause and laughter can be heard, as spectators go mad over the sight of The Hulking, Kettlenian Elite's cape flowing majestically behind him.

Puerto facepalms in chagrin.

"Damn it Cornelius, no one's going to take us serious now..."

"Oh hush Honey." Replied Dunya. "Just look, the crowd loves us!"

"Yeah, it looks like we have our very own superhero." Said Wendy. "Cornelius, you should hold onto that. It'll make you an excellent distraction in a firefight, this way I can pick off all our foes from a sniper's nest far away."

"But wait," Said Cornelius. "wouldn't that put *me* in danger?"

"Oh Cornelius." Said Wendy. "I love you ya big oaf, but that's just a risk I'm willing to take."

Cornelius folds his arms and pouts in discontent.

The Mystic Marauders step onto the stage, taking their seats in the row before The Funk Munkeys.

"Ey brothas and sistas." Said Danba. "Good luck and many blessings on tha journey ahead."

"Thanks, Danba." Replied Wendy. "We have to come to one of your shows some time!"

"Oh for sure." Said Lukah. "Svenn, hit 'em with that *good* shit."

Svenn silently nods, pulling a pack of CD's out of his robe and a handful of disheveled event tickets. He hands them to Wendy and Puerto with a meek smile.

"Oh, uh... What are they?" Asked Puerto.

"Uh, duh?" Lukah replied. "Brand new copies of our mixtape, and a shit ton of tickets to some of our soonest shows. You're freaking welcome."

Puerto whispers to Wendy.

"These tickets are for shows from like, 2 months ago... And who even uses CD's anymore?"

"Shh just go with it!" Wendy whispers back.

The two awkwardly wave and smile back at the Funk Munkeys, turning back around in their seats before further embarrassment. Chairman Yang draws the microphone back to his chin.

"This next candidate is the first in *years* to successfully pass the Hired Blades Exam, completely on his own! He's a ruthless, ace of flamecast! The one man show; Bhujanga Garuda of The Emerald Flame!!"

Bhujanga steps out into the stadium, a stone cold expression upon his face as usual.

"Yeeeooooww!"

Many of the women in the crowd deafeningly purr, hoot, and holler at the handsome young flamecaster, as he lets out a vexed scoff.

"Tch, whatever..."

Bhujanga takes his seat beside the Mystic Marauders. He leans in towards Cornelius.

"I find these trivial proceedings to be irrelevant at best, what do you say?"

Cornelius scratches his head for a moment.

"I don't know what you just said, but what a banger that was in the desert right?!" He offers Bhujanga a fist bump. "It was *glorious* besting that titan's Eraser cannon alongside you, Blade brother!"

Bhujanga tries to stay serious for a moment, before a subtle grin begins to escape his face. He bumps fists with Cornelius in amusement.

"Yes, yes it was. Friend."

Parallel to each other within the entryway corridor, The Reaper Elite and The Hidden Blades lie in wait to be called to the stage. Lazlow Jr. decides to stir the pot.

"Hey dickbag." He says to Pilet.

Pilet turns to his rival, a contemptuous glare in his eyes.

"Hmph, 'the hell do *you* want?...

"Bet you they'll be cheering my name *twice* as loud as yours. If anyone even remembers your name!"

The Reaper Elite begin to laugh; save for Asger, who folds his arms and looks away in discomfort.

Pilet's brow furrows. His nostrils flare in rage as he begins to march towards The Gavel.

"Why you little-"

"Stop." Said Faith, as she barres Pilet with her arm. "Not the time, just forget about it."

"Grrrrrrrr..." Growls Pilet. "Punk bitch."

"Next!" Shouts Chairman Yang. "The crushing, overwhelming power of this team has put them ahead on the scoreboards throughout every test and trial; both in the academy and the exam! They're the Reaper Elite! Led by their courageous emissary-"

Yang notices Lazlow Jr. in the halls, getting ready to have his name called. He looks at the sheet of paper, seeing "Lazlow the Gavel" written under his name.

"Wait, isn't that The Enforcer's boy?" Thought Yang. *"It looks like they put his father's name here by mistake. What did Deadeye call him again?"*

He recounts their discussion after the auracast exam...

"Fuchsia the... Florist! His son is Fuchsia the Florist."

"Right!" Said Chairman Yang into the microphone. "Oh, sorry. Well yes back to it then... Led by their courageous emissary, Fuchsia The Florist!" Yang puts down the mic for a moment. "He can take one hell of a beating for a *Florist*, what a fascinating name indeed."

Lazlow's eyes widen in shock.

"I, what?! What did he just call me?!"

Asger, Dabria, and Arturo do their best to hold in their laughter; while Pilet, Yuuna, Max, and Faith drop onto the ground in hysterics.

"Baaahahahahaha!!" They let out a bellowing, deep belly laugh in unison.

Lazlow's face goes as red as a cherry with rage, as he walks into the stadium. Smoke might as well escape his ears and nose, as the peeved Kettlenian Elite leads his crew onto the stage with haste. Befuddled, mixed reactions can be heard throughout the crowd.

"The Florist?!"

"What a bold name, he must be so secure in himself!"

"How tough can the guy be with a name like that!?"

Name aside, they applaud nonetheless for the fearsome new Hired Blades. As The Reaper Elite take their seats, Faxion can be seen burying his head bashfully into his coat.

"I can't believe he remembered that..." He said.

A hand taps the Veteran Blade on the back.

"Hey now Mr. Faxion, I don't see my boy up there yet." Said Milo, Pilet's Grandfather. "We didn't come too late did we? I swear this city is so hard to navigate!"

Tecia, his Grandmother, leans over Milo to interject.

"Also, will they let me take this cotton candy fruit pie to him when it's over? I'd be absolutely devastated if I couldn't. The amount of love that went into this is just enormous."

Faxion smiles at his two guests.

"You made it!" He exclaimed. "How wonderful! I was beginning to lose hope... And yes, you've come *just* in time you have." Faxion gives Tecia a reassuring wink. "And don't worry about the pie, I've got some *pull* around here."

Sitting on the other side of Faxion, Kenzo Quinn can't help but notice the new guests. He reaches out towards them for a handshake.

"It is an honor to meet the father of such a skilled warrior!" Said Kenzo. "His skills on the battlefield are unparalleled! Well, save only for my son of course."

Shocked at the sight of a swordsman dressed in full battle armor, Milo and Tecia fall back in their seats for a moment. Seeing the confusion in their eyes, Faxion steps in.

"Ahem, yes I do apologize. Allow me to introduce to you the father of one of your grandson's new colleagues. This is Kenzo Quinn, a Chief of the Sanda tribe of Hachidori!"

After a brief pause, Milo vigorously shakes his head to clear the cobwebs of disbelief. He reaches out a hand, as the two proceed to shake.

"Wow!" Exclaimed Milo. "Those cutlery are really something, aren't they Babe?"

Tecia nods her head.

"We could've used you when Pilet was a little boy!" She replied. "My husband's about as good with a knife as he is with a spatula in the kitchen. When he taught our grandson how to cut fruit you'd better believe there was a bloody mess everywhere!"

Milo nudges Tecia in the ribs.

"Stop embarrassing me in front of the fancy swordsman, woman!" He said.

"Well, you must have done something right." Said Kenzo. "The years of scrapes and cuts must have done him some good, because that boy's skill with a shiv would give a Sanda warrior a worthy challenge! Now, to see the boy take a heat-seeking missile to the face like that... How did you teach him to repair his scorched and mangled flesh?"

Tecia and Milo both pause in confusion once more. Faxion dons an anxious face, as he turns to Kenzo and flashes a shushing finger across his lips.

"Well, he hasn't *seen* combat yet, right?..." Whispered Faxion with a nervous wink.

"Aah, so it is like that..." Replied Kenzo. "What a shame, I've forgotten he's not of a warrior's caste. Such interesting, trivial issues they have..."

Faxion turns to Milo and Tecia once more.

226

"Hahaha! Never a dull moment with this gentleman around, his sense of humor is unmatched!"

The couple from Chamboree glance at each other for a moment, before bursting out in laughter.

"Hahahahahah!" They bellowed.

Milo slaps Kenzo jestfully on the shoulder plate of his armor.

"What a guy! Oh I like you, you're a real riot!"

Kenzo flashes an awkward smile to the couple.

"I do my best, haha...ha."

Just then, The Chairman clears his throat on the microphone. He hocks a loogie off to the side before continuing with the commencement.

"Ugh, allergies." He said. "Right, so here we go! This final team has managed to win the hearts of the crowd during the beginning phases of the exam with their light-hearted attitude, quick wit, and at times even a sharp tongue."

He looks to Pilet in the hall, as The Fiery Prospect flashes two "M" symbols with his fingers. He reads Pilet's lips, making out the words "Minego Mayhem" incessantly escaping the boy's mouth. Yang shakes his head.

"An impressive stand out group, comprised of the only candidates this year *not* to attend The Hired Blades Academy. This ragtag crew has managed to come out on top of every challenge they've met, smiling in the face of adversity as they push forth into the fray!"

The crowd roars in anticipation. In the hall of the arena, Pilet turns back towards his team.

"Hey Yuuna." He said with a devilish grin. "Wanna have some fun?"

Yuuna meets him with a mischievous gaze of her own.

"Oh yeah? Let's cause a stir! Muahahahaha!"

Faith and Max give each other a concerned glare.

"Oh brother." Said the elder Sierro.

"Let's just try not to hurt anyone, at least not too bad...." Retorts the Sanda warrior.

Yang puts the finishing touches on his introduction.

"Led by their fierce and fearless emissary, Pilet, "The King Killer"! I give you, The Hidden Blades!!"

The crowd stands to their feet, cheering in jubilee.

Milo leaps out of his seat in joyous adulation as well.

"That's my boy! They said his name!!"

Tecia gently wipes heartfelt tears from her face with a handkerchief.

"It's too good to be true, did you hear dear? He's even the leader!"

The crowd continues to go wild, cheering and whistling in an earth shattering pitch. But, as the stadium erupts with intense praise, The Hidden Blades are nowhere to be seen. Chairman Yang tilts his head to peer down the corridor once more, as Pilet and the others have vanished from sight.

"What?" Thought Yang. *"Where the hell did the boy go? They were just there?! Someone's going to get throttled for this!"* He looks towards Faxion in confusion.

A bead of sweat forms above The Deadeye's brow, dripping down the side of his head as he slinks back into his seat. He gives The Chairman a befuddled shrug of the shoulders, before timidly twiddling his fingers.

"I'm going to kill that boy." Thought Faxion. *"I'm going to kill him in the two and a half milliseconds before Yang kills me..."*

Suddenly, a vicious whizzing sound, followed by an intense crackle can be heard throughout the arena. Faxion turns towards the action, as he sees vibrant stars of green and purple shoot forth into the sky. The audience oohs and ahhs at the beautiful lightshow before them, as the sky above the colosseum fills with small, vibrant auric stars. In the corridor of the arena, the sound of a sword unfastening from its sheath can be heard.

In an instant, a brilliant bolt of lightning flashes across the sky. The auric lightning bolt catches one of the vibrant stars hovering over the stadium, before jumping from star to star in a blazing flash. The surging electric current begins to form a spectacular image in the stars like an arcane game of connect the dots.

Suddenly, a massive sphere of ice and frost bursts forth from the corridor. The sphere of cold dances above the colosseum, as iridescent flakes of auric snow begin to fall before the crowd.

The audience cheers at the welcome climate change throughout the humid stadium.

As the arcane blizzard drops fluffy snow onto the thrilled spectators, the surging lightning begins to form the shape of a two-edged sword into the pattern of the auric stars. As the audience looks on in delight, a thick smokescreen begins to billow out from the stadium's corridor. Chairman Yang looks on in exuberant excitement. He puts the microphone down, clapping in delight at the spectacular exhibition.

"I knew I loved this kid!" He exclaimed, giving a thumbs up to Faxion in the crowd.

Faxion returns the gesture with a hesitant smile.

"Phew, I guess he thinks I planned it?..." Thought Faxion.

From within the corridor, a scarlet light begins to shine like a small sun in the thick fog.

"Hollowpoint!!"

In a flash, scores of blazing, bright red Hollowpoint casts whizz through the air. The flaming Hollowpoints explode onto the many stars making up the arcane constellation, leaving a hellish, flaming glaze upon each one. As the flaming, electrically charged sword of stars hovers above the night sky, The Hidden Blades begin to march forth from within the smokescreen.

High pitched whistling rings from the mouths of the many adoring fans. Crowd members begin to fling popcorn buckets and soft drinks into the air in sheer, uncontrolled hype.

Chairman Yang rushes to the microphone at the sight of The Hidden Blades advancing from the shadow of the fog.

"I give you... The Hidden Blades!!"

"Ooooraaah!!"

The audience jumps up and begins stomping in elation. The force of the crowds delightful celebrations shakes the very foundation of the building, as the ground quakes under the pressure.

As The Hidden Blades walk towards the stage, Faith clenches one of her fists shut; stopping the dark, arcane smokescreen from escaping her grasp. She then puts that hand on Pilet's shoulder.

"Alright, I'll give you this one." She said with a smirk. "Good idea, doofus."

Pilet grins, continuing to march through the stadium in a prideful stride. The scarlet glow of the flame Keycrystal still pulsating from around his neck.

Some of the other Blade graduates on stage react to the intense auric performance.

"What was that all about?" Said Wendy. "No one said we could pull some fancy stunt like that, and The Chairman's just gonna allow it?"

Puerto shakes his head in disbelief.

"Ooh King Killer..."

With arms folded, Bhujanga looks up at the flames glazed over the airborne, auric symbol. His lips perk as his brow lifts, ever so slightly impressed at The Hidden Blades work.

"Hmm. Basic shit, but not a bad flamecast..."

Lazlow Jr. slams his fist into his thigh in frustration.

"What kind of crap is this!" He exclaimed. "If I'd known they were letting us put on a show, I would've had a pack of Wisp Tigers brought in so I could slay them in front of the crowd!!"

Arturo gives Lazlow an unamused side-eye.

"You know those are sacred in my country, right?"

Lazlow grins.

"Tch. Oh I know, that's why I said it."

Stepping up the stairs to the stage, The Hidden Blades take their seats across from The Reaper Elite. The two teams glare intently at each other for a moment, before Chairman Yang walks over to Pilet in elation.

"You've really outdone yourself with this one, kid." He said, shaking Pilets hand with a firm grip. "I love this shit, keep it up and I'll see you taken care of around here."

"Ha! You ain't seen nothing yet, Chief." Pilet replied.

Max and Faith turn to each other in bewilderment.

"I can't believe that went over so well..." Said Max, scratching his head.

Faith shrugs her shoulders.

"Honestly, at this point I've stopped trying to understand how these people work." She said. "Just go with it. If Pilet gets us killed, I'll know it's to no fault of my own..."

Chairman Yang returns to the podium with mic in hand. He looks up at the blazing symbol of the blade in the air.

"I love the thing, but it's mildly distracting now..."

He lifts his right arm, as an auric tattoo of a crane begins to glow. Suddenly, a cloud of brilliant, white feathers begins to erupt from the palm of Chairman Yang's hand; floating up to The Hidden Blades auric masterpiece and dismembering it into thin air. He repeats this action, this time evaporating the sphere of frost floating above the crowd. Yang begins to speak.

"Now for the moment *you've all* been waiting for!"

He reaches under the podium, pulling out a leather bag from within. Yang then motions toward Caffo Gilwick, who's sitting in the front row. As Caffo approaches the stage, he takes an authoritative stance behind the Chairman with hands folded at the waist. Yang hands Caffo the leather bag and gives him a nod.

"Make 'em official." Said Yang.

"Right." Responds Caffo.

Caffo reaches his hand into the bag, drawing a golden HBA badge on a black leather lanyard. This one reads "Lazlow Lexington Jr.", engraved along the bottom. Caffo walks over and hands the badge to The Reaper Elite's Emissary, giving him a stern gaze as he does so.

"You're only getting this because your old man pulled some strings." He said with a snarl. "Pull some shit like you did in Devil's Tongue again and you can kiss this badge goodbye."

Lazlow scoffs, snatching the badge from Caffo and looking to his father in the crowd. With arms folded in a serious posture, Lazlow Sr. nods intently at his boy. A subtle grin creeps from the corner of Sr.'s mouth, as Jr. returns one of his own. Lazlow Jr. turns to Caffo in response.

"Piss off."

Caffo shakes his head, moving on to the rest of the graduating class in chagrin. As the weary proctor hands out badges, each graduate pins the illustrious badge to the leather patch on their left pectoral; proudly displaying the symbol of The HBA to the crowd before them. The Chairman continues on the mic.

"These who have gathered before us today have proven worthy of our adulation. They have shown great heart and grit, and have demonstrated that they have all the skills required to join the ranks of The Hired Blades Association. I hope to see these new Blades continue to shine in the face of adversity throughout their career."

As the Chairman speaks, Caffo hands Pilet his HBA License.

"Good job kid." Said Caffo. "Good thing I'm not a betting man, I honestly didn't think you had it in you."

"Tch, this was light work." Replied Pilet. "Keep an eye out for me, won't be long before I hit the big time around here."

"Sure, whatever you say." Said Caffo. As he moves on to the next team, he mutters under his breath. "Shit, now I owe The Deadeye like, 60 bucks. Could've swore the runt would've ended up splattered across the sand..."

As the faithless exam proctor departs, Pilet stares intently at the golden badge in his hand. The Fiery Prospect revels in the weight of the achievement.

"I can't believe I'm actually holding this right now. "He thought. *"The hours of training, all of those God awful ass whoopings from Fax..."* The image of Toste being swallowed by the Pyramid Morph's immense beam flashes through his mind. *"And Toste..."* He clutches the HBA badge tightly in his grasp, holding it firmly to his chest. *"This badge won't go to waste, I promise....."*

As Pilet remains deep in thought, Yuuna gets his attention.

"Hey Pilet, who are those old people pointing and waving at us?" She said.

"Huh?" Replied Pilet, snapping out of his fervent trance. "Where? Who are you talking about?"

"Over there." Said Yuuna, as she points into the crowd. "They're sitting with Fax and Kenzo, they look real happy to see you!"

Pilet scans the crowd curiously, pausing as his gaze affixes onto Milo and Tecia cheering and pointing towards him. Pilet's eyes widen in awe.

"Holy shit!" He exclaimed. "Those are my grandparents!" Pilet firmly holds the sides of his head in distress. "I was keeping the graduation a secret, Fax must've freaking told them!"

Max chimes in.

"You didn't want your family to know?" He said. "Why would you deprive them of seeing your crowning moment as a fearsome warrior?"

"I... What?" Replied Pilet. "Bro, not everyone lives like an action movie star. They run a hotel in the mountains, hell I worked at a fruit stand my whole life until this point! Look, they basically didn't even know we would see combat during this exam. They thought it would just be a written test! If they find out about everything, I'm gonna get an earful from the both of them..."

Confused, Max turns to his father in the crowd. Max curiously nudges his head towards Pilet's rowdy grandparents, to which Kenzo replies with a befuddled shrug of the shoulders.

"How very strange your culture is..." Said Max.

As Caffo finishes handing out the HBA Licenses, Chairman Yang turns toward the graduates, gesturing them to stand to their feet.

"From this day forth, I give you my blessing as the head of this Association." Said Chairman Yang. "May your weapon be ever guided by the Five Generals, may the sun always be to your backs, and may you find the strength, courage, and cunning to prevail even when it is not." He then turns to the crowd, hands outward in a celebratory posture. "On this day, I give you the graduating class of 2117! Welcome to the Hired Blades Association!"

The crowd erupts into a thunderous applause; as more Hired Blades emerge from the front row, using flame auracast to breathe massive streams of fire into the air. Following the mighty flamethrowers, starcasting Blades send forth crackling and exploding stars into the night sky.

The arcane fireworks put on a dazzling display up above, as Scott Diliger organizes a group of aquacasters in a circle around the stage. He gives his group an affirming nod, as each aquacaster summons a powerful geyser shooting upwards from their palms. Surrounding the stage like a massive auric fountain, the audience cheers and whistles in a hellacious uproar of excitement.

Within the confines of the auric fountain, Pilet gazes through the water towards Faxion. He locks eyes with his mentor, as the two share a brief moment of synergistic thought. Something to the effect of, *"This is only the beginning, the start of a lifetime of action and adventure."*

The Sweet Sorrow that is; Farewell

As the night drags on, the festivities continue within the circular walls of Grand Titanus Colosseum. The class of 2117 meet with friends and family, drinking copious amounts of Smoked Cedarbeer and Sparkling Lightning wine at a bar in the V.I.P. lounge. The Funk Munkeys take to the stage after hours, stringing up their guitars and playing a fantastic musical show for their many adoring fans. Amongst the chaos of the post-graduate celebrations, Pilet meets with his grandparents at the bar with Faxion.

"I can't believe this old fool actually invited you guys." Said Pilet, putting an arm around Faxion. "Chamboree is so damn far, you guys must have driven for hours on end just to get here. And for what, a half an hour of The Chairman monologuing because he likes the sound of his own voice?"

"Oh can it Pilet!" Said Milo, snatching Pilet by the ear and dragging him towards him.

"Ow, *shit!* Let go Grandpa!" Pilet exclaimed.

"When did you plan on telling us that you'd actually be fighting for this contest?" Said Milo. "Why, I heard there were monsters and giant scorpions in the desert that day!"

"Well, he's not wrong." Added Faxion.

Pilet hisses at Faxion as Milo continues to relentlessly tug on his ear.

"Shut the hell up and stay out of this Fax!" He exclaimed. "Can't you see *you've made* this mess?! Ow! Ow ow ow!"

Pilet winces in pain, as Tecia begins to mercilessly beat the back of his head with a wooden spoon from her purse.

"You told us it was just a written exam Pilet!" Tecia Hollered. "I was worried about you! I knew something was wrong... A mother knows these things!! Don't ever lie to us again!"

Milo laughs at his wife in response.

"Ha! Tecia, you know the boy is going to lie again so stop with your nonsense."

"Oh I'm totally gonna lie again... Ow!" Said Pilet, as his Grandmother continues raining punishing blows with her purse.

"You'd *better* not!!" Exclaimed Tecia, increasing the speed of her barrage by double.

"Crap! Ouch, stop!" Yelled Pilet, breaking out of his Grandfather's grip and putting some distance between them. "*Pant* Listen, I'm gonna be dealing with dangerous shit like this from now on, ok?" He cracks his neck in pain. "Ugh. Look, just get used to being worried... ok?!"

Pilet snatches the Dragonfly knives from his inside pocket. Engaging the infrared function, he brandishes the gnarly glowing blades before his Grandparents.

"Guys, Hired Blades do scary stuff on a daily basis around here. I can't promise you I'm not gonna get hurt in the future. In fact if anything, I *can* promise you that I *will* get hurt! Like honestly, probably pretty bad!"

Milo and Tecia take to a serious face, both taking a seat while deep in thought. Pilet holds the glowing, infrared blades up to his face.

"But one thing's for *damn* sure!" He said. "You see these? Anything that tries to hurt me, whether they succeed or not, is going to get *these* shoved *right* up their ass! I promise that I will return home in *one piece,* ok?!"

Milo wipes a tear from Tecia's eye, before wiping his own with his shirt.

"Pilet my boy, I have faith in you." He said. "We've known you've been special since the day you were born. Everything you put your mind to, everything that you chose to give it your all in, you manage to succeed somehow. I have no doubt in my mind that you'll make a fine Hired Blade. Isn't that right dear?"

Her face rosey and covered in tears, Tecia blows her nose into a tissue. Suddenly, she crinkles it up and throws it at Pilet.

"Yuck Grandma!" Said Pilet, as he deftly dodges the projectile.

"That's what you get for scaring us like that!" She exclaimed. "I love you so much, you'll always be my precious baby! You're all we have left in this world to remember your Mommy by. Never forget that, ok?!"

Pilet sighs. He takes a deep breath, choking back tears of his own before embracing his grandparents in a group hug.

"I know. I'll never forget. I promise..."

Faxion whispers in Pilet's ear from behind.

"You know, real Hired Blades don't hug their grandma's and cry like that..."

Pilet whispers back.

"Shut your trap geezer, I'll deal with you later."

Faxion laughs, reclining in a lounge chair whilst sipping a pint of Smoked Cedarbeer.

After their brief, heartfelt moment, Pilet separates from his grandparents to find his team mates. He spots Max, Faith, and Yuuna standing by another bar in the far corner of the lounge.

"So what do you ladies have planned?" Said Max. "You know, now that you're *officially* Licensed?"

Yuuna takes a shot of tequila, putting a hand drunkenly on Max's shoulder to lean on.

"Buddy, I got no idea." Said Yuuna. "I didn't even think I'd make it this far. I wanna go home and smoke ass-tons of Cosmic leaf with my Wind and Star pals. In fact yeah, I think I'm gonna go do that." Yuuna tries to leap into the air, attempting to cast "Kitestream", before her sister drags her down to her seat.

"Sis stop." Said Faith, laboredly holding her sister down. "What did we say about drinking and flying? Do you want to end up crashing into a flock of geese again? You're making a fool of yourself, it's really unbecoming."

"Oh hush!" Exclaimed Yuuna, fighting to stay airborne. "I was born to *flyyyy-*"

Suddenly, Pilet's Jean jacket drops onto Yuuna's head, blinding the young wind and starcaster and causing her to fall to the ground.

"Aahhh!" She exclaimed. "Ouch, where the hell did this come from?"

"Yo." Said Pilet, as he drags the jacket off of Yuuna's face. "This is a no fly zone, sorry to clip your wings."

"Oh, Pilet!" Said Yuuna. "How did things go with your grandparents?"

"Pretty shitty. Got my ass beat for a bit, but that's to be expected so it's no big deal."

Faith whispers to Max.

"It's no wonder he's such a brat..."

"I heard that!" Exclaims Pilet, stomping his feet in protest. "Whatever... Look, I just came to say goodbye to you losers."

Yuuna, Max, and Faith turn to Pilet in confusion.

"Well... don't look so surprised!" He continues. "I'm sure it's been going through all of your minds since the beginning. I mean, we knew that this time would come."

"Pilet..." Said Faith. "You don't have to be so negative about it. I mean, I'm sure we'll meet again..."

Max draws one of his Lacerates, holding it to his chest in an honorbound gesture.

"My friend, I've said it before and I'll say it again. A friend of The Sanda is a friend for life. We are linked on the branches of time from this day forth."

Pilet scoffs at his Sanda ally.

"Dude, can you be *any more* of a walking cliché?" He replied. "Look, the four of us are gonna go on our merry way. I'm spending the night with my folks back at Chamboree, and in the morning I'm taking the first Blades job I see. Max, you're probably going back home, and I'm 89% positive that Faith's going to go playing in the sand again in some ancient ruins. And Yuuna, I have no idea what you're gonna do, but I'm sure it's some crazy shit I'm not into. We're all about to split. This group is basically over and I just didn't want to leave without saying goodbye. Alright?!"

Max resheathes his fearsome weapon, folding his arms in contempt.

"Pilet. For your information, I will be staying in Kettlena for the foreseeable future."

"Wait, you are?" Said Yuuna. "Why wouldn't you go home Max? You're gonna leave your family and your luscious island behind to stay in this polluted dump?!"

"On Hatchidori, Warriors who join the ranks of The Hired Blades Association do so to use their resources. We travel far and wide, taking various jobs and learning the martial concepts of cultures all over the world. Clearly not all Sanda partake in this quest, but to those who do comes great honor for our experience."

"Aww Maxy." Replied Yuuna. "But isn't Kenzo gonna be really sad? I know my dad would be if..." She glances at her sister, as the two share a somber gaze for a moment. "Well I'm sure he would understand. But still."

"I've already attained the blessing of my father, we've planned this venture from the start. My mother and siblings had such great faith in my success that we said our goodbyes before I even left Hatchidori."

"Good for you Max." Added Faith. "I'm really happy for you man, I'm sure that you'll make an amazing Blade out there." She turns to Pilet in disdain. "As for *me*, mister know it all... Well you pretty much hit the nail on the head. So good job... But ya don't have to be such a dick about it." Faith draws her tome, gazing at the ancient lettering along the leather binding. "Yeah, I'm going to spend as much time as I can learning about The Rok-Senn people, and contributing to The Blade's knowledge on the matter. It's what my parents would have wanted..."

Yuuna looks at her sister in discontent. She mutters under her breath. *"So you say..."*

Pilet scans his friends' faces, still strucken by the fact that they will soon part ways.

"Promise me one thing, will you?" He said. The group members each give him a curious gaze. "Just, don't die out there alright?"

The trio look at each other, each one with a contented look on their faces.

"Wouldn't dream of it." Said Faith.

"There's not a beast, nor a bandit of *your* sorry homeland that could match my skill with a sword." Retorts Max.

Yuuna says nothing, as the others stare at her in confusion.

"..."

"What?" She said. "I mean, I might end up flying too high and fall off a cliff like I did that one time. I can't help that! Wind and Starcasters do some craaazy shit Pilet, so unless you're gonna babysit me, I can't promise I won't end up at the bottom of the ocean high on mushrooms...OK?"

"....."

"Bahahahahaha!"

The group breaks out in unanimous laughter, as the tension of the moment slowly begins to fade away.

"Let's keep in touch." Said Pilet. "You guys are pretty rad, almost as cool as me. It'd be a shame to miss out on each other's adventures from here on out, you know?"

Yuuna giggles at Pilet.

"Guys, I think Pilet doesn't have any real friends."

"What?! Shut up Yuuna! I do have friends! Why I'm, I'm the coolest kid in Chamboree!"

Faith and Max share a jovial glance. Max shrugs.

"Some things never change, do they."

"Ha," Laughed Faith. "I hope you guys never change..."

After enjoying the festivities of the evening; the new graduates, their families, other attending Hired Blades, and all manner of otherwise stated guests take their leave of the Colosseum. Pilet decides to leave with his grandparents, opting to spend the night in Chamboree to keep them company. He bids farewell to his mentor, imploring Faxion for a ride back in the morning. As the Fiery prospect hops into his grandparents car, he takes one last look at the colosseum that housed his illustrious graduation.

He once again holds his new badge in hand, gazing intently into the five swords of the emblem as cars whiz bye.

"I really did it." He thought. *"I really just became a Hired Blade. A real Hired Blade."* As his grandparents car passes by HBA headquarters, Pilet peers into the window with curious wonder. *"I wonder, what he would think...."* He takes a deep breath, sighing out the heat of the tension. *"Dad..."*

Slowly but surely, Milo drives through the daunting traffic of Grand Titanus City. Pilet scoffs at the "Oohs and aahs" of his grandparents, as they gaze in fascination at various Fossil creatures pulling carts full of passengers. Eventually escaping the bustling city streets, they pass through a toll gate and proceed out of Grand Titanus toward their mountain home. Lush, green fields and rolling hills orchestrate a concerto of crickets and katydids. A curious wind rushes through the hills, gently caressing the heads of each dancing blade of grass. Like an otherworldly mirror, the still waters of Lake Titanus reflect the image of the crescent moon off of their soft ripples.

As green pastures begin to slowly morph into rocky hills, the car carrying the family from Chamboree begins to creep steadily up the winding mountain path. Nodding off to sleep, Pilet's eyes blink and flutter laboredly. As Milo's car cruises through a meandering curve, the night sky hovering over the Minego mountain range is the last sight Pilet sees before drifting out of consciousness...

SIX

The End of the Beginning

The curious chirping of mountain canaries plays an uplifting tune; carried joyfully throughout the streets of Chamboree.

Pilet inhales deeply, blinking his eyes open and wiping the crust from his tired eyelids.

"Where, where am I?"

He sluggishly scans his surroundings, slowly slipping back into conscious thought. The sound of the rickety old bed springs crunching beneath his weight fills the room, as he sits up in his mattress. Dark, mandarin orange walls surround him, with rustic, oaken furniture scattered throughout. A decorative medal hangs around a lamp on the nightstand, reading "1st place, 2114 Track Meet". Random comic books and video games lay scattered across the emerald-colored, carpeted floor.

"Oh, I'm in my room. Did Grandpa carry me here? He knows his back is jacked up. Ugh, why didn't he just wake me up?"

Pilet composes himself, stepping out of bed and cracking his back to free himself from the morning stiffness. As he walks towards the door, he notices his Dragonfly long knives hanging by the handguards on the blinds of his window. He approaches his beloved blades, lifting them from the blinds and gazing through the window of the top-floor hotel room. The roofs of neighboring buildings and houses lie just out of a long jump's reach, overlooking the village streets.

Pilet scratches his head.

"You know, I've always wanted to try this. Ever since I started hurdling in track..."

He opens the window, breathing in the morning's crisp mountain air. Large enough to stand through, with a pane that cranks open via a rotating handle. Cranking the window open, he takes several paces back and drops into a runner's lunge. He breathes deeply, scanning the distance between himself and the first rooftop. On the exhale, Pilet flexes his calves, pumping fresh blood into the powerful runners muscles housed within. "Fleetfoot." He casts. An arcane glow erupts from the soles of his feet, as he lunges forth from the confines of his room.

"Hah!"

In a flash, The Fiery prospect dashes forward; leaping over his mattress, through the window, and easily landing onto the first roof in sight. He tucks and rolls on impact, sliding on the slate tiles with the force of his dash. Immediately, he continues to burst forth, sprinting ahead and leaping wildly from rooftop to rooftop.

"Woohoo! I'm the King of Chamboree!"

Dashing and hurdling across the roofs of Chamboree, Pilet feels the wind rush through his buzzed hair. He gazes in wonder at the view granted by his arcane sprint, soaking in the stunning mountainside.

The mighty rock formations and beautiful mountain flora sitting just outside the humble village skate by, as he bolts across Chamboree like a nimble wolf spider. He sees goats and sheep, peacefully grazing by a nearby stream. A pack of wolves dashes across the wilds, whilst a noble eagle soars high overhead, screeching fiercely into the sky. He gazes down at rows of cotton candy fruit trees; the big, round, blue and pink melon-like fruit, growing in meticulously cultivated rows behind the homes of some settlers.

Continuing his tirade for nigh half an hour, Pilet takes note of the desolate village streets.

"Where is everyone anyway? It's a Sunday morning. Nobody should *really* be at work right now..."

Having had his fill of excitement, Pilet decides to return to his humble hotel room. He sprints back, leaping deftly through his bedroom window and slipping on a rogue comic book as his feet hit the floor.

"Aaagh!"

He spins out of control, tumbling and rolling along the floor. He crashes into his bedroom closet, causing a mountain of unfolded clothing to fall on him like an avalanche of fabric.

"God dammit Grandma!" He exclaimed. "Why doesn't she fold my clothes anymore? It's like... She expects *me* to do it or something..."

Gathering himself, Pilet walks out of his bedroom door and departs down the winding staircase of "Dreams of Chamboree". As he approaches the first-floor lobby, he notices a hearty helping of balloons tied around the handrail at the bottom.

"That's weird..."

Coming around the corner, he immediately jumps back in shock, as at least two dozen villagers leap forth with party favors in hand.

"Surpriiise!!" They shout in unison.

The villagers let out a thunderous applause for Pilet, clapping and cheering for the first, Licensed Hired Blade out of Chamboree.

"Aah!!" Cries a startled Pilet, as he misses the last two steps and falls on his face.

"Oooooh....." React members of the crowd, a painful grimace across most of their faces.

"Haaahahahaha!!" One villager finds the fresh Blade's misfortune hilarious, as Pilet dusts himself off and leaps to his feet in protest.

"Who the hell's laughing?!" He snorts.

As the crowd falls silent, the laughing villager cuts through to the front, beginning a slow clap for Pilet. As Pilet sees the jovial villager, he shakes his head in lament.

"Oh, this prick." He said, as his best friend James emerges from the crowd. "Who invited *your* ass?"

"I did, dipshit!" Retorts James. "Is that any way to thank me for getting a welcome crew together for you?"

Pilet looks at the crowd in bewilderment, peering back at James in disbelief.

"Dude, you did this?" He said. "I mean... You didn't have to."

He walks over to James to give him a fist bump, as James pulls Pilet into a hug instead.

"I..." Pilet stutters in shock.

"I'm just glad you're alive, I didn't expect you to *actually* win... but I always knew you could do it."

Choking back tears, the two break off and shove each other apart abruptly in discomfort.

"Don't make it weird man!" Said Pilet, shamelessly wiping his tears in his tank top."

"Y-you're the one making it freaking weird!" Cried James. "Just shut up and smile for the pictures!"

"Awwww." The crowd chirps.

The teary-eyed companions look at each other, two sorry sights welled with hidden emotion. After a moment, their frowns turn into subtle grins, as the two friends begin uncontrollably laughing together. Arm in arm, Pilet and James march towards the bar in elation.

"He'll have a cold one on me!" Said James. "And I'll have what he's having! One round of the hard stuff!"

The bartender turns around, revealing herself to be Tecia wiping down a clean glass.

"Oh shit." Said Pilet and James.

"Root beers for the both of you, ya hear?" She said. "You're both 19, that's about as hard a drink as you'll get."

"Oh Tecia, let the boys live a little!" said Milo, as he exits the kitchen doors with a massive platter of food. The partygoers cheer at the sight of the elegant platter. "The boy's old enough to put himself into the line of fire, but not old enough for a damn beer?"

"And whose bright idea was it to let him go?!" She retorts. Folding her arms in disdain, she hands them both a glass of smoked cedarbeer. "Fine, just for today. Ok honey?"

"Woah!" Replied Pilet. "Thanks, Grandma!"

James and Pilet clank their glasses together, taking a deep swig of ice-cold beer. Unused to the bitter taste, the two of them try to hide the uncomfortable grimace on their face.

"*Cough* Good shit, right shit-eater?" Said James.

"**Gag** Oh yeah, real good." Pilet replied. "Looks like I drank more than you, I guess it's not as good as you thought?"

"Oh yeah?!" Replied James, drawing the glass to his face. "I bet you like, forty aurem I can finish before you."

"Oh you're on, prepare to get left in the damn dust!" Retorts Pilet.

They both begin to chug their cedarbeer incessantly, making all manner of uncomfortable faces in the process. The crowd goes wild, cheering and clapping for the hilarious contest. Tecia tosses a rag to Milo.

"You'd better hold onto that. You're on cleanup duty, mister, "Let the boys live a little.".

Milo watches, as James and Pilet chug unforgiving amounts of Cedarbeer before the crowd of party goers.

"Oh... This might not end well..."

On Matters of Love

Sometime later, as the festivities begin to wind down; Pilet and James sit at the bar, completely sloshed in a reclined posture. The partygoers eventually congratulate Pilet one by one, before taking their leave of the lobby. Being the last one left, James stands laboredly to his feet.

"Ugh, damn." He grunts. "That stuff hits hard..."

"Ha, careful there." Said Pilet. "Wouldn't want to pull a hamstring walking to the bathroom, fatass."

James grins.

"Tch, whatever." His face gets a touch more serious. "Listen man, all jokes aside... I just wanted you to know how awesome it is that you actually made it. I know you've wanted to be a Blade for a long time. And it's weird, I never imagined you would be one... but for some reason, I always *could* see you being one in my head. Does that make sense?"

Pilet scratches his chin.

"I mean, actually yeah. It does. We've always been buds. I feel like common sense was telling you that I probably wouldn't make the jump, at least not on my own. But because you know me so well, you knew that I definitely could."

"Right, that's it!" Replied James. "It's like, it seemed so wild to imagine something like this happening. But then again I feel like whatever you really want to do, you just kinda do it. I figure if you applied that to this then it can't go any other way. Well it could, you could end up getting straight-up killed. But yeah, if that doesn't happen then I could totally see you succeeding for sure."

Pilet remembers the multiple times in which he should have indeed perished. He gulps anxiously.

"Yeah well, I can't see that happening any time soon. Trust me. Anyway, you out of here man?"

James rubs his belly in discomfort.

"Yeah, I feel like shit after drinking all that beer. And my mom wants me home to clean my room or something."

"Ha, tough luck buddy." Said Pilet. "My Grandma is house cleaning for the hotel, so she just cleans mine for me!"

As he says this, an empty plastic food container bounces off of his head.

"Ow!" Exclaims Pilet.

Tecia stands at the end of the bar, giving Pilet a contemptuous side-eye for his remark.

"*OK* Grandma!" Said Pilet. "I'll clean it later!'

"Where have I heard *that* before?" Tecia replied, taking a stack of dirty dishes into the kitchen.

"Anyway." Said James. "I hope everything goes good out there, and you make it in the big leagues. Just remember your pal when you're making hero money, ok?"

Pilet stands to his feet, as the two look at each other in a heartfelt gaze. James comes in for a hug. But suddenly, Pilet rips a swift punch into James' gut, as James doubles over in pain.

"Baaahahahaha!" Laughs Pilet. "I told you not to make it weird! Ahahaha!"

Whilst bending over in agony, James responds with a heavy-handed shot to Pilet's groin.

"Gah!" Grunts Pilet, as he drops to the floor in a fetal position. "My dick! You, you dick!"

"Ugh, ha!" James lets out a labored chuckle. "That's what you get for letting your guard down punk. How'd a tough guy *Hired Blade* let a normal dude beat on him like that huh?! *Urp, blegh!*"

Mid-sentence, James vomits the contents of his stomach onto the floor. At the sight of this, Pilet holds his mouth, trying hard as he might to withhold his own upheaval.

"Oh *urp*, oh God."

But to no avail, as the Fiery Prospect empties his frothy, alcohol-lined tummy onto the hotel floor as well. As the two roll around in pain and filth, Tecia emerges from the kitchen doors. She facepalms at the sight of the boys rolling in throw-up.

"Milo!" She cried. "You wanted them to drink, you clean it up!" She grabs a handful of rags and tosses them at the boys, before marching up the stairs of the hotel. "I need to take a bath just looking at the lot."

Milo comes out, sees the situation and begrudgingly aids the boys in cleaning the God-awful mess that's become of them.

"This is what I get for letting you have your fun, hmm?"

Once the two clean themselves up, Milo marches into the kitchen with a trash bag full of soiled linens; tossing it to the side before getting to work on a sink full of dishes. James then takes his leave of Dreams of Chamboree, as he gets a disgruntled Chatch call from his mother about his unkempt bedroom. This leaves Pilet alone, sitting at the bar by himself; gazing at the random bottles of alcohol on the shelf. He recounts the bitter taste of the cedar beer.

"How do people drink this shit?..."

As he reflects, a notification on his Chatch pings, as Pilet scans the screen curiously.

From: "Old Douchebag".

"I'll be in Chamboree within the hour, hope you didn't miss me too much!" Followed by a smiley face emoji.

"*Sigh* Guess it's about that time." Said Pilet. He pokes his head through the kitchen doors, yelling out to Milo. "I'm outta here Grandpa, seeya later."

Milo takes a break from meticulously washing dishes, approaching his grandson and entrapping him in a savage bear hug.

"You give 'em hell my boy, ya hear me?!" He exclaimed.

"Ack! Shit, my spine!" Said Pilet, as a boisterous crackling can be heard. "Loosen up, I can't breathe dammit!"

Milo releases his grip, as Pilet holds his back begrudgingly.

"Say goodbye to your Grandmother, and don't forget her cotton candy fruit pie ok?" Said Milo, pointing to a pie standing on the end of the bar.

"Grandma made pie?" He replied. "Oh *hell* yeah!"

Pilet grabs the pie, marching up the steps until he reaches the top floor. He strolls down the hall to Tecia's room, curiously knocking on the door.

"Yo, Grandma. Fax is here, I'm leaving now."

"Oh, come in baby." Said Tecia.

Pilet enters, as Tecia finishes ironing some of his battle-worn tank tops, baggy blue jeans, and socks. She places the tanks neatly into a large navy duffle bag, handing said bag to her grandson with care.

"Here you go precious, I washed and folded all of your favorite clothes. Even the stinky shirts with the strange holes on them!"

Pilet grabs the bag, hoisting it over his shoulder with a Grunt.

"Damn, this is heavy." Said Pilet. "Well thanks Grandma, I appreciate it."

Tecia gives Pilet a sad stare, before reaching in for a hug and kissing his cheeks.

"I love you so much." Said Tecia. "Everytime I look at you, I see the face of your mother. My little Sarah, it's..." She pauses for a moment, her lip quivering unsteadily. "It's like her spirit lives within you."

"Grandma..." Said Pilet, unsure of how to respond.

Tecia holds his cheeks in her palms endearingly.

"Be safe my love, I'm so proud of you. Just, be safe. And good luck, making the world a little safer for the rest of us."

Pilet takes a deep inhale, tears welling up in his eyes.

"I, I will Grandma. I will." He wipes some of the tears from his eyes, doing his best to feign strength. He shoots his grandmother a look of subtle pride. "For Mom..."

After a moment of warm embrace, Pilet returns to his own room and quickly packs his belongings. With luggage in both of his hands, he rushes down the stairs in excitement; eager to meet with his mentor and continue his career path as a Hired Blade.

As Pilet pulls open the hotel doors, he is met with a shocking sight. His good friend Nivia, sits patiently on a bench outside Dreams of Chamboree. She twirls her long, auburn hair bashfully between her fingers. Pilet's heart sinks into his bowels at the sight of the girl, inadvertently dropping one of his large duffle bags in awe.

The sound of the bag thudding to the ground alerts Nivia to his presence, as she stops twirling her hair in embarrassment.

"Oh! Pilet, I..."

"H,Hey Nivia." Stutters Pilet. *"Get your head out of your ass and talk to her!!"* He thought. He shakes his head vigorously, clearing the cobwebs from his brain. "Ahem, uh yeah what's up! You missed a cool party a few hours ago, I was beginning to think I wouldn't see you before I left."

"Yeah I'm sorry, I uh..." Nivia looks around anxiously. "I had a dentist appointment that I just *couldn't* miss. I mean, not that I don't take care of my teeth or anything! But you know, sometimes those cavities just sneak up on you right?..."

"Uh, yeah right!" Replied Pilet nervously. "Oh for sure, dude I've had like a thousand root canals, they suck! I guess it's all the cotton candy fruit. Haha, ha...."

"..."

The two stand in silence for a moment, awkwardly twirling their thumbs in nervous tension. Suddenly Nivia breaks the silence.

"I saw a really big, fancy airship on the way here. It was just hovering over the edge of a cliff like a floating house! I'm guessing your Hired Blade friend with the cool hat is here for you, right?"

Pilet glances at the time on his Chatch.

"Oh shit, time freaking flies." He said. "Yeah that'll be him. I'm gonna head back to Grand Titanus City for a bit before starting my first job, whatever that is."

"..."

Another tense moment of silence goes by.

"Uh yeah so, I should probably get going then." Said Pilet. "It was nice seeing you, Nivia. I'm glad I caught you before I left."

"Yeah, you too Pilet!" She replied.

She reaches in for an awkward, half hug, as Pilet unwittingly pats her on the back like a dog. They both feel the sweat dripping down their own backs in embarrassment, neither one choosing to mention it.

"Yeah, so I'll see ya later then!" Said Pilet with a gulp. He grabs his bags and begins pacing nervously towards the edge of town.

But as he starts to walk away, Nivia bashfully calls out to him.

"Pilet wait!"

Pilet stops in his tracks, standing erect as a pole in fear.

"Oh crap." He thought.

"Did, did you ever get the chance to read my letter?" She said, tensely playing with some of the split ends of her hair.

"Oh, uh... I..."

His heart starts pounding faster than the drum of Danba the Witchdoctor. He gulps the apple of tension in his throat.

"You know the craziest thing happened..."

"I uh, *cough cough*, I was opening the letter by my window in this fancy skyscraper condo that my friend got me, and you know how high up those rooms can get right?" Pilet clears the sweat from his brow. "So you know, I was opening it and then..."

A strong mountain breeze brushes past the two teens, whooshing by and clearing some of the nervous sweat from either's faces.

"Aaaaand then the *God damned* wind took it! It snatched it right out of my hand and the damn thing flew like, probably halfway across the world by now! Crazy right?!"

"....."

"Phew"

Nivia lets out a sigh of relief, a disappointed, but much less tense expression on her face.

"Oh, oh that's ok!" She said. "Well don't worry about it. I was just wishing you luck in the exam, which it looks like you didn't even need! And also congrats! I forgot I hadn't said that yet. Anyway, you should get going with your friend. I'm sure he's getting impatient by now. It was good seeing you Pilet, I'm so happy you made the grade!"

"Uh yeah thanks!" He said. "And, good luck finding a college you like. I know you were having trouble getting accepted with your first few picks, but keep your chin up!" Pilet smiles, the most genuine look on his face since starting this conversation. "You're the smartest girl in this town, one of these colleges is gonna see that. And then you'll make big waves out there, I promise."

The sincerity in Pilet's eyes melts Nivia's heart. Her face radiates a rosy red, as the girl from Chamboree begins to unrelentingly blush. The two wave innocently at each other, as Pilet hoists his bag over his shoulder and begins to take his leave. As he gains some distance, Nivia calls out once again.

"Take care Pilet!" She smiles. I'll be worried about you, even if you don't want me to."

Pilet looks back to her as he walks off.

"Ha! You should be worried for whoever stands in my way." Pilet smiles back, pointing at his bashful friend. "I'll come back in one piece, next time I'll take you to the city to see the Dinosaurs and hover cars."

The two share a warm grin, as The Fiery Prospect takes his leave of Chamboree.

The Proposition

Pilet treks across the rocky mountain top, playfully kicking up dust and little stones beneath his feet. Lizards and small snakes rush into their homes under small rock formations, as the young Hired Blade jovially twirls the hilt of a Dragonfly knife like a whirling propeller. Wistfully strolling through the mountain top, Pilet begins to reach the ledge of a particularly high cliff. As he approaches the cliffside, the young Blade is taken aback by the stunning view of the Minego Mountain range. Hawks, eagles, and all other manner of birds of prey glide effortlessly across the wind. A dense, white fog envelops the cliffside, as the height of the mountain peak literally pierces a cloud in the sky. Pilet stops himself towards the end of the cliff.

"The highest point in the Minego Mountain range." He breathes in the crisp mountain air, gazing at the scenic view before him. "You know, I'm sure going to miss this place..."

Pilet pauses for a moment, curiously glancing to and fro in confusion.

"But wait. Didn't Nivia say there was an airship here?" He cups his hand over his brow, shielding his eyes from the sun for a better view. "I... did Fax leave? Did I take too long!?..."

Before his mind can play tricks on him, Pilet hears the subtle, mechanical whirr of a group of jet turbines in the distance. The pointed black tip of a mysterious rooftop begins to peek out from the mountain fog before him, parting the fluffy white cloud in its presence. Slowly rising through the cloud, the black-tiled roofs of The Crimson Pagoda begin to erupt from the skies beneath. The vibrant, crimson finish of the multi story vessel glistens in the light of the afternoon sun. Finally, the base floor of the vessel reaches the ground level of the high mountain peak, as its luxurious glass double doors begin to slide open.

A metal platform begins to extend from directly beneath the sliding, double doors; steadily reaching for the surface of the cliff like a spectral bridge.

"Phew! Looks like the old bastard didn't forget about me."

As the extending platform touches down to the ground with a loud klang, Faxion appears; standing in the doorway of the illustrious airship. The Veteran Blade strides along the bridge over the clouds, grinning at his pupil in subtle glee.

"What happened?" Said Faxion. He reaches the end of the bridge, ensnaring Pilet in a congratulatory hug. "I waited an extra half an hour for you, I was beginning to think you'd gotten cold feet!"

"Sorry Fax, I got a bit held up." Pilet replied. "So, this is the fancy airship Yang gave you huh? I gotta see the inside! Let's not waste any more time."

Pilet fastens his duffle bag over his shoulder, beginning to walk past Faxion onto the hovering bridge. But as he does so, Faxion holds an arm out in protest, barring the boy from going any further.

"Wait." He said, a serious tone in his voice. "I have a question for you before proceeding."

Shocked, Pilet steps back in hesitance. The gaze upon his mentor's face goes from one of gleeful excitement, to a much more grave expression.

"Uh, ok..." Chirps Pilet. "Do you still want to teach me? I mean, you don't have to if you're too busy man..."

A disappointed glaze seeps into Pilet's eyes, as the Blade from Chamboree sighs in anticipatory sadness. Faxion's expression begins to lighten, as he puts a hand on Pilet's shoulder.

"What? That's not it lad, chin up now." Faxion draws a cigarette from his coat pocket, lighting it and taking a relaxing drag. "Look, I've neglected to inform you of the true nature of your recruitment. Right before we met, the Chairman had implored that I take on a group of, shall we say associates. I'm putting my time as an independent Hired Blade on hold for the time being, in favor of a more urgent matter."

Pilet begins impatiently tapping his foot, holding his hands to his hips in contempt.

"Alright dude these bags are getting heavy, what are you getting at here?"

Faxion grins, laughing off the crudeness of his pupil.

"I'm putting together a small company, Pilet." He said. "A squad, a band, or if you will, a party. You're obviously familiar with the *Wurm* insurgents, yes?"

"The God-forsaken parasite I murdered? The one that gave me my nickname?" Pilet retorts. "Yeah, what about it?"

"These Wurm parasites are becoming seriously problematic. They're increasing in number, *and* in strength. What we know about them is extremely limited, and from said knowledge, there isn't really much of relevance." Faxion points to Pilet, tapping him in the chest. "That is, until *you* came around. There's no denying that there is a clear link between you and this menace, Pilet. You are very special indeed."

"I... What do you mean?" Pilet replied. "Are you blaming me for all this? I didn't even know about these things until *you* came along!"

"That's not it." Said Faxion. "Your "Fever Point" is extraordinary. When you fought the Wurm gorilla... To utilize the aura in the atmosphere around you without first being aurabroken is, well, simply nigh impossible. But to beat it, you did *just* that." Faxion takes another drag of his cigarette, blowing a deep cloud of smoke before scratching his head in bewilderment.

"And when you killed it, a mysterious aura sprang forth from the creature and entered you. I watched it with my own eyes. The same occurred with Kuweha in Devil's Tongue. Once, might have been coincidence, but *twice* is indicative or something more, Pilet. A right fool could see this, it's clear as the view atop these mountains."

Pilet holds his chin in his hand, deep in thought.

"I know Fax. I know. I haven't been able to figure it out man. None of this makes any sense!" Pilet begins holding his head in frustration. "I can do alot of crazy shit that first time auracasters shouldn't be able to.

Between the Fever Point, the quick healing, the fact that I can fire like, fifty damn Hollowpoints without breaking a sweat! The purple fur and the scorpion armor are just the icing on the cake, none of this makes any damn sense! It's cool to have these abilities but, I've just been trying not to feel like a *freak* in all of this..."

"Gifts are gifts Pilet, and the presence of such does not make one a freak." Said Faxion. "But gifts are *given*, and the ones *you* possess are of a mysterious origin. We need to analyze these talents of yours, to determine this peculiar, "gifter" once and for all. But that leads me to my initial question." Faxion finishes his cigarette, dropping the butt to the ground and stomping it out with his combat boots. "Understand something, from this day forth you are a free Hired Blade, let that badge you received be evidence of such. But with that in mind, would you be interested in joining my crew?"

Pilet pauses for a moment. It's as if everything he'd ever wanted had just materialized before his eyes. The respect of his peers, a formidable title behind his name, and now, the man in which he admires most in this world, offering him a spot at his table. Pilet speaks.

"Could I still take on my own jobs?" He said.

"Of course." Replied Faxion. "When not on a group mission, you have every right to take on independent ones of your own. Just take one of the Pagoda's auxiliary vessels to and from the job, or your mountain home, or Grand Titanus... Or wherever you'd like!"

"Alright. Then..." He pats the Dragonfly knives holstered to his hip. "You know, I still owe you for these. And room and board, and for covering exam fees..." Pilet grins ear to ear. "Screw it, I'm in!"

Faxion meets Pilet's elated smile with one of his own, as he wraps his arm around the boy's shoulder.

"That a boy lad, I knew you couldn't resist!" The two begin to trek onto the metal bridge, proceeding towards the Crimson Pagoda.

"So, this team..." Said Pilet. "You got anyone in mind?"

As he asks, the two take a step through the double doors and into the Pagoda's lobby area.

Luxury couches with black, bonded leather form an "L" shape before the massive 60 inch television, programmed into the wall. Beside the television lies a mahogany door with scarlet trim, leading to the ship's control room. A beautiful, light sandalwood coffee table sits before the couches, with gold trimmed coasters scattered atop. Left to the double-doors to which Pilet and Faxion enter, sits an extremely well furnished kitchen, with marble countertops and diamond-edged cutlery. Light gray walls line the Pagoda with a subtle elegance, promoting an energetic sense of focus in the rooms throughout. Finally, opposite to the kitchen and cockpit lies a narrow hallway, with the doors to various rooms scattered along. At the end of the hall is a spiral staircase, which leads to the luxurious vessel's second, third, and fourth floors.

Perched atop the back spine of one couch, Max Quinn meticulously wipes clean the edge of his Lacerate with a soft rag. Yuuna Sierro sits atop the coffee table in a meditative trance, slowly channeling aura into the quartz beads given to her by Scott Diliger. Suddenly, Faith Sierro bursts forth from the cockpit door. She turns to Faxion in chagrin.

"Fax, where is this kid? How long do you expect me to keep this thing suspended in mid air like this?"

Her outburst draws the attention of the others, as they turn to Pilet with a collective look of subtle gratification. Pilet looks at Faxion in disbelief, then back to The Hidden Blades with a gaze of unconcealable satisfaction.

Smiling deviantly, Max tosses his rag at Pilet's face.

"Looks as though Chamboree has had enough of your nonsense, they must have thrown you at *us* to deal with."

Yuuna snaps out of her trance, her eyes widening at the sight of her companion.

"Pilet! It got so boring without you!! These guys are such squares!"

Faith scoffs at Pilet, attempting to conceal a slight, jubilant smirk.

"Took ya long enough. Get your ass on board already."

Pilet drops his bags as he walks inside the door. Faxion puts a hand on his shoulder, drawing him closer.

"Welcome back to the Hidden Blades, Mr. *Emissary*."

Pilet shakes his head in disbelief.

"Wait, does that mean I'm the boss?" He said.

"Ha!" Laughed Faith. "Fat chance! It just means that if we do something wrong or make a mistake, you're the one taking the blame."

"Hwhat?!" Exclaimed Pilet. "I never agreed to this bullshit Fax!"

"Ohhh yes you did." Faxion replied. "That's part of being an Emissary, did you never read about that in the Blades handbook?"

"I, I skimmed that shit... I mean yeah, I knew that. I was just testing you losers!"

The group collectively laughs at Pilet's expense.

Flashing them all a contemptuous side-eye, Pilet takes a walk over to the windows on the opposite side of the lobby. He glances at the beautiful, scarlet afternoon sky.

"So, where to next, *boss*?" He said to Faxion.

Faxion taps away on his Chatch.

"Well look at this." Faxion opens an email, curiously scanning its contents. "It seems RepCo. West has lost contact with the capital a few days ago. The association has been tasked with scoping out the facility. Does this sound good to everyone?"

Faith ponders.

"RepCo., isn't that one of the Fossil labs?" She said.

"Ooooh!" Exclaimed Yuuna. "We gotta go! I've always wanted to see how they make FC's!!"

A voice rings throughout Yuuna's mind, coming from the black Onix stone in her bag.

"Don't forget about our deal, girl. The Dragon Sorcerer, my body, and your blood..."

"Oh quiet you..." She muttered. *"I know, I know..."*

Max methodically sheaths his prized Lacerate. A mesmerizing shing can be heard as the blade retreats into the scabbard.

"Yes, let's waste no time. Lord knows what distress those scientists may be in."

"Lost contact, huh?" Said Pilet. "What, is their Wi-Fi down or something? Doesn't sound too exciting to me. But hey, everyone else wants to go. So sure, why the hell not." Pilet brandishes his Dragonflies. "Maybe a rogue Fossil creature will get outta line while we're there, then I'll get to smack 'em around a bit."

"Then it's settled." Said Faxion. "I'll set a course for Crater Canyon. We'll be there by the morning, so get cozy!"

Faxion walks into the control room, beginning to set coordinates for the Pagoda's next destination.

Pilet steps through another set of double doors, out onto a balcony attached to the lobby area; taking a moment to soak in the sights. He spies the vast Minego Mountain range, scanning the many hilltops and rocky peaks that define the unique landscape. He peers once more, the world famous, colorful cotton candy fruit growing behind the settlers homes. In the distance, Pilet can make out the tip of the roof to Dreams of Chamboree, and past that, he spies the bustling bazaar to which he cut fruit for so many an afternoon.

"So long, Chamboree..."

Just then, Faith yells out to him from across the lobby.

"Pilet we're taking off, get inside before you get flung off the ship."

He takes one more glance, a soft smile strewn across his face.

"Next stop, adventure..."

The Fiery prospect steps back inside, as The Crimson Pagoda's many turbines begin to fire with increasing intensity. As the high-powered mercenary vessel retracts its metal bridge, the Pagoda's main engine comes to a wicked scream. The massive thrusters behind the esteemed airship fire a dazzling inferno along its posterior, as The Crimson Pagoda blasts off into the peerless sunset.

Evil.

As the Pagoda sets off into the sky, a vile wind rushes through the cliff it left behind. An Indigo snake, with glowing patterns running down its body, peeks out from within the crevice of a cracked stone. Its eyes, glowing with a ghoulish violet haze, tirelessly glare off towards the departing vessel.

Countless miles away; the entrance to a small, dark cave lay isolated, somewhere in the middle of a vast ocean. An immoral, dark fog blocks the small island inlet from sight, as a raspy voice can be heard from deep within the cave.

The shadow of a foul-smelling creature, with a spine hunched at a harrowing angle, begins to confide in another.

"My Lord." Said The raspy voice. "The subject is leaving with the troublesome Hired Blade. Should we not have put a stop to this sooner?"

Across from this foul creature, a shadowy figure sits upon a gory, blood-soaked throne. Skeletons line the corners of the room, as the throne itself seems composed of limbs covered in rotting flesh. They both peer into an arcane window, suspended in mid-air before them. Through this is the sight of the Chamboree cliff, seen through the eyes of the ghoulish snake. The coagulated blood of the hellish throne makes a wet sound, as the shadowy figure begins to wave its finger ever so slightly in protest.

"No my underling, yet again you misunderstand the root of my plan. To cut the fruit off of the tree before it is ripe, is a sure path to death by dissatisfaction." The shadowy figure opens its eyes wide, revealing a glowing pair of violet, vile irises. "The fruit needs more time. Intervene, and I shall make sure *you* are cut from *my* tree." The figure glances at the arcane image of Chamboree yet again. "You will have your time, fruit. For now............."

Printed in the United States
by Baker & Taylor Publisher Services